P

THE OTHERS

"Davis brings all the quirkiness of San Francisco to life like never before, seamlessly weaving together the modern and mystical. Depicting a secretive society in our midst, comprised of witches and fairies, demons and vampires, *The Others* is a delicious adventure, unconventional romance, and compelling parable for our politically wrought time."

—MIKE TRIGG, author of *Bit Flip* and *Burner*

". . . a paranormal romance and thriller for the intelligent reader. It has it all: political issues, social issues, family issues, witches, vampires, demons, time-walkers, fairies, werewolves, empaths, romance, violence, danger, and espionage. Davis does a laudable job by weaving an intricate storyline around a well-developed, blossoming romance. She ties storylines together and introduces backstories to explain complicated characters. Moreover, the protagonist is extremely likable and easy to relate to. This may have been a paranormal book, but I found her story to be motivational. Who hasn't wanted to turn their back on the world and throw in the towel? When Olivia begins her training sessions to get her life back on track, the book becomes nearly therapeutic."

—REBECCA SKANE, book reviewer at Seacoastonline.com

"Let me begin by first saying, WOW. I loved this book from start to finish. Evette Davis's book truly packs a punch and has plenty to offer, including the supernatural, romance, fantasy, politics, and more. This is a beautifully written book with an exceptionally strong plot."

—A.C. HAURY, *Bibliophile Book Reviews*

THE OTHERS

THE
OTHERS

BOOK ONE
IN
THE COUNCIL TRILOGY

By

EVETTE DAVIS

Published by SparkPress, a BookSparks imprint,
A division of SparkPoint Studio, LLC
Phoenix, Arizona, USA, 85007
www.gosparkpress.com

Published 2024
Printed in the United States of America
Print ISBN: 978-1-68463-270-1
E-ISBN: 978-1-68463-271-8
Library of Congress Control Number: 2024910034

Interior design by Stacey Aaronson

All company and/or product names may be trade names, logos, trademarks, and/or registered trademarks and are the property of their respective owners.

This is a work of fiction. Names, characters, places, and incidents either are the product of the author's imagination or are used fictitiously. Any resemblance to actual persons, living or dead, is entirely coincidental.

To Alec and Stella.
I love you both very much.

Careful now.

We're dealing with a myth.

This city is a point upon a map of fog;

Lemuria in a city unknown.

Like us, it doesn't quite exist.

—AMBROSE BIERCE

PROLOGUE

MOST OF YOU ARE PROBABLY FAMILIAR WITH THE FACT THAT San Francisco is a foggy city. What few people know is the real reason for the fog. San Francisco's weather, despite what the nightly news might say, is controlled by a powerful spell. This spell conjures up the cool, wet fog to keep people from seeing what is really going on around them. The fog tumbles across the hills and mountains like a great gray-white wave, pressing inward until it erases San Francisco from view. On the most foggy days and nights, people can barely see more than the hand in front of their face, and it can be difficult to know if what you are seeing is real. That's when the city's Others— fairies, witches, vampires, and werewolves—can meet. They attend to their business in the darkness of night, the light muted, the air damp and gray.

The Others leave behind no trace of themselves or their activities. The fog is their eraser, a privacy screen to shield humans from an unsettling truth: they are not alone in this world, and they are not in control.

San Francisco is also known for its colorful residents. It's no accident that so many outlandish people live there. The city is home to an enormous population of Others, alive and undead. That the Beat poets, the Free Speech Movement, the Summer of Love, the sexual revolution, and the gay rights movement all originated in San Francisco is no coincidence. Amid the tattooed, pierced, and corseted, the Others are free to live their lives. In San Francisco, it is easy to hide in plain sight.

MY GRANDMOTHER USED TO TELL ME STORIES, WHEN I WAS A child, of the time-walkers who visited her village in Scotland. In her tales, they brought news of dead loved ones and warned of impending dangers. Free to move between the past and the future, these witches were welcomed cautiously by the villagers and warmly by women like my grandmother, who had their own gifts. I always thought the stories were charming folklore, the stuff packed into books in the library.

Then, quite unexpectedly, I woke up one day and discovered that the legends might hold some truth.

It was an early morning in August. As I came into consciousness on my kitchen floor—my head thudding from a terrible hangover— the first thing I realized is that I'd been plagued by the dream again. The sleek black panther with the green eyes always walked near me yet never blocked my way. The creature always stayed close, as if it wanted to communicate.

As I woke up more fully, blinking in the light, I began to move my cold, stiff limbs gingerly. Why had I failed to make it into my bed? Slowly, I remembered the details of the previous night—and the previous week. Losing another big client to my competitor, the political consultant Stoner Halbert. Picking a fight with my best friend, Lily, while she was at work. Skipping work. Going on a totally uncharacteristic drinking binge.

I opened one eye, steeling myself to stand up, when I heard a voice speak.

"Let me help you," a woman's voice said.

"Lily?" I asked aloud. How had she gotten in? Maybe I had let her in last night, or maybe I had called her and she had used her key. Either way, I was glad that she was there.

"It's not Lily." Now I realized that the voice had a hint of a foreign accent I couldn't place. "Get up, Olivia."

I did as I was told and promptly let out a scream as I staggered up and spotted a strange woman standing on the other side of the kitchen. It was someone I'd never seen before.

"Who are you, and how did you get into my house?" I asked, wondering if I had managed to leave the door open. Maybe some deranged person had walked in off the street. I did live in a city, after all. I began calculating how quickly I could get to the phone and call the police. But as I looked at her more closely, I saw that she didn't look deranged. She seemed about my age and was tall, slightly more so than Lily. She also had long black hair, but it seemed almost darker than black, like the color of a raven's wing or, say, maybe a panther. She was wearing skintight leather pants and a dark sweater. The fingers on her hands were long and slender and adorned with several silver rings. She wore a small silver hoop through one of her eyebrows, which framed green eyes that almost glowed like a cat's. I was beginning to see a pattern that unnerved me.

"Are you the panther?" I asked, shocked at the absurdity of my question.

The woman nodded. "You did invite me here, Olivia. You asked me to come and tell you what I had to say."

Too stunned for words, I began to question whether I was losing my mind. For so many years, I'd worried that my artistic, substance-abusing mother would be the one to go off the deep end. But now it seemed I had it backward. I sat motionless and stared.

"This is your problem, Olivia," she said. "I've been watching you for several weeks, and you haven't lifted a finger to help yourself. So here I am. At last, we meet face-to-face."

The woman offered me her hand. I grabbed it and felt the warm flesh of a human being against my palm.

"How is this possible?" I murmured, staring into her extraordinary eyes. "Are you really here? I'm not hallucinating?"

"I'm real," she said. "As real as Stoner Halbert, only I have come to help you."

"How do you know about him?" I asked. "How do you know about me?"

"Your grandmother sent me," she said. "Bella chose me to watch over you when you were born. When you ran into trouble with Stoner, I expected you to summon me, but it seems you don't practice the old ways of your family. I've been forced to appear in your dreams to get your attention."

"*Summon you?* I have no idea how to do that," I said, my tongue slightly swollen in my mouth. "I had no idea my grandmother could do that sort of thing. I was drunk and angry last night. If I did have an outburst, well, I had no idea that it would result . . . well, that it would bring *you* here."

The woman laughed. "There is a lot about this world you don't know, Olivia, and that has put you in harm's way."

I walked slowly to a stool and sat down. It was too much. My head was pounding, and I was exhausted. Now, there was a strange woman in my house claiming to be my guardian angel. I couldn't imagine what would happen next. I decided to make an espresso and find out.

"Do you drink coffee . . . ?" I trailed off in a way that made it clear I was hoping to learn her name.

"It's Elsa," she said. "And tea, please."

"Elsa," I said back to her. "I have Earl Grey and green tea."

"Earl Grey," she said, and I began to fix our drinks.

I set two warm mugs on the counter. Elsa took the stool across from mine and sipped her tea. She seemed to savor it more than a normal person would.

"Don't they have tea where you're from?"

"It's been a while since I've been called to your world. I remember now how nice it is to visit."

"What do you mean *my* world? Are you dead?"

"No, not dead . . . unable to move on," she said without a trace of sarcasm. "As you may have guessed, I'm not from this time. But I do live in your century regularly now."

Perhaps it was the combination of fear and a raging hangover, but keeping up the light banter felt impossible. I had questions, and I wanted answers. "Why are you here? What were you trying to tell me when you appeared in my dreams these last few weeks?"

Elsa put down her mug and turned to face me. "I came because your grandmother feared what would happen if you continued to block your gift. Before her death, she summoned me and told me she had seen a vision in which you were in danger. She asked me to visit you periodically and ensure that you remain unharmed. For many months, I watched and saw nothing out of the ordinary."

"And now?"

"Now? You're in danger. It may have seemed wise to avoid using your powers, Olivia, but turning off your instincts has made you vulnerable. You're not even trying to sense when you're in danger. It's why Stoner Halbert's demon picked you."

This remark caused me to drop my coffee mug on the marble counter, where it promptly broke into several pieces.

"I'm sorry, did you say *demon*?"

Elsa sighed. "I can see we will have to start at the beginning. Your friend Mr. Halbert has been dabbling in black magic ever since his wife ruined him."

"That's ridiculous," I said. "I think I would have noticed if the former chief of staff to a prominent California state senator had morphed into the Wicked Witch of the West."

"Are you sure?" Elsa's voice sounded almost like a purr.

I wasn't. I'd built a successful consulting firm that catered to individuals and companies with political problems. As the head of Olivia Shepherd Consulting, I'd learned all about the depths that others would sink to in order to get ahead.

Stoner Halbert was a case in point. He'd lived the golden life: successful in politics, married to a beautiful woman who also happened to be the head of a successful investment firm, and invited to every function held by California's political and wealthy elite. Then one day in late 2021, the FBI charged Amber Halbert with insider trading and embezzlement. The ensuing news coverage detailing how she had stolen and defrauded some of the state's biggest names in politics and business became too much for Stoner to bear. He resigned from his post to shield his boss from further embarrassment. Amber pled guilty to avoid a more stringent jail sentence, and the two quietly divorced. Yet somehow, Stoner had come back from the dead. Over the last year he'd built up a brand-new and hugely successful consulting firm in San Francisco—successful enough to steal several of my clients.

"Yes, he fell from a great height," Elsa said, as if reading my thoughts. "Is it really any wonder that he sought revenge and became interested in the occult? He has managed to make it work for him. He was able to conjure up a minor demon that promised him great wealth. The demon has given him an advantage, a sort of influence— and he is using it against you and others."

"Why me?"

Elsa seemed to pause for a moment. "What's the expression? You are a 'sitting duck.' The Others can see that you have intentionally blocked off your senses. It makes you an easy target for their mischief. Halbert's demon has gone in search of the most vulnerable. An empath who refuses to listen her instincts? That is an easy mark."

"Why should I believe any of this is real or true?" I asked, feeling frightened beyond measure. To cover my feelings, I leaned down to clean up my mess. Either I was having a complete mental breakdown or there was a spirit guide in my kitchen discussing a demon.

Elsa smiled and put down her mug. "It's nice to see you get angry, Olivia. It's long overdue but welcome. Who do you think I am then, if not someone sent here to help you? I could have killed you while you were passed out in your kitchen. And yet, here I am and you're still alive."

"That's my point," I said. "You could be anyone. You could be some con artist off the street. Why should I believe you?"

"How would I know about your gifts if not for your grandmother?" Elsa asked. "You can try to pretend you're not connected to any of this, Olivia, but your grandmother was a great seer. And your mother, Rose, is extremely receptive. The fact that you have ignored your lineage doesn't erase the connections."

The mention of my mother sent my head spinning. How much did this woman know about the magnificent but overwhelming India Rose Shepherd? She hadn't been easy to have as a single mother, that was for sure. Not that we struggled financially—her wealthy family provided for us, until my mother established her career as a renowned landscape painter.

No, her struggle was with her gifts. Put simply, my mother can feel another person's emotions. She's an empath. India can read people, feel their nervousness, sense their hesitation to do something, detect their anger or sadness. She refers to it as "picking up on the energy of the universe." My mother, grandmother, and her mother before her were all empathic. All of the women on our side of the family carry the skill, including me. They call it the Gift, but I have never seen it that way.

From an early age, what I saw was my mother drinking herself to sleep at night to avoid feeling anything. She swallowed too many pills with her friends in order to maintain a barrier between the energy of the universe and herself. And then when she did focus on her painting, she would remain sequestered in her studio for weeks, inevitably collapsing in her bed for several days afterward.

As I grew older, I worried that my mother would kill herself, either through her excesses or through exhaustion. Now, at thirty-two, I understand my mother's moods and simply try to avoid her when she is on the dark side of the universe.

"Olivia." Elsa's voice drew my out of my reverie. "I'm still right here. We were having a conversation," she said crisply.

"I remember," I said slowly. "About demons. And spirit guides. Frankly, it's all a bit much."

I looked Elsa over again. I knew she wasn't a vagrant off the street. Her arrival could only be connected to my dreams, and her explanation about my grandmother was as good as any. But I wasn't ready to face her.

"I'm tired. I think you should leave and come back another time when I feel up to a discussion," I said, walking toward my front door and opening it.

Elsa stared at me, a look of fury in her eyes. "Do you really think you can avoid me like you've avoided everything else? You asked me to come!"

I nodded. "If I did, I didn't know what I was asking for. I don't know why my grandmother sent you, but I don't need your help. I'll get some rest and fix everything tomorrow."

"You cannot fight the demon without my help, Olivia. You need me."

"That's exactly my point," I said as I ushered her to the stoop. "I don't intend to fight."

I shut the door and managed to walk upstairs to my bedroom before I started to cry.

"Goddamn it," I screamed as I tossed a pillow across the room. "Goddamn it!"

Maybe I *had* asked her to come. Clearly, I did need help. But I truly meant it when I said I didn't know what I was asking for. What did I need? An exorcist? A psychiatrist?

The last time I'd seen my mother, she'd been full of warnings about this very thing.

When I'd arrived at her place in Bolinas the previous week—after I'd lost another client to Stoner but before my drinking had gone off the deep end—she'd abruptly began scolding me as I stepped into her painting studio. "Olivia, you are *not* yourself," she'd said, turning to face me as I entered. "I can sense it. And it's time for me to say this: You haven't been yourself for many, many years. You've intentionally turned off your own sixth sense for so long I think maybe it is finally catching up with you."

Remembering how I'd stormed off and left her home, well, suddenly it all felt like too much, and I hunched over the edge of my bed, sobbing. Then my iPhone vibrated with a text. I picked it up from my nightstand. There, staring me in the face, was a message from Stoner Halbert.

Olivia, where have you disappeared to? You're spoiling my fun by hiding. I'm just getting started. Where's your fighting spirit?

I put the phone back down on my nightstand, suddenly feeling sick to my stomach. I managed to make it to my bathroom before I began to vomit. Why? Why was this happening to me? I was a lover, not a fighter. At least not when it came to people. I'd never harmed a soul. My only flaw, if you could call it one, was that I refused to use my gift. I had forsaken my emotions for logic, relying on the power of reason to solve my problems. Now, though, it seemed that logic could be easily overpowered by magic, for no reason at all.

I leaned against the edge of my toilet, wiping a cold cloth across my lips. I hadn't given Halbert my phone number. I had to suppose my ex-client had turned it over. I felt trapped inside my house like a mouse in a cage. Would I find him waiting for me outside one day? Elsa was right. For once, I couldn't fix a problem on my own. I needed help. I knew she would come again if I called her.

"Come back," I said, more quietly than I intended, as I walked to my bed to lie down. "Please come back."

I awoke several hours later from a dreamless sleep. I climbed out of bed slowly and grabbed a robe from a chair nearby. I walked into the bathroom to look in the mirror. The face staring back, while worn and puffy, didn't seem any different. My long brown hair streaked with red and gold, a trademark of all the women in my family, looked exactly the same. I had no marks on my body—no bumps, no bruises or scars.

Whatever Halbert was doing to me, it was all in my mind. I shook my head ruefully. He would drive me crazy if things continued this way. In the world of consultants, I had a reputation as the queen of calm.

That kind of poise is essential in my field. Politics and public affairs aren't quite dominated by men these days, but we're still evaluated differently. When women do show up, we often get labeled as "ballbusters" or "bitches." I had long ago lost track of the number of times I'd been complimented on "taking the bit between my teeth," or been a "real bulldog." I'd heard male consultants complimenting each other as "relentless" many times; women showing the same quality were mainly compared to racehorses or loyal pets. All this meant I'd learned not to have emotional outbursts when I was insulted. I made a point to never show the world if I had a problem. This much upheaval was bad for business, though. I would never be able to keep a poker face in public now.

I began to panic again, thinking about Halbert. I sat down on the edge of the tub to calm myself. It was at that moment that I heard the sound of the television coming from the living room. I walked down-stairs and found Elsa sitting on the couch, her shoes and socks off, watching a reality TV program that appeared to center on second marriages and Botox.

"You know, that stuff will kill you," I said, relieved that she had returned.

"It's fascinating," Elsa said, looking away from the television screen. "Do people really spend their time watching this stuff?"

"Yes. Quite a few people; these programs are very popular. You can stream an entire season in the time it takes to eat a pint of ice cream," I said jokingly.

Elsa shook her head and clicked off the TV. "It's no wonder the Council is worried."

"The Council?"

"Later. It's too complicated. How are you feeling?"

"Better, but I've been thinking about what you said to me. I want to know what's happening to me, and I want your help."

"It's the demon," Elsa said, rising from the couch. "He is a minor demon of the lowest order—Halbert is not skilled enough yet in the dark arts to conjure anything more powerful—but this one is still a force of evil. Its job is to harm the adversaries of whoever conjured them."

"How?" I asked. "Do they use physical pain?"

Elsa shook her head. "Not this demon. He's not designed to cause physical pain; he's subtler. Have you been acting odd lately? Acting in ways that are unusual for you?"

I nodded. "I've lost my focus, my will to compete. Even my mother commented on it when I visited her recently."

"What did she say?"

I was about to admit that my mother had been right about something, and it made me uncomfortable. "She said that as long as I ignore my gift, I would never really be myself."

"She was right. You have cut yourself off from your true nature and the source of your power. When you do that, it is very easy for an Other to knock you off balance."

"What is an 'Other'?"

"An Other is someone like me, or a vampire or a demon. There are humans, and there are the *Others*."

"What do you mean, knock me off balance?"

"You said it: you don't feel like *yourself*. Have you been more argumentative? Have you been overconfident that things will be fine, when in reality they are getting worse?"

Again, I nodded.

"That's the demon."

It was a relief to hear someone tell me that I wasn't going crazy and that the events of the last few weeks were not totally my fault, and yet the joy of reassurance was overshadowed by her explanation. I was being plagued by a demon? To hear it described in such dispassionate tones was unsettling.

"Am I under the control of this demon now?" I asked, afraid to hear the answer.

"Yes and no. There have been moments when the demon cast spells that made you act badly. How else do you explain walking away from your work? He's also placing spells and charms on your clients, or why would they behave so oddly toward you? But the demon has not tried to possess you physically. Once I began to appear in your dreams, I placed a protective spell on you to limit his manipulations."

"Why just *limit* things?" I asked. "Can you stop this?"

"It all depends on you, Olivia. You were born with abilities that should make it difficult or impossible for a demon to target you. If you'd been using your full powers, you would have known that the emotions you were dealing with were not your own. It's even possible you would have felt the presence of the Other. We won't know more until we open your senses and see what kind of gifts you really have."

I shook my head. "I don't want to open my senses," I said. "I don't want to feel more emotion. I want your help to get rid of this demon and let me go back to work."

Elsa picked up her shoes and socks and began to put them on. "This time, *I'm* leaving," she said. "It's obvious that you're not prepared to deal with the situation, and I can't help someone who won't help herself. This isn't a school project that you can ask your parents to fix. You are a grown woman, and you're in trouble—a trouble only you can make disappear. If you won't help yourself, then there is nothing I can do."

"What happens if you go?"

"More of the same, only minus me in your dreams," Elsa said. "Halbert will continue to take what he wants from you until there is nothing left."

She used my pride against me, and it worked. I couldn't stand the idea of losing my business to him that way—stripped to the bone, all my clients and past successes erased.

"OK," I said, swallowing hard at what was unfolding. "What do I have to do?"

Elsa smiled. "I'm glad you asked."

ELSA ASKED ME EITHER TO CLOSE MY BUSINESS OR TAKE A leave of absence. Both suggestions seemed too dramatic, so I put her off, saying I would start with a vacation. I informed my remaining clients that I would be out for several weeks. Then I called my staff and apologized profusely for being inattentive, giving them all modest pay raises as encouragement to stay on and manage things while I was away.

My home in the Inner Sunset neighborhood, near Golden Gate Park, has three bedrooms. Built in 1936, it was a gift from my grandmother—part of a successful real estate portfolio she and my grandfather managed. I gave the smallish guest room with a double bed to Elsa, complete with a fresh set of sheets and the code for the Wi-Fi. It was obvious that wherever Elsa normally spent the bulk of her time, streaming Netflix was not the norm.

I went to bed that night and slept soundly for the first time in weeks. My peace was short-lived, though, when I was awakened at six o'clock the following morning by Elsa, who stood looming above me, a pair of my running shoes in her hands.

"Up," she said. "It's time to begin your training."

I mumbled something about it being too early and flipped onto my side. She pulled the blankets off and let the cold air roll over me. I shot up and tried to pull the blankets back, but Elsa was not budging.

"Up," she said. "You need to get into fighting shape."

"Where are we going?"

"I did a little scouting while you were asleep last night. There's a place nearby where we can begin our work."

"Are you going to feed me to the lions?" I grumbled.

Elsa snorted. "I am not quite *that* old, if that's what you were implying. Besides, they would not have fed their seer, possibly their local healer, to the lions."

That caught my attention. I didn't know anything about Elsa or where she had come from. For all I knew, she *did* exist when the Romans built their colosseums.

She seemed to know I had a few questions on the tip of my tongue because she quickly cut me off. "Later. I will answer your questions when we return."

Not long afterward, I was staring at a steep set of steps inside Kezar Stadium, an old football stadium nearby. "You want me to run the stairs? Why?"

"When I was your age, I could ride a horse for miles while holding a crossbow," Elsa said, her hands on her hips. "I've fired a rifle from horseback while hunting with my tribe. Can you do that?"

I shook my head, trying not to laugh at the image of me with a crossbow.

"You need to get into fighting shape to protect yourself," Elsa chirped. "After a few weeks with the demon, I fear you've lost some of your energy."

"I have no need to shoot anything from the back of a horse," I barked back. "I can't see how this will help me at all."

"Just run the steps," Elsa deadpanned. "I will see you at the top."

This was too ridiculous. Hunt? Ride a horse? I'm a modern woman. I have a Clipper Card and an Uber app on my phone. It was with that kind of mindset that I prepared to walk away. But where would I go? I had asked Elsa to stay, and more importantly, I hated to abandon a challenge. How hard could it be to run the steps?

I took off with gusto. The first few seemed easy. *Piece of cake*, I mused privately. As I climbed higher, however, my legs began to quiver. Then they began to ache, my hamstring muscles burning like a match to the strip on the box. I gasped for air, unsteady as my legs wobbled. As I was nearing the top of the steps, I tripped and missed breaking my nose on the corner of one of the wooden benches by mere millimeters. I barely managed to pull myself upright, still gasping for air.

As I sat down to collect myself, I watched Elsa, decked out in a pair of my yoga pants, come running up the stairs. She wasn't even out of breath when she reached the top. I hid my face as she approached.

"Don't be embarrassed," she said. "I didn't do that to humiliate you. But I did want to make a point. You need to know your body and know your emotions. The best way to do that is to be physically fit. Being fit also gives you mental endurance, and you will need that skill when you allow your gifts to return."

"I think I might throw up," was my brilliant reply.

"By all means," Elsa said in response. "But when you're finished, you need to run the stairs again. We're going to be out here every day until you can do this easily."

"Why?"

"I outlasted my enemies because I rode harder, rode faster, and rode farther," Elsa said. "Endurance is everything in war."

"War?" I said, a shiver running up my spine. "I'm not at war."

"Do you want your career back? If so, you will have to stand up to the demon and Stoner Halbert. That is not something that can happen without work. Think of it this way. I have been watching television, and the men of your era seem to like fit women. It is easy to distract men using physical beauty. It will give you one more skill to use to your advantage."

It was not the motivational speech one would normally hear

from a personal trainer, but it worked. And so, my training began, and in those first few days, Elsa and I settled into a comfortable schedule. We exercised for several hours each morning before returning home. The city, it turned out, was a wonderful boot camp, with endless hills to climb, many lined with hidden staircases. We drove to Crissy Field and ran the path to the Golden Gate Bridge. After a few weeks, I was able to run the bridge and back as a part of my regimen. My afternoons were left open, and I spent that time running errands, touching base with my office, and working in the garden.

Although I was feeling better, I wondered what Elsa had in store for me next. She'd asked me not to tell Lily about her, and so far, I had honored her request. Normally, Lily and I spoke every day, but our friendship had been strained the last few weeks since we'd argued over Stoner Halbert and how much she knew of his dealings with my clients. Since then, except for a brief meal, I'd kept my distance, and Elsa was giving me a great excuse to continue the new pattern. Besides, I knew Lily was pretty busy with her own life.

I'd met Lily Prescott a few years before when we'd been neighbors in an apartment building near the waterfront on the Embarcadero. I'd just gotten back to San Francisco from Washington DC, where I'd worked as a press secretary to a member of Congress. Lily had just arrived from Portland, Oregon, where she'd worked as a children's librarian. Eventually, we both left the building, but our friendship stuck. Now, she lived in the Mission District and worked for the San Francisco Public Library. I'd come to truly rely on her friendship—she was funny and loyal but had an exotic air about her that made her seem slightly mysterious.

Now, with so much going on, I missed my friend. One afternoon as Elsa and I were having tea—she'd banned coffee from my diet—I asked if I could see Lily.

"Not yet," was her reply.

"Why?"

"Because you need to focus," she said in a schoolteacher's voice. "If you bring your friend into this, she will only distract you."

"Distract me from what? It seems as if your work is almost done here," I said, feeling confident. "I'm exercising; I feel great."

"We are a long way from being done," Elsa said. "This is simply the conditioning you need to get physically ready. We have yet to unlock your senses and see how they work."

"No," I said. "How can allowing myself to feel more possibly help?"

"You will not help yourself by remaining ignorant," Elsa said. "The reason you feel well is because I'm here and because you're not in the direct path of the demon. The minute you step back into your office, you will experience the same problems again."

I didn't know what to say. I did feel better and I was growing used to Elsa, although I still knew next to nothing about this woman living in my guest room.

"Why are you doing this?" I asked. "I know you said my grand-mother summoned you, but why do you have to stay?"

"I don't *have* to stay," she countered. "But as a spirit guide, my job is to help you escape danger. My work isn't finished yet. And I have business with the Council that keeps me here."

"So you aren't necessarily staying for *me*," I said, certain there was something she wasn't telling me.

"Why are you so anxious to see me leave?" Elsa asked. "We have much work to do. I sense you have great power, Olivia. I feel the energy in you. But you are in danger as long as you fail to use your instincts to see what's happening around you."

"I'm afraid," I said. "This gift you keep referring to has made my mother's life difficult. I don't want to become like her."

"Mother, father, sister, brother," Elsa said, shaking her head. "We cannot escape the bonds of our family. Their blood is our blood."

"I don't have any of those except my mother. I never knew my father, and my grandparents are dead."

Once again, Elsa paused, as if she were acknowledging something important in my statement. "Your gift is passed through the women in your family, so it matters little about the rest. My mother was a shaman in our village, as was her mother before her. These skills pass through one generation to the next. One day, you will have a daughter."

"Stop," I said, holding out my hand. "I'm not getting married. I'm not having a child. Look at me. My life is out of control. I am having a conversation in my kitchen with a ghost about how to beat the devil at his own game. How on earth can you talk about a future with marriage and children?"

Elsa looked amused, but not in a good way. "Technically, I am not a ghost, and I have never seen anyone beat the devil at his own game," she said. "You are nowhere near ready to do that. I am asking that you take responsibility for your own life and use the tools you were given. By all the goddesses of the known world, I have never seen anyone reject her bloodline so readily. This wasn't a choice when I was your age. People in my tribe, in my village, depended on my mother to seek out the spirits—to learn about the harvest, to heal the sick, and to protect our elders."

"What about you?" I asked, angry at her lecture. "What did they depend on you for?"

Elsa turned her head away from me slightly. For the first time since she'd revealed herself to me, I could see hesitation. It seemed that she, too, had secrets.

"We are alike in many ways, Olivia," she continued. "I did not reject my skills when I was your age, but I did not manage them well either. I wanted to do more than help old men bring in good crops for the village. So I began to dabble in things that were beyond my measure."

Elsa got up from the stool and began to pace around the kitchen.

"Eventually, I left my village in search of someplace where I could learn how to gain more power. I wasn't content to *see* the future; I wanted to control it. After much searching, I found an old witch who promised to help me gain introduction to a school of magic where I could learn the secrets of casting powerful spells to control things. Nature, the weather . . ."

"So you wanted to be a powerful witch?"

"I wanted power," Elsa said. "I had no specific occupation in mind."

"Did you find the school?"

Elsa nodded, but her face was grim. "The school was in the mountains of Romania. It was very remote. It took several days to reach the top of the mountain and find the castle."

"And . . . ?"

"The witch was true to her word," Elsa said. "She sent me to the door of the Scholomance, where all things dark could be learned. I should have been more cautious, but I was eager to begin my lessons. I knocked upon a large wooden door with a raven engraved on the front. After some time, an elderly man dressed as a servant opened the door. He confirmed it was a school but said they accepted only ten students at a time. At first, I thought he was sending me away, but then he said that I had arrived just in time to be the tenth student. He instructed me to secure my horse in the stables nearby and return to the castle. Excited, I quickly did as I was told. But as I walked back toward the school, an angel appeared on the branch of a tree next to me."

I raised an eyebrow but did not interrupt.

"The angel called out to me by name and implored me to not enter the castle. He told me it was the house of the devil, and that of the ten students chosen, one would have to stay behind and be sent to hell as payment for the lessons. The angel was certain I would be the one to make good on the debt, and he urged me to reclaim my horse and ride away from the castle that very moment."

"Did you leave?" I asked, caught up in her remarkable tale.

"I was eager to become more powerful, but I certainly didn't want to give my soul to the devil. So I agreed to leave with the angel. But as I turned to retrieve my horse, the door of the castle swung open. The servant I spoke with was there again, but this time, he was dressed in the clothing of a gentleman. I realized I had been conversing with the devil himself."

At this point I was speechless. The devil? Was she joking with me to make a point?

Elsa sensed my skepticism. "If you decide to continue with your training, you will come to see that there is more to this world than meets the eye. I didn't believe I would ever stand toe-to-toe with the devil, either, until that day."

"Go on," I urged.

"The devil asked us both if we would like to come inside for a cup of tea. The angel laughed and said, 'You know very well that I will not walk through those doors.'"

"'Then I will come to you,' the devil said. I had seen many evil spirits in my time as a shaman, but I had never felt such evil as I did when he approached us. He was standing as close to me as I am to you. By knocking on his door, he said, I had already offered myself to him. The angel replied that he had been watching the school for more than a hundred years and knew very well that until I crossed the threshold, I was not subject to the devil's contract."

I have to admit, Elsa had captured my attention. I motioned rapidly with my hand to continue.

"To my surprise, the devil asked the angel if he would take a walk with him. I did not know at the time, but it seems that the devil enjoys making deals and negotiations. Testing the intellect of his opponents gives him great pleasure.

"The angel agreed to walk with him, but only if they stayed outside the castle. It was dark now, but the glow of a bright autumn moon illuminated the grounds. While waiting for them, I leaned against the tree, listening as the mountains came alive with the sounds of creatures in the area, including wolves. I vowed to myself that I would go into the barn and lock the doors if they didn't return quickly.

"After a short time, they did return. But while I waited, I had never been so frightened. I had climbed the mountain to the school full of the energy of an ambitious woman in her thirties, with no idea of the true expense of the knowledge I desired. Exposed at the doorway to the devil and his brood, I now understood that some things are too costly to pursue. And furthermore, I had angered the devil by refusing his wish. And all I could think was, *If he wins the argument with the angel, what will become of me once I am inside the castle?*"

I had the same question burning in my mind and was beginning to imagine all kinds of torture—images straight out of all the late-night horror movies I had seen.

"The devil seemed to enjoy my apprehension, for he grinned broadly and took his time to speak. 'You are free to leave,' was all he said, and then he disappeared into the darkness."

"Is that it? You walked away?"

Elsa was about to finish her story when my doorbell rang. We both looked at each other, wondering who it could be. I shrugged and got up to find out. When I opened the door, Lily was standing outside.

"Where have you been?" she asked, pushing past me. "Why are you blowing me off? Please don't think I'm mad at you about the Stoner Halbert thing—"

She stopped abruptly when she saw Elsa standing inside. Both women grabbed me, as if they were trying to tug me to safety. I yanked free and yelled at them both.

"What is the matter with you two?" I asked. Gesturing with my hands to make introductions, I said, "Elsa, this is Lily, my best friend. Lily, this is . . . well, this is Elsa."

Elsa responded by asking me a question. "Your best friend is a fairy?"

Lily, not to be topped, asked, "Why is there a time-walker in your house, Olivia?"

This clearly was not going to be a typical girls' night in. I wasn't sure which question to answer first.

"Elsa is the panther from my dreams I told you about. She's here to help me. It's a long story. But why does Elsa think you're a fairy?"

Lily spoke to Elsa, ignoring me. "Who sent you?"

"I could ask you the same thing," Elsa said. "Are you supposed to be guarding her?"

Lily looked slightly defensive as she turned to me to give her reply. "I met Olivia when we were neighbors. I don't usually take humans as close friends, but I could see she was special. I am not officially her guardian; I never asked for permission. We became friends. I have always tried to look out for her. She's flying blind, you know."

"Have you seen the demon?" Elsa asked.

Lily shook her head. "No, but I sensed his presence. I placed a few minor charms around Olivia's home to keep him away, but since I'm not her guardian, I couldn't intervene."

This seemed to satisfy Elsa because she took a step away from me as she nodded in agreement. But I was not happy being an invisible third party.

"Hello," I said, waving my arms at them both. "I'm standing right here. Can you two tell me what's going on? Lily, you're a *fairy*?"

Lily smiled. "Yes, but honestly, is that so shocking to you, after seeing Elsa appear? You must know by now that there is another world of creatures beyond what humans can see. When I first met you, I could tell right away that you had extra gifts. I expected you to notice what I was, but you never did. After a while, I realized that you weren't even trying to use your senses."

I was feeling a little embarrassed. A few weeks back, when we'd gone out to dinner, I'd noticed a tattoo with strange writing on the back of her neck, which in retrospect, was clearly some kind of fairy marking. Yet she had not revealed herself to me. Everyone in the room seemed to know more about me than I did.

"So what is this? Are you my friend out of pity? I've been telling you everything that's happening to me. Am I some kind of project for you to look after?"

"I'm a fairy, Olivia," Lily said, clearly annoyed. "We don't reveal ourselves to *anyone*. I'm your friend because I want to be. If I pitied you, I would have asked my clan to assign a real guardian to watch over you, someone you would never have seen or met."

"Is it against the rules to be friends with humans?"

Lily and Elsa looked at each other and laughed. "It's not encouraged," Lily said.

"Why?"

Elsa held her hands up. "I think you've heard enough for the time being, Olivia. Why don't we go into the kitchen and make some dinner?"

3

"MAKE SOME DINNER" ACTUALLY MEANT ORDERING CHINESE food from around the corner. Once the food arrived, I started streaming a San Francisco Giants baseball game. We sat for a few moments eating pot stickers and listening to the local announcers calling the plays.

There are probably plenty of people who wouldn't expect sports to be an interest of mine, since I'd grown up in a house with only my single mother. But they would be wrong; I love baseball. My grandfather loved the Giants, and his passion was infectious. I have fond memories of listening to the play-by-play at my grandfather's house—he had a radio in almost every room—when I would visit him.

My mother is more enthusiastic about soccer, a result of her many sojourns to Europe over the years. I'd learned to like it too. Both she and I are true Francophiles. My introduction to the French language began in kindergarten, when my mother insisted that I attend a bilingual school in Marin. There, a kindly older woman from Toulouse taught me my earliest French words. In addition, during college I did a brief exchange program in Paris. My mother's occasional art shows in Paris gave me even more of a chance to relish European culture.

My dinner companions appeared not to share my love for baseball or soccer, however.

"Baseball is not a sport," was all Elsa could muster as she sampled another dumpling. "There's no blood involved."

Changing the subject seemed like the best idea. "Tell me about being a fairy, Lily."

Lily put down the container of garlic green beans. "What do you want to know?"

"Why do you work in the library?" was my first question, followed by, "Where is your family, and what kind of powers do you have?"

"I come from a clan of fairies that has always lived in the human world," Lily said. "We've dedicated our lives to public service. Although we make visits to the Other Side, we mostly stay in this world. I'm one of a long line of librarians. And yes, I have added a little magic to the library system. Who would return to a library if it never had the book you wanted? Having a well-run, popular library system is good for San Francisco."

"Why libraries?"

Lily finished chewing before she spoke again. "Because fairies are voracious readers of books and texts in many languages. Working in a library affords us the luxury of being surrounded by words and information. Obviously, there's the Internet and social media, but for me, there is no better way to learn about humans and the world in general than to work in a library."

"What does that have to do with public service?" I asked, putting another dumpling on my plate.

"That's easy," Lily said. "Libraries are important for humans. In the human world, being able to read is the key to all of your activities. It's pretty clear that the less people know, the worse their fate is. Allowing all people to have access to the same kinds of information for free is important. When people are uneducated it . . . well, it creates opportunities for others to manipulate the situation."

Elsa snorted. "Humans want to be controlled; they appreciate limited choices."

I decided to ignore Elsa's pointed remark for the moment. "What about the rest of your family?"

"Everything you know, everything I've told you about my family, is true. My father and mother are retired but did work as librarians. They do live in San Jose. My sister really lives in Seattle, and my brother really lives in Portland. He's a firefighter, but that's rare; normally, we're terribly afraid of fire."

"And your powers? What kinds of things can you do?"

"I'm not a circus act," Lily said, sounding slightly annoyed. "I don't do tricks."

"I'm sorry, Lily. That came out wrong."

Elsa inserted herself into the conversation, turning to me. "I think we need to focus our energies on freeing up your gifts."

"And how do you plan to do that?"

"I have to run an errand," she said. "But tomorrow we're going on an overnight adventure."

"Overnight? Are we camping?" I asked, wondering what destination she had in mind.

"You could say that," Elsa said with a smile. "I need to leave in a few moments to look for some supplies. Assuming I'm successful, we will leave here tomorrow night after sunset."

"Can I give you a ride someplace?" I asked, not expecting an unusual reply.

Elsa looked at Lily when she spoke. "No need. I travel using a portal in the park."

"Can I come tomorrow?" Lily asked.

Elsa nodded. "Yes, it will be better if there are more of us."

I was beginning to get worried. "What's a portal?" I asked.

Lily and Elsa exchanged knowing glances. "It will be better if we show you," Elsa said.

"OK," I said, feeling relieved to avoid, if temporarily, yet another hidden detail about the world I'd missed. Lily and Elsa left the house together, and I watched as they walked down the street into the night's thick fog. One minute I could see them very clearly, and the next, they were gone.

4

FOR THE FIRST TIME IN MANY DAYS, I WOKE UP ALONE IN THE house. I confess I missed my new roommate, or at least I missed the feeling of having someone nearby.

I don't have a great track record with men. There have been no great romances in my life. To be sure, there have been a few multi-week excursions, but they never transformed themselves into repeat engagements. Instead, I have amassed a collection of single-night memories.

It would be nice to feel great passion for someone, to feel my body long for another with every fiber of my being. But that has not been a sensation I've experienced. Perhaps watching my mother's struggles over the years has made me timid. From where I sit, spilling over with emotion looks messy and, if unreciprocated, humiliating. As a result, the only male voices heard emanating from my living room on a regular basis are the baseball announcers Jon Miller and David B. Flemming.

Even without Elsa, I followed my normal schedule, rising early to eat a banana and then heading straight for the park to work out. I entered at Ninth Avenue and ran west toward the coast. I managed to reach the graffiti-scarred retaining walls of Ocean Beach in less than an hour.

To cool down, I decided to walk onto the broad beach and stretch on the sand. The fog from the night before had retreated, perching along the edge of the horizon as if it couldn't decide what to do next. The sun was coming up into the sky, and the air around me was cool and mild. It felt delicious to be outside. I decided to prolong the feeling by walking over to Judah Street for a cup of coffee at a nearby beach café.

Java Beach Café was fairly busy, but I managed to find a table outside and started scrolling through my Apple News feed. I sipped my cappuccino, alternating between catching up on current events and gazing at the sea until a headline on my screen caught my attention: INTERNET CEO SEEKS RETURN TO CONGRESS. I read with interest a story about my former boss, Levi Barnes, and his decision to run for office again, this time as a congressman representing Silicon Valley. My first job in Washington, DC, had been with Levi when he was a congressman representing Salt Lake City, Utah. After losing a particularly tough reelection bid, he'd left politics and moved to the Bay Area to become an entrepreneur. It seemed unthinkable that, after losing so badly before, he would give up his privacy and success to reenter national politics. What had changed for him? It had been more than a year since the two of us had spoken, and I made a mental note to call him to catch up. I was also curious to see who he'd hired to run his campaign.

The high-pitched squeak of the N-Judah streetcar jarred me out of my thoughts. It was time to head home. Seeing that a train had reached the end of the line and was turning east toward downtown, I decided to hop on and ride back to my house.

By midafternoon, a few hours later, Elsa had returned. She walked straight into the kitchen and began brewing some kind of concoction that gave off quite an unpleasant aroma. I came into the kitchen just as she was placing small button-shaped fruits into boiling water with what looked like cinnamon sticks and a vanilla bean.

"What are you making?" I asked, trying to breathe through my mouth.

"It's going to be a tea," she said. "You're going to drink some tonight before we go out."

"Is it going to taste as bad as it smells?"

"Actually, it's going to taste worse," she said, keeping her back to me as she hunched over the stove brewing her potion. "The trick is to drink quickly and not think about it."

"What does it do?" I asked, thinking that I should at least know what I was getting myself into.

"It should help you regain your senses," Elsa said. "It's an old recipe that has been used by many women over the years."

"Where did you go last night?"

Elsa kept her back to me. "New Mexico, mostly. I had a few other stops to make."

"I take it you didn't fly on a commercial jet," I said, hoping to provoke a discussion about portals and time-walkers.

For the record, it's not that I find it difficult to imagine that there is more to things than what we see at first glance. And I don't doubt that the world has more complexity to it than most people think. I've just never wanted to accept it.

What I want from life is something more rational. If I'm going to pay attention and care, then I want to know how the mysteries work. If I can understand the mechanics, then I can manage my fear. After years of living in a very logical fashion, now I was expected to be Alice in Wonderland, throwing caution to the wind and drinking my potion so all can be revealed.

"You know I didn't take an airplane," Elsa said. "I used a portal. It's a door between places, and they are scattered across the city."

"Where do you go when you use them?"

"With a little practice and focus, you can go anywhere," Elsa said.

"Am I going to use one tonight?"

"No. Tonight you're going to work on finding those instincts of yours so we can see what kind of empath you really are. I sense you

have great abilities, Olivia, but you have stuffed them so far beneath
your skin that only the most drastic efforts will draw them out." She
removed the pot from the stove and strained the contents into a
ceramic pitcher, which she placed in the refrigerator. "It will be better
chilled."

"I'm scared," I said, admitting the obvious. "What's going to
happen to me tonight?"

"Lily and I will be with you," Elsa said. "Whatever happens, and
maybe nothing will, you will be with us and we will take care of you."

"This is not a reassuring speech," I said.

"I'm not here to reassure you," Elsa remarked, her voice stern.
"I'm here to protect you and to get you to stop living a half life."

"A half life," I repeated. "How is running a business and owning a
home a half life?"

"Olivia, you were born with a sixth sense—a set of instincts that
allows you to read people before they even know something themselves," she continued. "Instead of using those skills, you buried them
and left yourself vulnerable to all kinds of danger and mischief. At
minimum, you might have been able to stop Stoner Halbert's demon
from stealing your clients. Do you think a man with eyesight would
knowingly blind himself? That's what you've done."

"I haven't blinded myself," I responded, my pride wounded once
again. "Did it ever occur to you that maybe I see more clearly than
you do?"

Elsa snorted. "After tonight we will see if that's really true. You
should go upstairs and rest. You won't get much sleep tonight."

5

NOT LONG AFTER DRINKING THE TEA, I STARTED TO FEEL ILL.
Elsa must have known what was coming because she was already at
my side, quickly guiding me toward the sink, where I began to retch.
Lily was also there, rubbing my back in an attempt to soothe me.
They both murmured calming words in my ear, but I was in no shape
to understand. Large sounds filled my head—vibrations really, that
resonated off my sternum as I grasped the edge of the sink. A great
freight train was barreling through me, and I could feel it coming
down the tracks through every bone in my body.

"What's happening to me?" I asked, my heart racing.

Elsa grasped my shoulder and whispered in my ear, "Don't be
afraid. Whatever happens, Lily and I will not leave your side. Just
remember: not everything you see tonight will be real."

We must have left the house after Elsa's remarks, but the particu-
lars of our exit are a bit fuzzy. Next thing I knew, we were walking
through a pair of ornate green iron gates that featured delicate-look-
ing vines and leaves. We strode onto a red brick path sheltered by a
canopy of trees. Moonlight illuminated the path, and suddenly I felt
as if I were a bride in a wedding, although who I was about to be
joined with remained a mystery.

In the middle of the path sat a well-worn sundial perched on a
stone pedestal. The metal glowed with a golden light. Fascinated, I
reached out to touch the illuminated dial. The moment my skin

made contact with the triangular piece, I felt a jolt of energy run through my body as a cacophony of voices began to pierce my skull. I laughed aloud as if I understood the joke and tried to listen to the conversation.

Before I could lock onto a single word, Elsa removed my hand from the dial. I turned to face her and exhaled suddenly. She was awash in color; shimmering waves of yellow, orange, and green poured from her body.

"Oh my God, oh my God!" I exclaimed, reaching out to touch the light waves. "You're so beautiful."

"What do you see?" she asked.

"I see colors," I said. "I hear voices and I see colors."

"Good," Elsa said. "Don't worry—you're not crazy. The peyote is working. Let's see what happens next."

I looked up to see billowing strands of moss hanging from a Monterey pine. A strong wind arrived, blowing in a wicked fog bank, which rolled across the park at a furious speed. I should have been cold, but instead my skin burned like I was on fire as the crisp air enveloped me. I quickly shrugged out of my fleece and flung it to the ground. Again, I lost track of time, and when I refocused, I found that we were standing in the music concourse of Golden Gate Park, near where the de Young Museum and the Academy of Sciences are located. I swallowed hard, my tongue feeling too large for my mouth.

The park was bursting with noise. Every living being, it seemed, made some kind of sound as it moved. The night was awash in color. I absorbed all of these sensations and felt them take root, as a young tree establishes itself in new ground. I laughed again, feeling an uncanny sense of new knowledge.

I was ruminating on the meaning of the sounds I was hearing when my attention was abruptly drawn to a fountain in the center of the concourse.

The bowl of the fountain was illuminated by lights below it, and in the center of its pedestal stood an enormous stone saber-toothed tiger. Trapped between its massive claws was a serpent that was partially coiled around the cat's body. Locked in a fierce battle, the cat, with its massive, muscled arms, looked more human than feline and seemed to be moving, wrestling with the snake.

I sat down on a wooden bench nearby, unable to tear my gaze away from the fountain.

"It's Elsa!" I yelled aloud, surprised at the sound of my voice. "It's Elsa taking on the devil."

Now Elsa laughed. "What do you hear, Olivia?"

Responding to her question, I strained to listen. At first, I couldn't detect any sound coming from the fountain. But as I focused, I began to feel a vibration moving through my body, and I stood up, unable to sit still.

"Up," I said. "It's saying, 'Get up and come in.'"

Elsa preened like a proud mother. "Very good. That's exactly what it's saying. One day soon we will go inside, but for now, we have to say good-bye to the Guardian."

"The Guardian," I whispered to myself. As I murmured the name, I caught sight of a light coming from a large tower in front of us. I could also *feel* the intense light. "Bright!" I screamed as the light expanded behind my eyes, momentarily blinding me.

"What light, Olivia?" Lily asked. "Where is the light coming from?"

I pointed up, toward the tower of the de Young Museum. My already sensitive stomach was roiling again.

Elsa turned me so that my back was to the tower. "You must breathe deeply and try to push the light out of your mind, Olivia. Focus on the light and push it away."

Eventually, I was able to do what Elsa asked. I inhaled and exhaled, slowly bringing my attention to the center of my forehead, where the pain was the strongest.

Meanwhile, Elsa had begun shouting at no one in particular in a language I didn't understand. While Lily stood nearby looking grim, Elsa walked briskly to the fountain, touched the edge of the cement, and disappeared.

Hand outstretched, I shouted her name. Lily was at my side immediately, pulling me away. She grabbed my fleece and we began to run, setting a brisk pace through the wet, foggy night. As we passed through the damp, muddy trails of the park's forests, I removed more clothing, dropping items along the way. My body temperature continued to climb, despite the fact that I was now wearing nothing but a running bra and bike shorts.

"I need water, Lily," I said.

She opened a backpack and handed me a bottle. "Drink," she said. "The effects of the tea will start to wear off in a few hours."

"Is Elsa coming back tonight?"

"I'm not sure," Lily said. "She had to go see someone."

"She disappeared," I remarked absently, distracted by the buzzing in my ears.

Lily nodded. "Yes. But she will come back."

Very quickly, we found ourselves back in the land of glowing flowers, strolling through an open meadow, dotted with pink and purple foxglove. We crossed a road, climbed a dirt path, and, after a few minutes of walking, came to stand before Stow Lake, a man-made lake established in Golden Gate Park in the 1890s. Half-dressed and disheveled, I paused on the sidewalk, transfixed by a small island a few hundred yards from where I stood. The island, shrouded in mist and almost completely covered by a fallen tree and overgrown flowering vines, seemed to be calling to my overheated body.

It didn't take much for me to heed its call.

"Hot!" I cried out, and I waded into the lake.

"Olivia, noooo!" came Lily's frantic cry as she jumped in after me.

We swam to the island, but never made it out of the water, thanks to a ring of thorny blackberry bushes lining the shore. Rebuffed, we made our way back onto dry land. Standing on the side-walk, dripping wet, Lily removed a small towel from her pack and handed it to me.

"It's not much, but it will help dry you a bit," she said, rubbing the water off of her arms and legs as she spoke.

I sat down on a nearby bench and began to listen to the world around me. A cacophony of sounds rang in my ears. I could hear the fish swimming below the surface of the water. I detected the faint rustling of owls in the trees. Smiling, I took Lily's hand in my own.

"This place is alive," I said with conviction.

Lily smiled and squeezed my hand. "See what you've been missing," she said gently. "Now, *you* are really alive, too."

6

MY FIRST SENSATION WAS THE FEELING OF SOMETHING COLD
and hard pressing into my lower back. Then the smell of damp,
rotting plants filled my nostrils. I remained motionless, trying to
recall what had happened. Where was I? Then I remembered my
adventure in the park and the tea Elsa had given me that caused me
to hallucinate. I lay still, testing my body. I wiggled one limb, and
then the next and the next, waiting for injuries and pain. I moved
my head from side to side and slowly opened my eyes.

I recoiled, for there, not an inch from my face, was an egret. The
small white bird was studying me.

I smiled at it. "Either you're in the wrong place, or I'm sleeping in
your bed," I said quietly to the bird.

The egret opened up its wings and flew away as I sat up to survey
my surroundings. I was sleeping on a small patch of dirt next to a lily
pond near the side entrance of the de Young Museum. *Why here, of
all places?* I wondered, and then I recalled hearing a man's voice at the
end of the evening. The voice was insistent, urging me to leave my
old life behind to join him. I had followed the voice, getting as far as
the museum, but I could not find its source.

At some point, I must have lost Lily and come back here to fall
asleep, choosing to slumber beside a statue of Pan with his flute. Now,
as the light of day pressed against my sensitive eyes, the nature of my

situation dawned on me. I was a half-dressed woman trespassing on city property, and I needed to get up and leave before someone saw me. The good news is that given the kinds of characters who inhabit San Francisco, I wasn't too worried about looking odd when I strolled back to my house. I was certain my unkempt appearance wouldn't raise so much as an eyebrow.

I wondered what had happened to Elsa. I concentrated for a moment, and then, one by one, the images of the night returned. I recalled with clarity that Elsa had disappeared into the fountain. I remembered the bright light and her attempt to shield me from it.

My running shoes were sitting next to me, and I reached over to slide them on to my filthy, bare feet. As soon as I climbed out of the dirt and hopped onto the sidewalk, I spotted Elsa sitting on a bench nearby. Her eyes were shut, and she appeared to be dozing lightly. I intended to gently tap her on the shoulder, but as I approached, she opened her eyes with a start.

"Olivia," she said, smiling. "You've returned to this world. How do you feel?"

"I feel great," I said. "My back is a little sore from sleeping on a rock, but other than that, I feel fine." As I stood looking at Elsa, I began to see some of the same colors I had seen the night before. Elsa was gently giving off waves of yellow and orange as she stood before me. "You're giving off colors again," I said.

As soon as the words left my mouth, I felt a rush of warmth invade my body. It was the feeling of pleasure, but the feeling was not my own. It belonged to Elsa.

"I can feel your pleasure, too," I said, shaking my head. "Is that what you hoped would happen?" Again, a rush of warmth ran through me. "You're pleased. I can tell."

"I *am* pleased," she responded, rising from the bench to stretch. "How much more you can do with your gift remains to be seen. We're going to work on it a bit, and then I'm going to introduce you to a group of people who are very interested in meeting you. They'd like you to come and work for them."

We walked back to the house in silence, my mind too preoccupied with the show unfurling before me. As I passed people on the street, I could clearly see the outline of their auras and feel their emotions. Unfiltered, it was disorienting, and by the time we got to the front door, my stomach was churning with all of the morning angst I'd picked up as my neighbors headed off to work. I placed my hand against the doorjamb and closed my eyes, remembering Elsa's advice to breathe deeply. After a few moments, I regained control of my senses. I'd nearly been overwhelmed by other people's emotions, but with some measure of confidence, I realized that I could calm my mind when necessary.

I was about to reach for my hide-a-key when the front door flew open. Lily was standing in the doorway half-awake, wearing one of my bathrobes. Evidently, she'd had the good sense to come home and sleep in a bed.

I watched velvety green light flowing off my best friend and felt her happiness at my safe return deep inside my heart. In the color chart of aura reading, which had been taught to me by Elsa, green and blue appeared to be the colors of good temperament, kindness, and peace. It was lovely to feel that kind of friendship from another being.

"Thank you," I said. "I'm very glad to see you too. What an adventure we had last night. Did you know that your light is as green as that island we swam to?"

Lily giggled. "It worked. You can see my aura. I'm usually green, and sometimes a little blue comes through. Most fairies are green. If you ever see a red color coming off a fairy, you should run and get away as fast as you can. It means something horrible is about to happen."

I nodded, but I was distracted by my stomach, which began to grumble. "I'm starving. Let's have some food and we can talk some more."

"I can't stay," Lily said. "I have to go to work. You know the library is open seven days a week."

"Suit yourself," I said. "I'm making pancakes."

After I had eaten and taken a shower, I came downstairs to find Elsa sitting on the floor in the living room, meditating. Legs folded and eyes closed, she was chanting softly. I could see very strong orange-and-yellow pulses coming from her body as she took in breaths of air. I wondered what colors my body gave off, but when I looked in the mirror after my shower, nothing appeared.

"Yellow, orange, and a twinge of red," Elsa said. "I can hear your thoughts now, Olivia. Your mind is very powerful. We need to be careful so that you don't telegraph what you're thinking to those who would use the information against you."

I flopped down in a chair and sighed. "You can hear my thoughts, and I can feel your emotions. How is this supposed to be better for me? I feel more vulnerable than ever."

"You *are* more vulnerable . . . for the moment," Elsa said. "It will pass, and you will come to learn how powerful a woman is when she uses her sixth sense."

I sat for a moment contemplating my future. It certainly couldn't get any worse, I reasoned. I now had the power to read people and know their emotions. If I could figure out how to protect myself, maybe I could get back to work and retrieve my clients from Stoner Halbert.

"What about the demon?" I asked. "Will it go away now?"

"Soon you will be able to keep him out of your head, and then he'll have to move on to someone more vulnerable."

Thinking about being vulnerable reminded me of the horrible light and pain from the night before. "What was that light last night? Why did it hurt my head?"

Elsa paused a long while and then said, "It was someone trying to read your thoughts."

That didn't sound good at all. "But why? Who was it?"

Elsa frowned. "He's the head of an organization that's very interested in humans who have extra skills like yours."

"Really? How odd," I said. "He sounds like a freak. How does he even know about me?"

Again, Elsa didn't answer immediately. Then, "I am a member of a group called the Council, and it was my responsibility to tell them that I was leaving my post temporarily to help a human," she explained. "When I told the director about your gifts, he became very interested."

"The Council," I said aloud. "It sounds like a John Grisham novel."

"I don't know who John Grisham is," Elsa said, her stern voice returning. "But I assure you, the Council is very real. Gabriel Laurent is the current director. He's the one who tried to contact you last night."

"Does he always try to blind people to say hello?"

"I told him it was too early to try such a thing," she acknowledged. "I asked him to wait a few days and promised that I would bring you to meet him."

"Is that where you went when you left? To see him?" I asked. "You touched the fountain and disappeared."

Elsa nodded. "I used the portal to jump to the top of the museum, where the Council keeps its headquarters."

"How did you do that? I mean, how do you make sure you get where you want to go?"

"I use my mind. It will guide me to where I want to go."

"And what does Monsieur Laurent want with me?"

"It's nothing, really; he wants to speak to you about a job."

I knew right away that Elsa was lying.

I HAD TO WONDER WHAT ELSA WAS HOLDING BACK. I COULD feel her hesitation. By now, I also knew her well enough to know I should back off and wait to ask her again later. So I let the matter pass and dressed and readied myself for my first day of learning how to use my reclaimed skills.

We were headed to the Mission District. Elsa insisted we use the streetcar to travel downtown. Riding the public trains, she said, would be a good place to practice. As soon as we boarded the N-Judah line, Elsa leaned in and whispered my assignment.

"Focus on one person, and try to block out the rest. Find one person and tell me what you see and feel."

I scanned the people on board, looking for a good target. A few seats away, I locked on to a well-dressed woman who looked to be about twenty-five. She was tall with long blond hair, held in place by a tortoiseshell headband. Her hair, which looked like it had been brushed until it shined, cascaded down her back. She seemed successful and content—an easy first assignment, I told myself.

When I examined her more closely, though, I began to see a different story. She was encased in a solid red line of fear. She was worried. I could feel it. Her heart also held another emotion: longing. I sat down on a nearby seat and watched her.

"She's worried," I said to Elsa under my breath. "She's trying to reassure herself about something. Well, maybe not reassure, but I think I can feel her trying to soothe herself."

Elsa pulled me up and led me to the second car of the train. "Try again."

I was feeling more confident, so I decided to try someone more challenging. This time I locked on to a slightly disheveled homeless man, his belongings piled high on the seat next to him. When I focused in on his coloring, I saw something odd. He gave off a grayish hue, which looked like smog hovering over the hills. And as soon as I tried to read his emotions, he turned around to face me, and I could tell he knew I was trying to read him. Although he smiled at me, his behavior was anything but friendly. He began to press back, sending some very dark emotions my way. I felt a rush of sadness and realized that he was trying to drive me to despair. He persistently pushed negative feelings into my head.

"That's a demon, Olivia," Elsa said, appearing at my side. "Can you feel him trying to drive a wedge through your soul? Block him out."

Once again, I practiced using my breath to lower a blind over my mind's eye and close off my nervous system. Soon, I began to feel like myself again. The demon turned away from us and looked out the window.

"He gave up very easily," I said.

"He probably knew he had no chance with you," was Elsa's reply. "Demons, in general, are a lazy lot. They don't like to work hard. I think he knew better than to test your will."

"Are they always gray?" I asked as we made our way out of the train station.

"Always. You must have a soul or some connection to humanity to give off an aura. Remember that. Gray is the absence of color. As servants of the devil, they have no humanity left inside them and, therefore, give off no color."

"Wow. That's scary. What would have happened if he'd succeeded?"

"You would have left the train feeling like your life was not worth living," Elsa said ruefully. "Demons are responsible for a lot of the suicides you read about that happen in public—the stories about people who jump into the path of a moving train or leap from the Golden Gate Bridge. Their deaths are often incomprehensible to the people who knew them. Now you know the reason for their actions."

I shuddered slightly as we rode the escalator up from the bowels of the subterranean train station, trying to shake off the gloom of the demon and Elsa's story. Would that have been my fate, too, had Elsa not appeared? Would I have been doomed to toss myself over a bridge when Stoner was done with me? I didn't want to know.

We exited the station at Sixteenth and Mission. From there, we moved west, walking through the crowds on Valencia Street. There were dozens upon dozens of bodies moving through the neighborhood. I held still, allowing myself to feel the energy of the people passing by.

"Don't lock on to it or try to absorb it; let it move past you, as if you were browsing titles in a bookstore," Elsa said.

If I had been in a bookstore, the floor would have been a mess. It felt as if I were bumping into everyone who passed. A jolt here, a jolt there. I was being brushed by anger, anxiety, sexual longing, happiness, and true love. My senses were tickled each time someone passed. I began to regulate it, as if turning a dial to find a radio station. I concentrated, focusing my mind to pull in from one person but not the next. A rainbow of colors passed behind my eyes, and I was enjoying my newfound skills until something began pressing on my skull again.

I looked up, trying to discover the source of the pain and found myself staring into the dark-green eyes of a man with long hair and a nose ring. His piercing gaze seemed to be picking at my head. It was a very specific kind of pressure, but it came with not a trace of emotion.

"Elsa, that man over there is trying to force his way into my head."

"Vampire," was all she said.

"Vampire?" I replied. "In the Mission?"

"Especially in the Mission," she said.

"He's picking at my skull like a woodpecker."

"Make him stop."

I closed my eyes and forcefully shut him out. He smiled, saluting me with two fingers as he passed.

"He doesn't give off any emotion," I said as he passed. "Only that pecking sensation."

Elsa laughed. "Vampires don't feel emotions the way humans do. It has something to do with the absence of a beating heart. But if you ever get to know a vampire well, you will learn to read their feelings."

"Wow, a vampire and a demon, all in the last hour in San Francisco," I said, shaking my head. "I never imagined it was possible."

"And now?" Elsa asked.

"I'm not sure," I said honestly. "But I do know that everything I thought I knew has changed."

"That is a good beginning," Elsa said, putting her hand on my arm. "Let's go find a place to meet Lily for dinner."

We settled on a quaint bistro on Valencia Street. Lily arrived at about five thirty, looking exhausted. Seeing her made me realize how tired I was too.

"I don't think this will be a late evening," I said. "We both look like we could use a good night's sleep."

A waiter took our order for three glasses of wine and a sampling of house-made meats and cheeses. I added on a bowl of warm olives, and Lily asked for some bread. Once our drinks and small plates arrived, I quizzed my magical friends on what really was going on around me.

"You're very lucky to live in San Francisco," Lily said, licking a drop of olive oil off her fingertip. "This city is the most magical of any in the world."

"You don't mean picturesque, do you?"

Lily smiled. "Nope. I mean magical, with a capital *M*. After a while you'll feel it. You were amazing last evening," she continued. "But I did have a brief scare. After Elsa left and you began to run toward the lake, I thought at one point that I'd lost you. You seemed to disappear from my line of sight, but then I found you again at the foot of the water. I think my eyes must have been playing tricks on me."

"I was running around like a crazy woman. Maybe a tree or a bush blocked me from view," I said as I nibbled. "My memory of the evening is hazy on details, but I do remember one thing. I heard a man's voice. He asked me to leave behind my old life and join him. I followed the sound of his voice all the way to the museum, but I never located him. I'm guessing it was just a hallucination."

My companions both laughed. "If we ever do this again, remind me to brew a weaker tea," Elsa said lightly.

Elsa shifted in her seat, and just for a minute I felt apprehension coming from her. Then, very quickly, the emotion vanished from my radar, almost like a shadow that disappears from the corner of your eye when you turn your head to find its source. But, for the second time in one day, it was clear that Elsa was hiding something from me.

THAT NIGHT I SLEPT DEEPLY. I DIDN'T STIR FROM MY BED
for ten hours. I woke up feeling stiff, but otherwise remarkably well,
considering my discovery that I shared the city with fairies, demons,
and vampires. At dinner, Lily had also briefed me on witches, who
seemed to find San Francisco especially welcoming to their lifestyle.
We humans were not alone, it turned out. We actually walked side by
side on Valencia Street, although most of us had no idea. Nor did
many people realize they were stuffed into the N-Judah streetcar with
the undead during commute hours.

What was I to do with this newfound knowledge? Was I supposed
to return to my old life, knowing there were two parallel worlds in San
Francisco? I was prepared to let those questions percolate at the back of
my mind as I got on with my day, but magic, it seemed, was in the air. I
started watching the Giants game and noticed that one of the pitchers
was a vampire. With his long black hair and pale skin, this starting
pitcher had always caught people's attention. It was rare, I realized, that
he ever pitched a day game, and now I knew why.

Sure enough, as the sun began to retreat from the plate and the
shadows grew longer, his pitches gained in velocity. In the ninth in-
ning, he was relieved, and as I stared into the bullpen, I noticed that
one or two other members of the team were also Others. A vampire
and a demon playing for a major league baseball team—it seemed the
world I knew was really gone forever.

Elsa had left the house earlier in the day and did not return until almost dusk. Normally a woman of few words, she had not been in the house ten minutes when she suggested we go out for dinner. "I was thinking of the place that used to be called the Moss Room," she said.

"Are you buying? That place is pricey," I said. "And it's impossible to get a table."

"Actually, we've been invited to dinner," Elsa said, a bright smile on her face. "The director of the Council, Gabriel Laurent, has invited us to join him."

"What's the catch?" I asked. "First, he tries to blind me, and now he wants to wine and dine me?"

"No catch," Elsa said. "He wants to meet you and, if there is time, discuss a job. I think we should go. Your old job is going to seem quite boring now, anyway."

"I'm not so sure about that," I said, feeling slightly bullied.

"It's just dinner," Elsa said lightly, but I could sense some uneasiness. She needed me to go to this dinner.

"OK," I said. "What time are we meeting him?"

Elsa looked relieved. "One hour."

"Great. I'll go upstairs and change."

The private dining room inside the Academy of Sciences was once the Moss Room, named after the moss that grew on one of the subterranean walls inside the restaurant. Tucked underground, guests dined inside a snug room adorned, on one side, with moss and trickling water and, on the other, brick and glass. It was designed as a terrarium for the culinary set, and those lucky enough to obtain a table from the finicky chef with a nameless restaurant had to descend a long glass stairway that terminated at the broad elbow of a majestic wooden bar to enter the dining room.

As we came to the last step, a man seated at the bar turned to face us. Instinctively, I knew this was Gabriel Laurent. Impeccably dressed in a gray cashmere sweater, jeans, and a black sport coat, he was the picture of casual French elegance.

"Hello, Elsa," he said, revealing an accent. "This must be Olivia."

"Hello," I said, turning to face him, resisting the urge to show off and *parler*. Eventually, he would come to know that I was fluent. "It's a pleasure to meet you, *monsieur*."

Gabriel stared at me for a moment but did not speak. He was glowing with a deep-blue aura that sparkled like a sapphire.

"You're so blue," I blurted out before I could stop myself.

I could sense his pleasure at my remark, but like Elsa, he, too, held something back.

"I can see what they say is true," he said. "You are quite adept. I am anxious to discuss your gifts in greater detail. *Alors*—let me tell the hostess we are ready. I have reserved a private room." His word for her came out as "Oh-stess," spurring me on to speak in his native language.

"*Comment allez-vous?*"

Gabriel turned around and smiled. "*Bien, merci. Vous parlez très bien, mademoiselle.*"

"Thank you. I've studied French for many years," I replied. "It was a sort of requirement with my mother."

Once again, he stifled some emotion, but I felt a drop of it. It was curiosity.

"You must tell me about your mother . . . eh . . . your family sometime," Gabriel said as the hostess led us to our private quarters. "I am curious to know about your background. There are not many humans with the kind of powers you seem to have."

The private room, it turned out, was a clear box off the main dining area. The small glass-walled salon was soundproof but transparent to the rest of the diners. It made for interesting theater. We could see everyone as they came and went through the dining room, and they could see us, but they could not hear a word we uttered. I didn't think this was a coincidence at all.

Almost immediately after being seated, I began to feel nervous. It took a few moments to realize that the emotions were not my own. Thanks to my training, however preliminary, I knew the difference between my feelings and those of others. They felt too sudden, the emotions, when they belonged to someone else. The question now was which one of them was nervous, and why?

Gabriel ordered a bottle of wine and asked that it be decanted as we looked at the menu. Once the wine had been arranged and we'd been sitting for a few moments, Gabriel spoke again.

"You've had quite an eye-opening experience in the last few weeks, Olivia," he said, gently rotating his wineglass between his fingers. "For most of us, the knowledge that the universe is divided between two worlds is introduced gradually by our peers as we grow older. You have had to absorb the entirety of the situation quickly. Do you know why your parents never told you the truth?"

Interesting. Elsa, it seemed, had not told Gabriel about my mother. "I'm afraid you can't blame my family," I said. "The blame, if it must be assigned, is all mine. My mother and grandmother did try to educate me, but I refused."

"Refused? I don't understand."

I snorted. "That seems to be a running theme these days. I didn't want to use my skills. I've watched my mother nearly drink herself to death trying to avoid her feelings. She's a brilliant landscape painter. Her artistic skill, combined with her *gifts*, has made her quite in demand, but it has never made her happy. She has been overwhelmed with her emotions, and everyone else's, for a long time."

"And your father?"

"I don't have one. At least that I know about," I said, feeling a rush of anxiety. "My mother told me my father was a man she loved deeply but could never marry. Beyond that, she has never said a word. I stopped asking after a while."

"She never married?"

"No," I said. "She's had a few boyfriends over the years, but she has never had a serious relationship. She often said she'd been in love once and it was enough."

"And your *grand-père*?"

"He's dead. So is my grandmother. I have an uncle, but my mother and I are the last two of our immediate family. I'm an only child."

That brought an odd look to Gabriel's face. "I see," he said, quickly recovering as he poured wine into our glasses. "And now that you have learned more about your skills?"

It was my turn to feel nervous. "I'm not sure. It's remarkable to see people in, well, in a different light, but I'm not certain how all of this will affect my life in the future."

"Your honesty is refreshing," Gabriel said. "Most humans would be eager to find a way to use their skills to their advantage. To make money or to gain power."

"Are you human?" I asked, knowing I was being too forward with the Frenchman.

"It's a good question, Olivia. One I will answer in time."

"Why does everything always take time?" I was losing my patience.

"Because when you step out of the human plane, you can see that time is infinite," Gabriel said. "The world is an old place, and history is repeated every minute, every second that humans spend on the planet . . . in the tiny gestures and major decisions they make every day."

"Those who fail to understand are doomed to repeat . . . ?"

Gabriel nodded. "Exactly. When you are in the stream of time, it is difficult to see all sides to an issue. One advantage the Others have is the gift of perspective. When you have lived a century, you can step back and examine issues differently. War, religious intolerance, and famine—they all take on a different significance decades later. But as a human, you are bound by the moment."

I looked over at Elsa, who had remained silent during the conversation. "Do you see humans as such frail creatures?"

She nodded. "Not frail, but blind. They don't make decisions for the long-term, only for what feels good in the moment."

"This is fascinating, but what does it have to do with me? I'm not sure how I fit into this discussion. I *am* human, living in *this* time, mortal and destined for dust one day. Not long ago, I had a successful business and a nice house with a garden. But now . . ."

We paused as our meals were brought in. Once we had taken a few bites, Gabriel spoke again.

"You want to know what comes next. You wonder if you can continue doing things the same way, knowing what you know now. The answer is yes and no." Gabriel turned to Elsa. "Does she know about the work of the Council?"

Elsa shook her head. "No. I was waiting for you to tell her."

"Are you familiar with the United Nations, Olivia?"

"Yes, why?"

"You know that their mission is to promote peace and stability among nations."

"Well, their success is debatable, but yes, I'm familiar with their mission."

Gabriel responded with a grim smile. "As you said, their success is mixed. Why? The governments of the world, in my opinion, are no match for religious intolerance, xenophobia, and renegade dictators. Millions of dollars are spent globally, and where are we? Half the world's female population remains uneducated; old wives' tales and superstition still reign. Do you know a person can still be accused of being a witch and stoned to death in some parts of the world?"

This remark caused Elsa to involuntarily flinch.

"Have you been hunted?" I asked her.

Elsa nodded. "Small villages are breeding grounds for that kind of hysteria."

Gabriel continued. "Even here in your country, religious zealots would like to dictate who you can marry."

I nodded. "Don't forget banning abortions," I added.

Gabriel leaned forward to continue. "Can you imagine how dangerous it would be if the religious extremists were able to take the reins of your government? Can you imagine if the president of the United States were a religious fanatic, or perhaps, the men and women in your Congress were? As you know, extremists have taken control of some aspects of your government. Autocrats rule other countries with impunity. Can you imagine if it continues to spread?"

"I can, but I try not to," I said. "Some days, it seems like that's already happening."

Gabriel glanced at Elsa, and I could feel their anticipation as she finally came to the point.

"Things can actually get much worse," she said. "Many of us have lived through the days of witch hunts and inquisitions. We know the damage one ambitious official can cause when he sows superstition and distrust among the disenfranchised."

"I can't imagine the United States ever being that provincial," I said, feeling a little overwhelmed by their comments. "After all, we were founded to avoid the rule of one man or woman. There are plenty of people who still believe in Democracy in this country." I wondered if what I was saying was a fact or wishful thinking.

Gabriel reached for his phone and held it up. "This little device is full of more hate and misinformation than any one person can combat. The lies, the conspiracy theories floating around on social media. There are people ready to set the world on fire so they can reap the benefits."

"Your country is growing more polarized by the day, which is causing many people to avoid elections," Elsa said. "Only extremists show up on both sides."

"We are at a tipping point where intervention is necessary," Gabriel said.

"Intervention?" I asked, once again feeling alarmed. I had the feeling I was being recruited into some kind of battle. "What do you mean?"

Finally, I was able to connect the nervousness I'd been feeling all evening with its owners. Both of them shared the anxiety equally, but it was Gabriel who spoke first.

"I'm the leader of an organization of Other, designed to help with these matters globally, with this intervention I spoke of—the Council. It's devoted to maintaining stable governments across the globe," Gabriel said. He paused to order a second bottle of wine. "Do you know the story of 'the watchers' from the Bible, from the Old Testament? It's about a group of angels sent by God to live on the earth and help humans."

"No," I said, shaking my head. "I'm not all that familiar with the Bible."

"I see. Well, we are like them. The world is full of magical beings— Others, as we refer to them. We, *they*, do not want to be visible to the outside world, hunted for religious reasons, or perhaps exploited for financial gain or political power. For decades we have lived among humans and co-existed. The equation is simple: the more educated and stable the population, the more insulated Others are from harm and persecution."

"How does it work?" I asked. "Do you have an army? Is there fighting?"

Gabriel waved his hands emphatically, as if to dismiss the comments. "Olivia, I am not asking you to fight in a war or join an army. Here in the United States, and in Europe, we use the political process. We work to ensure that stable, moderate people are elected to every level of government." Gabriel let out a sigh. "I used to believe that there was no need for violence, that managing the political process would be enough, but now I'm not so sure. Politics has grown more volatile. We've never advocated for warfare, but if there is a need to protect Democracy and the fate of humankind, we will not hesitate to act."

"What do you want me to do?" I asked, although I wasn't sure I wanted to hear the answer.

"For now, I want you to do what you already do—run a campaign," Gabriel said, smiling. "But I also want you to use your newfound skills, to help *increase* the odds of success."

"Increase the odds?"

"Yes, of course," he said. "It's much easier to win an election when you know what voters are thinking ahead of time. You can help a candidate correct their messages in a matter of seconds. You can sit in a room with a journalist and sense their intentions before they even begin an interview. It all makes for much better odds."

"Why should I do this for you? I could just go back to running my company."

Gabriel nodded. "True, but you could never tell your clients or colleagues about your talents. Who will believe that you can see someone's aura or read their emotions? And if your competitors *did* come to believe that, they would try to get you fired or disqualified. Who will you share your gift with? Who will you ask for advice? Elsa can't stay with you forever; she must return to her own work.

"I've seen your record," he continued. "You're a talented consultant. Surely you must see the value of using your skills to help make a difference? You can shape the future and help ensure that zealots don't continue to run governments or never make it into office in the first place."

I set aside his pitch to help save the world for the moment. It was difficult to imagine my contributions amounting to that much, but his other remarks hit home. I couldn't share my secret with other humans. They would think I was crazy. Then again, maybe I didn't have to; maybe I could enjoy my new skills in private.

"I know what you're thinking," Gabriel said. "That you can keep it all a secret and continue on with your life."

I nodded. "Why not? No one has to know."

"True. But don't you think you would be living a half life, Olivia? You have been given the rare opportunity to see what's behind the wizard's curtain. In your case, there is real magic to be found, not some cheap parlor trick."

"Maybe, but I never asked for these gifts," I said. "All I've ever wanted was to live my life in peace."

"*Mon Dieu!* Who doesn't?" Gabriel said, offering a sympathetic smile. "But that is not always what fate has in store."

9

I WOKE UP THE NEXT MORNING KNOWING THAT I NEEDED
to clear my head. I decided that a bike ride out of town would be just
the thing. The red wine and conversation had made my night's sleep
less than solid, but I managed to wake up feeling rested enough.
Gabriel had closed the evening asking me to consider his offer, but
the truth was that I had bigger issues to contemplate.

I knew that Gabriel was right when he said I would never be able
to reveal my skills to my clients or colleagues. But that wasn't the part
that bothered me most. What I worried about was not being able to
share everything I knew with anyone else. Beyond Lily, who could I
tell about this new world of mine? And was there any man out there
willing to date a woman who could tell his true colors on the first
outing? To see the world so differently and to be so limited in talking
about it—well, it didn't sound appealing.

I thought rigorous exercise and reflection would help me work
through these issues, so I pedaled my way through Golden Gate Park,
up into the Presidio, and across the Golden Gate Bridge. I rode past
the Marin Headlands and on to Mill Valley, stopping in the town's
village square for a break before heading back toward home again. It
was a classic San Francisco day—sunny but with a cold, biting wind. I
slogged through the tourists in Sausalito and rode up Alexander
Avenue, turning right to climb the hill toward the lookout points.

But now, after several hours on relatively flat terrain, my leg muscles rebelled against the abrupt change in grade. I was also pressing against fierce, chilling headwinds. Although my body ached, it felt good to push so hard. I used the confusion I was feeling as my energy source. The wind wicked the sweat off my torso, and I felt the delicious tightness of my skin as it reacted to the frigid air.

My efforts were rewarded when I reached the top of the road and gazed out at the stunning view of the city's skyline, the beautiful twin spires of the bridge across the Golden Gate, and San Francisco Bay. To one side I could see Baker Beach, and to the other, the skyscrapers of downtown San Francisco. It was beautiful, and my heart felt lighter as I looked out at the city I called home.

I decided to walk through the old World War II tunnels and examine the view from behind one of the gun turrets, so I locked my bike into a rack and walked toward the opening of the tunnel. As I approached, I heard music coming from inside. And when I entered, I saw a man in the distance, sitting against one of the walls. I couldn't see his face, as the bright sunlight made it impossible to see more than his silhouette.

It was the music, though, that caught my attention. The notes were rolling off the guitar with great sadness and melancholy. It was beautiful, but I hesitated to walk closer. A bit of pressure was building in my head. I took a sip of water from my bottle, thinking that I was dehydrated, before it dawned on me. The pressure was coming from him. I was being pecked at again, which meant that the man I was staring at was actually a guitar-playing vampire. I was in no mood for examination after such a long ride and immediately shut him out.

Out of the shadows I saw him raise his head and laugh, and then he looked away and continued to play his guitar. But as I turned to head back toward my bike, the mystery musician spoke.

"Don't worry," he said in a voice that carried a trace of a Southern drawl. "I won't try again. I didn't realize who I was dealing with."

I decided not to answer. I don't normally speak with strangers under any circumstances.

"Don't you want to finish what you started?" he asked, a touch of sarcasm in his voice. "It's worth it to get to the other side."

I wasn't sure what he meant. The previous evening's discussions had further opened my eyes to the world around me; there were two dimensions to everything. Was he saying I was afraid to go through the tunnel, or did he mean something else? I wasn't afraid, although I had never been alone with a vampire in a dark tunnel before.

Now that I was really focusing, I could detect a greenish-yellow aura surrounding him. He was very calm, and I didn't feel threatened in any way. Instead, his stance made me curious: who was this mysterious guitar-playing vampire down at the end of the tunnel? I walked toward him to find out.

Briskly, I closed the gap between us, but he made no effort to move or rise to meet me. As I approached, I could make out a cowboy hat, bright-red hair, and a pair of faded jeans beneath an old acoustic guitar. Whoever he was, it was clear he was not prepared to speak with me again.

I had been raised to never chase boys or men—a policy I amended on the spot to include the undead—so I gave him a feeble wave, and he tipped his hat back in acknowledgment. Then I walked out of the tunnel and into the clearing.

It was growing colder, and I could feel the fog beginning to push its way in. The chill in the air convinced me that it was time to get myself back across the bridge and into a hot bath. When I got home, Elsa would want to discuss Gabriel's offer to come and work for the Council. The fee he had offered me was enormous—certainly more than I made on my own in a year. Although I didn't need the funds, it was intriguing to be offered a king's ransom for doing a job I loved.

I finished gazing at the churning sea below and walked back to the tunnel, hoping to catch a glimpse of the guitar player again. But when I stepped into the shadows, I discovered I was alone.

✳

By the time I returned home ninety minutes later, I'd decided to accept Gabriel's offer. Whether it was the encounter with the vampire in the tunnel or Gabriel's remarks, I now knew I had to make some changes.

Despite my resolution, I decided to call my mother to gauge her reaction. After all that I had experienced, including the visions I'd seen of my grandmother, I felt I needed to talk to her. We had parted ways badly a few weeks ago, and I was anxious to clear the air.

Within seconds of my dialing, she picked up. "Olivia," she said warmly. "You have found your gifts. I can feel the energy pouring out of you."

"Wow," I said. "Even over the phone, Mom?"

"Your energy is very powerful," she said. "How did this happen?"

"I met someone, a woman who's been helping me. Her name is Elsa, and she has been a sort of, umm, a mentor. She said Grand-mother sent her."

There was a pause on the line. "That is exactly the kind of thing she would think to do. Interesting that she appeared now. Well then . . . are you OK? It's a lot to understand at your age."

"That's funny. A man I met said something very similar."

Again there was a pause, but then she said, "A man? You mean someone your age?"

"No," I said. "Elsa introduced me to a man who runs an organi-zation that protects people like us, and others, from harm. His name is Gabriel Laurent."

For the third time, my normally verbose mother was silent. "I see," she said finally. "He's French. What did he want?"

"He offered me a job, to work for an his organization—it's called the Council. I would run political campaigns here, and maybe in states across the country."

"I don't know, Olivia. This is all very sudden," she said. "Maybe you should take some time off and think about things. Perhaps you'd like to take a trip to France? I have an exhibition coming up in Paris. We could travel there together and relax and see the city."

"Mom, I would love that, but I need to work and stay busy," I said. "I feel like I have already been on vacation, the way I've abandoned my company these last few weeks."

My mother sighed into the phone. "It's not as if you need to work, Olivia. Your family has ensured that you have plenty of money. What can it hurt to take things slowly? You don't know anything about this Laurent fellow. He may not have your best interests at heart."

I was now able to clearly map the outlines of my mother's state of mind. She was worried, but whether it was for me or in general, I couldn't tell. "Don't worry, Mom," I said, wanting to reassure her. "I like Gabriel. He seems very nice. Maybe it's because of our years in France, but I felt very comfortable around him."

She hesitated for a moment, then spoke. "Very well, honey," she said warmly. "Perhaps you will come to Paris for a few days and take a break with me."

I was about to say good-bye and thanks when she spoke again.

"Honey, remember that there is a lot still to come. I hope you will be ready for all that there is to know."

"Don't worry," I repeated. "Elsa is helping me. I feel better than I have in a long time." After we hung up, I turned to Elsa, who had been listening from the hallway. "Well, what do I do next?"

"We should visit Gabriel at the Council offices," Elsa said. "We can go tomorrow evening. I'll confirm with him."

"Can't we go tonight?" I asked, anxious to get started now that I had made the decision.

Elsa shook her head. "He's not there. Tomorrow we'll go. The Council convenes after dusk," she said. "It must be dark when we approach their offices. If it's foggy, we can use a portal. If it's not, then we use the main entrance."

"What does fog have to do with it?"

"Come into the living room and sit down, Olivia. If you're going to work for the Council, then I might as well begin your education." Elsa walked toward the couch. "Once you cross their threshold, there will be no turning back. You will be privy to some of the world's greatest secrets."

"You make it sound dangerous. What happens if I change my mind?"

"That's exactly my point; you can't change your mind. Once you've been exposed to the Council, you are bound by their rules. It is a serious commitment, one that I know well. I have been working for them for many years."

"How did you get started?"

Elsa began to rearrange the pillows on the couch, avoiding my gaze. "I told you the story of how I almost gave my soul to the devil," she said. "But I never told you what happened when I was released."

I nodded. "What happened?"

"After the devil told me I was free to leave, I ran back to get my horse. As I was adjusting my saddle—I planned to ride through the night to get off the mountain—the angel who had bargained for me came into the stable. I asked him to tell me how he had won the argument with the devil, but he wouldn't reveal their conversation."

"That's it? He never told you?" I asked.

"He did not, but he did tell me that there would be a price for my foolishness."

"A price?"

Elsa nodded. "Yes. He told me that to repay my rescue from the devil, I would have to pledge myself to helping others for an undetermined period of time. I have been a time-walker since then, moving through the centuries, helping humans and Others."

"How long do you have to do this?"

Elsa sighed. "For as long as it takes. It's been hundreds of years, and I have yet to see the angel again. When he reappears, I will know my payment has been made."

"Well, that doesn't seem fair," I said. "You've been at this for a long time."

"Yes, but to ask God to save your soul from the devil when you almost willingly gave it away . . . well, who knows what had to be promised to free me."

I watched Elsa closely. She was beautiful to look at, sleek and powerful like the cat that appeared in my dreams. Her punishment not only had made her immortal, but it also had frozen her in time. She didn't age. Perhaps when she finished her penance, she would be allowed to grow old. "Is that how you came to work for the Council?"

Elsa nodded. "I discovered them during my travels. I had no idea how to repair the damage I'd done. It made sense to work for them. They gave me a way to have a purpose and fulfill my obligation."

"Are there others like you?"

"If you mean people who travel through time, yes, there are. But are there others doing penance? Not that I know of. Yet I can't imagine I am the only person on earth who almost gave their soul away to the devil in the pursuit of power and knowledge."

Elsa's tale reminded me of Stoner Halbert. *We all, it seems, have to make our own beds.* How did a rising star in politics come to call for the devil? I tried to imagine that much burning hatred or shame —a feeling of despair powerful enough to bypass God and ask for help from the dark side. I couldn't imagine ever wanting that kind of revenge or power. "Is that what Stoner Halbert has done? Given his soul to the devil? What will happen to him?"

Elsa shrugged. "It's hard to know when these things catch up

with you. It can take years for evil to be rebuffed, or it can be immediate. The circumstances are never the same."

"What happens if I decide that I don't want to do this?" I asked,
the proposition of my "new life" suddenly weighing more heavily
on me.

Elsa rose from the couch and began to pace. "I don't know what
would happen. No human has ever been allowed to work for the
organization before. But for Others, once you join the Council, it's
hard to turn your back. I can't make the choice for you, but I
strongly encourage you to take Gabriel's offer. This is your destiny."

"How can you be so sure?"

Elsa hesitated, and I experienced a brief sensation of nervousness again.

"Come on Elsa, tell me what you know."

Then it was gone; she was good at hiding her feelings from
empaths like me.

"I have been doing this for a long time, Olivia. Your gifts deserve
to be used for greater purposes than building condominiums."

Elsa's words stung a bit. I'd never set out to change the world, but
she made my career seem insignificant. We get up, we go to work, we
do a good job, and we come home. Why does life have to be more
complicated than that? And yet, it is. I now had the ability to read
people and sense their emotions. I was either going to Las Vegas to
make my fortune, or I needed a place to use my skills where I
wouldn't frighten people.

"Text Gabriel," I said finally. "I will join the Council."

10

THE NEXT EVENING AS WE LEFT MY HOUSE FOR THE PARK, we stepped into a dense wall of wet fog. The humid mist on my face jogged my memory.

"I forgot to ask you last night about the fog," I said as we pulled our collars up around our necks.

San Francisco's fog is legendary. Summer in San Francisco means hardly ever seeing the sun, at least in my neighborhood. Sometimes the fog rolls in gently, bringing a quiet, sultry climate to the city. Other nights, the fog rides the heels of a wicked wind that bends trees and howls through the narrow alleys between the row houses.

"The fog is one of the Council's most important tools," Elsa said as we walked. "San Francisco is enchanted; a coven of witches created a spell that would summon the fog in order to protect our kind from prying eyes. When the fog is present, it's easier for the Council to operate and for magical creatures to move about the city."

"Seriously?"

"Seriously," she said. "It's the perfect device for maintaining a curtain between our worlds. It can be summoned at any time, especially if the Council has called a general meeting at its headquarters."

What Elsa said made sense. Things that look odd in the shadows are probably easily explained away to humans. The fog obscures light. It muffles sound. I remembered my peyote-induced trek through

Golden Gate Park, and how foggy that evening had been. Perfect for hiding a half-dressed woman running toward the sea.

"Huh, it's a brand-new world," I said, only half-aware of how true my words were.

Before I knew it we were standing at the foot of the Music Concourse, gazing up at the tower of the de Young Museum. By day, it's the fifth most visited museum in the country. By night, it is the headquarters of the Council. We looked across the plaza at the building sheathed in copper, gleaming in the evening light. According to Elsa, the fog was not quite thick enough to use the portal so we walked to the side of the museum, passing Pan's island and the lily pond where I'd spent the night. We didn't go in the side entrance reserved for museum members. Instead, we made our way along a sidewalk partially obscured by ferns. Almost immediately we were facing what looked to be a solid wall of copper. Elsa placed her hand on the wall. The area beneath her palm began to glow.

"Fingerprint recognition," Elsa explained matter-of-factly as the outline of a door appeared, then clicked open slightly to let us pass. Once inside, Elsa turned left toward a bank of elevators. "We're going to the top of the tower," she said as she pressed the button on the wall.

I scanned our surroundings; the museum's lobby looked exactly the same as it did in the daylight. The elevator, which was taking us up twelve floors to the observation tower, also looked the same. I wondered whether the museum's iconic top-floor viewing deck would also be unchanged. I was, I realized, slightly disappointed. I'm not sure what I expected. Maybe I'd watched too many *Star Trek* episodes, but in my mind I had conjured up a different world. I'd imagined a series of rooms with glowing flat-panel screens featuring rotating three-dimensional orbs that depicted faraway destinations and tactical information.

When we arrived at the top of the tower, however, my imagination was rewarded by the sight of a room full of several flat screens mounted to the walls. A dozen men and women were seated at desks, hunched over their laptops and iPads. At first glance, it could have been an office anywhere in the world. Except it wasn't.

I looked up to see Gabriel walking across the room toward us.

"*Bonsoir*, Elsa, Olivia," he said as he shook my hand.

"It looks so normal," I said, gesturing at the scene before me.

Gabriel nodded. "Modern technology almost makes witchcraft unnecessary at times. We can track people and issues far easier than our predecessors."

"How is this possible? Do you pack up at the end of every evening?" I asked.

Gabriel smiled. "There is not much to put away, and the panels on the walls are enchanted. Humans cannot see them as they stroll through the deck during the day. The rest is portable. Thanks to wireless technology, our offices transport easily and, for the most part, are paperless."

"Is the museum aware of your presence?" I asked, imagining rumors floating through the city about the de Young's haunted galleries. "What happens when people here work late?"

Elsa and Gabriel exchanged a knowing glance.

This is where they begin to bind you with their secrets, I thought to myself, *the way they fold you in.*

"They know," Elsa said. "The museum knows we're here."

"It's true," Gabriel said, seeing my raised eyebrows. "The museum spent a fortune to build this magnificent copper building. Copper, as you may know, is an ancient metal dating back to the Romans. It is a very important metal in the supernatural world. You are standing inside a building that has the ability to conduct energy back and forth between individuals and the spirit world. It acts as an amplifier for our thoughts, for sending and receiving psychic communications. Can you imagine? No better building could be constructed for our purposes.

"When we learned of the plans to build the museum, we contacted their executive director," he continued. "Although human, she is quite the diva and has a reputation as a bit of a sorceress herself. She was only too happy to accommodate our request in exchange for a sizable donation."

I nodded. "It all makes frighteningly good sense."

"But," Gabriel said, his head cocked to one side. "There is something on your mind."

"It's nothing. I'm amazed at the businesslike way in which this all operates. You have a state-of-the art building, wireless technology. It all seems, well . . . routine."

"Did you expect us to fly around on broomsticks?" Elsa asked sharply. "That's a children's fantasy."

"What Elsa means," Gabriel interjected diplomatically, "is that we've adopted today's standards like the rest of the world. We cannot survive if we fail to adapt to our surroundings. But I will take credit for the businesslike way in which things run. In my other life, I'm the CEO of an AI company that generates special effects for movies. Our offices are near Marseille. I started my career in the mid-1970s at Industrial Light and Magic in Marin."

Before I could think too much about anything he'd said, Gabriel grabbed my arm and led me away.

"It's time for your grand tour," he said.

Elsa said she would stay behind, in the main arena, as it was called, to monitor things.

Although I remained wary, there was something very comfortable and familiar about Gabriel. I found myself easily led by him, and before I knew it, we were back in the elevator. We went down one floor and stepped out into what looked like ordinary office space filled with cubicles—complete with more young workers, heads down at their computers.

"We use most floors of the tower," he said, gesturing toward the desks. "A director and one deputy manage the Council. Our positions rotate every five years. You'll meet my deputy, Aidan Burke, in a few minutes; he keeps his office on the floor below. He's a crafty Irish shape-shifter; we've been friends for years. We're in the fourth year of our term. Next year the deputies for Central and Eastern Europe will take control."

"You're not very excited about that," I remarked, feeling a deep sense of ambivalence coming from him.

"Very good, Olivia," he said. "Your skills are becoming second nature to you. Yes, I have reservations. Zoran Mikic is a werewolf. By day, he is the governor of the Croatian National Bank. His deputy, Nikola Pajovic, is a vampire, as well as a wealthy Serbian developer who builds casinos on the Adriatic coast. They have a unique partnership, with Nikola acting as more of the leader. I worry, at times, about their commitment to the mission of the Council."

I was at a loss myself to understand what the Council's purpose was. Why did it need deputies and rotating staff members to monitor humans? "Gabriel, I hope you don't mind my asking, but why is all of this necessary? What exactly is it that you, that *we*, do?"

Gabriel nodded. "Yes. Let me explain. As I mentioned, the Council is divided by region, with directors holding positions for North America, Central and South America, Western Europe, Eastern Europe, Asia, and finally, Africa and the Middle East. Each sector monitors elections and shifts in government. We try, when possible, to intervene in elections to ensure that moderate candidates take seats in government."

"Why not every time?"

"That would be a little too obvious," Gabriel said. "We're a clandestine organization, looking to protect the interests of our kind. If we influenced every election, it would draw too much attention to ourselves."

"And why is this necessary?"

Gabriel walked over to a desk and picked up one of the spare tablets. He returned to me and called up a news article. "Read," he said, gesturing at the screen.

CONGRESSWOMAN ASKED TO LEAVE RESTAURANT

(DENVER) – Pansy Thornblower, a Colorado congresswoman and Internet sensation, was asked to leave a chic neighborhood bistro Wednesday night after vaping at her table and yelling obscenities at nearby patrons, whom she referred to as "communists." Diners at the restaurant posted videos on the social media platform X, formerly known as Twitter, of a visibly inebriated Ms. Thornblower requiring help from her dinner companion to exit the restaurant.

"Come on, everyone knows she is crazy," I said, shaking my head. "Why should you worry about her? There are far more dangerous people lurking around national politics."

"It is easy to laugh here in San Francisco. She seems very remote from your life. But do you remember the story of the Trojan horse, Olivia? The people of Troy believed the horse to be a gift to the goddess Athena and allowed it to pass through their walls into their village, only to be destroyed by the Greeks hiding inside. One woman like this may be a joke, but you've already got six members of Congress who can block a vote, thereby holding this country hostage to their views. What happens if you elect an entire Congress full of them . . ."

"So Thornblower is a threat because she further normalizes this behavior?" I asked.

"*Exactement.* The civilized world is a mile wide and an inch deep. We've already seen what can happen when unfit people are elected to the White House. We've had riots and incursions, election deniers...if you create the right settings, religious fanatics could control half the world. Already in Europe we see the beginnings."

"I admit things are getting worse, but there will always be those who try to counter the extremism."

Gabriel looked out through the open windows at the darkened sky beyond. "Only if we stay the course and continue our work," he said. "We can't afford to look away for a second."

"And how do you see me in all of this, again?" I asked.

"I see you running a campaign. Levi Barnes, your old boss, is running for Congress. It's a new seat created by the latest redistricting process, so it's wide open, no incumbent. He's declared, but he hasn't picked his campaign staff yet."

"And he's going to hire me . . . because you asked him to? It's been a decade since we worked together."

Gabriel smiled. "I know him well because of my work. Some years ago, he invented an impressive cloud-based cash application. He sold the company for an enormous sum. An amazing man, really."

"I'm not surprised," I said. "But you still haven't answered my question. Why is he going to hire me?"

"Because you're the best person for the job," Gabriel said. "And because I will strongly suggest that he does."

"Suggest," I repeated. "You mean cast a spell?"

"If that's what it takes to get him on board, yes."

"Why would you go to the trouble to gain one congressional seat in Silicon Valley?"

Gabriel smiled as he walked us back toward the elevator. "What makes you think it's one seat? I told you it's about the total number of seats held. Our job is to ensure that rational, moderate people win seats."

"I should think the hardest part would be to get rational, moderate people to even run for office."

Gabriel nodded. "It is increasingly difficult."

We descended one more floor, walked out of the elevator and stopped outside an office with its door closed. Gabriel knocked, and the door was quickly opened by a tall, slim man with dark black hair and bright blue eyes.

"Hello, Aidan," Gabriel said warmly. "This is Olivia, the empath I told you about."

Aidan, whose handsome, dark features were slightly distracting, even for a man easily a decade older than me, gave me more scrutiny than I would have expected. He seemed to be examining me closely, although I could not detect an ounce of emotion coming from him.

"Hello, Olivia," he said cordially, a hint of an Irish accent coming through. "Welcome to the Council. Gabriel has high hopes for you inside this organization."

"'You can check out, but you can never leave,'" I said with a smile. "Oops, I said that out loud, didn't I?"

Aidan tossed back his head and laughed. Now I could feel his warmth bubbling up. "Yes, something like that, I'm afraid. In fact, we need to get you set up for your work. I told Gabriel I would manage that task so he could see to other business."

I said good-bye to Gabriel as Aidan shut the door to his office. For a moment we sat in silence, but then Aidan began to speak, fixing his blue eyes on me.

"I'm a shape-shifter," he said. "In my village in Ireland, every other year one boy is born with the skill to shift. It's considered good luck to be the family whose child is born with the talent. My parents, however, were not as thrilled as others might have been. I didn't stay at home for long. I met Gabriel one evening outside Aix-en-Provence. He was walking in the hills under the glow of a full moon and we . . . ran into each other."

"Is it painful to shift?" I asked, knowing the questions must sound so utterly human.

"At first, when we're young, yes, but not now."

I could feel genuine friendship coming off of Aidan in waves. I felt a sense of loyalty and duty from him. I wondered why he'd taken such an instant liking to me. "Why did you volunteer to help me?" I asked. "Don't you have an HR department like all global bureaucracies?"

"Because I wanted to meet you myself," Aidan said. "It's unprecedented for a human to work for the Council. Gabriel is impressed with your skills and hopes you will be able to increase our chances of winning elections."

"I hope I can live up to everyone's expectations," I said. "What happens to people who lose elections?"

Aidan's eyes twinkled. "We send them out with the werewolves."

"I see. So my fate will rest with Zoran," I said jokingly.

Aidan's smile disappeared, and I detected a momentary sense of loathing. "Oh, I do hope that is never the case," he said. Then quickly he changed the subject by opening a drawer in his desk and pulling out a small device that resembled an ear-piercing gun.

"Is this going to hurt?" I asked.

"No, but it will be weird," Aidan said. "I am going to embed a tracking device in your skin. No matter where you are, in this time or another, we will be able to find you."

"Did you say, 'in this time'?"

Aidan smiled. "I did. You know about the portals. It's possible that you will use them to go back in time one day. We all wear tracking devices. Well, most of us do, anyway."

I held out my arm as instructed, and Aidan stamped the skin on the underside of my arm, near my wrist. I felt pressure and heard a pop of air, but there was no blood, only a tiny blue dot under my skin. I glanced at my arm and then back at Aidan.

Aidan nodded, seeming to understand my thoughts. "It's semipermanent, but it can be deactivated if necessary. And it will convert to a homing beacon if you're in trouble."

"How can I get in trouble running an election for a congressional seat?"

"Olivia, you should know better than anybody that politics is a dangerous business."

11

BEFORE LEAVING THAT EVENING, AIDAN GAVE ME SEVERAL binders of information to read. It looked like mostly organizational charts of the various Council directors, as well as the Council's mission statement. I gave him a slip of paper with my bank account number on it, and he promised that funds would be transferred into it almost immediately.

"Normally," I said, "I do some work before I get paid."

Aidan laughed and said that Gabriel had wanted to compensate me for the time I had lost in transitioning to my new life.

I knew my mother would be furious if she found out about the funds. A group that was willing to pay me before I'd even been on the workforce a day would only confirm for her that there was something strange going on. But I was happy to take the money. I wasn't convinced that Levi Barnes would hire me. If this new arrangement didn't work out, at least I would have extra funds in my account to support myself until I decided what to do next.

It was decided my first night at the Council's offices that I would keep my firm open and use the same employees. Since I already had a track record running campaigns, it was a perfect cover for my work with the Council. Gabriel returned to Aidan's office and handed me a binder with information about Superdistrict 15, the new congressional district Levi would be running for.

Previously made up of two other districts, the new territory was enormous, encompassing two counties, all of Silicon Valley, part of the state's breadbasket near the city of Salinas, as well as the coastline near Santa Cruz. In my opinion, it was political suicide to try to represent such a huge district, since the interests of urban, suburban, and agricultural voters were certain to clash over the years. I couldn't wait to hear why Levi Barnes wanted to return to the United States House of Representatives.

The last thing Gabriel told me that evening was that we were having lunch with Levi the next day at the Four Seasons Hotel on Market Street.

"You work fast," I said in response.

Gabriel smiled and said he would meet me in the restaurant.

At home later that night, I read through the materials I had been given. After his defeat, Levi Barnes left Congress and Utah for California. During the following decade, he became a very wealthy entrepreneur thanks to his digital payment app, ensuring that he, along with his children, would never need to work again.

I wondered how much he had changed in the decade since I had worked for him. We had parted ways on good terms but had taken different paths. His life had been consumed with entrepreneurial pursuits and mine with politics. He was married with a family. I was single with my own business in the City. Time had passed quickly. But now, here we were again, being reunited by Gabriel Laurent, a man whose connections and background I was only beginning to grasp.

I arrived at the Four Seasons at one o'clock, as directed. The host led me to a table where Gabriel and Levi were already seated.

Levi Barnes was aging very gracefully. His short black hair had grayed somewhat in the decade that had passed, but his blue eyes looked as crisp and aware as ever, and he had managed to keep his tall frame fit and trim over the years. Gabriel, once again impeccably dressed in dark jeans and a white oxford shirt with driving loafers, was almost vibrating with feelings of approval toward me. And while he was holding something back—I was sure of it—there was no hiding that he felt proud of me as I strolled to the table.

Both men stood up to greet me. Gabriel gave me the traditional *bisou* on both cheeks, and Levi clasped my hand in the two of his.

"Olivia, it's so nice to see you," he said. "I'm embarrassed that it's been so long since we've seen each other."

Right away, I opened myself up to Levi, curious to know what he was feeling. His aura was bright yellow, glowing like the sun on a summer day. This was a good sign, as yellow tends to indicate people who are positive, have strong intellect, and are imbued with the power to inspire—excellent attributes for someone trying for elected office. He was also feeling a deep sense of curiosity but was otherwise happy. For someone who had to quickly assemble a team and jump into a congressional race, he struck me as remarkably calm. I wasn't sure if that was his nature—I didn't remember him being that calm before—or if it was Gabriel's influence.

We all took a seat as I spoke. "It seems you have been a bit busy."

Levi laughed. "Yes, I guess I have," he said. "Silicon Valley is a remarkable place. There are so many ideas to pursue, so many businesses to start. Well, it captured my attention."

"And now," I asked as the waiter came by with a menu for me, "you're ready to return to Congress?"

Levi nodded. "Utah was unpleasant, and I didn't think I would ever return to politics. But a lot of time has passed and I have changed my mind. I have enough money to last a lifetime. My children are grown and living their own lives. I'm ready to do something new —or old I guess, in this case," he said, smiling.

The waiter took our order. I was almost too excited to eat and requested only a bowl of soup. Gabriel frowned and added a piece of fish to my lunch, saying, "The sole here is too delicious to be missed." He also ordered a bottle of Sancerre to go with the meal. It struck me as sexist and annoying, his desire to order for me, but despite my efforts, I could not detect any untoward motives on his part. He was obviously old school and bossy. I made a note to tell him I could order my own lunch in the future. If Levi found it inappropriate that a French executive was ordering lunch for me, he didn't show it.

Gabriel told Levi that we knew each other because of his business interests in San Francisco. "I have toyed with the idea of relocating some, possibly all, of my employees to San Francisco or the surrounding Bay Area," he told Levi. "France has an amazing startup culture, but I don't have to tell you that the epicenter of everything is Silicon Valley. It has the money, the universities, and the talent pool to do anything. I spend so much of my time coming to California that it makes sense to move. Olivia has been kind enough to put up with my halfhearted efforts to look at various buildings and provide me with a political analysis of my chances to renovate them. There are rules, you see, sometimes about having actual offices inside industrial buildings and we need both for our work."

"This is a great time to come to San Francisco," I said, going along with the charade. "The city has incredible incentives to offer companies willing to relocate here."

Our plates arrived, and we ate in silence for a few minutes, until Gabriel spoke again. "Levi, you've declared your interest to run for Seat 15. Are you certain? If so, you need to assemble a campaign team immediately."

I could sense Levi's concern about my role very clearly. "Maybe I can step in here," I said, feeling confident for the first time in weeks that I knew what I was talking about. "Levi, you know me as a twenty-something press secretary. I didn't help run your first campaign. But like you, I have been busy since we closed down your office in the Rayburn Building ten years ago. I have built a very successful political consulting business here in San Francisco, which includes running campaigns."

I had managed to catch Levi's attention, and I could feel his growing interest.

"I represent a number of both national and international corporations, as well as individuals, in their dealings with both the media and government officials," I continued. "I have run a number of campaigns to protect their interests. I have an extensive background in business and development in the Bay Area. And I understand the dynamics of election politics. In short, I believe I have the leadership, skills, and required relationships to run this congressional campaign for you."

"She is considered one of the best," Gabriel said, pouring more wine into Levi's glass. "And then, there is the fact that you two have already worked with each other."

"You know my work ethic," I said. "I was the first one in the office and often the last one to leave. This will be no different."

Levi was curious but not sold. "How do you think I can win this race?" he asked.

I smiled. "Well, it's not magic," I said, cringing inwardly. "Your money is not enough. Look at Hillary Clinton. She spent millions on her campaign, but at the end of the day, she couldn't connect with enough voters. Voters support people they like, people who understand their issues. On paper, you are the perfect candidate. You came from another state to chase your entrepreneurial dreams, and after years of hard work, found success. You've raised a family, nurtured a marriage, and now after your success, want to return to a life of public service. You have a background in both business and education; you are exactly the kind of person California needs to represent its interests in Washington. But will voters relate to you? It's all in how we frame it."

Once again, Gabriel vibrated with happiness. He was very pleased with my speech, and, luckily, so was Levi Barnes.

He agreed to hire me right then and there, offering his apartment in San Francisco as a temporary campaign headquarters. We were nowhere near ready to open a campaign office in Silicon Valley, so using his apartment, along with my office, as a base of operations was perfect. I offered to work for free for the first few weeks so that Levi could decide if I was a good fit for the job. I didn't need the funds since Gabriel was paying me, but Levi just laughed and said money was not an issue.

Within a matter of days, he'd paid my first month's salary and deposited one million dollars into a campaign account "to get us started."

AIDAN WAS SITTING AT HIS DESK INSIDE THE DE YOUNG, deep in thought, when I arrived one evening a week later to brief him on my progress.

"Knock, knock," I said as I walked into his office.

"The intrepid consultant returns," he said, swiveling his chair away from his computer to face me as I took a seat across from his desk. "How are things going?"

"So far, so good. I'm writing a campaign plan and interviewing pollsters," I said. "Most evenings after sundown, I'm here, training with Elsa."

"And the campaign?"

"The campaign seems almost too good to be true," I said. "How often does an open congressional seat appear with few competitors vying for it? It's a district representing a huge portion of the state's population and wealth. Admittedly, not nearly as sexy as San Francisco, but it's still home to billions in venture capital and agriculture. So far, press coverage has been sparse. But I think we have a few days to get this campaign up and running before we're in the spotlight."

"And then what?" he asked.

"I'm certain opponents will appear and begin to evaluate their chances. Why not? There's nothing to lose, since it's an open seat," I said. "The big question is whether another Democrat will challenge

Levi. I'm going to speak with the head of the party and see if I can preempt a challenger."

"Do you need someone to come with you to help persuade him?" Aidan asked. "Gabriel is good at that kind of thing, you know."

"I don't think we need to bewitch Paul Levant, not yet at least," I said. "He's been chairman of the California Democratic Party for more than twenty years. I know he's salty and irascible, but he does have one soft spot: he loves women's rowing. I've already checked the race schedule. There's a regatta coming up in a few days at Lake Merced. I'm going to approach him then."

"Do you think you'll be able to read him clearly?"

"Yes. Every day it gets a little easier," I replied. "Besides, Levant isn't one to hide his emotions. I won't have to work hard to know what's in his heart."

"That's fortunate," Aidan said. "We've had great difficulty in some of our other races trying to get ahead of the opposition. Too much magic is too obvious, so we take baby steps."

"Why can't you just put a spell on an entire town?" I asked, only slightly in jest. "Who would know?"

"We would," he replied. "I'm afraid it's against the rules."

There were, it turned out, a myriad of rules to follow when it came to the Council. Secrecy was reinforced at every opportunity. We were to monitor and possibly intervene on behalf of humans but without drawing attention to the organization or ourselves. I was never to discuss my skills with anyone, even my family, which in my case seemed like an unnecessary rule since my mother already knew what I could do. We also were forbidden to attract the notice of the police or other authorities. That rule caught my attention.

"That reminds me—I've been meaning to ask you something," I said, changing the subject. "I was reading the rule about not attracting the interest of the police, and it got me wondering if there are Others who break the law."

My question brought an immediate rush of Aidan's anxiety to my solar plexus.

"There are Others involved in every facet of life: Navy SEALs, astronauts and, yes, even criminals," he said, a reluctance in his voice.

"Criminals," I repeated, as if it were the first time I'd heard the word.

"You'd be surprised," he said.

I was surprised. I wanted to pry further, but a glance at my watch told me I was now late to my appointment with Elsa, so I nodded and left the room.

Elsa was engaged face-to-face with a man in a heated argument. There were looking at something on his laptop, but I was too far way to see. Watching their body language, it was clear there was little love lost between them.

"Hello," I said, interrupting them. "I don't mean to intrude, but it's time for our appointment, Elsa."

"You must be Olivia," the man said, offering me the sort of bitter smile reserved for competitors and enemies. It took only seconds for me to realize he was a vampire—one who, for some reason, did not like me at all. "We are, it seems, to have a human in our midst."

"Olivia, this is Nikola," Elsa interjected before I could respond. "He's a member of the Eastern European delegation and next in line as deputy to the director."

He was also up to something; his energy was as dark as a lump of coal. Darkness suited him. Tall, lean, and looming, Nikola was the perfect embodiment of the stereotypical menacing undead.

"Hello, Nikola," I said, intentionally ignoring his remark about humans. I made sure to look him in the eye before I turned my attention to his computer, leaning in to get a better look. The story up on the screen announced that a former Serbian army general from the Balkan Wars years ago had just been convicted of war crimes at the International Criminal Court at The Hague.

"Why are you two talking about this?" I asked, pointing to the screen.

"I'm sure it does not concern you," Nikola said.

"I'm a member of this organization, and—"

"We can discuss it later," Elsa said, cutting me off again. "We need to get started on our work. Nikola, if you'll excuse us . . ."

Before I could ask any questions, I found myself herded into a private conference room. "You know," I said, "the first time we came into this building, I didn't notice so many private rooms. Can you create new rooms to suit your needs?"

In response, Elsa pointed to a piece of paper on a large conference table. It was some kind of map of the city, but not the type normally drawn by the US Geological Survey. Instead of the usual lots and blocks, the map contained numerous vibrant color drawings, including a picture of the windmill at the far west end of Golden Gate Park and a drawing of the archway on Grant Avenue that marks the entrance to Chinatown. On another part of the map there was a lone dragon floating above a doorway and a statue of Willie Mays in front of Oracle Park. I also recognized the fountain in the Music Concourse outside the de Young Museum.

"It's a map," I said, knowing I was stating the obvious. "But what are these drawings?"

Elsa ran her fingers along the images. "These are the locations of the portals hidden across the city. Although you can carry a copy of the map with you, it would be easier if you memorize the locations."

Memorizing was never one of my strong suits. "That doesn't sound easier," I said. "I'd rather have a copy."

"You can't walk around with a paper copy of the map in your hands," Elsa said. "If you choose to have a copy, it will have to be imprinted onto your skin with a spell, but . . ."

"But what?" I asked.

"Well, I don't recommend it," Elsa said. "For one thing, it introduces your body to a powerful form of old magic that is painful, and two, it can be difficult to be on the run and try to conjure the map up onto your skin."

I was trying to decide which part of her remarks to deal with first: the part about it being painful, the fact that that you could use witchcraft to do something like that, or the part about being on the run. Day by day, the Council was beginning to feel more complicated. I said, "Could you elaborate more on the part about 'being on the run'?"

"I'm not trying to frighten you, Olivia, but our situation is different," she said. "Like humans, we have a mix of good and bad people, but in the human world, you can walk away when someone bothers you. In our world, now *your* world, you won't always be able to do that. You will need the portals. They also can be a great shortcut if you are ever running late."

I could tell that Elsa was being honest. She wasn't trying to frighten me, but she was worried about my safety. What she was hiding, I couldn't really say. I wasn't sure if her worries were about an immediate danger or the result of living centuries on high alert. Our conversation brought me down to earth again. My responsibilities for the campaign were lengthy and serious. I felt the weight, but I welcomed it. I was happy to be involved and challenged to do my best. I knew how to do that.

Elsa, in her own way, was making sure I understood. It was clear that she did not mean to harm me. She did not even mean to warn me. It was well past the time for that. I was already tagged and ready for duty. Elsa, it seemed, was trying to accomplish what my mother had hoped to do. She was preparing me for my life, my new life. She wasn't my mother, and maybe that made it easier. It wasn't her fault that the things I needed to know were intimidating.

"I'm really not that good at memorization," I said, looking her straight in the eye. "If it's all the same to you, I'd rather have the map imprinted on me."

She nodded, her green eyes signaling comprehension. "We will need to find the old witch who lives nearby. Nadia will bind the map to you."

After that, we practiced blocking, another skill Elsa insisted I needed to have. Blocking is the act of keeping people out of your head so they can't read your thoughts or harm you. I thought I had mastered that skill in the first few days after my peyote trip when we had ridden trains around the city. But she was not backing down.

"Didn't I already do this on the train?" I asked. "What else is there to know?"

Her reply was swift. Elsa pushed against me with her mind with so much force that I almost fell off my chair. As I feebly tried to block her, my nose began to gush blood.

"See what I mean?" she said, handing me a tissue. "Blocking is like one of the baseball games you love so much. Energy shifts. One distraction, one error, and you can be behind in the count, as you like to say."

My task for the remainder of the evening was to focus and maintain my blocking. No matter how hard Elsa pushed, I was to resist. I had to focus and not divert my attention for even a moment. That was somewhat easy if I was standing still watching her. But then she insisted we go outside and run. Trying to block while moving was a whole other story. I had to look ahead to see where I was going and try to keep her locked out of my skull. As I tore through the forest behind the museum, jumping over logs and trying to avoid obstacles in the dark, I could feel her pressing on me.

At first, I was too distracted to keep her out, and she wasn't even trying very hard. Then my eyes finally adjusted to the darkness, and I began to use my senses more efficiently. I calmed my mind as Elsa had instructed and began to imagine a huge force of energy surrounding me. It both protected me and propelled me. I could see the glow in my mind's eye—a sensation Elsa had told me to expect. I was generating a field of energy around my body and my mind. For a short while I was able to run with ease with no pressure in my head. Then, for one moment, I got distracted. My mind wandered and just like that—wham!—it felt like Elsa had taken a bat to the back of my head. I went down in the mossy loam of the path and curled up into a ball.

"Why did you stop concentrating?" Elsa asked as she ran up and bent over me.

"Why did you wallop me in the back of my head?" I gurgled from the forest floor.

"I didn't mean to use so much force," she said, trying to help me up. "You were doing so well. You were aglow. I was testing you and then—poof!—you weren't blocking anymore."

Elsa stopped talking when I abruptly put my hand to my nose, where I could feel the warm trickle of blood starting up again.

"Let's go inside," she said. "I'll help you clean up."

AFTER A COUPLE OF WEEKS AVOIDING NOSEBLEEDS AND working what amounted to a double shift, I was ready for a break from my duties. Luckily, my need for a diversion coincided with the arrival of the annual bluegrass festival. Planned and paid for through the generosity of a local philanthropist, the event is a three-day tribute to the twangs and twinges of guitar, fiddle, and banjo. The music is performed in several large meadows and groves in Golden Gate Park, where bands play continuously from late morning until dusk. Because it's free, tens of thousands of people stream into town to enjoy the music. I couldn't think of a better way to spend the last days of San Francisco's Indian summer than outside at a concert.

On the first day of the festival, I scanned a map online of the five stages and the program of performers. As I perused the lineup of bands, I plotted a strategy for moving as little as possible while enjoying maximum sun and music. After some quick deliberation, I decided to make camp in an area featuring local bands. Most of the big names I wanted to hear, like Shakey Graves and Sierra Ferrell, wouldn't play until early evening. I knew some people would stake out a place now for those shows, but I didn't have the heart to sit through music I didn't like for several hours.

I had invited Elsa to join me, but she declined, saying she had some work to review with Aidan. Alone, I grabbed my camp chair and a thermos of rum and Coke and headed for the park. With little trouble, I found a good spot to sit in an open grassy field, directly in front of one of the smaller performance stages. I opened my chair, put some sunscreen on my face, and prepared to enjoy the day.

Technically, you are not allowed to bring alcohol into the park. I say "technically" because, although the law is very real, it's rarely enforced. In fact, it seemed to me that I'd rarely been in the park at a festival where alcohol and other assorted goodies were not being passed around.

Although I was beginning to think of the park as a gigantic hideout for magical beings and as the headquarters of the Council, the park was also a human refuge. In a city as dense as San Francisco, with more apartment buildings than single-family homes, the park is a backyard to thousands. It's a place to run, walk, think, and get high. Today was clearly one of those days when getting high took precedence over other activities.

As I unscrewed the cap on my thermos and poured a bit of my cocktail into the small plastic cup, someone tapped me on the shoulder and offered me my own pre-roll. When I'm working, I usually go easy on the cannabis. I'm paranoid that there will be some kind of emergency at the same time I'm peaking on a gummy, and I'll be too out of it to solve the problem. It was also true that Elsa would have been less than thrilled at any attempt to dull my mind, which she was working so feverishly to sharpen. But I am human. It was too beautiful a moment not to light up.

Not long after, I was feeling right as rain, and I leaned back in my chair to enjoy the music. I pulled out my schedule and read the name of the first band: Three Blind Mice. Two people came onstage: a woman carrying a fiddle and a man with a stand-up bass. A few seconds later, another man sauntered out with an acoustic guitar in his hands.

He was pale, amazingly so, with a slight sprinkling of freckles across the middle of his face, and fiery-red hair that hung straight to his shoulders. Before he began to play, he pulled a hair band out of his pocket and tied his hair back in a ponytail. This made it easier to see a small hoop earring in his left ear and to see his eyes, which were a green similar to the moss on the shady side of a log. He had a long, narrow nose that sat above a set of pale-pink lips. He was tall and slim in a way that appealed to me, as I have never been one for bulky, muscular men.

OK, I'll admit—I was intrigued.

But I couldn't say why he caught my attention. In San Francisco, there is no shortage of tall, gaunt, waifish men to gawk at. I noticed also that he had a fabulous set of tattoos around his wrists and elbows—again, not a rare occurrence. With him, though, there was a certain *je ne sais quoi*. Maybe it was the way his gray shirt and faded jeans hung on his body. Maybe it was the pre-roll. I was trying to put my finger on what it was that caught my attention when the trio began to play. The moment I heard the music, I knew he was the vampire from the tunnel.

The recognition was immediate for us both. When I looked back at the stage, his green eyes were gazing directly into mine and he had a slight smile on his face, as if he also was satisfied to find me. I held his gaze. I sank back in my chair, eyes locked on to him as he moved his fingers up and down the neck of the guitar, fret to fret to fret, hitting every note while never taking his eyes from mine.

I've never put much stock in love at first sight, but honestly, I was quite dazzled by the gorgeous musician making eyes at me. He periodically switched instruments, using a banjo instead of a guitar, and now and then I would look away to chat with someone or to take in the swelling crowd, but the moment I turned my head back to him, he would meet my gaze.

I was enjoying myself, but I realized that I needed to bring our staring contest to an end and leave before the vampire got the idea I was actually interested in getting to know him better. It's been well established (by me) that I don't have boyfriends. I slept with men occasionally when I felt the urge, usually the kind of men who didn't want to be called again, and this suited me fine. I'm not interested in dating. I don't believe that people meet, fall in love, and live happily ever after.

Of course, this vampire never said he wanted to date me. I had no evidence that he wanted anything to do with me. Last time we were alone, he'd abruptly stopped talking and disappeared. In fact, I didn't even know if vampires liked humans, let alone dated them. But the biggest black mark against him? He was already dead, which meant he had a lot of free time on his hands. To me this was the fatal flaw. The last thing I needed was a guy with too much time on his hands hanging around.

Having had this entire conversation quickly in my head, I reluctantly packed up and abruptly set off as the band was ending its set, walking into the massive stream of people surging toward the other stages. I was never so relieved to be swallowed by a crowd. I was allowing myself to be pushed along with the general direction of the mob when I felt a whisper of breath against my ear.

"I see you still can't finish what you start," he said, his Southern drawl sounding stronger today.

Whoa. Vampires are fast. And quiet. I didn't even hear him come up behind me. I turned to face him, prepared to indignantly deny all when I found myself looking into eyes far darker than they had seemed from the stage. I exhaled before I could stop myself. My God, he was beautiful. And calm. He was still giving off the calmest waves of energy I had ever felt. I, however, did not feel calm. I was feeling anxious. How exactly had he found me so quickly in such an enormous crowd?

"Have we met?" I asked, using my haughtiest voice.

My remarks caused him to throw his head back and laugh. "You spent my entire set ogling me, and now you're going to pretend we don't know each other? That is downright cruel."

"I was not ogling," I said, unable to steel myself against his charm. "I was watching you play. I happen to like bluegrass music."

"Liar," was his reply.

We were at a standstill. As I stood watching him, trying to control my breathing, it occurred to me that he was standing in the midday sun.

"Are you going to burst into flames if we stay here?" I asked, genuinely not wanting to draw that kind of attention to myself. I mean, how would you explain that to the police?

He smiled. "No, I will not burst into flames, but I would like to get my hat and my guitar and find some shade. Would you care to join me, ma'am?"

It was the *ma'am* that finally got me. It was delivered in a velvety drawl that sent shivers down my spine. And just like that, all of my "I don't date; I don't get involved," disappeared, and I followed a strange vampire into the middle of a music festival.

We walked back to the stage where his band had performed. He pulled several lanyards with plastic badges from inside his shirt and showed them to a guard, who let us both behind a makeshift fence. As we headed toward the back of the stage, I found myself ready to ask questions.

"Do your band mates know?" I asked.

"Know what?"

"You know," I said. "What you are."

"They know," he said, picking up the same straw cowboy hat he'd been wearing in the tunnel. "They don't much care as long as I show up for our shows."

"They must live in the Mission," I blurted out before I could stop myself.

My Southern man of mystery smiled. "You mean because in the Mission no one would notice a vampire walking around?"

"Exactly," I said, glad he understood.

"I'm William Ferrell, by the way," he said, extending his hand.

I took his cool hand into mine, and for the second time I could not control a gasp. He was an old soul. I could tell now why he was so calm. He had lived lifetimes; the energy he gave off spoke of conservation and time. I was amazed at what I could feel coming from him. But more than that, I could feel his strong interest in me. He was burning with curiosity about what I was and was clearly letting me read him to see what would happen.

"Why are you letting me do this?" I asked.

"Tell me your name," he said, holding on to my hand.

"Olivia. Olivia Shepherd," I said.

"Well, O-liv-i-a," he said, stretching the syllables out. "I am trying to figure out what you are."

Although we were in a crowd full of people who had been partying for hours, I was leery of saying anything. The Council had been explicit that I was not to discuss my skills or the existence of the Others with regular humans.

"Shhhh," I said, laughing. "You'll scare people. Let's get out of here."

William grabbed his guitar, and we began to walk. We left the festival compound and headed east along the sidewalk until we got to the entrance to Stow Lake. I don't know why I took him there. I guess I thought it would be quiet, and it has some nice shady groves.

By now it was late afternoon, and the clouds were moving in. The light around the lake was slightly dulled, and the sun had to push through the clouds to be seen. It was still beautiful, and I was pleased to see a flock of geese flying across the lake, honking as they came overhead. I led William to the inner ring of the lake, where a dirt path climbs to the top of what locals call Strawberry Hill. He walked wordlessly next to me. When we got to the top, I gestured with my hands to show him the panoramic view of the city. He smiled.

We sat down on a large boulder and looked out at the Pacific Ocean and Marin Headlands in the distance before us.

"Are we alone?" he asked, knowing the answer. "Is it safe to ask—what are you?"

"I'm not sure what to tell you," I said, feeling apprehensive. "I've only begun to understand myself. I am human, but I come from a long line of women with the ability to read people. I can read their emotions and auras. Sometimes I can read minds. Actually, it's closer really to reading their *intentions*, not their actual thoughts. And I only recently learned that I can do all of this."

"Recently," he said, sounding surprised. "Where I come from, this kind of talent is passed from mother to daughter. Why didn't your mother tell you?"

Gosh. Was I really going to divulge my family history to a strange vampire who I hardly knew, in the middle of the park?

"It's complicated," I said. "My mom did try to tell me. She's an artist, and she can easily pick up on people's emotions, but it over-whelms her. She has a major substance-abuse problem. Her paintings are these mad, amazing landscapes that display the energy of the land in a way that really captivates people. And she's an amazing hostess who loves to entertain. People adore her, and we used to have parties at our home that would last until dawn. It's too much for her, though. She can't separate out what belongs to whom. The energy eats her alive. She has a house and a studio, where I grew up. She's very wealthy but very fucked-up. I never met my father.

"Anyway," I continued, "I had no desire to be like her. It was scary to watch as a child. She could be so happy, but then . . ."

"So what have you been doing all these years?" he graciously asked, helping to change the subject.

"I'm a consultant for companies, and sometimes I run political campaigns," I said. "Lately, though, I've had some bad luck and some major changes in my life."

"Hmm," William drawled. "Are you getting married? Is it something like that?" he said, laughing.

I slapped him on the shoulder, shocked at how solid he felt to the touch. "Don't tease. I am pouring my heart out to a complete stranger with a Southern accent. The least you can do is be sympathetic."

"Darlin', my accent is real," he purred back. "I was born and raised in Tennessee."

"In what year?" I asked, hoping he would tell me.

"All in good time," he said. "Eventually, I'll answer all of your questions."

"Are you really a vampire?" I asked, wanting to firm up my assessment.

He turned to look at me and asked, "Are you really a human who can size people up for what they truly are?"

"I am," I said, pleased with his explanation for my gifts.

"I'm glad we got that all sorted out," he said. "Now, what do you mean bad luck? In my experience, there's no such thing as bad luck. There is bad information, bad planning, or bad execution. If you have one of those three, then you usually have bad luck."

He did have a point. I suppose when you've been alive for as long as he has, you have the luxury of seeing things more clearly and separating out your own emotions. I guess in a way I did have some or all three of those in my basket. I had failed to use my gifts and missed opportunities in my work. "I suppose you could say I had a triple whammy. Thanks to a demon unleashed on me by a competitor, I managed to get myself fired from a project. Then I tried to compete for another big campaign, and I made a mess of the presentation and lost the work. At that point, I got mad at myself and sort of let things go."

William nodded, indicating I should continue.

"I got angry. Then I grew depressed. Around that time, I began to have dreams with a great black panther in them. And she seemed to want to speak to me."

"Oooooh, now that is spooky," William said. "Are you telling ghost stories up here on the mountain top? I feel like I'm back home with my kinfolk."

I slapped him again on his very solid, tattooed arm. I was growing to like his sense of humor. And there was no denying that he was incredibly sexy. There were worse ways to spend my time.

"Actually, I am telling a ghost story," I said, smiling. "I have a sort of ghost of my own. Her name is Elsa. One morning after a night of heavy drinking, I awoke to find her standing in my kitchen. Elsa was the panther. It scared the shit out of me—I won't deny it. It's not that I didn't believe in spirits; I really never gave it much thought. Now, of course, I know that the earth is really divided into parallel worlds, but it was a bit of a shock to see an ancient time-walker sitting in my home."

I could see this story had actually shocked William because he was now looking at me with what seemed like a new appreciation for my situation.

"Where is she now?" William asked, sounding a little worried. "And what happened to the demon?"

"The demon," I repeated, realizing I didn't know. "I don't know exactly what happened. When Elsa appeared, everything bad that was happening stopped. Then she gave me this peyote drink, and I ran through the woods and saw colors." I was babbling a mile a minute, the same way a child would quickly try to tell a story. "Why do you care? Are you worried she won't like me talking to you?"

William nodded emphatically. "She's here to help you accomplish something important, Olivia. Few humans in the world manage to catch the attention of a time-walker. You have what my dear departed mother would have called a powerful spirit."

I laughed. "I don't think Elsa will care. She . . ." I was about to say that she works with vampires, but I wasn't so sure I should tell William about the Council.

"Did you tell her you were going for a walk alone in the woods with a vampire?"

I shook my head. "I didn't know myself," I said, hoping this wasn't the end of my evening. "It's none of her business," I added, suddenly worried I would never see William again.

William shook his head to disagree. "This is powerful magic that should not be interrupted."

"I don't want to interrupt," I said, raising my voice. "I'm happy to learn what Elsa wants to teach me, but I don't like being told who I can be friends with."

William bent his head down and began to laugh softly. "My dear, sweet Olivia, you have a lot to learn about the world you've entered. Vampires don't make friends," he said. "They take lovers."

And then he leaned in and kissed me. Kissed me until my lips felt like they would blister from the heat. I had no idea how powerful sexual energy could feel until that moment, when I opened myself up to it. It was easy to understand now what someone meant by being lost in a kiss. In fact, I was so lost that it took me a few moments to realize I was actually no longer kissing him. At some point, he'd disappeared—like he had that day in the tunnel. Once again, I was alone in the dusk light. This was the second time he had managed to vanish on me. I vowed there would not be a third as I grabbed my things and headed for home.

14

MY SLEEP HAD BEEN RESTLESS, BUT THIS TIME I HAD THE vampire to thank for my insomnia. His kiss had seared my soul, and I'd spent the evening tossing and turning, yearning for him in a way I had never wanted a man before.

The timing of our meeting, I realized, firing up my espresso machine, was horrendous. I was running a multimillion-dollar campaign and assuming a new role as a consultant. My window for romance was slim at best, assuming I could even find William Ferrell again.

I must have been daydreaming because I didn't hear Elsa come into the kitchen.

"How was the concert?" she asked.

"Good. Fun," I said. "I met a vampire. His name is William."

"You met a vampire, as in he came up and introduced himself?"

"Yes. Sort of. What I mean is . . . I had been staring at him . . . er . . . watching him perform. He's in a band," I managed to stutter out, sounding like a teenager.

"And, what happened?" she asked, sounding like my mother, which got my defenses up.

"I am over thirty years old," I said, sounding even more like a teenager. "I can take care of myself."

Elsa was shaking her head in a way that oddly reminded me of William. Once again, I was going to be lectured on all the things I didn't know. I held my hands out in front of me to indicate I wasn't in the mood.

"Listen, he already told me I didn't know what I was getting into," I said. "And he told me you wouldn't approve at all."

"He was right," she said. "Vampires are serious creatures, Olivia. They do not *make friends* with humans."

"So I've been told," I said. "Listen. I'll probably never see him again, so let's drop it."

Elsa nodded, and I went back to making myself a cappuccino. Once that was out of the way, we discussed how to contact Nadia, the witch versed in old magic who would transfer the map of the portals onto my skin. It would not be hard to locate her, Elsa said; she could be found most days feeding the ducks and geese at Stow Lake. All we had to do is walk over and look for her.

The sun was already high as we climbed to the top of the stairway at the foot of Stow Lake. The trees were lush and green, and our surroundings seemed brighter against the brilliant October sky. There were turtles sunning themselves on logs and ducks resting on the grass as Elsa scanned the perimeter of the lake.

"There she is."

"She" turned out to be an elderly woman, who, despite the heat, was dressed in tights, a floral dress, and a large cardigan sweater. For good measure she had a floral scarf tied around her head and knotted at her chin. Next to her was a worn red wagon stuffed full of bags of bread pieces and birdseed. Nadia, it seemed, was well stocked for her work.

"That is Nadia?"

Elsa nodded. "You were expecting a pointy hat and a magic wand?"

"When you said old magic, I guess I got an image in my head of someone more scary looking," I said, cringing at how stupid I sounded.

"I said *o-l-d* magic, not black magic," Elsa said with a laugh.

"But don't be fooled. Nadia can be very scary when she needs to be."

Nadia looked up and acknowledged us as we approached. She and Elsa began conversing in a language that sounded like Russian. The two chatted for a few minutes, each one periodically looking over at me. Finally, Nadia turned to face me completely. "This is going to hurt," she said, sizing me up. "But it will be over quickly."

I glanced around the lake, taking in our surroundings. There were a few other people strolling nearby, but for the most part the area was empty. I wasn't sure how this old magic was supposed to work, but I was pretty sure we didn't want any witnesses. Nadia picked up on my thoughts and shook her head.

"I will come to you, to your home, in a few days," she said. "In the meantime, I need something of yours: a hair or a fingernail."

I looked over at Elsa at a loss, never having been a party to this kind of request before. In response, she yanked a hair off my head and handed it to Nadia. The elderly witch immediately reached into the pocket of her cardigan and took out a white handkerchief. Carefully, she put the hair inside and folded it closed. Then she returned the cloth to her pocket.

"How will I know when to expect you?" I asked, once again exposing my ignorance.

The old woman smiled and patted my arm. "Don't worry," she said. "I will find you."

I wasn't worried. I'd read Nadia's intentions while we were standing together, and I was certain she meant me no harm. After a few more pleasantries, we said good-bye.

A few days later, I was working on my laptop at home when there was a knock on the door. Lily was over, sitting on the couch reading a book. Elsa was in the living room doing yoga. "It's Nadia," Elsa said from the other room, rising from her mat to open the door.

It seemed rude to stay seated, so Lily and I both got up and walked to the door to greet her. In the dusk light, Nadia looked much younger. She arrived with another colorful scarf covering her hair, but up close, her skin was moist and pale, almost flawless.

She caught me scrutinizing her. "Thanks to the old ways, I age more slowly than one might think," she said, looking at me directly.

Before I could ask what her secret was, she urged the four of us to move in to the kitchen. I took a seat at the peninsula, and Nadia stood at the counter, unpacking a small bundle she had removed from her sweater pocket. Slowly, she unrolled the cloth to reveal a paintbrush and a small brown glass jar filled with a clear liquid. The brush was made of a dark wood and was ornately decorated with symbols I couldn't decipher. The hairs of the brush were stark white and shaped into a point.

"Are you left-handed or right-handed?" Nadia asked, diverting my attention away from her supplies.

"Right," I said.

"OK then. We'll do your left hand because it will be sore for a day or two."

This conversation made me a little uneasy. I had a vision of my left arm blackened and hanging limply from my side.

Lily came up behind me and placed her hand on my shoulder. "Don't be scared," she said quietly. "I've seen this kind of old magic before many times. It will feel a little like getting a tattoo. A short sting, and then the next day your skin will feel as if it has been burned."

I washed my left forearm in the sink and dried it. Then, following the witch's directions, I laid my arm on the counter. Nadia removed her heavy cardigan, saying she was warm, and instructed Elsa to bring her a candle and some salt. Elsa brought both items to her and took a step back.

"Dim the lights," Nadia said to no one in particular. Lily got up and turned off most of the lights in the kitchen, leaving a single bulb above the stove for illumination. Then Nadia lit a small white candle and picked up the glass bottle. She ran the flame under the bottle several times and then tilted the candle until it began to drip wax onto the counter.

"North. South," she chanted in her Russian-tinged English. "East. West. These are the directions in which we travel." She continued to drip wax until the face of a compass appeared. When she was done, she asked Lily to slowly sprinkle salt along the wax pattern as she spoke. Nadia ran the flame of the candle under the bottle one more time and then began to murmur the words of a spell under her breath. Slowly she unscrewed the cap on the bottle and handed the candle to Elsa. Then she picked up the paintbrush, and symbols on the handle began to glow. Nadia dipped the brush into the jar and continued to speak.

"*Subnoto. Signum. Terminus.*"

As soon as the brush touched my arm, it began to sting. I had expected her to draw the images on my arm, adding each site I had seen on the map. Instead, she was running the brush up and down the length of my arm, much the same way a painter would try to cover a wall. When my arm was coated with the liquid, exact copies of the line drawings I had seen on the map began to appear. I'm not sure how long it took her to complete the process. I was transfixed, watching the map take shape on my arm. The pain was no less and no more than what Nadia and Lily had promised. It stung and my arm burned, but I was almost too distracted by the magic to be uncomfortable.

When Nadia was finished, she asked Lily to put the last of the salt on the wax compass on the counter. Then the old witch placed the brush in the flame of the candle and said, "*Termino.*" The hairs of the brush glowed but did not catch fire.

I looked down at my arm. There were a half-dozen line drawings sitting at the surface of my skin, all angry red and swollen at the edges.

"Can I touch it?" I asked, hoping I could put a cold cloth or some ice on my arm.

Nadia nodded and took a small clay jar out of the other pocket of her sweater, which I was beginning to suspect was bewitched to hold anything she needed. She opened the pot and moved it under my nose several times so I could pick up the fragrance. "Calendula flowers," she said as I smiled at the scent. "It will help your skin heal." Nadia rubbed the salve on my arm and asked Elsa to bandage it for the night. "In the morning, you can remove the bandage," she added as she began to pack up her belongings.

"What will it look like tomorrow?" I asked, worried it would be a big, ugly mess.

"The map will be visible for the next few days, but only to you," she continued. "Then it will disappear, and it will only return when you request it."

"Request," I repeated, but Nadia shook her head.

"Not out loud. All you need to do is think about the map to see it. There's one more thing: the map will change."

This caught everyone's attention. "How do you mean?" Lily asked.

Nadia fixed a stare on the three of us, much like a schoolteacher dealing with inept students. "The magic that binds the map is a part of the same spell that creates the portals. If the locations change or a route is blocked, you will see it."

"And if I leave San Francisco?" I asked, thinking this handy information.

Again, Nadia fixed me with eyes that spoke volumes about my inexperience. "The map will display the portals located in the place where you are. If your arm is blank, it means there is no exit."

That sounded ominous.

"I think it's time for tea," Lily interjected, thankfully.

Relieved, I joined with the others in making Nadia a cup of tea, and the four of us sat in amicable silence for a few minutes. Finally, the old woman stood up abruptly and declared that she was tired.

"I'll walk with you," Elsa offered, but Nadia declined, saying a walk alone in the crisp night air would do her some good.

When we reached the door, Nadia asked for my hand and began to examine my palm. She stood quietly for a few moments and then spoke. "You are destined for great things, Olivia. You have a long life line and . . ." Nadia stopped speaking.

"And what?" I prodded.

"You have a great adventure ahead," she said, almost squinting at my palm. "Two great loves will enter your life."

I replied with my own question. "Did I make the right decision joining the Council?"

Nadia squeezed my hand and stepped closer to me to ensure that only I could hear her whispered words. "That was not your choice, *miloska,*" she said. "Women kings are born and must accept their fate."

"There's no such thing," I said back.

Nadia began to leave. "Oh, but there is," she said nodding. "There is." And then she quickly walked down the stairway, onto the sidewalk, and into the night.

I remained in the doorway, unsure of what to think. I decided it was better not to mention too much to Lily or Elsa, who'd stayed in the kitchen. I knew Nadia wasn't crazy, but she was old and maybe a little bit nostalgic for a different time. I walked back into the kitchen to find Elsa tearing a linen dishrag into strips for my arm.

Lily broke the silence. "OK, tell us: did she read your palm?"

I nodded. "Yes. She said I would live a long life and have two great loves. I assume she meant the two of you," I said, trying to make a joke out of it. But neither Lily nor Elsa was laughing.

"Nadia is a great seer," Lily said. "If she said 'loves,' she means it."

I found the entire conversation a little overwhelming after my cartography session. "How will I ever find one love, let alone two, when I've got a campaign to run and you two as my chaperones every evening?"

"Whatever Nadia told you is going to come true, Olivia," Lily said, undeterred. "So you'd better be prepared."

15

LUCKILY, I DIDN'T HAVE TIME TO DWELL ON FORTUNE-cookie predictions or the mysterious old woman who doled them out. My arm, while tender, was healing nicely, and, as Nadia had promised, the images were invisible to everyone but me. That made my next job easier, as I was off to find the head of the state Democratic Party and convince him to not run a candidate against Levi.

The expression "three is a crowd" holds true for both romance and politics. A three-way race is a disaster in a local campaign because it splits the ballots, making it almost impossible to gain a majority of the votes. It usually results in a runoff.

I was determined to help Levi avoid that fate. I drove over to Lake Merced and found my target. As I expected, Paul Levant was ensconced on a bench, watching a regatta. No one was seated next to him, something I thought was probably not a coincidence. Throwing caution to the wind, I slid alongside him.

Levant, a small bag of popcorn in his hands, turned to look at me, shook his head, and chuckled. "I figured you would come to see me, sooner or later," he said, popping a piece into his mouth.

"You must have ESP," I said, watching the women of the University of San Francisco glide across the water.

"Maybe," he said. "Or maybe I read somewhere that you're running Levi Barnes's campaign for District 15. I do try to stay current on my political news."

"I liked it better when I thought you had magical powers," I said, enjoying myself.

Levant handed me the bag of popcorn and smiled. "On second thought, I do have ESP because I know exactly what you're going to ask me."

"You do?" I asked, feigning ignorance for the sake of our conversation.

"You want to know if the party is going to support someone else for that seat," he said. "The answer is no; no one wants it." Levant was agitated. I wasn't the cause, but there was an undercurrent of worry running through him; it felt old, like it had been with him for a while. "The Republicans are looking for a candidate, Olivia. They want a MAGA rep for that seat, someone who can appeal to the conservative money in Silicon Valley and the farm belt."

"You think an engineer working on AI is going to vote for someone who thinks the world is flat?" I asked tartly.

Levant shook his head. "Don't be so flip. They won't be as obvious as that," he said. "It will be about taxes and regulation. It will be about immigration and education, maybe a tad bit about water rights in the Central Valley. Stuff your guy is not as good at."

"What do you mean, 'no one wants it'?" I asked, not wanting to discuss Levi yet.

"Just what I said," Levant replied, taking back his popcorn bag. "Politics is a rough business these days. There isn't a lot of demand to take on the far right and their base. The demographics are changing. More voters move back and forth between the parties. It's difficult to raise a million dollars even with tech money. At this rate, the Democrats will be lucky to keep the seats we currently have in Congress."

Here was my opening. "Fortunately for you, money is no object for Levi Barnes. He's prepared to spend to win. And he's a Democrat."

Levant shook his head. "At this point, I am glad someone is willing to run for the seat. I'm getting too fucking old for this shit. As far as

I'm concerned, a Bible's main use is to swear in a candidate, and that's about it. In my day, we didn't let these fights become so personal. Your guy is walking into a shitstorm of hard feelings in Washington."

"Paul, don't worry," I said, feeling the need to reassure him. "Levi is a former member of Congress and a successful businessman. He can stay above the fray, and he'll be a bright star for the party. You wait and see."

"If he can win, kid. If he can win," Levant said, turning his gaze to the boats on the water.

"Maybe if you use some of that ESP you've got to help us, it will be a sure thing," I said, gathering up my belongings.

"I think I'd rather send you a check," Levant said. "Be in touch with me about your campaign plan; the party will support you."

I waited until I was on the road back to my house before I made the call to Levi.

"Levant is backing us," I said, feeling jubilant. "The party will bankroll our efforts."

"I don't need their money, Olivia," Levi said. "I'll tell Paul to use it for another race, for someone who needs the help."

"We should take a little help from the party," I said. "For one thing, it will look better if they're seen spending some resources on us. We don't want anyone to think our campaign is operating out there alone."

After I hung up with Levi, I called Gabriel. He didn't pick up, so I left him a message letting him know that I'd secured Levant's backing.

With Paul Levant's promise in my back pocket, I was free to continue with a research project I'd started a few weeks back. It took patience, but finally one Sunday, as I was reading the entertainment section of the paper, I was rewarded. There, in a small box, was a listing for Three Blind Mice. They were playing later in the week at the Treasure Chest, a nightclub on Divisadero Street.

This was my chance to see William again. Now that the campaign was on the right path, I didn't see why anyone would object to me taking a night off. Nadia's pronouncements aside, the truth was that I couldn't stop thinking about him. I wasn't sure what bothered me more, being caught in the horrible cliché of pining for a vampire or my actual yearning for him. Regardless, I was determined to see him.

When the night of the show arrived, I was pleased Elsa had forced me into such a rigorous exercise regime. I pulled a pair of very slim black jeans out of my closet, along with a beat-up pair of brown cowboy boots, and then searched in my drawer for the sexiest bra I could find. I knew I was playing with fire—not to mention being pretty presumptuous—but if there was a make-out session in my future, I wanted to be wearing the most provocative underwear possible.

I rummaged around for the black T-shirt I was looking for and grabbed a khaki safari jacket off a hanger. I looked in the mirror and liked what I saw. I was stylish without trying too hard. At the very least, if I missed William, I would no doubt meet someone interesting, and the truth was that I was in the mood for a little night magic.

I called an Uber, and within ten minutes, a car arrived at my doorstep. It was approaching nine-thirty when we pulled up at the club. I began to feel nervous. What if I walked in and he was there with another woman? What if he didn't want to speak with me? I was rethinking the whole idea in my head when I looked up, and there outside, leaning against the wall in a pair of faded jeans and his signature cowboy hat was William. It seemed likely he had picked up on my thoughts and knew I was coming when I got within a few blocks of the club. I sighed, realizing there would be no sneaking up on him.

As I paid the driver and stepped onto the curb, my nervousness ramped up. I'd never really chased a man before, and now I felt my whole life depended on what I would find when I looked into William's eyes. I glanced up slowly and was relieved to see he had a wide grin on his face.

"Well now," he said emphasizing his accent. "What do we have here? Have you gone AWOL from your barracks?"

"No, sir," I said. "I gave myself a pass for the evening."

"Allow me to escort you in," he said.

William took my hand in his and gave it a slight squeeze. He was wearing a plaid flannel shirt with the sleeves rolled up to his elbows. The red of the shirt accentuated his tattoos and made his hair seem to shimmer in the club's subdued lighting. I thought that after we got inside he would let go of my hand, but he didn't. He continued to hold it as he led me through the nightclub and beyond a door marked with a sign that said STAFF AND BAND MEMBERS ONLY.

William greeted a security guard sitting on the other side of the doorway and then guided me along a short hallway to another door. He continued to hold my hand as he led us into a small dressing room. Inside I found his bandmates lounging on a couch. They were both smoking. A bottle of Jack Daniel's with three glasses stacked next to it sat on the table in front of them.

"Cat and Jack, this is Olivia," William said, pouring whiskey into a glass. His bandmates both nodded and said hello as if they had been expecting me to show up. In fact, I could tell from their emotions that they were not the least bit surprised to see me. I was flattered but unsure if their feelings meant he *wanted* to see me or just knew that, eventually, I'd come looking for him. William passed the bottle to Cat and then took a sip from the glass in his hand. I must have looked surprised because William turned to me and said, "I can drink alcohol and have been known to eat lightly from time to time."

I nodded, taking the glass from him when he offered. I took a sip and immediately began to cough. I don't usually drink hard alcohol without something mixed in. William laughed.

"A tenderfoot, I see. Let's go find you another drink at the bar."
He grabbed my hand again, and we retraced our steps through the
same set of hallways and doors.

When we arrived at the bar, the bartender greeted William by
name, and I soon had a rum and Coke with lime in my hand. We
were standing side by side at the bar. He had ordered another shot of
Jack and was slowly sipping his drink while gazing out at the stage.

"I have to go on in a few minutes," he said. "Will you stay until
I'm finished?"

I turned and laughed. "I think the better question is: will you?
You're the one with the habit of disappearing."

William took my hand and focused his dark-green eyes on mine.
"I don't plan on disappearing again." And with that, he bowed slightly
at the waist and turned to walk onto the stage. Not long after, Cat and
Jack joined him, and they launched into a set like the one I had heard
in the park. This time, though, I really listened to the lyrics.

"I was born more than one hundred years ago."

"I am one of the oldest souls you'll ever come to know."

It turned out that William was also a songwriter. Who knew
vampires had so many talents? It was one of the few details I knew
about him. He, on the other hand, knew a great deal more about me.
I guessed that was probably not an accident. When you live so long,
you must have to keep yourself hidden from view or at some point
people will notice that you never grow old or that you rarely eat food.

Yet after everything I had seen and done during the last few
weeks, I was beginning to realize that most humans noticed very little.
As long as their paychecks arrived and their Wi-Fi worked, they were
happy to live very limited lives. It worried me that I lived in a country
full of people who could be made content so easily. I suppose that's
why the Council existed—because humans were content with their
ignorance.

I drifted off, lost in my thoughts. After a few moments, I caught myself. When I glanced up, I saw that William was watching me. For the remainder of his set I focused on his performance, appreciating his skill with a guitar. He seemed to be able to make his instrument ache with sadness, and I knew without a doubt that William Ferrell had seen his share of misery. Twenty minutes later, they finished their set and were quickly besieged by friends and fans. I stayed back at the bar, unsure of my place, but it wasn't long before William separated himself from the crowd and walked over.

"Don't you want to stay with your friends?" I asked.

He shook his head. "They're not my friends."

"So what should we do now?" I asked, feeling a little like I was back in middle school.

"Now we get out of here," he said, grabbing my hand. We packed up his guitar and banjo and said good night to Cat and Jack. Once again, they didn't seem at all surprised.

"Did you know you would see me again?" I asked, hating myself for needing to know.

"Yes."

"Did you expect me to come find you?"

"Yes."

"Why didn't you come find me?" I asked, feeling like I was doing all the work.

"How do you know I didn't?" he said.

"Did you stay away because of Elsa?"

"I know enough to stay out of her way. Let's put it like that."

"So what changed your mind?"

"Nothing. I'm playing with fire, just like you are," he said. "I wanted to make sure you had the courage to try. This life is not for the faint of heart."

We walked outside with his gear and strolled around the block. There, parked on a nearby street, was a brand-new black Subaru wagon. I laughed.

"You were expecting a black horse maybe," he said sharply. "I'm not a character in a novel, Olivia. I live in this world, just as you do."

"Ouch," I said, laying my hand over my heart. "I laughed because it seems like such a practical car. I was expecting something more rebellious. Like a motorcycle."

"A motorcycle," he said. "Darlin', those things will kill you."

I laughed, once again reminded of how much I liked his sense of humor. He unlocked the car and opened the passenger door so I could climb in. I realized I had no idea where we were going, but I couldn't wait to find out.

Minutes later, after passing through the Castro and by Dolores Park, we were pulling into the driveway of a lovely Victorian home on the edge of the Mission. William pressed the button on an opener fastened to the sunshade of his wagon and pulled inside the garage. From there he led me up a set of stairs.

William lived in a very old, well-restored two-story home. At the top of the stairs, we faced a small living room with a fireplace. The room was decorated just the way I would have done it myself, in a combination of old and new: a bohemian mix of deer antlers, wooden antique furniture, and a smidgen of modern touches that respected the age of the house.

"Can I have a tour?"

William nodded and walked me from room to room. Next door to the living room was another small room that had been converted into a library. Floor-to-ceiling bookshelves lined the walls. A brilliant red-and-orange antique Afghan rug covered the wooden floors, which looked to be the home's original planks. In one corner of the library sat a chocolate-brown leather chair with a brass library lamp leaning over its arm. The shelves were neatly arranged, but I could see that William had been collecting books for decades.

There were first editions of Hemingway and Fitzgerald. I spied an original copy of *The Hobbit*, all of the books in Ursula K. Le Guin's

Earthsea Cycle, several biographies of past presidents as well as an entire section of poetry by T. S. Eliot. He also seemed to like Cara Black mysteries and books by Margaret Atwood. For a voracious reader like me, it was mesmerizing, and I must have looked intrigued because William broke the silence with an offer to let me borrow anything that interested me.

From there, we toured the rest of the house. There were two bedrooms on the main level, both decorated to look like guest rooms. On the floor above, there was a large loft space with an enormous bay window at the front of the room, and surprisingly, several skylights had been cut into the ceiling. Lovely blackout shades made from a rich fabric were bolted into the skylights. But for now, because it was evening, the shades were open, leaving us a clear view of the full moon in the night sky. There was no bed in the room, just an old drafting table that had been converted to a desk. There were more bold rugs on the floor, and a set of leather chairs that looked to be companions to the one in the library.

The most striking aspect of the loft was the collection of guitars and banjos on display. William had at least five acoustic guitars sitting on stands, as well as three or four more banjos. A brand-new Denon turntable sat nearby, along with a series of storage racks holding hundreds of vinyl albums. Like his taste in books, William enjoyed a wide variety of music. Aerosmith and the Eagles were intermixed with Billie Holiday, John Coltrane, Led Zeppelin, and Willie Nelson. Amy Winehouse and Nina Simone were sitting alongside Serge Gainsbourg, the Jam, and the Clash. I smiled inwardly at the depth and variety. This was clearly the room where William spent most of his time. The space was full of his calm energy, and it was obvious to see from the design that he did everything in his power to create and maintain that sense of peace.

We walked back downstairs and into a kitchen that could have passed muster with any editor at *Sunset* magazine. The sunken white porcelain sink and six-burner Wolf range complemented the large stainless-steel refrigerator.

"Cook many big meals?" I teased, thinking the fridge would most likely be empty.

"As you know, I am not much of an eater," he drawled back. "I have a small property management business, and over the years, I have acquired a few investment properties in San Francisco and other cities. One day I might sell or rent this house. It will be more valuable with a working kitchen."

"I can't imagine ever wanting to leave here," I said, thinking of the beautiful home my grandmother had given me. "I have a nice old house too. My grandmother left it to me in her will. I hope to live in it until I . . ." I was about to say more, but then I stopped.

"It's OK," William coaxed. "You want to stay in the house until you *die*. You are human, Olivia. You can discuss your life in a normal way."

"I didn't want to seem insensitive. I have no idea how you feel about being a vampire."

"Living forever has many advantages," William remarked thoughtfully. "I have amassed a lot of interesting objects and wealth. But there are moments when time does drag on."

"Are you going to tell me how you became a vampire?" I asked, hoping there was a bottle of wine and a fireplace in my future.

I must have pushed that wish out very strongly because William immediately followed up with, "Red or white?" I chose red, a lovely Pinot Noir from the Russian River, and we went back to the living room to sit down.

"The fireplace doesn't work," William said. "And these days there are so many laws about when you can burn wood that I haven't bothered to have it repaired. The last thing I need is someone knocking on my door to cite me for burning wood."

We sat down on a very comfortable chocolate-brown leather couch—I was beginning to detect a theme in his tastes—and he poured us both a glass of wine. I was using all of my self-control not to blurt out the long list of questions I had for him: How old are you? Where are you from? How did you come to live in San Francisco?

I was sitting at one end of the couch, using the corner as a sort of brace. I had no idea what to do. Should I sit closer to him? Should I stay away? Was it hard for him to be around humans and not want to drink their blood? My mind, I was beginning to realize, gave off strong signals to those who knew enough to pay attention. I was hoping he would say something before I burst with pent-up anticipation.

"Try to relax, Olivia," he said. "I promise to tell you everything you want to know, but first I want something from you. If we're going to do this—share our secrets—then I want something from you in return."

"What do you want?"

"I want a kiss," he said, smiling. "You and I, we're making a deal of sorts . . . and I want a kiss to seal it, as a commitment that we will keep each other's secrets."

Another kiss? How dangerous could that be? In my short but intense training in Magic 101, I'd never heard of a kiss being any sort of binding contract. If you discounted the fact that I was agreeing to kiss a man who appeared to have been dead for more than a century while sitting alone in his living room with no way to get myself out or drive myself home, then, yes, the request seemed rather harmless.

"OK," I said.

"OK?" William said back.

"What do you want me to say?"

William looked slightly wounded. "Madam, I have kissed other women before, and usually they have shown a little more enthusiasm."

It turned out that even the undead have egos, but I was more than willing to ease his mind. "I haven't stopped thinking about you since the moment you kissed me in the park," I said, taking a sip of wine for courage. "It's possible that I am being quite irresponsible, but of course I want to kiss you. I want to do much more than that. But at the same time, I feel that I'm completely out of my depth. You have to admit this is all a little out of the ordinary."

"No, darlin'. I don't think so," he said. "That's not the way I see it. I am a man who wants to kiss a pretty woman, and that is something that hasn't changed since the dawn of time."

And then in a blink of an eye, he was right next to me, kissing me again in that way that made my lips feel like they would catch fire. This time, though, I was prepared, and I kissed him back with equal intensity. His lips were cool to the touch, which was initially a bit disconcerting, but as I grew hotter, the coolness was soothing.

As we continued kissing, his hands explored my back and made tentative advances toward the front. I felt more than ready for him to slip his hand under my shirt. I had been exploring his body, marveling it how lean and hard it felt. I was certain he could pick up on my thoughts, and I reached to unbutton his flannel shirt.

William pulled back from my advance. "Olivia, you are a handful," he said, making a noise that almost sounded like the exhaling of breath. "There is no rush. I haven't even told you my story yet. There will be plenty of time for us to get to know each other better. Besides, taking a vampire lover is a complicated business, and you may want to know more before you sign up for that responsibility."

Honestly, I would have signed over the deed to my house at that point. I was so aroused, it took a few moments for his words to even register in my brain. I have never been much good at delayed gratification; it's one of my weaknesses.

Still, he had a point. I didn't know anything about taking a vampire as a lover, but honest to God, at that moment, nothing sounded better. Then I thought of Elsa and her reaction if she believed I'd slept with William. Reluctantly, I came back to earth.

"OK," I said, taking his hand. "You're right. And I do want to hear your story."

William poured us both more wine and began to speak.

"You know my name is William Ferrell. My full name is William Aubrey Ferrell. I was born in Tullahoma, Tennessee, in 1830. My father was a farmer who left South Carolina and took work with the railroad. I was one of six brothers and sisters. As you can imagine, we were pretty poor. We had some land to grow our food and raise a few chickens, but it was a difficult life. I was born in the house we lived in. When I grew older, I trained as a carpenter and made decent money for the family making furniture and repairing things for the people in our village.

"I started playing music when I was a child," he continued. "There was a man in town with a guitar, and he taught me how to play in the spare moments when I wasn't helping my mother tend to my brothers and sisters. I made my first guitar myself out of some extra wood I was given for a job. I carried that guitar with me everywhere. In fact, it was with me in Louisiana when I died."

Once again, I heard William make a noise that sounded similar to breathing. He was occupied with the past now, and I could feel his emotions becoming more intense. "When the war broke out, I was living in Knoxville, where there was more work. I enlisted in the spring of 1861. I can imagine you're wondering about my politics. You have to remember, I was born in another era and while our family did not own slaves and I felt no real need to fight for the right for others to do so, there wasn't much of a choice. Deserters were shot on the spot."

William's story was a lot to process, especially the part about fighting for the Confederacy. I was relieved to hear he did so begrudgingly. I was also doing the math in my head. We were sitting in William's living room in late October of 2022, which meant I was sharing a couch with a vampire who was 192 years old. There was no doubt, I mused silently, that I was making the moves on a much older man.

"One year later I was dead," William continued. "I died in Louisiana at the Battle of Baton Rouge."

"You don't have to tell me any more," I said taking his hand in mine. "At least not tonight."

"Actually, I'm fine," he said, looking intently at me with his moss-green eyes. "I haven't told anyone the story of my life for a very long time. Truthfully, it's nice that you want to know."

"I do, very much," I said.

"So, we were in Baton Rouge. We had started with a thousand strong men, but by the time we arrived, there were barely a hundred healthy souls remaining in the division. We arrived with no tents and little gear. Many of the men had neither a coat nor shoes. Imagine, walking for days on end, your feet bloody and raw. There was no food, and our bellies ached with hunger. Many were ill with dysentery. The filth and disease were overwhelming. The horror of watching your brothers, cousins, and friends killed or maimed . . . I think for some it was probably a blessing to die."

"Did you feel that way?"

William shook his head. "No. After all the death and destruction I'd seen, I didn't care much about winning or honor, but I didn't want to die. I wanted to survive and go back home to my family."

"But you didn't survive the war."

"Sadly, no," William replied. "I remember the day of the battle very clearly. It was very humid and also foggy. The air was heavy and wet, and I couldn't make out the landscape beyond my feet. It was a bloodbath; almost five hundred men were killed on the battlefield, out of two thousand, maybe three thousand soldiers. I remember lying on the ground, listening to the screams of the wounded, while civilians from town ran their hands through my pockets looking for valuables. There I was, thirty-two years old, miles away from my family, and I had never even kissed a girl."

"Wait. What do you mean, you'd never kissed a girl?"

William chuckled. "Women were not quite as confident as they are today. And I was too shy to say anything. And then there was the fact that I was too poor to offer for a lady's hand anyway. What would I have given her? I had barely enough money for the roof over my own head. In those days there were few women from good families who would have consented to marry me."

It was a shocking story, but it did make sense. It also made my kisses all the more intriguing. "I guess you learned to kiss after you became a vampire," I said, hoping for more of his story.

"I did, but I haven't had the wild life you may imagine. Anyway, I was turned right there on the battlefield. I had been lying on the ground for a while, having been shot several times in my leg. It must have hit an artery because I started to bleed out. There was no doctor in the camp and no medics to come and help me. Believe me, as bad as war is today, at least soldiers have the proper tools and support in battle.

"My second 'father' was a Union officer. I mistook him for a priest because he came so close to me. I thought he had come to take my confession. Of course, he had something different in mind. He told me that I was minutes away from dying but that he could save me. He asked if I wanted to see the world . . . live a life of endless travel and immortality. I felt my limbs growing cold as the blood left my body, and I knew I had little time left to live."

"Were you scared?"

"Of course," he said. "I was human like you and as afraid of death as anyone, but I was also intrigued. As a poor man in Tennessee, my life's prospects were limited. What my new father offered was a life beyond what fate had in store."

"So you agreed?"

"I did, and I walked out of Baton Rouge the next day and on to a new life."

"Where did you go?"

"Paris. It was an interesting time to be abroad, and my new father was convinced that the United States would never evolve into a civilized country."

"So you speak French?" I asked, feeling odd at the way our lives seemed so neatly connected.

"*Oui, je parle français. Et vous?*"

"*Oui. Bien sûr.*"

"*Bon,*" he said. "If you're nice to me, maybe we'll visit France together."

I was ready to be very nice to him. I was also very tired. I looked at my watch and realized that it was after midnight. I didn't want to go home though. I didn't want to leave William. Once again, he was not far behind my thoughts.

"You can sleep here tonight. As you can see, I don't have a bed in my room. I don't normally sleep, but you can use one of the guest rooms."

I suddenly had a vision of being one of many who had walked down that path. I must have made a face because William took my hand.

"I am flattered at how popular you think I am, but the fact is I've never brought a woman home with me. You're the first."

His confession was my undoing. Baton Rouge . . . a dying soldier who had never been kissed . . . I considered that maybe it was all a fabulous lie to seduce me. But I was holding out hope that it wasn't. Regardless, my emotions got the better of me and I burst into tears, overwhelmed. I knew I was in serious danger of falling in love with this old Southern gentleman. OK—this old *dead* gentleman, but there was no doubt he was different than anyone I'd ever met.

I managed to get out an "I'm sorry" before he picked me up and carried me to one of the bedrooms. He pulled down the sheets and laid me on the bed. With little difficulty he pulled off my boots and tucked me in.

"You see, Olivia," he said gently. "I told you there is a lot to consider when you bring a vampire into your life."

I nodded but said nothing else. I was asleep in seconds.

When I opened my eyes the next morning, it took me a few minutes to realize where I was. I was still in my clothing from the night before; everything was buttoned and snapped into place. I glanced at my Apple Watch, shocked that it was already nine thirty.

Horribly off schedule, I jumped up and opened the door of the bedroom. I padded down the hall to the bathroom and freshened up. When I came out, I heard the sound of guitar coming from upstairs. Slowly, I climbed the steps and stepped into the loft. It was a lovely image, and I worked hard to keep my mouth from hanging open.

There, sitting in one of the leather chairs was William, shirtless, a guitar in his lap. His red hair was loose around his shoulders, and as he leaned forward to play his guitar, I could see more of the tattoo work on his back. There was an enormous angel with its wings outstretched across his shoulder blades. It was magnificent work, and I wondered whether the angel was in honor of the man who saved him that day on the battlefield or for something else.

"Good morning," I said, knowing he was already aware of my presence.

"Hello, sleepyhead," he drawled. "I was beginning to worry you would snooze the day away."

"It seems I might have. I don't remember sleeping so deeply for a long time."

"You got an earful last night," William said. "I can imagine it was a bit of a shock. How are you feeling?"

"I feel great," I said, and I meant it. I was happy to have found William. I knew it was going to make all of the rest of what I had to do more complicated, but I didn't care. "Mind if I come over and say hello?" I asked.

William set down his guitar and opened his arms. I sat on his lap and laid my head on his shoulder, eager to feel his skin against mine. He smelled delicious, lemony, like a very sweet, sugary lozenge, with a hint of rosemary. I sat there for a while not saying anything, sitting in the cocoon of his body. I'm not sure how long we sat in the chair together. Time stopped. We kissed, but it was nothing urgent. After a few moments, we paused to talk, revealing the small details of our lives.

I told him more about my campaign, describing Levi and explaining how I had worked for him before. I didn't mention the Council. I'm not sure why. I guess I had a feeling that maybe this thing between us was too fragile to be laden down with such complicated issues right away. In fact, it all felt a little complicated. I'd never spent the night at a man's home before when we didn't have sex. I'd never spent the night at a vampire's house. I wasn't sure what to expect, but I was out of time to wonder. I looked at my watch and thought of the long list of obligations I had pending. I was long overdue at work.

"I have to go," I said. "I don't want to, but I'm really running late for what will be a very busy day."

"Can I see you again?" was his reply, which sounded so normal that I laughed.

"Forgive me," I said. "It's just that this sounds like a conversation any man or woman would have. Are you asking me out on a date?"

"I am asking you on a date," he said, crossly. "Please keep in mind, darlin', that I'm not a character in a pulp-fiction novel. I won't be using mind control to lure you to my side."

"Bummer," I said. "What about bats? So you won't be flying in through my window?"

My remark seemed to defuse the moment. I had no desire to offend him, and I was relieved when he shook his head and smiled.

"No bats, no flying. I have none of those tricks up my sleeve. I meant what I said last night. I'm simply a man who wants to date a pretty woman."

"You are a man who drinks blood," I said looking him in the eye. "That does seem like a topic worth discussing."

To his credit, William did not break our gaze. "I might take a taste, but I will not *drink* your blood unless you offer it to me, and even then I might refuse."

"How do you survive if you don't drink human blood?"

William turned away slightly from me as he spoke. "I do not need to eat as often as young vampires do."

"Yes, well, you are one hundred and ninety-two," I cut in.

William smiled. "I can see you're good at math. So when you are as old as I am, you do not need to feed daily."

"But when you do feed, what do you drink?" I asked. "And why wouldn't you drink from me if I offered?"

"When I first became a vampire, my hunger was overpowering, but now I can survive for weeks without feeding. When I do need to eat, I drive up into the hills and search for wildlife. Deer are plentiful nearby, so I never have much of a problem."

"I saw you drink alcohol last night."

"Interesting, isn't it? All of the myths about vampires, and most of them are as untrue as we are undead. Alcohol is something I've grown accustomed to over the years. Newly made vampires require a lot of blood to survive. Alcohol is too disruptive to their nervous systems. But later, as you are able to feed less, you can introduce other forms of pleasure back into your life. For me, it's whiskey, sometimes wine. I like to eat raw fish and meat occasionally. It's good to blend in with people, and eating and drinking makes it easier to disappear in a crowd.

"As for you," he continued, "you might offer your blood to me for all of the wrong reasons. Drinking your blood would bind you to me, and that, darlin', is a permanent thing."

"But if I offered?" I said, a hint of pleading slipping into my voice.

"I would have to be certain," he said. "It's a different life, a complicated life. Unless I was convinced you understood the responsibility, I wouldn't accept. Vampires don't share, Olivia. We don't compromise, and we're not very patient."

I wasn't ready to let him drink, but being stubborn by nature, his lecture was igniting a challenge within me. "Then why are we doing all of this?" I asked.

"I can see I got your back up a bit," he said. "Don't mistake my intentions. I want to be with you, Olivia. But after almost two hundred years on this earth, I have had my share of heartbreak."

He meant it. I felt his sadness—really, his disappointment. To be alive for almost two hundred years must have meant a few bad relationships. I nodded and kissed him gently to convey that I understood.

William quickly dressed and dropped me at my house. I would have invited him in, but I knew Elsa might be there and I really needed to get to work, so we said our good-byes. As I walked in the door, he sent me a text asking me if I would join him in two nights for a paddleboat ride at Stow Lake. It was so old-fashioned and romantic, I accepted right away.

Unfortunately, my exuberance at being in the midst of a full-blown romance ran straight into a wall of disapproval standing in my kitchen. Elsa was there, decked out in black leather pants with an actual silver dagger stuck in one of her boots. Lily was standing next to her.

"Lily, what are you doing here?" I asked.

"Elsa texted me when you didn't come home last night," she said, looking sheepish. Being a mother hen did not suit her at all.

I turned to face my housemother. "What's this all about, Elsa? What did you think had happened to me?"

Elsa was angry but also relieved. I'm not sure what she thought had happened to me, but she was experiencing real relief that I was home safely. I hadn't told either of them where I was going. I didn't want company, and I hadn't wanted anyone to try to talk me out of being with William. Looking back, my secrecy was probably impractical.

Elsa didn't reply, so I posed another question. "I suppose you both want to know where I was last night?"

Two heads nodded in unison.

Elsa spoke first, "Why didn't you leave word where you were going?"

Lily looked pensive, as if she knew bad news was coming. She was always worried about a conflict between the three of us.

"I should have left a note or texted one of you," I said. "But can I ask why you were so worried?"

Elsa didn't want to tell me exactly. Her fury was dying down a bit, but she still had to work to restrain herself. "Olivia, you are the only human agent working at the Council, and you've been the target of a demon attack. Gabriel was . . . er . . . I mean, you report directly to the director. Anything could have happened to you. There are plenty of people who would be interested in your talents and connections."

It sounded reasonably plausible. I wasn't alone anymore. I was a part of a team. "Look," I said raising my palms up in surrender. "I am sorry. I should have checked in. Next time I will be more considerate."

Lily was relieved. Apparently, fairies didn't like conflict.

But Elsa wasn't finished. "Are you going to tell us where you've been?"

"I was with William," I said, my chin up slightly in a defiant pose.

Now we were back to two against one. Lily and Elsa were exchanging glances that spoke of serious hand-wringing.

"You spent the night . . . with a *vampire*?" Elsa asked.

"Yes and no," I said, resenting the tawdry emphasis. "I slept at his house, as in a pillow and a blanket. Not, you know, *with* him."

Lily was craning her neck to get a good look at mine.

"No, he did not drink my blood."

This was met with more raised eyebrows and sideways glances.

"Really. He didn't ask, and I didn't offer." This caused them both to calm down, but I resented the image they had painted. "I need to take a shower and jump in my car to get down to Palo Alto, but I want to tell you both something before I leave. William isn't the villain you imagine. I scanned the newspaper advertisements every Sunday looking for a listing for his band. I took an Uber, unannounced, to his show. And I am the one who pushed to have sex . . . and he turned me down. *I chased him.*"

This seemed to catch Lily by surprise. "Olivia, honey," she said gently. "Are you sure you want to go for something so complicated for your first serious boyfriend?"

Ouch. Leave it to my best friend to state the obvious. Of course, I hadn't planned on having a boyfriend. I hadn't planned on a century-old vampire catching my heart.

"William is different," I said, sounding like a cliché. "He's not like anyone I've ever known. He's intelligent and funny—"

"He's dead," Elsa said, interrupting me. "He drinks human blood. Can I ask where you see this thing going? Did you tell him about the Council, about your work?" It was clear Elsa didn't like vampires. She didn't seem to trust them. It was a deep-set feeling that I knew I couldn't change at the moment. So I didn't try.

"I'm not sure where it's going," I said. "And he doesn't know about the Council. Now, if you'll excuse me, I'm off to a campaign meeting."

16

Despite being thrown off my regular routine, I managed to check in with them by phone at a time that was still within my normal schedule. It was thrilling to have the first part of my day occupied by a make-out session with my boyfriend rather than campaign duties. I hoped I wasn't overstating things too much by calling him my boyfriend. Maybe a human man would have said we were just dating, but I'd been the first woman to sleep at William's home. I didn't believe a vampire would compromise his privacy for just a date, especially one that hadn't involved the removal of clothes.

I quickly put all of my giddiness behind me as I set out on Highway 101. My calls to both men were brief but important. We were opening a new campaign office in Palo Alto, a wealthy community and the home of Stanford University. We were planning to open the office with a kickoff party that evening; volunteers could come after work and celebrate with a glass of wine before picking up their supplies. Gabriel and Levi would be arriving at five thirty. The party would begin at six.

I hung up just as my office called and patched me through to Patrick Wright, the day-to-day manager of the campaign. "The first shipment of door hangers has arrived," he said.

"What about window signs?" I asked in response, hoping they, too, had been delivered.

"Yep, they're here," Patrick said. "All two thousand. Now all we need is an army of volunteers to deliver them."

"Amen," I said. "I hear you. I'll be there in thirty minutes, and we can go over the rest of this."

As promised, half an hour later, I pulled into a parking spot on University Avenue and walked toward the headquarters, which had already been decorated with LEVI BARNES FOR CONGRESS and BARNES FOR SEAT 15 campaign signs. As I got closer, I noticed a man peering in the window, his hands cupped around his eyes to shield out the glare. His face was framed by curly dark-brown hair that had been cropped short. He was wearing a blue-green plaid shirt with a navy sweater vest and jeans.

"Can I help you?" I asked as I approached the front door. A set of brown eyes focused on me with suspicion. He was human, I detected very quickly, and very curious.

"Is this Levi Barnes's campaign office?" he asked.

I nodded, glancing at the dozen posters in the window. "It is, but we don't officially open until tonight." I then repeated, "Can I help you?"

"I'm JP Ellington," he said, grasping my hand tightly. "I'm a reporter with the *Silicon Valley News*. I'll be covering this race."

I responded in kind. "I'm Olivia Shepherd," I said. "I'll be managing the campaign." I'd had this kind of conversation dozens of times before but never when I could read a reporter's emotions. JP was surprised, about what I wasn't sure, but I had a few ideas. "You seem surprised," I said, deciding to see what would happen.

"I am," he said, showing no hesitation. "I guess I expected to see someone I know."

"You mean a man?"

"Yes . . . uh . . . I mean you're not from Silicon Valley," he said, sounding a little sheepish.

I ran through my résumé and let him know I had been part of Levi's staff previously. He seemed satisfied, or at least a little less skeptical.

"Can you come back at six fifteen tonight?" I asked. "I'll make sure to introduce you to Levi right away." I was trying to sound casual, but the truth was that I wanted to begin on a positive note with a reporter who would be covering the campaign. "We're not open yet," I said, smiling. "I need a few more hours with my staff to get ready."

JP agreed to return in a few hours. We exchanged business cards, and I wrote my cell on the back of mine. We shook hands to seal the deal, but as I turned to leave, he held on to my fingers a second longer than I expected, causing me to look up into his brown eyes.

"OK, so I'll see you in a few hours then," I said, pulling my hand away.

JP smiled. "You'll definitely be seeing me again."

True to his word, JP returned and stayed for most of the party, interviewing guests and, of course, Levi. I kept a close eye on him, but I couldn't detect anything but professional intentions when it came to the candidate. Levi, having already been a congressman, needed very little help with the media.

The kickoff party had been a success, the festivities lasting longer than any of us had expected. As I was cleaning up later that evening, I thought for a moment about how things had gone. More than one hundred supporters dropped by to celebrate and take home a campaign sign. It may seem odd, the fixation with campaign signs, but for a candidate they're important. To drive or walk through an area or a specific street and see a sign in every window is a powerful visual. It's street-level advertising, and it can be quite successful. It also can be intimidating to your opposition—although we didn't know quite yet who that would be.

The success of the evening was one of the topics I was prepared to review with Gabriel and the rest of the team at our debriefing meeting later the next day. Pleased, I went to sleep that night happy that things had begun so smoothly.

The next morning, I woke up early to go for a run in the park. I pulled on my running shoes and slipped a spare front door key into a small pocket in my running tights. By the time I made it out the door, the pink light of dawn was peeking over the edges of the sky from the east, but racing to beat it was a cold, wet fog. I could hear the horns blowing off the coast as I set off. By the time I made it to the Music Concourse near the de Young Museum, the fog had made it all the way into the city. I was curious to know if today's wet mess was the result of nature or something else.

I wasn't aware of anything special going on, but it was likely I didn't know everything that went on with the Council. I was only a human consultant for them, after all, and not a full-fledged member. I quickly passed the museum and headed down a side path that cut behind the building and onto another road. By the time I turned the corner to head west and go deeper into the park, the mist was so thick I couldn't see more than a few steps ahead.

The low pitch of the foghorns could be heard every few seconds now, no doubt warning large cargo ships away from danger out on the bay. I was so distracted listening to the repeating rhythm that it took me a moment to register that there was a man standing on the sidewalk in front of me. I stopped myself abruptly mid-stride and waited. Thanks to the fog, he seemed to have appeared out of nowhere. That would have been startling enough, but what was more shocking was his appearance.

He was tall, with black hair in tight curls, and he wore a garish suit consisting of a bright-red velvet blazer, a red shirt, and black trousers tucked into cowboy boots. A straw cowboy hat sat perched on his head. He was overdressed for any occasion, but in this situation, his clothing appeared even more absurd. The combination of his attire and physical build gave him the look of a menacing rodeo clown.

But I knew instinctively that there was nothing silly or good-natured about him. I also knew our meeting was probably not a coincidence. The figure in front of me was a demon. I could feel him trying to trip me, to flood my mind with despair. Maybe if he'd dressed like another runner in the park I would have been caught off guard. But his gaudy costume had alerted me immediately. I stopped directly in front of him, prepared for anything.

"Olivia," the thing purred. "We share a common connection. Stoner Halbert sends his regards."

Ah, so this is Stoner's demon, I thought, wondering how he'd managed to land a demon with such outlandish taste in fashion.

"I'm not sure you can call it sharing," I said. "But I know Stoner. What does he want?"

The demon smiled, revealing a set of very brown teeth. "He wants you to know that there will be another candidate in the race for Seat 15."

I'm not sure why, but Stoner's involvement didn't surprise me. Stoner Halbert was after my life—mostly because he thought it was easy to take. But he didn't know what I'd been up to these last few weeks. He didn't know about the Council. The fact that I was even able to hold this conversation was proof that Elsa had saved my life.

"You tracked me to the park on my run to tell me this?" I asked. "Why not hold a press conference and make an announcement like other candidates?"

It was a little childish of me to spar verbally with a demon—essentially a bag of bones with bad intentions. After my quip, the demon became angry, and I felt the full force of him against my skull. I knew I could hold him off for a while, but not indefinitely, and I began to wonder what would happen if I tried to run past him. In the end, I decided to take a different approach, in the hope that I could cut our visit short.

"Listen," I said cordially. "You can tell Stoner that I have received his message and that I said, 'May the best candidate win.'"

This seemed to take the demon's temperature back down to normal.

"OK then," I said. "If you don't mind, I am going to go now."

Once again, I was treated to a smile. The big red demon pivoted his body so that I could pass on the sidewalk. I slipped by gingerly, thankful that I noticed a path leading up a hill back in the direction of my house. Curtailing my run and heading directly home to avoid any more trouble seemed like the best idea. I ran at a brisk pace toward home.

Now that I had managed to put some distance between Halbert's messenger and myself, my adrenaline kicked in, causing my hands to tremble as I put the key in the lock to my front door. I closed the door behind me and leaned against the wood to catch my breath. Elsa wasn't home. She had been staying away for longer periods of time, and I was beginning to wonder whether my roommate would be moving on shortly.

Staring down a demon is tiring business. Feeling depleted, I went upstairs and took a warm shower to calm my nerves and heat up my bones, which felt hollow and chilled from the encounter.

Once I was dressed, I returned to the kitchen to make myself a cappuccino and plop some bread into the toaster. While I waited for the toast, I checked my phone for messages. I had several texts from William, reminding me that we were supposed to go out tomorrow night. I smiled and texted him back that he could pick me up at five. I also had a second set of texts from JP asking if I could talk. I clicked on his name and called his cell. He picked up right away.

"JP, it's Olivia," I said, stating the obvious.

"Thanks for getting in touch," he said.

"What's up? I asked. "Are you calling to tell me that Levi has an opponent?"

I could feel his disbelief over the telephone. He thought he was going to surprise me. I liked being able to surprise him; it almost made the visit from the demon cowboy worth it.

"How did you know?" he asked.

"I ran into someone who knows Stoner Halbert," I said. "He let me know there was going to be an opposing candidate. But I don't know who it is."

"Her name is Lacy Smith," JP said. "She's an attorney and Republican in the Trump camp."

I was listening to JP and formulating my statement. I knew he wanted a comment, an official one from the campaign. "I assume you're looking for a quote from the campaign?"

"Yes," he said.

"OK. Here it is," I said. "We welcome Ms. Smith's entrance into the race and look forward to a spirited debate about the issues as the campaign progresses."

JP snorted into the phone. "That's it? You don't want to comment on her credentials?"

"I'm really not familiar enough to make any further statements," I said, knowing I sounded very much the reticent campaign manager. "So . . . is that it?"

"Actually, I have one more question," he said. I knew before he asked that whatever he was about to say, he felt nervous. "Do you want to have dinner sometime soon?"

His request surprised me. Setting aside William and my already head-over-heels feelings for him, it was a plain old bad idea to date the reporter covering your campaign. It was unprofessional and downright dangerous, since the line between lovers and adversaries can get blurred in a hurry. And let's face it; the press is often a campaign's adversary. I decided a work-related brush-off was my best tactic.

"You know, these days my schedule is pretty jam-packed with work," I said, trying to sound nonchalant. "Why don't you ask me again in a few weeks?"

This elicited an "OK, will do," and we said our good-byes. I turned the ringer volume up on my phone, expecting more calls from reporters during the next several hours. I decided to make another espresso and work from home until it was time to meet with Gabriel.

I left a voice mail for Gabriel telling him about Lacy. Then I called Levi and briefed him on both Lacy and the quote I'd given to JP. Levi asked if he should make a statement. I discouraged him. "You can comment when she says or does something that deserves your attention," I said. "In the meantime, let me be the one who speaks."

When I'd finished with Levi, I called Paul Levant, to let him know his prediction had come true.

"Shit, that was fast. Love the name, though. *Doonesbury* has a character named Lacey, except she's a tough old Democrat. Nothing like what you're facing."

"And what am I facing?" I asked, knowing I would enjoy his answer.

"It's like I told you before," he said. "To me, a Bible is something you put your hand on to make a point. With her, it's a manual for living."

"I'm not sure if you know, but Stoner Halbert is running her campaign," I said.

"Interesting," he said. "That guy seems to pop up everywhere. It should make for a great race; the two of you will both give as good as you get."

A LARGE PICTURE OF LACY SMITH WAS STARING DOWN AT
me from a screen on the wall when I walked into the conference
room to start my meeting with Gabriel and other members of the
Council. Joining us were Elsa, Aidan Burke, and an older woman in
her fifties with beautiful, long gray hair. She was introduced to me as
Madeline Klein, the Canadian ambassador to the United States, as
well as a witch and longtime member of the Council.

The meeting began with a briefing about some of the other campaigns the Council was working on in the United States. Political
issues in Europe and beyond were not going to be a part of my agenda
for the time being.

Aidan opened up his laptop and began reporting on a number of
political races: some in California, some in other states. There was a
congressional race in Alabama, along with several contests to retain
the seats of incumbent superior court judges in Pennsylvania, Ken-
tucky, and Ohio. All told, the Council seemed to be involved in or
monitoring more than two dozen races.

"Why do these particular fights interest you?" I asked Aidan as I
was getting ready to give my report.

"We're looking for situations where we can make a difference,"
Aidan said. "But, as you may recall, we have to be careful not to be
too obvious."

"Yes," I said. "You scoffed at my request that we just cast a spell on an entire town."

"Exactly," Aidan said, laughing. "But occasionally you do read about candidates that have an amazing comeback from behind. There are moments, you see, when voters can be persuaded to have a change of heart."

"Don't you wish you could win every race?" I asked.

"We're not a political party," Gabriel said, joining the conversation. "We don't want to control the balance of power absolutely."

"Why not? It seems like things would be much easier."

"Be careful. Those words or some facsimile have been spoken by many a dictator," Gabriel said grimly. "We're here to help maintain a balance, not dominate the fate of mankind. There must be some room for humans to make bad decisions and live with the consequences. There must be some opportunity for them to fight for their own causes."

"So you don't care if I win the campaign?"

"*Bien sûr*. I do care," Gabriel said. "I want you to win, but that is not what we were discussing. You asked why we don't just bewitch entire towns and states. We choose races where we know we can make a difference. We identify individuals who we know will go on to play a major role in the advancement of human society. So, yes, when we send you in to work, we want you to win. But using magic is not like painting a house. You can't just cover everything up and hope it will endure through the years."

"I understand," I said, feeling slightly humbled by his remarks. "Shall I start my report?"

"Please," Aidan said, offering me a reassuring smile.

I started the discussion by describing my encounter with Halbert's demon in the park.

"I really credit Elsa," I said, four pairs of eyes fixed on me as I described the creature's red attire and cowboy hat. "Without my training, I don't know if I would be here now describing all of this to you."

Elsa grimaced. "You were wise to limit your time around him," she said.

"Why do you think he came to find me in the first place?"

"It's a good question," said Aidan. "One we will look into. We expected Halbert's demon to move on to easier targets, not to go looking for you."

"Maybe someone sent him," Madeline offered, speaking for the first time.

"I would have thought Stoner did," I said.

"As I said," Aidan said, "we will look into it."

"Olivia," Gabriel said, smiling at me. "Perhaps until we get this sorted out, you could refrain from running alone in the park. We can't afford to have something happen to you in the middle of the campaign. I would be happy to pay for you to join a fitness club."

"Wow," I said. "Do you treat all of your campaign consultants so well?"

The emotional response was quick, and I felt the communal dismay at my words immediately. Then, very quickly, it disappeared and everyone in the room was all smiles.

"Olivia, you're helping elect a candidate who is destined for great things," said Madeline. "I come from a long line of witches who predict the future. Levi Barnes could be a great leader for your country; his contributions to peace would be immense, but he must be elected first."

"OK, I will stay out of the park, unless Elsa is with me." With my own security issues out of the way, I circled back to the woman staring down at me from the screen on the wall. "Lacy Smith is a svelte fortysomething conservative woman who believes that God should control everything, right down to how the government establishes the tax code," I explained. "She's generally regarded as a decent public speaker, but she does have a few on-the-record incidents of making outrageous statements. I'm hoping we'll see some of that during the campaign."

After providing a few more personal details about Lacy, I moved on to give the group an overview of what had been accomplished so far, touching on everything from the need to develop a poll to the final design of the campaign's logo. I told them about the campaign office in Palo Alto and the success of the kickoff party.

"Good briefing," Aidan said. "We'll expect you to provide another update in a few weeks."

After the meeting ended, Gabriel asked me if I would have dinner with him. I agreed easily, glad for an opportunity to spend a little time alone with the man who had changed my life so greatly.

Aidan and I walked into the main area of the Council's offices, chatting about the full moon arriving the next evening. "Will you be going out?" I asked.

"Oh, yes," he said, his delight obvious. "I shall go for a long run in the park."

Suddenly I had an image of myself galloping across the forest the night Elsa had given me peyote. "I highly recommend it," I said giggling. "A good run in the middle of the night can be very satisfying."

After saying good night to Aidan, I waited while Gabriel fetched his coat. As is my habit, I started to scan the area, watching what other people were up to. One corner of the room caught my attention. It was at the far end of the main hall, where Nikola Pajovic kept his office. The door to his private quarters was closed, but outside, seated next to the door, was a man vibrating with anxiety. Broadly built, he had the body of a soldier or a bouncer at a nightclub. His hair had been shaved so that only dark black stubble remained. It matched his beard, which was also closely shorn.

A prominent red outline hovered around him. His energy was all wrong: dark and full of anger. He wasn't human, either. Knowing the company Nikola kept, I suspected he was a werewolf. Whatever he was, whatever his intentions, he didn't like being left in the hallway. The minute Nikola opened the door, the man jumped up and disappeared inside.

Nikola's door slammed shut at the same moment Gabriel arrived and escorted me out of the building.

"An odd man just walked into Nikola's office," I said. "His aura was dark, very damaged."

"Nikola often keeps grim company," Gabriel said. "It's a function of his time in the Balkan Wars. A lot of his associates are veterans. Serbs, I think. As a rule, they're very reticent people."

A black BMW sedan was waiting for us at the curb in front of the museum. Gabriel greeted his driver warmly as the man stepped out of the car and came around to open the door for the two of us. "I am old-fashioned and prefer to let someone else do the driving," Gabriel said. "I hope you don't find it too ostentatious."

I laughed. "I don't mind at all," I said. "My mother also likes to use a car service, but with her I think it's safer for everyone if she doesn't operate a vehicle. She gets too distracted to watch the road."

"Too distracted?" Gabriel repeated.

"Oh, yes," I said. "She can never look at the scenery as just a driver; she has to look as an artist, which is not very safe for anyone. By the way," I asked, changing the topic abruptly, "where are we going for dinner?"

"You must know that to a Frenchman this question is of paramount importance and must be considered carefully," he said, a faux gravity in his voice.

"*Oui, monsieur,*" I said, my hand over heart. "*Mais j'ai très faim!*"

I could tell our banter delighted him, a thought I said very clearly to myself.

"I *am* delighted," he said out loud. "It's a pleasure to meet someone who enjoys the French language and culture."

Our exchange reminded me that for some reason both he and

William seemed to read my thoughts very clearly. I made a note to ask him about it later.

"I was thinking we would have dinner at an old favorite of mine called Bix," Gabriel said. "Do you know it?"

Anyone involved with San Francisco politics knew Bix, a former speakeasy located on the lower lip of North Beach. It was a quintessential San Francisco watering hole that attracted the high-flying set. Once, while dining there, I had been asked to move from my table to make room for the actor Keanu Reeves.

I nodded, replying in mock seriousness, "*C'est très cher!*"

"Olivia," Gabriel said, his dramatic voice returning, "how can you put a price on a good meal?"

After a few minutes, we arrived at the restaurant and I allowed him to lead the way. I assumed two things as we entered the ornate dining room: first, that Gabriel knew the owners, and second, that he must have called ahead. He managed to walk in at eight-thirty and secure a table immediately.

As we were being shown to our seats, I had the terrible thought that the headwaiter might mistake me for Gabriel's mistress. Once again, Gabriel turned around quickly, having heard my thoughts; he wagged a finger at me as he scolded, "You worry too much. Relax."

It should have been spooky to be read so easily, but with Gabriel, for some reason, I didn't mind. I knew he was shielding some emotion from me, but I also knew instinctively that he did not intend to harm me nor did he harbor any romantic intentions.

Once seated, we quickly ordered. "Two champagnes," Gabriel said. "And I will have the oysters."

I wrinkled my nose and asked for the steak tartare. Our server tilted his head slightly in approval of my choice and then took our order for salads for the next course.

After taking a sip of my drink, I decided to ask Gabriel about something that had been bothering me. "You know," I said, "the one topic we didn't discuss tonight is the connection between Stoner Halbert and Lacy Smith. Does his demon work for her now?"

Gabriel shook his head. "I don't think so, at least not in the way you suggest. She is a fiercely religious woman, so I don't think she would be comfortable with it out in the open. But Stoner and his demon, they would be quite attracted to her and the kind of extreme energy her conviction gives off."

"It doesn't make sense to me that Stoner—a lifelong Democrat—would work for a conservative candidate," I said.

Before either of us could speak again, our waiter appeared with a platter of oysters, picked fresh fifty miles up the coast in Tomales Bay. He left and returned a few minutes later, pushing a wooden cart toward us with a small metal bowl fixed to its center. In the bowl was the beginning of my steak tartare.

Around the edges of the mixing bowl were other small containers with various ingredients: minced shallots, capers, salt, pepper, and mustard. I watched intently; I enjoyed the attention to detail that the dish required and the briny smell of the capers. As the server pointed to each ingredient, I nodded slightly. Once all of the ingredients had been placed in the bowl, he took an egg from inside a small drawer and cracked it over the mixture. Then he gently tossed it all together, forming a small mound, which he served to me on a plate, along with several small warm toasts.

When I looked up from my dish, I found Gabriel watching me. "I know," I said. "Sometimes I feel as if I am secretly part French."

For a moment, Gabriel's eyes reflected a shadow of melancholy but then very quickly it was gone. "Eat up," he said. "You want to enjoy it while it is fresh."

We ate in silence for a few moments until I steered us back to our conversation. "Please finish telling me why Stoner is working for Lacy."

Gabriel took a sip from his second glass of champagne. "That was his old life, Olivia," he said. "He made a deal with the devil. Now, he has no alliances, no allegiance to anything. His goal is to win and to be powerful."

"There is something perverse about the forces of evil working to elect an evangelical to public office," I said.

Gabriel let out a burst of laughter. "Yes, yes, *bien sûr*! And how delicious to be sitting right under her nose; even the devil has a sense of humor, you see. How satisfying to work to elect a candidate that appeals to the worst in human beings, eliciting their fear, their paranoia, and their insecurities. To help a candidate who excuses their shortcomings and those of their supporters by blaming their misery on another culture or religion."

"Are you saying that the devil likes to elect conservative Christians to office?" I asked.

Gabriel shook his head. "No, not at all. You look at it too literally," he said as the waiter removed our dishes and placed our salads on the table. "The devil has no political agenda in a Republican or Democratic way. He cares nothing for elections. What he enjoys is watching humans reap what they sow."

"But you don't want that to happen," I said.

"*We* don't want that to happen," he corrected, pointing his salad fork across the table. "You are a part of this now."

"I've never placed that level of monumental importance on my campaigns," I said earnestly. "I can't function under that kind of pressure, the kind where the world ends if my candidate loses. Now the stakes feel so much higher. No one knows about Stoner Halbert but me. No one knows that he is only running the campaign to cause trouble."

Gabriel smiled back with a glint in his eye. "It only takes one person to change the course of something," he said, pausing to ask for a dessert menu. "Besides, no one knows about you either. *C'est la même chose.*"

"Do you really think I will make a difference in this race?"

"Yes, I do," Gabriel said. "Campaigns are unpredictable things. Your intuition and ability to read people will be invaluable."

I nodded, feeling more confident. It was getting late, but I had one more question I needed to ask. I waited until our sorbet arrived, and then I pounced. "What are you?" I asked, taking a spoonful of chocolate sorbet.

"You already know, but you didn't ask me," he said.

"How do you do that?" I asked. "Read my thoughts so quickly."

Gabriel took a spoonful of lemon sorbet and paused. "I am a witch," he said. "One of many from a family that can trace its roots back to the dawn of France. More recently, the Laurent family hails from Aix-en-Provence, where we settled in the sixteenth century."

"Do you mind if I ask how old you are?" I asked, watching Gabriel's bemused expression. "*Pardon*, what I mean is, are you actually aging, or are you like Elsa?"

Gabriel smiled at me, a slight sadness in his voice. "Regrettably, I am aging," he said. "Even I do not possess the ability to stop time."

"Can you walk through time like Elsa?"

He nodded but turned to the waiter to ask for two glasses of calvados before he said, "I can, but it's not my main skill. My skill is telepathy."

Now it all made sense. "So can you read all my thoughts?" I asked, an image of William popping into my head. I wondered if he had the skill too.

Gabriel let out a snort. "Olivia, when you push them to the front like that, then, yes, I can hear everything. Curiously, there are times when I feel like you are trying to send me your thoughts directly. Is it possible you are also telepathic?"

"I don't think so," I said. "I believe my mother would have told me if she thought the trait ran in the family."

"Hmm. It's something for you to think about," Gabriel said, signaling for the check.

We sat in amicable silence for a moment or two as he looked over the bill and placed his credit card on the table. "By the way, about this man you're seeing . . . what does he do? *C'est ton ami? Qu'est-ce qu'il fait?*" Gabriel asked. "You know you are driving Elsa crazy."

"I'm not sure yet," I said as we walked out the door to our waiting car. "It's a work in progress. What about you? Do you have anything to say about William?"

Gabriel raised his hands to his chest in surrender. "Not a thing. *Rien, mademoiselle.*"

From the restaurant the driver drove straight to my house. As I turned to walk to my doorway, Gabriel called out to me.

"Olivia, remember what I asked. Please do not go into the park alone."

"Yes, I promise," I said, and thanked him once again for dinner.

18

was that I would be seeing William that evening. We had been texting each other every day, but tonight would be our first opportunity to be alone since I tracked him down at the nightclub. The days had passed quickly, the campaign occupying an ever-greater portion of my attention. Now that Lacy was entering the race, I knew the pace of the campaign would accelerate since we would be forced to respond to any criticisms she might level against Levi in the press.

In anticipation of the deluge, my day was booked solid with meetings with our opposition research team to comb through her records and our own. Clients are often shocked that I ask them to pay for the privilege to dig up their own dirty laundry, but it is always better to know what your opponent will find *before* they find it.

I pondered these details for a few more moments as I got dressed and walked downstairs. When I reached the foot of the stairs, I caught a glimpse of Elsa in the living room in the middle of her usual morning yoga-and-stretching ritual.

"Good morning," I said softly as I padded into the kitchen for an espresso. I made her a cup of tea before walking back to the living room. "Do you want to come into the office today to listen in on these briefings?" I asked. "There may be something that turns up that interests you about Halbert and his demon."

Elsa was in the middle of completing a sun salutation series and did not respond immediately. I set her mug of tea on the coffee table and waited patiently. There was no rushing a time-walker.

Finally, she finished and looked at me, grabbing the tea. "I would like to get a good look at the demon if he comes around again," she said.

I nodded. "You are welcome to come with me wherever I go," I said, and then paused. I was about to say, "Except when I'm with William," but I decided we were having too cordial a conversation to muddy the waters. "I mean, you can come with me whenever it interests you."

"You were going to mention him," she said, not bothering to use William's name.

I smirked. "I'm just saying you don't have to hang out with us if he bothers you. I wouldn't ask to join you on a date either," I said, trying to make light of the situation. "You do date, right?"

Elsa made a quick sound of exasperation. "Of course," she said. "Lately, I prefer the company of women to men," she said.

"Are you saying that you're a lesbian?" I asked, not that it would bother me either way. But I was curious to know.

Elsa shook her head. "I don't like labels," she said. "I base my attraction on desire and seek out people I'm attracted to, male or female. It's just that often after I have sex with a man, I feel like being in the company of women."

I laughed. "Elsa, that's a very common sentiment among women, regardless of the century."

We both finished getting ready and left the house together for the day. Elsa stayed with me for the majority of the briefings but then left after receiving a call from Aidan. The two of them were spending an ever-increasing amount of time with each other. I began to wonder whether he was interested in Elsa for more than her experience with weapons. Given her lack of ability to read the bigger picture, I was certain she would never have a date in this century without some serious intervention on my part. I resolved to ask her more about it when I saw her next.

As I had predicted, the day flew by. I was able to make it back to my house to shower and change before the doorbell rang. I stood upstairs listening to the chimes. There was a vampire ringing my doorbell, something I could not have imagined a few short months ago. I quickly ran downstairs to open the door, delighted by the sight waiting for me. William was wearing faded jeans, a navy T-shirt, and a brown corduroy jacket with a lamb's-wool lining. A brown wool ski hat sat on top of his head, pulling his red hair close to his face. I didn't imagine for a moment he was cold. I assumed he did it to fit in, since the night air was growing increasingly chilled as we approached winter.

"Come in," I said as I opened the door wider. When he was inside, I shut the door and turned to kiss him. He pulled me into an embrace and gave me a deep kiss.

"Now that is much better than a text message," he said, keeping me close.

"Mmmm, I agree," I said, enjoying his touch. We stayed in our embrace for a few more moments, and then I pulled back and asked him if he would like a drink.

"No, thanks," he said. "I thought would we take a detour someplace first before we start our official date, if that's OK."

"Sure," I said. "What did you have in mind?"

"A friend of mine is having a jewelry show at a gallery on Polk Street," he said. "I thought we might go and take a look."

"OK," I said. "Then are we going to the lake?"

William had a playful smile on his face. "Actually, I'd like to take a rain check on the lake. I have someplace else in mind, if you're up for a surprise."

I didn't really care about the destination as long as I was with him. "I'm game for a surprise," I said, and opened the door.

Hooks and Catches made its name as a gallery by featuring one-of-a-kind handmade jewelry. Open since the 1970s, it catered to women who did not want to run into their friends at social gatherings wearing the same necklaces and rings. Tonight they were debuting an exhibition entitled "Carbon Spot," a term used to describe a black mark often found on copper coins. It was a play on words since the exhibit featured several artists working with copper and gold—but there were no black smudges to be found.

We stopped at a table for a glass of wine, then began our gallery tour.

The first artist we encountered was William's friend. She made necklaces featuring colored beads, cut glass, turquoise, and copper charms. They were striking pieces, very primitive and provocative. One necklace in particular caught my attention. It was a mix of elements: a series of copper feathers, several strands of smoky gray glass beads, and a small turquoise teardrop charm hanging from a ribbon of copper and brown leather woven together. I asked the owner of the gallery if I could try on the necklace. He walked over to the case and pulled a small black velvet tray from a shelf underneath the counter. He carefully laid the piece on the tray, then placed a small handheld mirror in front of me. I glanced at the price tag. At $450, it was one of the more expensive objets d'art I had looked at in a while, but I had no reason to worry about money.

I tried on the necklace and stared at myself in the mirror. It was an unusual piece, and dressed in my current outfit, lent me sort of a rebel image. I was trying to imagine wearing it with a suit and realized I probably would never have to worry about presenting myself that way again. I worked for the Council now. I wasn't going to have to wear that conformist uniform. I must have drifted off in my thoughts because when I turned to ask William what he thought of the necklace, he was gone. I scanned the room and found him at the cash register handing the cashier his credit card.

He walked back toward me a satisfied smile on his face. "That necklace was made for you, darlin," he said.

"You didn't have to do that," I said, feeling a little awkward at receiving such an expensive gift on a first date. "I can afford to buy it for myself."

"I know that," William said, fingering the necklace. "But my friend made the necklace, and it suits you. It seems right that I would buy it for you. Besides, I am of the opinion that women should never buy their own jewelry. That is the purview of husbands, boyfriends, and lovers."

Before I could ask which category he fell into, William moved me along to the main room of the gallery. There were three cases in the middle of the floor, all housing copper and gold bands embedded with sapphires, rubies, and diamonds. I realized they looked suspiciously like wedding rings, and I tried not to glance at any one ring too intently. Still, I couldn't help myself when I came upon a set of three thin bands made of copper. The middle of the trio featured several sapphires. It was a beautiful piece, very romantic and old-fashioned, a bit like a sepia-tinged photograph. I concentrated on relaxing my facial features and clearing my mind. I didn't want William to think I was getting ahead of myself.

Thankfully, as we approached the end of the cases, he said he was ready to leave. "OK, so now it's on to my surprise," I said, fingering the charm hanging from my neck as we walked out of the gallery.

William didn't reply immediately. He seemed to be looking for something. "There's a liquor store near here," he said. "It's called the Jug Shop. Do you know it?"

"I do," I said. "It's one block up."

We stopped by the store and picked up a bottle of wine. As we walked toward his car, we passed a cheese shop, and William encouraged me to go inside and buy something for dinner. I didn't like the idea of eating alone, but my stomach was grumbling. It had been hours since I'd had lunch, so I ordered a ham sandwich with butter on a baguette and grabbed an apple from a bowl near the cash register. William paid for my dinner and asked the clerk if he could have a small bag to carry the food. Soon we were back on the sidewalk, William carrying a petite brown paper bag with handles that said CHEESE DEPOT in one hand while holding my hand with the other.

"I want to take you someplace special," he said, glancing at me. "Time is running out to see it, so we have to go tonight."

"I'm all yours," I said. "Let's go."

I looked out the car window as we left Polk Street and criss-crossed the city, leaving downtown in the rearview mirror. William drove the length of Valencia Street to Cesar Chavez and then on to Bayshore Boulevard. We were moving southeast toward the old Hunters Point shipyards, where the Navy had once maintained a thriving base during World War II.

"Where are we going?" I asked, finally unable to control my curiosity.

"I'm taking you to a castle," William said nonchalantly.

"A castle," I said. "Here in San Francisco?"

"Yep, in fact, here we are."

True to his word, we pulled up in front of a large compound that was hidden behind a massive stone wall. The wall was partially obscured in places by a number of very old oak trees. William leaned in front of me to open the glove box. He pulled out a set of keys and a small black Maglite. He kept the keys and handed me the flashlight.

"This is for you," he said. "I can see in the dark, but you might need some help."

I looked around, regarding the city's skyline in the distance. We were in the middle of nowhere, with nothing but the pale light of a quarter moon to guide us. I focused my flashlight on the path ahead of us. It led to a gate shut tight with an enormous padlock. I shined the beam of the light on the gate while William flipped through a set of keys and unlocked it.

"Welcome to Albion Castle," he said as we walked through the gate. "You're now entering an official historic landmark. It was built in 1870 by a man named John Burnell, a Londoner who came to San Francisco to start his own brewery."

"Why here? This is the middle of nowhere."

"Good question. He wasn't motivated by the landscape. He was compelled by something lurking beneath," William said ominously, guiding us through the grounds. When I shined the light on him, I saw that his face was animated in mock horror for good effect.

"Sounds spooky," I said, giggling. "Maybe we should go in so you can give me the tour."

The set of keys jangled in William's fingers as we stood in front of a massive wooden door with its ornate metal fixtures. He quickly opened the door and led me inside. I ran a beam of light around the perimeter and caught a glimpse of an enormous main hall with vaulted ceilings and wooden crossbeams. A scattering of furniture had been left behind in the room: an old couch with a sheet draped over it, a few rickety chairs, and an large oval mirror still hanging on a wall.

"Don't move," William pleaded, disappearing into the dark. I heard his footsteps, then a drawer opening, and the strike of a match against its igniter strip. He returned, illuminated by the light of a large candle. He looked every inch the vampire tonight, pale and shimmering in the light of the taper. He had taken off his hat in the car, and now his red hair gave off an amber glow from the lit flame.

For the moment, I felt utterly human, struck by the difference in our situation. He could walk through the dark without assistance. It made me uneasy, and though I tried to brush it aside, my throat tightened with a feeling of doubt. What was I doing here alone with a vampire?

William must have sensed my discomfort because he quickly

handed me the candle and left to retrieve several more. Soon we were sitting on the floor, a sea of candles of various sizes illuminating the room. "Don't be alarmed," he said gently. "I know it's weird that I can see in the dark, but we'll hardly ever be in these kinds of situations. I'm not so different from you, really."

With the room half-lit with candles and my sandwich and the wine laid out on the floor, my survival instincts retreated. It seemed silly to have been so nervous, and I tried to put it behind me. "I'm fine," I said. "For a moment in the dark, it was a little unsettling."

We sat for a few minutes and had a glass of wine. Despite my grumbling stomach earlier, the darkness killed my appetite, so I asked if we could take a tour. William smiled, clearly happy to oblige.

"I read online today that the castle has been sold," he told me as we walked into the gardens. "I know the caretaker for the property, so I asked if we could pay a visit tonight before the new owner takes possession."

We crossed the grounds, coming to a small gate that opened on to a set of steps. The steps led to an underground passage, which in turn, led into a series of caverns, some of which were filled with water. "What's with all the water?" I asked, feeling slightly claustrophobic underground.

"It's the reason Burnell came. The castle sits on an underground spring. It has its own source of water," William said, clearly delighted to be sharing this with me.

I raised my flashlight and let the beam of light skim the top of the pools. Burnell had carved deep stone pools hundreds of feet beneath the castle to collect water from the springs. Each pool was adorned with a lion's head, their mouths slightly open. It was a gothic spectacle. Although certainly a noteworthy feat of engineering, I couldn't see how it could ever be anything but unsettling down here, trapped beneath the surface. The room was damp, the air thick and rank-smelling. I shuddered, overcome again with an unaccountable feeling of discomfort, perhaps a reaction to the energy trapped beneath in this long-forgotten place.

William gently took my hand and pulled me away. "Come on," he said, a tinge of disappointment in his voice. "This place is bothering you. I can feel it."

It didn't take us long to retrace our steps and return to the main room. We sat down once again at our makeshift picnic, I with my sandwich and apple and he with a glass of wine.

"Well, this didn't turn out to be the best first date ever," William said as we sipped our wine. "Sorry, darlin', I generally try not to alarm my companion within the first few minutes of an outing. I'll try harder next time."

I let out a long breath and laughed. "It's OK. I'm fine," I said, touching his hand with mine. "Why did you decide to bring me here?"

"This castle is almost as old as I am," he said. "I have visited here a few times over the decades, invited to parties by various artists who have owned the property. Now, though, an anonymous buyer has purchased it out of probate court. It's about to become an Airbnb rental."

"Why did they stop selling beer?" I asked.

"Prohibition. All of the breweries in San Francisco shut down," he said. "After that, it sort of languished. It was also the site of a spring water company, but the main house and grounds were neglected. As I said, a few artists have owned it through the years, but mostly it's been abandoned, a relic out of sync with the times."

"Maybe you should buy it," I said. "Then you could fix it up."

"I wish I had known it was on the market. I might have. Then I could have built you a castle."

I took a sip of my wine. "I'm not sure I'm regal enough to live in a castle," I said. "I might be more of a barn or bungalow kind of gal."

"I don't see it that way at all," he said and then stood up abruptly, grabbing my hand. In his other hand he held a candle as he led me to the mirror that had been left hanging on the wall. "Look at your reflection," he said, gently cupping my chin in his palm. "I have scanned thousands of faces in my time, Olivia. You were meant to be a leader. It's etched in every line of your face . . ."

We were inches apart from each other as he spoke. No one had ever said anything like that to me. I wasn't sure how to respond. As usual, my emotions around William were a mess. I was worried about how vulnerable I'd felt earlier. I was agitated by the energy of the building and yet so desperate to feel his touch. In the end, I decided to say nothing. Instead, I stood up on my tiptoes and kissed him gently on the lips.

"Thank you," I whispered, bringing my lips back for a second kiss.

This time, he was ready and kissed me back passionately.

We were combustible elements, alone in a 141-year-old castle with nothing but a bottle of Côtes du Rhône and some lit candles for company. Once we began kissing, neither of us wanted to break the connection, sinking onto the floor where we had been standing. My doubts quickly disappeared, replaced instead by unbridled lust.

William had managed to quickly remove my jacket and T-shirt, leaving only my bra covering my upper body. The cold air hit me and caused me to shudder. He ran his kisses down my neck and across my collarbone. He used his fingers to explore, eventually arriving at my breasts and moving aside the lace of my bra. We both gasped as his fingers made contact with my nipples. The differences in temperature made the experience both excruciating and delicious. I was overheated, and William's mouth and the air around us were cool as he explored my body. The sting of the cold was both unbearable and pleasurable. I shivered and moaned, bucked and arched. I felt inconsolable and insatiable. Our kisses were long, luxurious affairs. Cradled in his arms, my body felt strangely like one of his guitars, being played fret by fret, note by note, transformed into a beautiful song.

Somehow we'd managed to overcome the awkwardness of the evening and had recovered our connection to one another. I should have been content to stay that way for a long while, but a practical thought popped into my head. I hadn't told William of my work with the Council. As much as I wanted this to turn into something more, I didn't want to get too much further in our *entanglements* without telling him. I had a nagging feeling that he would want to know. With regret, I broke our kiss and placed my hand between us. William looked down at my hand and smiled.

"Am I going too fast for *you* this time?" he asked.

I shook my head. "No, but I think I need to tell you something before we get more . . . um . . . involved." It was the only euphemism I could think of at that moment. We separated, and I grabbed my shirt, suddenly chilled by his absence.

"OK," he said, cautiously. "You have my attention."

"Do you remember when you told me that Elsa's arrival was unusual, and that it probably meant I was about to do something important?"

He nodded, an inscrutable look set on his face.

"You were right. She introduced me to an organization called the Council. Do you know it?"

William nodded, his face registering a hint of surprise. "I do, but finish your story first."

"Not long after I started training with her, Elsa introduced me to Gabriel Laurent, the current director. He told me that it was rare for a human to have such acute skills and offered me a job. I told you I'm running a political campaign, but I didn't tell you that it was Gabriel who helped me get the job."

His silence caused me to ramble on a bit.

"Anyway, it seemed important to tell you about my connection. You say you know about them? I don't know much about how life works for Others. Is the Council something everyone knows about?"

"You must be the first human to ever work for the Council or, at the very least, one of the few ever asked," he said. "Congratulations, Olivia. It's quite an honor."

It didn't sound as if he were thrilled. "Why don't you like the Council?"

William did not reply immediately; he seemed to be choosing his words carefully. "I once worked for the Council."

"Once, as in past tense," I said. "You don't now?"

"I haven't been in contact for some time," he said. "It never occurred to me that Elsa would lead you to them. I didn't see that connection coming. It's funny, I didn't think that part of my past would come up for some time."

"And now?" I asked, sensing that he was holding something back.

"Now, I suppose I should tell you a little bit more about myself," he said. "But first, let's get out of here. We can talk on the way back to your house."

I'd always heard the advice that couples should not discuss work in bed, and now I could see why. Reluctantly, I got up from the floor, dressed, and followed William to his car. Once we were inside, he started to speak.

"I know the Council. Remember, darlin', my father was a US Army officer. He had a deep sense of honor and patriotism that did not die when he became a vampire. I was no different; perhaps it's why he and I lived so easily together over the decades. As I've told you, after I was reborn, we left for Paris. We arrived in 1863, long after cholera, the Revolution, and even the Prussian Army had ravaged its citizens. We managed to live in relative peace for many years, watching the Eiffel Tower rise along the way as a part of the World's Fair. Finally, though, the whims of humans caught up with us.

"When World War I began," he continued, "my father wanted us to join the Allied forces—France and Britain—against Germany. He felt a deep loyalty to the French for their assistance in the American Revolution. He convinced me to become involved, to support France. But I was not a full-fledged French citizen, so I had no papers to enlist. I found the perfect solution in the American Volunteer Ambulance Drivers. The United States had not yet joined the war in 1916, but money was pouring in to support the allies.

"A group of men founded a volunteer ambulance service to help reduce the distance injured soldiers had to travel from the Western Front. My father went back to America to see what he could do to hasten the entry of the United States into the war, but the United States had little appetite for getting involved." William paused for a moment. "How much do you know about the war?"

"Only the obvious details," I admitted.

"It was horrific, I can tell you," he said. "Humans are so fragile. These men were living in enormous damp trenches that were filled with the blood of the dead. I could smell the rotting bodies for miles."

"You must have realized the value of your work," I said. "You were able to withstand things a human couldn't."

"I might have seen the value if I had witnessed a shred of common sense from the generals. It was so similar to the Civil War; man upon man massacred, as if humans could be reproduced indefinitely. On any given day, France easily sacrificed sixty thousand men. Russia lost more than one million solders. Over and over, the generals sent their men to slaughter, often never moving their lines more than a foot or two in the process. And here I was, racing to drive these mangled young men to a hospital so they could be patched up and sent back out on a fool's errand."

"I don't understand, William. How does the Council fit into this?"

"One evening I was out in the forest near Lille hunting for something to eat when I came across a group of men traveling in the cover of darkness. They were like me. There was another vampire, a werewolf, and a powerful witch. His name was Pierre Laurent—Gabriel's great-grandfather. Pierre recognized what I was immediately and asked me what I was doing in the area. I told him about the ambulance corps. He in turn told me he would find more drivers to assist.

"The next day he arrived with additional drivers, including himself. Over those days and weeks, he slowly introduced me to the Council and its mission. The war was not supposed to be the Council's main focus, but no one wanted to sit by while the human leadership of the world slowly killed off an entire generation of young men."

"And then what happened?" I asked. "Did you continue to work for them?"

William didn't reply immediately. He was looking out the window, and at first I thought he wasn't going to answer me. "I did," he said after a while. "I spent many years working for them, traveling back and forth between the United States and Europe. Eventually, I quit."

"Why? Why did you stop?"

"I stopped because I began to feel that humans deserved their own fate. I started to believe that our intervention was a wasted effort."

By now, we had reached my house and William had pulled into the driveway, letting the car idle while we spoke. I thought of asking him in, but didn't think he would accept the invitation. I knew I had to choose my next words carefully.

"Look, I'm not sure yet what this is all about, but it sounds like you made a difference during the war. We don't always have a choice in the bigger decisions that are made, but you helped save lives and reduce suffering. My job isn't nearly as important, but I am trying to do something helpful. I'm trying to ensure that good people get elected—people who will work toward fewer wars and more opportunities for stability and prosperity."

William shook his head. "I'm sorry, but I don't see it that way.

The Council gives your candidate an advantage. I know the Laurent family; they can bend people to their will. You are highly empathic and probably a little telepathic; you know what the crowd wants, and you can help make sure they get it. As far as I'm concerned, you're changing the fate of another human being. Maybe he isn't meant to be elected to office. Maybe humans deserve to live with electing the wrong person."

Now it was my turn to object. "Well, I don't see it *that* way," I said, repeating his words. "Levi is a good person. I can't make him *into* that. I'm not deceiving voters. I'm making sure Levi communicates to the best of his ability."

"And what if the voters want a warmonger or a racist?" William asked sharply.

"Then I can't help them," I said, confused about the direction our discussion was going. "What is it you really object to, William? I'm not controlling the minds of voters. I'm listening to them and helping Levi win by really connecting with people. Not by making up catchy slogans or sowing fears about far-off dangers that may never happen."

"I object because I don't think we should meddle in the lives of humans, period," he said. "They're incapable of learning from history. They're incapable of resisting their worst urges for power. They should be left alone to their own devices."

Our conversation had certainly hit a wall, and I felt the need to put some distance between us. "One thing about humans that you should probably remember," I said as I reached for the car door, "is that I *am* one, and I don't have such a poor vision of our collective destiny as you do. So I'll say good night. I'd say 'Thanks for a lovely evening,' but I wouldn't want to say something trite because I think that's what you want to hear." I slammed his car door behind me and turned to walk away.

I was barely up the walkway when he reached me, his quick vampire reflexes giving him the advantage of speed.

"Olivia, I'm sorry," he said. "That was a lot to drop at your feet."

"I can see you have strong feelings about the Council," I said. "The question is whether they're stronger than your feelings for me."

William frowned. "I thought we were having a discussion, Olivia. Can't I express my opinions?"

"I don't know. Can you do it without making me feel like a carny sideshow?"

William let out a sigh. "I am sorry. Years of living alone can do that to you," he said. "I will try to be more careful with my opinions." He walked me the rest of the way to my door and kissed me good night.

I tossed my keys and purse on the floor inside and laid my head against the door, wondering how it could be that after everything I had experienced recently I could still be so naive. What did I think William had done with all of the years of his life? He had died as a soldier in America's bloodiest conflict and been reborn a vampire. The tattooed angel on his back made more sense now. It was astonishing to think I had been sitting in the car with someone who had walked the fields of Europe in 1916, who was connected to major events in world history. The only problem was, William didn't seem to have emerged with a very good opinion of the human race.

I decided I would try not to take it personally.

MY FIRST THOUGHT THE NEXT MORNING WAS THAT I NEEDED to become more educated if I was going to have a meaningful relationship with William. My degree was in American history, not world history, and my education felt incomplete. The man I wanted to be with had walked across the Western Front and watched the dawn of Prohibition. To truly understand William's perspective, I would need to delve deeper.

While there was plenty I could review myself on line, having a best friend with unlimited access to the library system was a good backup. Lily could locate fabulous books to round out my crash course in world history. I texted her on my way over to to the Main Library make sure she was free.

When I arrived at her office, she was sitting at her desk, reading her email. I noticed she was wearing new eyeglasses, a pair of super large, rounded frames in a shade of light pink.

"I like your glasses," I said as a way to pull her attention away from her screen. "You look very fashionable."

"Why, thank you," Lily said, fingering the frames with one hand while still clicking with the other. "I know they're a bit of a fashion cliché, but I like how they look." She turned away from her monitor and looked up at me. "What brings you to the Main Library today?" she asked. "I thought you were off to Palo Alto."

"I am going to head down there for a few hours," I said. "But

Levi's out of town, and after last night, I've decided I need to do some homework."

"Hmm," Lily said. "What happened last night?"

"If you must know, the main thing is that I've been acting like a silly, moonstruck child," I said. "William is vastly more complex than I ever imagined."

Lily stood up from her desk and walked to my side. "I don't want to say 'We told you so,' but that is what Elsa and I were trying to tell you."

I didn't reply. I was too busy sulking. I slumped onto the edge of her desk, burying my face in the crook of an elbow.

"What did you find out last night?" Lily said, the alarm in her voice audible.

Her concern caused me to laugh. "It's not what you're imagining," I said. "In fact, you'll be quite surprised to learn it's the opposite. I'm the one with the dark secret *he* doesn't approve of."

"What?" Lily said. "Listen, let's get out of here and grab a cup of coffee. I'll drop a few books off at your house while you're on your way to Palo Alto."

I followed Lily out, and we walked up Van Ness to a nearby coffee shop and ordered cappuccinos.

"OK, now tell me everything," she said. "And start at the beginning."

I sighed. "Like I was saying, William's life is much richer and more complicated than I gave him credit for," I said, sipping my drink. "I saw him as a handsome man in faded jeans who played in a band, but that's a one-dimensional biography. And he's not human. Maybe I could take a human man at face value, but William was born in 1830. It turns out those one hundred ninety-two years make quite a difference."

"That makes sense," Lily said.

I tilted my head back and closed my eyes as I tried to think about where to begin. "He was a Confederate soldier who was killed in battle, then reborn as a vampire. He was a citizen of Paris at the time of the World's Fair and a volunteer ambulance driver during World War I. And that gets us to only about 1917."

Lily was obviously delighted at my predicament. "Yes, I can see what you mean."

"Wait," I said, holding up my hand. "I haven't told you the best part yet."

She raised an eyebrow but didn't speak.

"He used to be a member of the Council. He ended his involvement at some point, but we didn't get that far in our conversation."

Lily's eyes were wide with surprise.

"Yes, I think you may be starting to appreciate the situation," I said. "But here's the real kicker: I found out about his work for the Council when I told him what I was doing. And you know what? He didn't like it at all."

"I'm confused," Lily said. "Why not?"

"He said that humans deserve to live out their fates and that intervention is wasted on them," I said, again growing anxious as I thought about William's reaction.

"And then what?" she asked. "Did he ask you to stop working?"

I shook my head. "He didn't ask me to do anything," I said. "I'm not sure he had to though. I mean, it's clear that he disapproves."

Lily shifted in her armchair. "I wouldn't jump to any conclusions," she said, patting my hand. "As you said, this isn't just some regular guy from the Mission who plays in a band. He's much more complicated than that. I think you need to discuss this with him further before you can understand what he wants. I'll bet he won't ask you to do anything."

"Why do you say that?" I asked, wondering how Lily could be so sure.

"For a number of reasons," she said. "To start with, he's not the first Other to feel strongly about not intervening in human events.

This is a frequent topic of discussion in my own family. It's a common theme, and one that *you* will encounter more often as you wade deeper into the Council's affairs. Second, William has lived a long life and may have seen what ultimatums do to relationships. It's possible he would never ask you to change your life, but he is certainly entitled to question what you're doing."

"Why is there opposition to the Council's work?" I asked, realizing I probably should have learned about this before I allowed myself to be tattooed by a witch.

Lily walked over to a window and regarded the passersby on the sidewalk before she spoke again. "They're called the watchers, the invisible hand. The work of the Council is hidden from view," she said. "It goes unnoticed by humans and, in the opinion of some, doesn't always make much of a difference in the long term."

"But if you know you're going to live forever, why wouldn't you try to ensure that the world is a pleasant place to live?" I asked.

"I'm not William, Olivia," she said. "I think you need to ask him why he left the Council. That's an important part of his story, and it may tell you a lot about why he feels the way he does. But one theory is that after many years he came to realize his actions were only a drop in the bucket."

"Yes, but if you get enough drops, the bucket will slowly fill up," I said, feeling slightly defeated.

Lily took my hand in hers. "Olivia, are you falling in love with William?"

I nodded. "I think I fell in love the moment I first encountered him in the tunnel, even before I knew who he was. I know it's silly."

Lily smiled. "No, it's not," she said. "But I do think it's time you introduced him to your friends. If you love him, then he needs to know the people in your life."

"He's playing at a club tonight. I was planning on going after I get back from Palo Alto. Do you want to come?"

Lily nodded. "I'll text Elsa and ask her to come too," she said, smiling. "You might as well expose him to everything at once."

"OK," I said with a laugh. "You're right."

Lily grabbed my hand once again. "If you really love William, you must try to accept his perspective of the world. No matter what you do, it may always be less optimistic than yours; he's been around longer, which means he's had more time to be disappointed by humans."

I knew that this was good advice, but the human in me was itching for a rebuttal. "You know, Lily," I said as we were gathering our things, "it's possible that one day an Other will do something to disappoint a human."

Out on the street, we went our separate ways, Lily promising to choose a few books for me about the Civil War and European history. I picked up a few files at my office and then got in my car to drive to Palo Alto.

It was an easy day of reviewing website text, editing fundraising appeal letters, and creating a schedule for house parties through a network of volunteers. I left feeling that I had put in a good days' work in Levi's absence.

During the afternoon, I texted with Lily, who confirmed that she'd dropped a few books off at the house and left a couple eBooks waiting for me to check out on my tablet. She also reminded me that she and Elsa would be joining me at the Treasure Chest for William's show. My stomach tightened at the prospect of assembling the whole group, but Lily was right. I couldn't separate him from the rest of my life. It was time I brought everyone together.

Elsa and Lily were in the kitchen having a drink when I got home. Lily was educating Elsa in the ways of mixing a dry martini, and she had assembled the shaker and other tools of the craft. Just as I was almost finished getting ready upstairs, I heard the doorbell ring. Elsa answered the door, and I was surprised to hear not one, but two men's voices coming from downstairs. As I descended, I found both William and Aidan in the entryway.

"Hello there," I said, amused at the picture before me. "I assume you two met on the sidewalk?"

"Something like that," Aidan said quickly, turning his attention toward Elsa. "Is that a martini you're holding?"

She smiled and nodded. "Lily has been trying to convince me that this is a good drink, but I don't care for the gin. Would you like it?"

"Don't mind if I do," he said, his Irish lilt more on display than usual.

"Everyone, this is William," I said, stating the obvious. Heads nodded in acknowledgment as I looked over at him. "Follow me and I'll get you a drink." William came along, and as soon as we were alone in the dark of my dining room, where I kept a small bar, he grabbed me and pulled me close.

"You smell good," he said, burying his face in my hair, and then he kissed me. "And you taste good."

"Thanks for being such a good sport," I whispered. "I hope you don't mind being with all of these people."

"I've been waiting to see if you would introduce me," he said. "I wasn't sure you wanted them to know about us."

"I wasn't sure either," I admitted. "It's less complicated when we're alone."

William kissed me again. "Darlin', complicated is my middle name. Now come on, or your friends will think we've run off."

We walked back into the kitchen, everyone suitably outfitted with cocktails. After a round of drinks, Aidan said he would take Elsa and Lily with him in his car. I tried to gauge Elsa's response, but she wouldn't let me catch her eye. *Even hard-as-nails time-walkers need lovers*, I mused, and I was happy she had found someone who suited her. As we walked to our cars, I gave Aidan directions to the club.

William opened the door to his car and helped me in. "Aidan

and I know each other," he said, moments after pulling away from the curb. "I don't think he wanted to be the one to tell you, so he sort of changed the subject back at your house. I didn't realize that he was Gabriel's deputy. Otherwise I would have said something last night."

I wasn't surprised. After everything I'd been through in the last few weeks, I was prepared to hear just about anything. "How do you know each other?"

"Occasionally, I have worked for the Council unofficially to help them locate things," he said. "Aidan has been my contact for some of the assignments in Europe."

His connection to Aidan struck me as too close for comfort. "Did you know about me from Aidan before we met?"

"I knew you would ask me that," he said. "Honestly, I didn't. It's a coincidence. Call it fate, but I swear I had no idea of your involvement with the Council. I've never even met Gabriel."

It was obvious he was being honest from the moment he began to speak. I also knew he was aware I would pick up on any deceit in a second.

"You're right," he said. "I know you can read me, and I can often hear your thoughts too. Makes for an interesting relationship, don't you think?"

"How easy is it for you to hear my thoughts?" I asked as we pulled up in front of the club.

"It varies. Sometimes it's so clear it's as if you're in my head. Other times, it's more of a vague whispering. Why?"

"I'm taking a survey," I said, climbing out of the car. "You'll find out later."

We walked into the club together but split up inside. He went backstage to find Cat and Jack while I scanned the room for my friends.

I spotted Aidan standing near a booth in the corner of the club with a clear view of the stage. As I walked over, he slid in, inserting himself between Elsa and Lily. I slid in next to Lily, arriving at the same time as our waitress, who came to take our drink orders.

"I recommend we start with champagne, or in this case, sparkling wine," Aidan said, frowning at the wine list. His dismay made me laugh. The Treasure Chest was definitely a beer kind of nightclub; any wine on their list should come with a label that said DRINK WITH CAUTION.

"OK," I said enthusiastically. "I'll let you lead tonight."

"Won't that be nice for a change," Elsa said, drawing laughter from all of us. I did have a tendency to take the lead. Maybe tonight was a sign that I was ready to let go a bit.

A bottle of sparkling wine was delivered to the table just as William's band came out to play the opening set. He took his place onstage, picked up a guitar, and gave me a wink as he began to play. Not surprisingly, given the group I was with, everyone noticed our interaction.

"Are you and William quite serious?" Aidan asked.

"You know William," I said. "What do you think? Is he serious? He told me the two of you have worked together."

Aidan looked at Elsa, and then back at me. "I think anytime a man with William's background decides to share his life with a human, it's serious."

"His background," I said. "You mean because he's a vampire?"

Aidan stared at William playing for a few moments before he said, "It's really not for me to say, but William is a tracker, Olivia. He has a long history of finding objects and people that have gone missing. When the Council needs help locating something, he is one of a handful of individuals we've called over the years. Has he told you anything about his life?"

"A little," I said, "We've barely made it past the 1800s."

Aidan nodded. "I'm sure he will tell you the rest by and by. In the meantime, let's drink to our friend William," he said, raising his glass.

After our toast, we sat together watching the band, our conversation kept to a minimum because of the music.

When William's set ended, he walked directly from the stage to sit with us. I made room at my end of the booth and he slid in, pressing snugly against me. He glanced over at the glass of sparkling wine in front of me. "I'll remember that," he said. "I knew I was right about you and castles."

I called the waitress over and ordered William a Jack Daniel's, neat. William gave me a tip of his cowboy hat, a gesture that reminded me of the day I first saw him in the tunnel above the Golden Gate Bridge.

"You're sure that day in the tunnel was a coincidence?" I asked, hating myself for still doubting him.

William crossed his fingers over his chest, where his heart had once beaten. "Scout's honor," he said. "I go up there sometimes to play my music and get away from the city. I never expected to run into someone like you, much less see you again at the bluegrass festival."

"OK, I believe you," I said, turning to face the other three pairs of eyes watching our conversation. "It's just that it's an incredible coincidence."

Aidan sipped his drink, contemplating a reply. I could see him formulating a response; his eyes gave him away. Elsa was leaning in against him, watching him intently as he began to speak. "The world is a smaller place than you realize. We all share common interests and similar talents," he said. "Our paths, while different, have led us all to the same place. And I, for one, am glad. After all, the best breeds travel in small packs."

"That sounds suspiciously like another toast," I said, cajoling the group to clink glasses for a second time.

Afterward, Lily got up from the booth to stand at the bar with William's bandmate Jack. The first time I'd met him, I was so nervous that I hadn't studied him closely. Now, upon further inspection, I realized that he was quite striking. He was as tall as Lily, with long brown hair and green eyes. Dressed in skinny black jeans and a gray T-shirt, he was handsomely disheveled. Lily must have liked what she saw, because she was leaning quite close to him, hanging on his every word.

"Is Jack single?" I asked William, who had been following my gaze.

He laughed. "Darlin', Jack is in a band in San Francisco. Need I say more?"

I looked over at my best friend, a fairy hiding in plain sight of humans, and decided she could take care of herself.

"Olivia," Elsa said, breaking into our conversation, "Aidan and I are going to leave. We're going to look for a place to grab a bite."

I remembered that it was a full moon tonight and wondered if Elsa would go running with her boyfriend in the park. It was sort of a romantic vision, the two of them frolicking in the moonlight.

"You should go to Stow Lake. It's a good place to swim at night," I said. "Just don't try to get on the small island. It's covered with sharp blackberry bushes."

Aidan laughed. "Do you know this from experience?"

I nodded. "Elsa gave me peyote tea when we first met. I spent an entire evening running through the park, seeing colors and hearing voices. Lily thought I'd disappeared."

"We all agreed I made the tea too strong," Elsa said. "But it worked. Olivia regained her sixth sense."

"It was extraordinary. Even the part where I woke up at the lily pond next door to the de Young."

"You slept at the pond?" William asked.

"I was drawn by a voice in my head," I said. "What I thought was a voice, anyway. It was just a hallucination."

I noticed Elsa gently place a hand on Aidan's leg, and I knew she was eager to leave. I signaled for our waitress to come over so we could settle our bar tab. William waved her off, telling us that the drinks were on him tonight. Aidan slapped William on the back.

"If I had known that, I would have stayed for another round," he joked, and then he bade us good night.

Not long after, William and I gathered up our belongings. I looked around to find Lily and saw she was still standing at the bar. "Do you think Lily will be OK with Jack?"

"I think Lily can take care of herself, Olivia. She isn't some naive human woman. I suspect it will be harder on Jack when it's over."

I caught Lily's eye as we exited the club, and she turned to me and waved, clearly delighted to have a playmate for the night.

William and I walked along Divisadero Street for a few blocks until we reached his Subaru. It didn't take long to load up, and soon we were on the road to my house.

"I'm sorry I can't invite you in," I said as he pulled into my driveway. "I have a busy day tomorrow, and I need some rest."

"Not a problem," he said, walking me to my door. We agreed that we would see each other soon, but I was hesitant to make specific plans with all of the work I had coming in the next few weeks.

William kissed me deeply.

"Remember," he said, "I don't sleep. You can call me anytime."

20

ALTHOUGH THE CAMPAIGN OFFICE WAS IN PALO ALTO, I continued to spend a few days a week in San Francisco, or at least part of the day. Most of the members of the campaign team, including our pollster, RJ Peterson, had offices in the city. RJ ran his company out of a small suite on Sutter Street near Union Square.

As was my usual routine during campaign season, I met with RJ alone to map out the contents of a poll. In politics, nothing is left to chance, even with special skills like mine. Polling is one tool consultants use to learn what voters want so they can win their support on Election Day. After asking a voter's opinion on a certain issue, we asked questions about their age, income, and education. With those kinds of demographic details, I could ensure that Levi's messages were targeted to various audiences. It's a backbreaking business, one that takes hours of work to plan, analyze, and execute. Our collaboration that morning was successful, and by early afternoon, when I left RJ's office in search of lunch, I had a draft poll in my email.

After grabbing a lentil-and-bean salad at the French café next door, I headed back to my car, which was parked in a nearby garage. It was a pleasant, sunny day in San Francisco, and I enjoyed a stroll past some of the country's most prestigious boutiques and jewelry stores.

After living with my new skills for several weeks, I'd decided that being an empath was a lot like having a bad acid trip. All of the colors and sensations that come zooming at you can be a shock to your system. Early on, there were moments when I was barely able to enter a busy street without feeling overwhelmed by the totality of people's emotions. Now, thanks to hours of training and focus, I had learned to shield myself from most of the chatter of everyday life.

Today, however, it felt as though I were a novice all over again. There was a terrible buzzing in my ears, and it was growing worse as I neared Post Street. It took me a moment to make sense of the feeling in my head: something very powerful was nearby. I could feel the force of the energy vibrating through me. Behind the energy was a wall of emotion: fear, anxiety, and excitement.

As I approached the corner of Post and Grant, I carefully looked around for the source of the disturbance. I definitely didn't want to meet whatever was throwing off such intense energy until I had a chance to see it first. I pushed myself to pick up the direction of the forces I was feeling. I did a visual scan of all four corners of the intersection, but I didn't detect anything or anyone out of the ordinary. This, however, did nothing to diminish the sensation.

In addition to the vibration resonating through my sternum, I also felt a pressure building behind my eyes. I realized I needed to redouble my focus on shielding myself before the feeling overwhelmed me. As I worked to get my defenses in place, the whir of a car accelerating caught my attention. I looked up to see a black sedan speeding toward me. The darkness of the emotions inside the car, which was careening down the one-way street, left no doubt that its passengers were not human. Despite the pressure on my skull, I felt drawn to the energy. I began to walk toward the oncoming car—I had to get a peek at the passengers inside.

Before I could glimpse so much as an eyebrow, however, the sedan turned abruptly and jumped the curb, crashing through the majestic gold-trimmed doors of a jewelry store. I missed being hit by the car but collided with a man on the street, throwing us both down onto the sidewalk with a horrible thud. I felt the full force of the impact on my right shoulder as I hit the pavement. As we lay there trying to untangle ourselves, my shoulder throbbing, the car slammed its way farther into the store, sending shards of glass from the picture windows and bits of two smashed stone planters onto the sidewalk.

Finally, I was able to extricate myself. I stood up and approached one of the store's windows to get a better look at what was happening inside. Peabody Jewelers has occupied the corner of Post and Grant Avenue since the Gold Rush. Through all that time, it seemed safe to say, their salespeople had never watched an automobile plow through their main entrance. I'm also fairly sure they'd never witnessed four men exit a vehicle parked in their showroom, fire off several rounds of ammunition from semiautomatic weapons, and then smash the glass display cases containing millions of dollars in rare jewelry and timepieces.

As I peered through the window, another thought was rapidly forming in my mind: the beings inside wanted to limit my senses. Someone inside the store, a member of the robbery gang, had sensed me and was trying to blind me. I couldn't tell whether they were aiming for a temporary condition or something more permanent, but the pain behind my eyes now was excruciating. I tried as best I could to ignore the pressure in my head and continued to watch.

The men were brazen. They wore no masks or disguises, a detail that only reinforced my conviction that they were Others and supremely confident they would never be found. The thieves used small rock hammers, the kind geologists favor, to shatter the glass cases and scoop the jewels into generic black backpacks. The four tall beings didn't speak to one another nor to the frightened salespeople and customers cowering below the gold-plated display cases. And yet I knew they were communicating, the same way I knew they were trying to blind me.

I continued to squint through the window, my right arm hanging awkwardly at my side. Probably only a minute or two had passed since the crash. I could hear sirens coming and decided it was time to leave. My efforts to block the force against my eyes were proving feeble: the pressure in my head continued to build, my vision was growing dimmer every second, and I felt the unmistakable warm trickle of blood run down from my nose to my upper lip.

I caught sight of my hands, covered in blood from my fall, when I fumbled around one-handed in my purse for some tissues. Having none, I wiped at my face with my fingers, and then used my pant legs to clean my hands. I knew I wouldn't be able to drive with my vision diminished; I was going to have to use the portal at the Chinatown gate. It seemed risky to walk the three blocks covered in blood, but if I moved quickly, perhaps no one would mistake me for more than one of the disheveled homeless people usually wandering nearby.

I willed myself, despite the acute pain in my head, to start toward the gate. I felt a bit like Richard III, limping up the street, hurling one side of my body as if it were a deadened limb. I could feel my heart beginning to speed up, my adrenaline finally kicking in. Whoever was in the jewelry store did not want me to see them, and I was worried that if they had their way, I would never look upon anything again.

What a mad sight I must have been for the tourists as I approached the stone lions at the foot of the green tile gate. I mumbled a hasty "sorry" to a man I bumped into as I approached the lion's mouth. I knew I was making a bit of a scene just with my appearance, and now I was going to disappear from plain sight. But I had little choice. I had to get away from the thieves.

This was my maiden voyage using a portal solo. Elsa had practiced with me, but I had never traveled alone. Despite being rattled, I managed to remember the instructions. I placed my fingers inside the beast's open mouth, visualized the doorstep of my house, and then uttered one word: "*Aperio!*"

The moment the word left my mouth I was transported into

darkness, then light. I felt a gentle pull as I dropped out of thin air onto my doorstep. I lay on the landing in a crumpled heap, disoriented and unable to see. I wanted to scream for help, but I was afraid to attract the attention of strangers on the street. I didn't need the police coming to my house. I would never be able to explain how I managed to leave the scene of a robbery, injured and blinded, without the aid of a taxi or a companion. Instead, I lay still, pushing my anxiety out to my Other friends with all my might.

"Help," I exclaimed at the top of my inner voice. "I need help!"

Those were my last thoughts before I lost consciousness.

When I woke up, I was afraid to open my eyes. The memory of the pain I'd experienced returned, and I began to cry, tears streaming down my face from my tightly closed eyelids. The first voice I heard was Gabriel's.

"Olivia, please try to open your eyes," he said. "We're all here with you. You needn't be afraid."

I shook my head. "Too painful," I murmured. I felt someone sit down next to me on what must have been my bed, a familiar set of fingers taking my hand.

"I heard you, darlin'," William whispered in my ear. "I heard you call to me. So whatever happens, I am here. You can open your eyes."

I began by blinking to get myself ready; quickly, I opened and closed my lids, not sure my pupils would accept the light. *The light*, I thought to myself. *Thank God I can see the light!* Eventually, I opened my eyes normally and found myself staring into the faces of William, Gabriel, Lily, Aidan, and Elsa. It seemed they were destined to be my permanent entourage.

"Hello," I said feebly. "I see you got my message."

Elsa let out the breath she'd been holding. "I was inside the house. I heard you loud and clear, and so did Gabriel and William. By the time I pulled you inside, they were practically at our doorstep. How did you manage to do that?"

"I pushed the words out," I said. "I was afraid to make a sound. I couldn't see and didn't want any strangers calling the police and connecting me with the robbery."

"Robbery?" Aidan asked.

To tell my story properly, I needed to sit up. As soon as I tried to use my hands to prop myself up, however, the sharp pain in my injured shoulder caused me to wince.

"Careful," William said.

With William's assistance, I pushed myself upright on the bed before I began to speak. "I went downtown early to work on a poll with RJ. When I was finished, I stopped for a quick lunch before driving to Palo Alto. But as I was walking to the parking garage, I noticed something, a sort of buzzing in my ears. I felt like I was walking toward an energy field. I was curious, so I followed the sensation until I got to the corner of Post and Grant, in Union Square. Then right when I got to the corner, a black sedan came careening toward me. It jumped the curb and crashed into Peabody Jewelers."

"Was it an accident?" William asked.

I shook my head. "No, they meant to crash into the store," I said. "When the car stopped, four men with guns smashed every display case inside to bits and took all the jewelry."

The three men exchanged grim glances.

"Did the men see you, Olivia?" Aidan asked.

I shrugged. "I don't know. I was knocked down by the force of the car crash. That's how I cut my hands and hurt my shoulder. But I managed to crawl up to a side window to peek in, because I wanted to see who was inside. It all happened quickly. I think the whole thing was over in less than three minutes. I don't know if they noticed me. I pushed out toward the energy, and that's when my head began to ache and it got hard to see."

"Can you see now?" Gabriel asked, stepping into my line of sight.

I nodded. "Yes, but my eyes feel sore and scratchy."

At that moment, Elsa, who must have slipped out of the room earlier, returned carrying a tray with a mug of something warm and a small mirror. She handed the mirror to William, who turned to face me.

"Don't be alarmed, but you look a bit like a zombie," he said holding the mirror up to my face.

I gasped at my reflection, startled to see two red dots staring back at me; whatever had been tracking me had used enough force to burst the tiny blood vessels in my eyes. My pupils were barely visible through pools of crimson.

"They were trying to blind me," I said. "Will this heal?"

"I think so, to both things," Aidan said. "Someone in the robbery party must have been an Other and knew there was an empath nearby. My guess is they never actually saw you; they only felt your presence, the same way you could feel theirs. That would explain the nature of their attack."

"Are you saying that if they had seen her, they would have done something even worse?" William asked.

Aidan raised his hands in frustration. "I am merely speculating," he said. "I cannot say for certain what would have happened if they'd actually seen her, but I think we can all guess it wouldn't have been pleasant."

"Who were they, the guys who crashed into the jewelry store?" I asked.

"From what you have described, it sounds like the Serbian mafia," Gabriel said.

"The Serbian mafia? Here?" William asked. "Isn't this a bit far afield, even for them?"

Aidan shook his head. "I'm afraid not. Since the Balkan War, they have branched out far beyond Europe. This kind of robbery has become a signature of their work."

William's face was grim as he faced Aidan and Gabriel. He regarded them both, a deep look of frustration upon his face. "We need to make sure she doesn't show up on any video. Someone needs to begin searching now. I know a person who can help us delete any footage without leaving a mark."

His response caught my attention, if only because it sounded so tactical—as if he had done something similar before. I wanted to ask him, but I knew better than to bring it up in front of everyone else.

"Can I have some eyedrops?" I asked, interjecting myself into the conversation. "My eyes feel like someone ran a rake over them. And maybe some ice for my shoulder."

My remark caused Lily to wince, and she quickly came over and handed me a small bottle. "These will help take the sting out," she said. "I'll go get an ice pack from the kitchen."

I examined the green glass bottle closely before she left the room. It had no label or markings of any kind. "What is this?"

"Nadia made it," she said. "She said it would help speed the healing. She also said to remember your fortune and not to be afraid."

"Who is Nadia?" William asked, his curiosity piqued.

"An old witch who lives in the park," Elsa said as Lily left the room. "A healer."

"What did she tell you, Olivia?" he asked. "Does it have anything to do with this?"

It was a good question, and I thought, *Ni oui et ni non* . . . yes and no. Nadia never mentioned a robbery or being blinded, but she did mention adventure and a great love. But I didn't think this was the time to explain.

"It was nothing," I said. "She read my palm and told me I would have a long life. Listen, if you don't mind, I'd like to get back to the robbery. I think we should check the videos; maybe there will be something there. A clue."

"Good God, darlin', what do you mean you want to go search for a clue?" William was clearly agitated. "Do you see the damage these men are capable of, even from afar? Why would you go looking for trouble?"

"They're criminals. Supernatural ones, at that," I said. "Don't you think we should find out who they are?"

I'd crossed a line somehow. William looked at the two other men in the room with a pleading look that also spoke of exasperation at my remarks. "No, I don't think you need to go looking for anything," he said.

Before I could reply, Gabriel intervened. "Olivia, it's late. We should be going. You need some time to recover from this attack. We have a lot of work to do with the upcoming poll and our first major house party in Carmel," he said. "Elsa and Aidan will search for images of the robbery, and if there is anything promising, I will arrange for a screening at our offices *after* the party. They will also make sure *you* don't show up in any video that is floating around out there on the internet. The last thing we want is for the mafia to track you down. In the meantime, you must rest. I think we can leave you in William's capable hands."

I was being shut down, at least for the time being. "OK, I see where this is going," I said, sounding mildly petulant. I managed to say good night to the group in a civil tone before William walked them to the door. I heard the door shut and the dead bolt lock in place.

"I'm going to get a cool cloth for you," he said when he returned, wandering off to the bathroom. He brought a wet washcloth and insisted I lie back with it over my eyes. "The cold will soothe your eyes and help them heal faster."

"You seem to know a lot about what's going on," I said, ignoring his first aid. "Are you going to fill me in?"

Silence followed as I lay there, my eyes pressed shut under the weight of the cloth. Finally, he spoke.

"I've told you about my time as an ambulance driver and how I came to know the Council," he said. "I didn't linger in Europe after World War I ended. In 1920, I took a ship to New York and from there spent considerable time traveling across the United States. My father was living in Wyoming, of all places. He had purchased a small plot of land in a remote area near the Snake River. It was very beautiful and full of good game to hunt. We lived there for a time, but we missed Europe and decided to return to France. There was an apartment for sale at a decent price in Paris, near Place de la République, so we purchased it and settled in."

I felt William rise from my bed, gently lift the cloth from my face, and leave the room. As I blinked to test how my eyes were recovering, he returned and once again placed the cloth, freshly rinsed with cool water, over my eyelids.

"So, as I said, we went to Paris and we enjoyed ourselves for several years. But by 1940, things in France turned very dark, as you know. We found ourselves with a choice: leave France or live in occupied territory. Of course, slipping out of the country wasn't a problem for us, but I decided to stay behind. My father traveled to England to offer his services. Then, after the Germans invaded, it became clear I would need to join the Resistance, the Maquis. Do you know that name?"

Indeed I did. All over France there are memorials in tribute to the men and women who fought courageously against the Nazis and lost their lives. I had once visited the war memorial and museum in Caen, with exhibits that went on in great detail about the brutal deaths Resistance fighters faced. "Yes, of course," I said. "They were heroes. You were a part of the Resistance?"

"Yes, and so was the Council," he said, pausing. "The Nazis were the most evil people on earth, Olivia. They despised everything that failed to meet their vision of racial purity, including vampires, witches, and werewolves. They were happy to torture and kill anything they could not control or use to advance Hitler's cause."

Somewhere in the last few minutes, this had become a conversation that required eye contact. But when I tried to remove the cloth so I could see William, he stopped me. "No, leave it on," he said. "It will help you heal, and I prefer to tell this story without you watching me."

I nodded, the heavy, wet cloth sliding slightly off my eyes. "What did you do during that time?"

"Everything—though sometimes, it seemed, nothing. The goal was to hobble the Nazis and make it impossible to move men and supplies. I blew up train tracks, killed German soldiers, and helped to free Allied prisoners," he said. "I infiltrated the highest levels of Parisian society, *bien sûr*, and fed the intelligence back to my father in England.

"I was a perfect operative," he continued. "No need to eat or sleep. I could travel great distances in the dark of night, and with my reflexes, I was able to sneak up on German troops without them hearing a sound."

"Did anyone suspect you weren't human?"

"Perhaps," he said. "But it was war. It was better not to look too long at anything or ask too many questions. To be ignorant was safer. Those who were betrayed faced unimaginable torture."

I realized that this was the second story I had heard about William's father in the past, but I had never heard him mentioned as part of his current life.

"William, where is your father now?"

"He's dead, murdered in a village in Normandy," he said. "My father never did anything by half measure. As the war dragged on, he volunteered for extremely dangerous missions, dropping in by plane to deliver supplies. On his last assignment, he was caught. There must have been an informant; the Nazis knew we were expecting radio operators and their guides by parachute. It was a moonless night, perfect for Others to make a jump. But the Germans were watching and waiting. Before I could even get to the field, they ran in and beheaded him, along with his colleagues. It was a well-planned ambush, right down to the silver bullets in their guns."

"How did they know?" I asked.

"I never found out, but I have always suspected it was one of our own," he said. "Who else would have known? It was 1943. No human had set foot inside the Council."

This time I did remove the cloth from my face. I sat up, reached for William's hand, and brought his palm to my lips. "I'm sorry about your father," I said.

He pulled me close and kissed my forehead. "Thank you. The worst part was watching and not being able to do anything," he said. "To do so would have put the whole operation at risk."

"And after?"

"I waited until the bastards had left, and then I collected my father. His head had been severed from his body, and the silver bullet had shot clean through his heart. I couldn't risk a fire or a lantern, so I dug a grave in the darkness and buried him. I've returned to the area many times, but I've never located his grave. Finally, I gave up. After the war, I purchased a plot in a cemetery outside Caen and bought a proper tombstone for him."

"Is that why you left the Council?"

"No. If anything, his death inspired me to work harder to create as much mayhem as possible," he said. "My reasons for quitting were more complicated. It was the cumulative effect of the Nazis and their concentration camps, the Americans and their atomic bomb. And then there was Stalin," he said. "When I think of all the blood that ran through the fields of Europe, not once, but twice—and in the end, it changed nothing. The result was more bad human behavior."

"I don't mean to be disrespectful, but you're being unfair," I said. "The Americans' use of the atomic bomb, however cruel, doesn't compare to the horrors unleashed by the Nazis and Stalin. And some humans *did* try to make a difference. The United States helped end the war, however brutal the means. The Resistance was also full of humans trying to stop fascism."

"You weren't there to see the lapses in judgment, the betrayal, the bottom-feeders living off the misery of others," he said bitterly.

"That is the essence of being human," I said. "We don't have the luxury of watching from hundred-year-old seats. We make a choice in the moment. Some of us make poor choices; some of us rise to the occasion. Life is the struggle we all face to eke out a meaningful existence." I had no idea where my impassioned speech had come from. I'm generally not that philosophical.

"You've proved my point," he said, his voice rising. "Humans are incapable of change."

It was my turn to get angry. His bias bordered on the ridiculous. "OK, I get your point, although I fundamentally disagree with your perspective," I said. "Let's move on. Tell me what happened after the war."

"The year 1946 marked the end of my formal connection with the Council. I didn't have the heart for it anymore," he said. "Eventually, though, the Council began to contact me to work on small projects. My years in the Resistance were fruitful. I had connections across Europe. I was discreet and could assimilate into any environment. I agreed to search for things that had disappeared."

"Disappeared?' I said. "What kinds of things?"

"When an Other wants to hide from this world," he said, "they can do it quite successfully. I helped track them down."

I laid my head back down on my pillow and closed my eyes. I was relieved to finally learn more about William's life, but his view of humans was bringing me down. I hoped I could restore some of his faith in humanity. "Have you ever been asked to track one of these Serbian mobsters?"

"I have, which is why I'm asking you not to go looking for trouble," he said. "Hopefully, no one saw you and you can just forget the robbery ever took place."

As far as he was concerned, I was an interventionist and he was the isolationist. "I'm not looking for trouble," I said. "But I would like to know more about the people who tried to blind me. Don't you think I'm entitled to know?"

"You know what they say about curiosity," he retorted. "Why are you so stubborn? Why can't you take my word for it and agree not to search for them?"

Here we were again, facing William's lack of confidence in human decision making, only this time it was the merits of *this* human and *her* judgment. I'd had enough. My eyes no longer ached, but the rest of me did, chiefly my heart.

"Listen, I don't think I can discuss this with you anymore," I said. "I'm feeling better, so I'd like to ask you to leave so I can go to sleep."

"You're kicking me out?" William asked incredulously. "I thought I would spend the night and look after you."

"I appreciate the offer," I said, trying to keep a brave face. "I think I would rather be alone."

William stared at me. "Olivia, I'm really sorry. I think I may have said too much," he said. "I'll try to be more open to your point of view."

I patted his hand. "I'm exhausted, and I really need to be alone," I repeated.

Begrudgingly, he rose from the bed.

"Come down and lock the door behind me," he said as he left my room. When we were at the front door, he turned to me. "Promise me you won't do anything until we can talk again?"

I nodded, allowing him to kiss me good night. Shutting the door, I could feel the tears forming at the corners of my eyes. I didn't see how we could continue. It seemed impossible that I could have a relationship with a man who had such a low opinion of humankind and who was so opposed to the things I wanted to do.

21

DESPITE MY INJURIES, I MANAGED TO GET OUT OF BED THE following morning to do some work. I turned on my laptop, pulled out the draft of the poll, completed it by phone with my staff, and sent the final version to a call center in Omaha.

Now, almost two days later, we had the first results, and they were promising: Levi was ahead in the race.

Things were looking up. I was also starting to recover from my injuries. My eyes remained a shade of pink, but at least I no longer looked like a wandering zombie. Elsa was my constant companion, watching my every move, under the guise of needing to apply more of Nadia's healing remedies to my shoulder.

Although I had no proof, I suspected William had contacted Gabriel and Aidan to tell them I'd kicked him out. If they knew, then Elsa did, too, but she didn't mention William, and neither did I. The last time I'd seen him or been in contact had been at my front door when we'd said good-bye.

Thoughts of our last conversation continued to churn my stomach. It felt futile to try to convince him of my views, so I kept my distance. The fact that my heart was broken was irrelevant. There was no room for prolonged conflict in my life. Thanks to my walk-on role as an accidental witness to an otherworldly jewelry heist, I'd already lost precious time I needed for the campaign. I was determined to focus on my work and set thoughts of William aside, at least until I could figure out how to deal with him.

By the third morning, thanks to Nadia's magic drops, my eyes were clear. My shoulder was tender, but not terribly bruised. Inspecting myself in the mirror, I decided I looked "safe" enough to make an appearance in Palo Alto.

It felt good to be out of the house. For the next several days I spent long hours at the campaign headquarters writing direct-mail pieces and running impromptu meetings with the campaign committee, which consisted of me, Levi, Gabriel, and Richard Lyon, a close friend of Levi's and the founder of a hugely successful venture capital fund. Lyon's seaside home in Carmel was scheduled to be the site of our first house party, a meet-and-greet with potential donors and friends in an informal setting.

The party, which was about a week away, was being organized by Richard's office, which was managing the catering and event staff. A separate fundraising firm had been hired to send the invitations and identify major donors. All that was left for me was to manage the press and escort the candidate—easy tasks I was more than prepared to do. It all would have been simple, if my phone were not chirping every few seconds, signaling I had a text.

Olivia,
Finish what you start.
Please don't walk away . . .
again.
William

I didn't respond. By the following day, the texts had turned into phone calls; then, the missed calls turned into voicemails. I can't say it felt like stalking since I knew I'd hurt his feelings terribly, and he just wanted to speak with me. He was a vampire, after all, and not a regular human male. If I were almost two-hundred years old, I would expect someone to return my calls, too. But I wasn't, so I put my phone on Do Not Disturb and moved on. Gabriel, who'd come to help me with the party, must have heard through back channels that I was ignoring William because he reached across the table and grabbed my phone, holding it up for me to see.

"You're avoiding William?" he asked.

"He doesn't approve of my work," I said. "What's the point?"

"*Ce n'est pas bon*, Olivia," he said. "*Il n'est pas un vautour.*"

"He's not a vulture? What's that supposed to mean?"

"You know what I mean. A vulture is always buzzing around, looking for an opportunity. William is the opposite; he's a good man."

"He's too complicated."

"And you?" Gabriel said. "Aren't you a bit complicated, too?"

I dodged the question, changing the subject. "How are the videos of the robbery coming? Any luck?"

"You must wait until after the party," Gabriel said. "Then, and only then, will I show you what we found."

Grudgingly, I agreed to wait, and Gabriel headed back to San Francisco.

Later that day, my reporter friend, JP, walked into the headquarters and asked to see me. We'd been emailing regularly, but this was the first time I'd seen him in person for a while. The campaign sent out press releases weekly, sometimes daily, announcing key milestones, such as a notable endorsement. JP contacted me after every release for a formal comment, and then we would chat amicably for a few minutes. He hadn't asked me out on a date again, but today, for some reason, he was here in the flesh, carrying a whole lot of nervousness.

Earlier that morning, the campaign had sent out a release announcing Levi's position on raising income taxes for billionaires, an important issue among younger voters.

JP, it seemed, had decided to come for his quote in person. He asked if Levi would agree to tax himself at a higher rate.

"Absolutely," I said. "Like Warren Buffett, Levi Barnes believes the wealthy have an obligation to pay higher taxes."

"Yes, but can a billionaire ever really relate to the average American?"

I leaned back in my chair, ready to play press secretary. "It's not wealth that defines a person, but their actions," I said. "Levi Barnes wasn't born into wealth. He acquired it by living the American Dream. He was a university professor who used his education to start companies. Those companies created technologies that were embraced by consumers and the business community. Any entrepreneur can follow that path."

I watched as JP furiously scribbled in his pad. I'd grown used to the long silences while reporters tried to capture my words. I used to feel compelled to fill the silence with more talking, but I had learned over the years to be patient. I knew JP had gotten his quote. "Did you get what you needed?"

JP nodded as he closed his notebook.

"OK, then if you don't mind, I have some work to get back to."

"Wait," he said, his nervousness reaching a peak. "I was wondering if you had reconsidered having a coffee with me, or maybe dinner. I thought perhaps after Lyon's party next week."

"That's a private event," I said in my haughtiest voice. "I don't recall the media being invited."

JP laughed. "Wow, that was an excellent campaign-spokesperson reprimand voice," he said. "But you'll have to stand down because Richard Lyon invited me."

Not good, I thought to myself. Overconfident FOC—friend of candidate—invites reporter to lavish party in Carmel full of Silicon Valley insiders. I had to wonder who would benefit from that kind of exposure.

"If Richard invited you, then we're done here," I said. "I assume you'll keep everything off the record?"

More laughter. "Yeah, right. Now about dinner, do we have a date?"

"OK," I said. "But let's keep it light. This is more of a casual meal than a date. Deal? "

"Deal," he said, and he collected his notebook and left.

The next few days whirred by. There were plenty of preparations to make, and our tax policy release had managed to get Levi a space on *Nightline* and CNN. And I had been swamped with calls from other TV producers seeking Levi for interviews. Levi was thrilled with the exposure, and Gabriel was excited to see the campaign going so smoothly.

Gabriel had managed to keep Elsa and Aidan out of my reach, and I was dying to know what they had found in their search of the videos and media coverage of the robbery. The minute the party in Carmel was over, I had big plans to install myself at the Council's offices.

All of the activity kept me busy, and very quickly I found myself standing in the living room of Richard Lyon's home, watching the sunset. After all of the buildup and anticipation, I was relieved that the house party was going well. The view from his floor-to-ceiling windows of the Pacific shoreline had never looked more beautiful. Even more glorious, the home was full of Levi's supporters; the most wealthy and influential families from the region had sent at least one person to attend. The 1950s ranch-style home was basking in the last rays of the sun, and Levi was basking in the acceptance and encouragement of his peers. I was loving the energy buzzing in the room, for these people were truly hopeful—that Levi would make a difference, that the government could make a difference. Maybe it was all the wine and sunshine, but the vibe in the room felt right. It felt hopeful. It felt like . . . victory.

Out of the corner of my eye, I caught JP interviewing some of the guests. I sighed. In the days that had passed, I'd grown increasingly uncomfortable with Richard's decision to invite him and, for that matter, with my acceptance of JP's dinner invitation. He was a thorough, competent reporter, but whether he was suitable as anything more remained to be seen. JP was certainly interested in me, but I was missing in action. It was true that he and I had something in common: we were human. But there was no spark there. I was deeply in love with someone else. Of course, that someone didn't seem to approve of my choices in life, so from my viewpoint, there was no hope for the three of us.

Fortunately, I was too busy working the room to reflect more on the futility of the situation. Moving through the dining room, shaking hands, I was relishing being part of a well-funded campaign. I caught Levi's eye and began to make my way across the room. I gestured with my hands to ask if he would like a drink, and he answered with a subtle nod while holding a conversation with a well-dressed couple. I stopped and began to backtrack toward the deck, where the bar had been set up. I took a few steps, but ran into JP before I reached the bar.

"Where would you like to go for dinner?" he asked quietly under his breath.

"I don't know," I said. "Maybe Il Fornaio? It's sort of old-school, but they have a nice patio."

JP nodded. "That does sounds nice. There's also a café here in Carmel. It's named after a bicycle in French, I thought maybe you would like that."

I nodded. "La Bicyclette. Sounds good," I said, suddenly distracted by an uncomfortable feeling of pressure against my skull. I turned my head to try to identify the source of my discomfort and saw something I did not expect. Standing next to Gabriel in the living room was William. Were it not for his red hair, I might not have recognized him. I had never seen him wear anything but jeans and a T-shirt, but tonight he was dressed in an expensive Italian khaki linen suit that had been altered perfectly to fit his frame. He had paired the suit with a striped shirt and a yellow tie bathed in the pale color of the sun at high noon. He looked wealthy, successful, and above all, *invited.*

Although I was dismayed by his presence, William's cleverness tickled me. For him, fitting in here this evening was likely no different than infiltrating one of the Vichy cocktail parties he'd described. He understood the dynamics of political theater well and had managed to stroll into the room as if he had been on the guest list. There wasn't a single woman in the room whose gaze wasn't fixed on him. I felt a deep twinge of regret for avoiding him. But really, what choice did I have?

At the moment, however, he was impossible to ignore. I smiled at JP, trying to find a way to make a graceful exit. "I'm sorry to run off, but I see someone over there I need to speak with."

JP turned his gaze to William and locked on. It was just my luck to have an intrepid reporter and a stubborn vampire sharing the same room. What were the odds?

"Who is that?" he asked, no doubt noticing the unfamiliar face in a sea of insiders.

"No one," I answered casually. "A friend of a friend. But I do need to go and say hello."

I walked across the room, trying to keep my face as blank as possible, my body relaxed, my head held high. I acted as though I didn't have a care in the world. JP's curiosity was burning a hole in my back, his uncertainty about my truthfulness palpable.

"Gabriel," I said, offering a relaxed smile for the room to observe.

"Olivia," Gabriel said. "As you can see, I invited William. I believe the two of you need to speak," he said, raising his eyebrows in a sympathetic expression.

I looked at Gabriel and then back at William. He had the advantage, as they say, of the element of surprise. I was on the clock, being watched by a prominent reporter and a room full of wealthy donors. While I was tempted to be petulant, I couldn't afford to make a scene or express even the slightest emotion in front of this audience. This was not the time and place to rebuke William, and to be honest, I'd missed him.

"I don't believe there is anything to discuss," I said lightly. "We seem to have reached an impasse."

Gabriel smiled nervously. "*Pas grave.* I think I may have softened the beaches in that area."

I was on alert now. "*Vraiment?* I hope you didn't promise anything on my behalf, Gabriel," I said in hushed tones. "I must be free to make my own decisions."

"I only promised that the Council would not let you do anything alone," Gabriel said, sounding a tad defensive. "And we won't. The robbery is a matter of concern for the organization. There is no need for you to investigate this by yourself or take any unnecessary risks."

I looked at William, who had been standing silently throughout this exchange. My focus had been about managing my emotions, so much so that I had failed to read his. He was quite angry. Apparently, looking on silently while I restated my position was not what he'd had in mind.

"Gabriel," William said crisply. "Olivia is leaving with me. Can you please make her excuses?"

Kidnapping may not have been what Gabriel expected as the outcome of the evening, but the French are never vexed for long. "I suppose that will be OK. The event is almost over and has been a tremendous success. I will tell Levi that you caught a ride with a friend."

I let the two men enjoy plotting my exit for a moment before I made it clear I would not be cutting out early unless it was on my own terms. "If you fellows don't mind, I will make my own exit from the party."

I glanced at my watch. It was seven thirty. The event was set to end in a half hour. I didn't think it would be a problem if I left a little early. But first I had to think of how I was going to break my dinner date with JP.

"William," I said, a terse smile on my face, "I'm going to make another pass through the room and check in with Levi, then I will be ready to leave. I'll meet you at the front door in ten minutes."

He nodded, fixing me with a stare that was unfamiliar. His eyes revealed a look of profound exasperation. Clearly, I had pushed my luck by avoiding him for so long.

I came up behind Levi, his long-ago requested drink in my hand. "I'm going to leave in ten minutes or so," I whispered into his ear. "A mutual friend of Gabriel's has offered to give me a lift back to San Francisco."

"Tonight has been fantastic," Levi said, beaming. "This thing is in the bag."

His remark spooked me. Even without the supernatural connection, campaign consultants are a superstitious lot. We don't believe in tempting the gods by calling a race too soon. "Shhh," I said. "You'll jinx us. You have to knock on wood and hope for the best."

Levi laughed. "Next thing I know, you'll be reading my horoscope. Now go on. I'll touch base with you tomorrow."

I smiled and walked away, tapping a wooden chair as I passed, hoping the gods would accept the gesture. Moments later JP caught up with me. I was working furiously to maintain a neutral expression as I tried to concoct a story that would sound even vaguely convincing.

"Listen," I said, trying to sound serious but not too grave. "I hate to do this, but it turns out I need to return to San Francisco to deal with a few things this evening. I'm really sorry. Can I take a rain check?"

JP didn't believe a word I was saying. I could feel his skepticism as he gripped his reporter's notepad. "What could be so pressing that he would ask his campaign manager to leave a fundraiser early?"

Again, I strived to keep my face relaxed. I managed to laugh and placed my hand on his arm. "He didn't ask me to leave," I said. "I remembered something I need to work on before tomorrow. That's the nature of campaigns, I'm afraid. Things like this happen. But I don't have to tell you that, right?"

I could tell JP was debating. He was scanning the room for William. William, meanwhile, was waiting in the corner, his eyes locked onto me. My excuse seemed thinner in the harsh light of the living room, and for a moment I thought JP was going to take another pass at breaking me down.

"Rain check, then," he said, smiling.

"Rain check," I agreed, and I headed for the door.

don't think either of us knew where to begin. I'd been ignoring his texts and emails for more than two weeks. After our last conversation, it was apparent we had no way to break our impasse. Now, though, Gabriel seemed to have smoothed things over, at least temporarily. I wondered why he cared if William and I were together; it was hard to know what Gabriel's motivations were when it came to me.

William opened the door to his car for me, and I slid inside. He closed the door, got in the driver's side, slowly fastened his seat belt, and started the engine, all without saying a word. The silence was oppressive. Our anger and hurt feelings were rising up inside the car until it was difficult to breathe.

"I have mixed feeling about all of this," I said. "I'm a professional. You can't just show up and expect me to walk off the job."

"You were ignoring me," he said. "I tried to tell you the rules for dating vampires were different. If you want to break up, at least have the courage to discuss it with me. "

"Where are we going?" I asked, knowing he was right but not ready to admit it.

"I thought we would take a drive to a friend's house," he said, offering nothing more.

I leaned back against the leather seat and looked out the window. I'm not sure if it was the intense silence that ensued, or the fact that I had been working long hours, but within minutes I fell into a deep sleep. Sometime later I awoke, propelling myself toward the dashboard as I jerked out of my stupor.

"Oh my God," I said, rubbing my eyes. "I'm sorry."

William smiled, his normal relaxed demeanor back in place. "It's OK," he said. "It gave me time to calm down."

I looked out my window but didn't recognize the landscape. "Where are we?" I asked, rubbing my eyes again.

"We're about to enter Hearst Castle," he said calmly.

"This is an old friend's house?" We were nearly a hundred miles from Carmel, heading in the opposite direction from home. "Now you're going to tell me that you knew William Randolph Hearst?"

"We were acquainted," he said. "But it's his groundskeeper that I'm close with. Frank is a vampire and a former ambulance driver; he took this job after World War I war. Over the years, he's taught me every inch of this place. I thought you might like to go for a swim."

"You thought I might like to go for a swim? We haven't spoken in two weeks, and the first idea out of the gate is to kidnap me and take me to another castle for a swim?"

"I told you . . . you belong in a castle," William said as he pulled the car in to a spot along an entrance road and turned off the ignition. "Besides, you needed a nap and I needed a private place to speak with you. You've been avoiding me, Olivia, and that won't do at all. I was willing to wait only so long."

As I was about to give him my opinion of the situation, he took my hand and admonished me to stay silent until we were inside.

Hearst Castle is not just any castle. Conceived and built during an almost thirty-year period beginning in 1919, the sprawling complex was designed by architect Julia Morgan for newspaper magnate William Randolph Hearst. After his death, the Hearst family donated the property to the state, and it's been run as a historic park since the late 1950s. Hearst had an appetite for big things and he spared no expense for his so-called "country house," which by my calculations was about four hours from San Francisco.

William led me along a dark path to a small cottage at the end of the service road we'd parked on. He fished in his pocket for a key and opened the door, which swung open into a hallway. The hallway became a long tunnel that led to the main complex of the castle. We walked along the well-lit secret passageway that crisscrossed the property.

I tried to stay calm, but I was overcome by a series of conflicting emotions. I was angry with William for showing up at the party but also happy that he had come to find me. I was irritated he thought it was okay to take me miles away from San Francisco without asking permission. I was nervous about trespassing in the middle of the night, but secretly pleased that this time he had remembered to keep me out of the darkness. Using the hidden system of tunnels that it's said Hearst had built so his guests could swap lovers discreetly, William and I made our way slowly to a subterranean pool built at the east end of the castle.

I stood in awe as we entered. William bowed at the waist and waved his arms in a sweeping gesture.

"Welcome to the Roman Pool," he said.

I watched the light bounce off of what seemed to be a million small, square blue glass tiles. The blue seemed a shade deeper juxtaposed against similar-size gold tiles that formed a border on the walls. The tiles shimmered in the dim light of the lamps that illuminated the room. The blue also made the water of the pool look endlessly deep.

As I walked farther in to the room, I noticed a tray sitting in one corner; it held a small bowl of fruit, a bottle of champagne, and two glasses.

"Would you like a drink?" he asked, stepping in close to whisper in my ear. I nodded and soon had a flute of champagne in my hands.

"What did you mean about waiting for me?" I asked. "The last time we spoke you made it clear you didn't approve of what I was doing."

William crossed the room, returning the champagne bottle to the tray. "I may have mixed feelings about you chasing after gangsters and meddling in the affairs of humans, but that doesn't mean I don't want to be with you. You were injured in the robbery, almost blinded. Did you really think I wouldn't have an opinion?" he asked, taking a bottle of Jack Daniel's from a small backpack he had carried into the castle. "You seem to think I'm not entitled to have a view on things. And then, as usual, before we could really discuss it, you just gave up and threw me out."

"I didn't see the point," I said, trying to hold my quivering chin high. "How can I be with a man who won't support my work?"

"Darlin', that is overly dramatic, even for you," he said, laughing. "And, of course, untrue. But I am curious, is that why you were planning to have dinner with that reporter?"

William, it seemed, knew more about my activities then I realized.

"Why not?" I said, but with half the defiance I intended. "He's human. He likes politics. Seemed like a good start to me."

If a rule book existed for how to deal with vampires, the first piece of advice would probably be not to provoke one when he's feeling possessive. William quickly came to stand in front of me and grabbed my chin in his hand.

"Yes, but does he know you and Gabriel like to fix the races?" he asked, his voice low and angry. "Were you going to tell him what you do for a living, or would you have him believe you're just especially lucky in your career?"

He was right, of course. I wouldn't have shared my secrets with JP, at least not right away. The truth was that I had no interest in having a relationship with him. I wanted to say as much, but I found myself mute, unable to reply.

"Did you plan on sleeping with him?"

Without thinking, my hand came around and slapped William square in the face. "You bastard," I said. "Why would you ask me something so insulting?"

William rubbed his cheek, a look of satisfaction on his face. "I warned you about friendships with vampires. Did you really think that I would let you into my life, my inner circle, and then let some human come in and walk away with you?"

I didn't reply. Instead, I scanned the room for a ladder to dip my feet into the pool. I needed to cool down. Unfortunately, Hearst's pool was ten feet deep everywhere but at the far end, where a small wading area had been created.

"Let's get in," I said, walking toward the shallow end.

William blocked my path. "Let me help you out of your dress," he said, reaching around to unzip the back of my black sheath, then letting it fall to the floor.

Very suddenly I was wearing nothing but black lace boy shorts, a matching bra, and heels. William ran a finger under one bra strap, pulling it down around my arm.

"There you go, walking away again, but I want to finish our discussion. I saw the way he was looking at you, Olivia," he purred, and then he pulled down the other strap, exposing my breast. Slowly, he ran his thumb across my nipple and then leaned in closer. "There is no man alive who wouldn't want you, the way you were dressed tonight."

I grabbed his hand where it rested on my breast and brought his thumb to my lips. "You fool," I said as I slipped his finger into my mouth and gently bit it. "I'm not interested in any man alive. I'm in love with you. Only you. But if you want me to stay, you're going to have to accept me for who I am—my work, my ideas, all of it—or this night will be nothing but a waste of time."

William brought me into his arms and held me. We stood there for some time, until finally he lifted his head and began to speak.

"It's been more than a decade since I've had a lover," he said. "In fact, for almost all my nearly two hundred years I have lived my life alone, and that's how I planned to stay. Then one day, you walked into that tunnel, throwing all my plans to the wind."

I smiled, squeezing his hand.

"What I'm trying to say is, yes. I agree," he said. "I'll change. I will learn to be more flexible."

I kissed him then, thinking it was the most economical way to express my thoughts. It was hopelessly impractical to bind myself to a vampire, but I was in love for the first time in my life and had no wish to sacrifice my happiness for practical purposes. I had been that person who jettisoned her emotions in exchange for a well-ordered life, and it had nearly killed me. I was ready for a change—damn the complications. I wanted a lover who understood me, maybe better than I understood myself. So I kissed him again and threw my fate into the hands of the supernatural, just as my ancestors had done.

We undressed and climbed into the pool, bringing our bodies together. I kissed his cheek, then his eyelids. He pressed his lips into the small of my neck and nibbled on my earlobe. We clung together in the warm pool for some time before he spoke.

"Would you have slept with that reporter?"

I shifted in his arms so I could look at him more directly. "No," I said. "In fact, I'd been dreading the date since the moment I agreed to it. If you hadn't kidnapped me, I'm certain the evening would have ended badly."

"I didn't really kidnap you," William said, smiling. "I knew you'd come with me."

"How can you be so sure of yourself?"

"I'm not sure of myself, far from it," William said. "But I'm sure about *us*. I know we're meant to be together."

"I don't know if I would have come for you," I admitted. "I was convinced you'd never be OK with my work for the Council."

William nodded, pulling me closer. "Darlin', I'm also certain you and I are destined to get under each other's skin. But that doesn't mean we shouldn't be together."

Before I could reply, William kissed me again. Our kisses became more frantic as we pressed our bodies together in the salt water. Finally, he picked me up and sat me on the edge of the pool. He parted my legs and asked me to lie back, leaving me exposed to him. He started at my ankle, placing feathery kisses along my leg. Then he moved his lips back down to the tender skin on the inside of my thigh, where, without warning, he bit me. At the same moment his teeth pierced my skin, he slid a finger inside me. My body bucked and rocked as I screamed at the shock of the pain and the pleasure.

Hard to believe, but I had forgotten for a moment that I was making love with a vampire. Your imagination only goes so far when it comes to daydreams of moments like these. Imagining being bit is nothing like the real thing. It's shocking, but not as scary as you might think. This wasn't an attack, at least not the lethal kind. He was a gentle lover, and true to his word that night at his house, seemed to take only a sip before he raised his head to gauge my reaction. I sat up and smiled, beckoning him to join me. William climbed out of the pool, his long red hair matted against his shoulders, glistening from the water. He was beautiful and menacing to behold, pale and thin, his body marked with tattoos and ancient scars. He sat down next to me.

"Darlin'," he said, his Southern accent seeming more pronounced tonight. "Are you ready? 'Cause this is the point of no return."

"Which point?" I said playfully as I lay down, pulling him with me. "The trespassing on state property or the part where you make love to me?"

"Both," he said, smiling as he slipped inside me. "Both."

Our first time together was slow and languorous.

"This is why you belong in a castle," he whispered. "Good things happen to you here."

The second time, after he had fed me strawberries and more champagne, was different, rougher. William approached me from behind, running his hands down my back and bending me over at the waist. I could feel his sharp nails, the ones he used to play guitar, as he ran his fingers along my spine to the top of my neck. Then he ran his sharp teeth along the same path, grazing the skin at my nape of my neck. Then the rest of his body took over as he penetrated me. My senses were overloaded, overcome by his sensual nature and the lust and desire pouring through my body. Sex had never been this good or this intense before, and I wondered if it was because I was allowing myself to feel so greatly now or because I was with someone who made me feel so much.

When we were finished, I slumped over onto the pool floor. "My God," I said, deciding to leave it at just that. I looked over at William and knew he was thinking the same thing: we had truly given ourselves to each other tonight. Our emotions had been as exposed as our bodies, but neither of us had any regrets. I could feel it.

We dressed and walked hand in hand back to the car. My body began to ache as soon as I slid into the seat. I was sore in places I knew many women would never be. I smiled, amazed at what I had done with William and how badly I wanted to do it again.

"You tasted my blood," I said as we pulled onto Highway 1.

"I promised myself I wouldn't," he said, his voice drifting off a bit. "In the end, I had to take a small taste. Did I hurt you?"

I yawned, overcome with fatigue. "I'm fine," I said. "It was magnificent, but I have to tell you I don't think I can stay awake much longer."

"Go to sleep then," he said. "I'll wake you when we're home."

As I drifted off, I wondered which home he meant.

It was disorienting to wake up in bed and feel another body next to mine. It wasn't something I'd experienced very often, and at first my mind couldn't reconcile the facts. A moment of panic set in as I tried to retrace my steps from the night before. A horrible image of

JP jumped into view for a moment. Then, slowly, my body began to register the sensation of the cool mass beside me. A tumble of memories came flooding in, causing me to blush, and I realized that it was William next to me.

Part of what had confused me at first was the bed, which wasn't there when I'd visited his house before. Made of a dark wood, the queen-size frame sat in his bedroom against the middle of one wall. I knew instantly that he had made the bed for us. I was touched at his thoughtfulness but also chagrined at his expectation of success.

I wanted to sit up to get a better sense of things. As I pushed down on the sheets, I became aware of something else that was new and unexpected; on my ring finger was the trio of copper bands with the sapphires that I had admired at the gallery. I examined my hand, not sure what to do next. An image from a vintage horror movie popped into my head—a scene where the innocent, impoverished girl is lured from the village to a fate worse than death . . . to be the bride of a vampire.

But I knew that wasn't my story. I had walked into the castle as a willing participant. I was curious to know what significance the rings had for William. I looked over at the body next to mine. My suitor seemed to be asleep or at least in a deep trance. Just as they do in fairy tales, I kissed my sleeping prince. Then I gently bit his lower lip and pulled the blanket away, running my tongue across his chest and savoring his cool, smooth skin. I found his nipple and bit it, too, to see if that would wake the dead.

Instantly, I felt his senses alight, and once again I experienced the merging of our desire. I was hungry and impatient, my teeth suddenly set in a clench. My awareness of his feelings was instantaneous, and almost before I knew it, William slid into me. My body was inexplicably ravenous, and I bit down on William's lip, impatient for something I couldn't say aloud. Despite my provocation, he did not drink from me.

After we'd finished making love, he left our bed, put on a robe, and wordlessly walked out of the room. When he returned, he was carrying a tray with a glass of juice and whole-grain toast.

"Wow, a bed and food," I said. "You were certainly confident your campaign to kidnap me would be successful."

My host looked mildly rebuked. "I was hoping," he said. "I figured I could always throw the food away."

"Yes, but the bed, that took some work," I said, sitting up to sip the juice. "What would you have done with the bed if I'd refused?"

"I would have kept working to get you into it, of course," he said, sitting next to me. "Eventually, I would have worn you down."

I held up my hand and wiggled my ring finger. "You have a good memory," I said. "Usually, though, people ask before becoming engaged."

William took my hand and stared at the rings. "My mother had a set very similar to these. When I saw you admiring them at the gallery, I knew I had to buy them for you."

"Are we married?" I asked, unsure if vampire courting rituals skipped some of the steps humans found necessary.

He shook his head as he squeezed my hand. "That would be a little fast, darlin', even for a vampire. Think of it more as a set of commitment rings," he said. "A sign that we're together."

"Are we bound to each other?"

"No, I didn't drink enough of your blood, and you have not drunk from me. But after last night I would say that we are unquestionably *committed*."

I was more than fine with that, but I wondered how people would react when I appeared with what looked to be a set of wedding bands on my finger with nary a mention of a man in my life.

"These are beautiful, but I think we need to ease into my wearing them in public—at least until the campaign is finished. I don't want to draw attention to myself, especially from JP. Please don't mistake me; I do want to wear them. But I can't show up overnight with three rings on my finger."

I could feel William's scrutiny, but eventually the former Resistance fighter saw the elegance of my strategy. "You're right," he said. "When you get home, take off two of the rings and leave the single plain copper band. That doesn't look like it has any significance, and no one will notice." It was good advice from someone who'd managed to blend in for decades.

I would have been happy to sit in bed and chat all day about rings and commitment, but the mention of JP had given me an uneasy feeling. I scanned the room for my purse, realizing that it had been a while since I'd heard my phone ring and I had no idea what time it was. I assumed it was late, given what time we'd left Hearst Castle and because the sunshades had been drawn on the skylights in the bedroom.

"Where's my purse?" I asked. "I need my phone."

William walked over to one of the leather chairs and retrieved it. I dove in immediately looking for my iPhone. The ringer was off. "Did you turn off the ringer?"

"We didn't get home until dawn. I thought it better to let you sleep."

"Very sweet of you, but campaign managers need to hear their—"

I would have said more, but my eyes fell upon the time, which read 11:00, and the number 50 next to the phone icon on my screen.

"Shit! Someone has been trying to get in touch with me. I missed fifty calls." The numeral 30 sat, unblinking, next to the text-message icon. And there were 250 unread emails waiting in my in-box, more than twice as many as usual for this time of day.

I knew without a shadow of a doubt that something had gone wrong with the campaign. My heart was in my throat as I opened my email. I quickly began scanning the subject lines to see what I had in store. The first headline I saw sent my pulse racing:

CANDIDATE'S CHIEF FUNDRAISER RAILS AGAINST "FAT,
LAZY AMERICANS" IN SECRET VIDEO RECORDING

"Oh, fuck," I said, skimming the rest of the story. JP, it seemed,
had managed to get lucky last night after all.

THERE IS AN OLD FRENCH SAYING THAT ONE OF MY TEACHERS would use to scold us for misbehaving when she left the room. *Quand le chat n'est pas là, les souris dansent.* When the cat's away, the mice will dance. In other words, leave the children alone and they'll get into mischief. The same holds true for campaigns. There is no rest until the end, no moment when you can let your guard down. Every word must be spoken with intent, and every action must be carefully vetted to weigh its potential impact. One step in the wrong direction can be the end. To be a good candidate requires discipline. Without discipline, you get chaos.

I let out a few more expletives as I scanned the emails.

"Darlin', you sound like some of the men in the trenches," William told me.

"I assure you I can do even worse," I said. "Listen, something happened last night after we left. I need to get in touch with Gabriel. I'll probably need to get out of here quickly and go back to my house. I need my laptop and my phone charger." I dreaded dialing Gabriel's number. I knew he would be furious at me for being out of touch. *C'est la vie,* I thought. *I can't take it back; I can only try to fix the mess.*

"Olivia," Gabriel said when he answered, his French accent weighing down the first vowel of my name. "Call Levi. He will explain everything. There is a video; that damn reporter Richard invited took it. After you speak with Levi, call me back."

I pressed the number on my speed dial for Levi. He picked up on the first ring.

"Where have you been?" was his only greeting. "I have been trying to reach you for hours. The reporter—you know, the one Richard invited—he took video of us, Richard and me. I don't know what happened. Last night I thought perhaps that he'd had too much to drink. But he said . . . some unfortunate things."

"I know about the video, but I haven't seen it yet," I said. "Let me take a look and I'll call you back in five minutes."

William, who had walked out of the room, returned with a brand-new MacBook. We sat at his desk, side by side, and called up Tik Tok. Even before watching the video, my heart sank. The clip had already been viewed ten thousand times. The video itself was shaky at best; JP had filmed it with his phone at a distance so the two men would not see him.

They were standing on the deck, near the bar, illuminated by outside lights mounted to the side of the house. Levi and Richard clearly were already in the middle of a conversation. Richard looked agitated; although he was holding a glass of wine in his hand, he didn't appear to be drunk.

"Come on, Levi. Do you honestly believe that woman has a chance? She thinks the Bible should be the basis for all of our laws, for the Supreme Court for Christ's sake. She's crazy, and so are her few meager supporters. They're pathetic, the lot of them. Those fat, lazy high-school dropouts—why on earth should they have forever jobs building houses or making cheap American cars no one wants to buy? There is no room for them in this new economy. What person in their right mind would support someone who wants to 'ask for a sign from God' to fix immigration? This is Silicon Valley, not *The Beverly Hillbillies*. People are smart enough to know better."

I watched the video five times in succession, trying to memorize all of the words and gestures. The one thing that stood out immediately was that Levi never said a word. He definitely never agreed with Richard. On the flip side, he didn't try to stop him either. At the end, when Richard had finished his tirade, Levi said, "OK, Richard. Let's go inside now. Let's let the voters make up their minds. I think they can be trusted to make good choices."

Levi's faith in voters was something I could use. It was a small thing, but it provided the foundation necessary to build a plan for responding. The bitter irony of the moment settled upon me. I had assumed Stoner Halbert would try to do something directed at me personally. Now, it appeared that either Halbert's demon had come in contact with Richard and egged on his outburst, or we'd been walking around with a ticking time bomb inside the campaign for weeks.

I'd warned Levi not to jinx us.

I pulled out my phone and noticed an alert from X, formally known as Twitter, with a set of posts from Lacy Smith's campaign.

Barnes must quit the campaign.

The intellectual liberal elite have no place in government.

It's of the people, by the people.

William leaned over my shoulder as I scrolled through the posts. "I call it constitutional haiku," I said. "It's a favorite of conservatives."

"Smart," William said. "They're striking while the news cycle is hot."

I nodded in agreement. I had to acknowledge their discipline, but I had no intention of letting Levi quit the race—at least not yet. I picked up the phone, resolved to put Humpty Dumpty back together again. I texted Levi and Gabriel a Zoom invitation.

"Levi, forward the link to Richard," I said, as he and Gabriel appeared on my screen while I rummaged around for a piece of paper in William's desk. I found a yellow legal pad and began to doodle to relieve some of my nervous energy.

"Richard isn't answering his texts," Levi said, sounding apprehensive.

"I bet," I said. "Listen, I've reviewed the video, as well as the story JP wrote. I also reviewed Lacy's posts calling for your resignation. It looks bad, but I think it can be fixed.

"Here's what we're going to do," I continued. "First, Richard is going to issue a big, fat apology for his thoughtless remarks, which I will write for him shortly. Next, we'll hold a press conference in Palo Alto tomorrow to discuss what he said. We're going to make sure everybody knows this is about Richard, not Levi."

"That's it?" Levi asked.

"No, there's more. I'm leaving shortly for Palo Alto to begin on-the-street interviews with voters, to gauge what they really think about the situation. In the meantime, my staff will conduct a quick phone survey, using some of the voters we identified in our poll.

"While we do our work, Levi, you need to come up with a gesture—a donation of some kind that will unequivocally demonstrate your respect and belief that no one gets left behind in this new economy. Unemployment is still high with blue-collar voters; you have to reassure them that you'll help them find work. The perfect recipient would be a major foundation that funds job training and career transition programs. Finally, both of you should plan on being in Palo Alto later this evening. We'll regroup then and put all of the pieces of this puzzle together. Is everything clear?"

"Sounds like a solid plan," said Levi. "What time is the press conference tomorrow?"

"I'm recommending three; that way we can make the five o'clock TV news cycle."

"Will you let JP into the conference?" asked Gabriel.

"Of course," I said. "It won't do at all to shoot the messenger. I'm leaving now to pick up my gear and go. I'll get us a suite at the Four Seasons. It's not as ritzy as it sounds; it's by the highway. Anyway, I'll see you later this evening." Time was ticking away, and I was anxious to get started. I ended the Zoom and gathered my things.

"You're as good as any general in the field," William said, standing in the doorway watching me.

"I don't know about that," I said. "I led our troops right into this mess. This is my fault."

"You think because you didn't go out to dinner, JP decided to write something negative?"

"Sure, isn't it obvious?"

"Darlin', you're a campaign manager, not an escort. If JP was basing his favorable coverage on your affections, then this was bound to happen, regardless. You were never going to end up in his bed; you said so yourself."

"I did. Shit. Why did Richard Lyon invite JP in the first place? Before I knew *you*, I used to tell people that reporters are a lot like vampires—you should never invite them into your house because you can't get them out."

William laughed as we walked downstairs to his garage. "That's a bunch of folktale nonsense," he said. "We can come and go anywhere we please."

William took me home, and I quickly picked up my gear and left for Palo Alto. I phoned my staff from the car and asked them draw up a script to use for the phone interviews. My plan was to conduct in-person interviews at Stanford Shopping Center and among small businesses along University Avenue.

Although it was unusual for a campaign manager to do work in the field, being able to read people's emotions put me in the best position to conduct in-person interviews. It's common knowledge in the industry that people often lie or minimize things when they participate in surveys. No one wants to tell a stranger they drink four cocktails a night or eat junk food for every meal. It's the same with their views on candidates and political issues. Most people won't tell you they don't like someone when they have to look you in the eye. None of that would matter for me, though, because I would know their true emotions whether they shared them or not.

Thankfully, traffic was light and I made it to Palo Alto quickly. As I pulled into the parking lot of the shopping center, I readied myself for an afternoon of reading people.

After several hours of speaking with voters, I took refuge in a café to rest my tired feet and type up my notes. I ordered a chai latte, Elsa's love of all things tea rubbing off on me. I sipped the frothy, fragrant milk, feeling both exhausted and exhilarated. I couldn't wait to relay the results of my discussion with the team.

I had been typing for about an hour when Stoner Halbert suddenly appeared in front of me. It was a shock to see him; we'd managed to sidestep each other for months, even when he was in the midst of stealing all of my clients. Later, when I joined the Council and thought I had given up any work connected to him, I'd become too busy to care.

Halbert took the chair directly in front of me. A changed man sat before me. It was difficult to fathom that this was the person who'd ruined so many of my days just months ago. Now his aura was hollow, as if someone had stolen his very essence. The blue eyes peering at me were flat and dark.

Sitting in silence, regarding each another across the table, it struck me that I should have been more intimidated to face such a creature, this weasel that stole from the nests of others to feed himself. But I was no longer flying blind; I could read people's intentions, see their true colors. It hadn't been easy, but I'd come to trust my instincts and my intuition, two powerful forces that have served women for centuries. Elsa had prepared me for a moment like this, when I could sit face-to-face with an old nemesis and breathe a sigh of relief.

"Look what the cat dragged in," I said. "What brings you here?"

Halbert licked his lips and sat for a moment before replying. His gestures were human enough to keep people from noticing, but to me, his air of decay was unmistakable, as if he would peel open at any moment and allow some malevolent beast to come pouring out of his center.

"I came to discuss the terms of your surrender," he said. "You must have known I would be the one to take you down. I felt I should deliver the message in person."

As odd as it may sound, I was delighted by his remarks because they showed that he didn't know what I knew: the majority of local voters cared very little about Richard's comments. My interviews had revealed that most people were too busy living their lives to tune in to these kinds of petty clashes. And the few who *had* heard about the video were more interested in Levi's words and actions than those of his friends. Everyone, it turns out, can relate to being at a party where someone you know says something embarrassing. Halbert, meanwhile, had to stick with the media and their views on controversy—something that didn't necessarily indicate voter interest.

"Why should I 'surrender,' as you put it?"

"To avoid humiliating yourself," he said, clearly enjoying the conversation.

"I see," I said, nodding as if it were the most logical thing in the world. "So you would like us to resign and let your boss run unopposed with six weeks to go in the election?"

"Exactly," he said with a sense of satisfaction.

His comments were designed to enrage me, but I knew that keeping my temper in check was crucial. Halbert had no gift to read thoughts or emotions. He was one-dimensional. If people looked like losers, then they were. Some in the press might already have made up their minds that our campaign was about to collapse under the weight of Richard's comments, but I knew better. Tomorrow we would put the campaign back on its rightful course, but I didn't want Halbert to know it. That secret was all mine, and for once I had something he couldn't steal. Now it was my turn to prolong the reply, and I sat back savoring the silence that stretched before us.

"I'll think about it," I said. "You had better ask Lacy to pray that I make the right decision."

Having failed to get the response he was expecting from me, Halbert's face twisted into a grimace. I was tempted to taunt him further but realized it was time to end our discussion. His overt waves of hostility were starting to alarm the other café patrons.

"I think it's time for you to leave, Stoner. You've delivered your message," I said. "Now you can go back and report that you've done your job."

"Yes, but what is your response?" he asked tersely. "Will you quit the race?"

"I said we would think about it. You don't believe I would actually make that decision for Levi without discussing it with him?" I said, feigning surprise. "I'm a campaign manager, not a puppeteer."

He rose from his seat, his eyes full of malicious intent. He was poised to say something, maybe make a threat. I decided to cut him off.

"Halbert, you mad, old stray dog," I said. "Look at you chained up at the post, waiting to attack. When you sold your soul to the devil, did you expect to become his pet? I'm through being your meal ticket, so you'll have to look elsewhere. Now, I think you'd better leave before my boyfriend comes over and disembowels you right here at the table."

That caused Halbert to look up and search his surroundings.

William had come into the café minutes earlier. I could feel his presence as he pressed gently to signal his arrival. As Halbert made for the doors, I turned around and scanned the room until I spotted William sitting in the far corner, reading a book. I knew he wouldn't approach me until we were outside. We had agreed on a plan to help protect the campaign. I would drive to Palo Alto alone. He would follow later by train, so there would be no second vehicle for the media to notice.

After Halbert exited, I rose slowly from my seat, giving my lower back a chance to catch up with the rest of my body. I grabbed my bag and left the café. William was already outside waiting for me.

"Miss Shepherd, my name is William. I'll be driving you back to the hotel," he said, his words intended for anybody who might be listening.

I nodded and stayed mute, as I was certain Halbert was nearby. I handed William the car keys, and he slowly walked behind the car toward the driver's side, keeping vigilant along the way. *One part lover, one part bodyguard,* I thought to myself, although he picked right up on the sentiment.

"With me, they are one and the same, darlin', one and the same," he said once we were inside. "How did the interviews go? Good news?"

I was almost too excited to speak. "Really well, and the phone surveys too," I said. "As far as our research is concerned, voters don't hold Levi responsible at all for his friend's remarks. If Richard issues an apology and disappears for the rest of the campaign, we should be able to right this ship."

"So that's what you told Halbert," William teased. "He looks awful, by the way."

"Wow, vampires have excellent hearing," I said. "What else did you hear?"

"Apart from threatening to have your boyfriend kill him, I think my favorite line was 'mad, old stray dog,'" he said. "I believe you could write your own bluegrass songs."

We both laughed, and I slid back in my seat, relieved to have him to talk to after such a grueling day. He took my hand in his as we drove, and within minutes we reached the circular driveway of the Four Seasons. William insisted we check in under his name; he booked us into a suite on the fifteenth floor. It made sense. We needed a large room to work in, and we didn't want anyone in the media to know our whereabouts while we prepared for the next day.

As we entered the living room, I checked for electrical outlets, the one thing hotel rooms always have too few of. This was to be our campaign's secret field office for the next several hours. Gabriel and Levi were set to arrive shortly. Maggie was on her way, with a portable wireless printer. We would need enough electricity to power a small city when everyone in our group showed up with their phones and laptops.

When Maggie arrived, William left the main room, leaving us to set up. As was his way, he'd wandered off into one of the suite's two bedrooms to read and play guitar. Since we'd met, I found myself repeatedly taken with his ability to sit quietly and soothe himself. I hoped when the campaign was over, he would teach me some of his methods, although I had serious doubts I had the personality to be so restful with my time.

Not long after, there was a gentle knock at the door. William walked out of the bedroom to investigate.

"It's them," he said, peering through the peephole, and he quickly opened the door.

Gabriel and Levi looked exhausted. Twenty-four hours is a long time to be in the churn of the news cycle, and from the look of things, it had been rough on them. I could feel Levi's deep sadness at the predicament he found himself in. Gabriel, on the other hand, was angry—with Richard, I presumed, or maybe even me.

He was also impatient, wanting to know what had happened today. His thought came into my head clearly, and I sent one back just as fast. *All in good time*, I pushed out to him. *I will set your mind at ease.* He looked up and nodded, a thin smile on his face.

Levi and Gabriel went into the living room, sinking into a pair of plush library chairs decorated with jaunty brown-and-blue French sailor stripes. Now that they were both comfortable, I jumped at the chance to give Levi a bit of relief.

"As you know, I spent the better part of today interviewing registered voters in person, while Maggie and Patrick conducted about fifty phone interviews from our campaign office, using numbers we got from participants of our poll who gave permission to contact them again."

Levi listened, trying to be patient, but it was clear he wished I'd cut to the chase.

"The bottom line is that after dozens of interviews with voters, we believe that this will not harm your campaign permanently, so long as Richard apologizes and you indicate very concretely that you disagree with his views. If we do those two things, we should be able to pull out of this."

"The donation," Levi said. "Is that still something we want to do?"

"Absolutely," I said. "Tell me what you have in mind."

Levi leaned back in his chair and closed his eyes as he spoke. "I have a friend who founded a charity in the valley called the Vocational Service Corps, or VSC. It's a nonprofit that helps people find employment and provides classes to improve job skills, rewrite résumés, those kinds of things. I am prepared to donate $5 million over the next five years to help start a drop-in program for people who've been notified they'll lose their jobs. Studies show people who have this kind of preparation are often better able to find work quickly. I'll place one hundred percent of the money in a trust for VSC and, they can draw the funds annually."

"*C'est bon*," Gabriel said.

"It's perfect," I said, "and very generous."

Levi shook his head ruefully. "The sad thing is that I had planned on doing something like this anyway, but now it's going to look like a gesture forced under duress."

"Yes, *mon ami*, but it's an elegant gesture, and that is what will be remembered," Gabriel said.

24

OUR GAME PLAN IN PLACE, I SAT DOWN TO WRITE LEVI'S
speech. The words were swimming around in my head, and I was
eager to get them down on paper. As I typed away, I raised my eyes
from the computer screen to glance at the others in the room. Gabriel
appeared to be introducing William to Levi, who glanced in my direction, a look of surprise on his face. William must have seemed like
a man conjured up out of thin air, and I wondered how Gabriel was
explaining my new paramour to his old friend. I decided not to
guess. At this point, it was more important to work than to speculate.

I wrote for a few more minutes and then looked up again,
amused to see the three men consulting what appeared to be a
room-service menu. Another test, I thought. William would have to
feign the absence of an appetite in front of Levi or find another way
to distract him from his lack of interest in food. Again, I forced
myself to work rather than worry. William had survived more than
a hundred years without me, so I was certain he would manage this
evening. By the time the food was delivered, I had a decent first
draft of a speech for the team to review.

Gabriel, it turned out, helped play a role in William's diversion.
The meal he'd ordered included raw fish. Sushi and sashimi are foods
I knew William's system could tolerate in small doses.

"It's better not to eat a heavy meal when we need to be thinking
on our toes," Gabriel said as the waiter wheeled in a cart with assorted

fish and a bottle of vodka on ice. "We can always order more if we're hungry later."

I watched William out of the corner of my eye as he picked up a pair of chopsticks and deftly nibbled on a piece of tuna. The shot of vodka went down more easily, his system long accustomed to hard alcohol. Still, his ability to blend in was admirable, and I concluded that vampires were the best chameleons I'd ever encountered.

I turned out to be the one with no appetite—too keyed up to eat. I managed a few bites and then took a shot of vodka for courage. It was difficult to believe, as I surveyed the room, that only the night before I'd been floating in a ten-foot-deep saltwater pool at Hearst Castle, making love and drinking champagne.

Elections once again were proving to be a lot like a long drive on a narrow mountain road; one false move and you were in danger of swerving over the side. This speech was to be our way of getting back on course safely. I hoped we could do it without any more near misses.

After the meal, I handed out copies of the speech. Levi walked to the desk and began making notes on his copy.

Gabriel handed his pages right back to me, saying, "This is his speech; I will let him make the first comments."

Levi soon returned to our circle of chairs, handing me his notes.

"You've always been a good writer, Olivia," he said. "But this has to come from my heart if it's going to be credible, so I've made a few modifications."

His changes were great. I nodded. "Let me update your remarks, and then we can rehearse."

By midnight, Levi had completed several practice runs, and we'd made minor tweaks to the language along the way. By twelve thirty we disbanded. Levi and Gabriel went to their own rooms in the hotel. Maggie was bunking in the spare room in our suite and had long since retreated to get some rest after what had been one of the toughest days of her young political career. I heard William lock the door to the suite as I stood at the window of the living room massaging my neck.

"I need to try to be more ergonomic," I said as he took over massassing the tender pressure points in my neck and back. "Political campaigns are hard on the human body."

"Seems that way," he said. "It feels like you have a rock embedded in your shoulder."

I laughed. "That's been there for a while. If you try to remove it, my arm will fall off."

"As soon as this campaign is over, we're going on a vacation," he said, kneading my muscles harder. "Someplace where you can relax and stop thinking about everyone else's problems."

"Hmm, sounds lovely," I murmured as the muscles in my neck finally relented and relaxed. "Let's get through tomorrow, and then we can start thinking about vacations."

I watched the reflection of William's face in the window break into a smile. "I've been observing you since this all began this morning. You always do what's necessary first, regardless of your needs or wants. I understand now how Gabriel came to choose you for his team; you seem to have an abundance of something that is rare in humans."

"What's that?"

"Discipline," he said as he led me to our bedroom.

I quickly undressed and collapsed into bed, managing only a feeble "good night" to William before I was fast asleep.

Discipline was definitely what I needed to get out of bed the next morning when my alarm went off. The beeps from the small plastic box on the nightstand had gone unnoticed, but when my phone chimed in with the backup alarm, I opened my eyes. It took a few moments to remember where I was, having failed to sleep in my own bed the last two nights. Finally, though, my brain brought itself up to speed and I rolled over. William wasn't there, but I hadn't expected to see him, since sleeping wasn't a vampire's main form of leisure.

I didn't I mind, though, since I don't like to snuggle when I sleep. Lying flat on my back with nothing, and no one, near me is my preferred way to slumber, so William was my perfect bedmate. Reluctantly, I got out of bed and went in search of the workout clothes I had hastily packed the day before.

I was always grateful to get in some exercise before the day started. Fortunately for me, the Four Seasons had a world-class fitness center only a few floors away. I pulled on shorts and a T-shirt, laced up my shoes, and padded down the hallway in search of William. As expected, he was reading in the living room, a guitar propped against his chair.

"What are you reading?" I asked, knowing he'd already heard me coming down the hallway.

"Come here and I'll tell you," he said, setting his book on a side table. "You slept well? Feel OK?"

"Despite the utter chaos of yesterday, yes, I do," I said as I settled into his lap. "I went to sleep feeling very optimistic; we'll see if my intuition holds true."

I received a kiss for my optimism, a very deep, long kiss, and then a second, more gentle kiss in the small of my neck near my shoulder. Such intimate, peaceful play was new to me, and it made my heart soar. It would have been wonderful to stay in his arms for the remainder of the day, but I came back to reality.

"I need to go to the gym," I said, rising from his lap. "I need to get some exercise in before the day grows too long."

"I'll go too," he said. "Just give me a minute to change."

True to his word, he reappeared quickly in a pair of black warm-up pants and a T-shirt, and we set off for the elevators. I was not at all surprised to see Levi and Gabriel jogging away on treadmills as we walked through the door of the gym. The only person missing was

Maggie, who I assumed, at her tender young age, had decided sleep was more important than exercise.

Feeling no need for pleasantries at this hour, we all jumped into our morning routines. I stepped onto the treadmill next to Gabriel and began what I hoped would be a three-mile run.

We left the gym as a group but went our separate ways, agreeing to meet at the campaign office at two o'clock, one hour before the press conference. William said he had some business to attend to and would see me at the press conference.

I stayed behind in the room, intent on working, hoping to call back reporters and review last-minute details before the event. My plans were disrupted immediately, however, by a series of taunting texts from Stoner Halbert, all saying essentially the same thing:

Resign.
It's not too late to avoid embarrassing yourself.

The last time Halbert had texted me, months ago, I'd rolled up into a ball on my bed and cried. Now, I felt like punching him in the mouth. My days of running from my enemies were over, so I clicked on Halbert's number, wondering if my nemesis would answer his phone.

"That was quick," Halbert sneered. "I had no idea you would fold so easily."

"I didn't call to resign, you idiot," I said. "I think all that black magic is rotting your brain."

"Then why did you call? Just wanted to hear my voice?"

"I called to tell you to knock it off," I said. "For someone allegedly mastering the dark arts, you're behaving like a desperate loser. I want you to stop bothering me."

"Or what?" he asked. "What will you do?"

I was on the verge of threatening him with some painful retribution involving his limbs being separated from his body, but then I remembered that cell phones could record conversations.

"You don't think I would be stupid enough to threaten you on the phone on the day of my press conference?" I asked.

Halbert was silent, and it occurred to me that perhaps he'd hoped for just that situation.

"Good-bye, Halbert," I said, "I'd tell you to go to hell, but then I'd only be encouraging you."

After I hung up, I tried my best to calm down and focus on my work. A few hours later, I was stuffing my laptop into its bag when I heard my phone ring. I picked up the phone with trepidation, hoping it wasn't Halbert.

It was JP, so I pressed "Answer" to hear what he had to say.

"Were you planning on inviting me to the press conference?" he asked, without offering so much as a hello. Even through the phone, I could feel his anger.

"Hi, JP," I said, trying to sound casual. "I believe your newsroom received an advisory from the campaign like every other news outlet."

"Yes, but were *you* going to call *me*?"

"You know, things have been a little busy these last twenty-four hours," I said. "I guess it slipped my mind."

"So you have no comment on the video," he pressed.

"We'll be commenting at three," I said, trying hard not to show my anger.

"I'm asking if *you* have anything to say yourself about the video," he said, his voice tinged with sarcasm. "Or about the fact that I saw you leave with that man. I saw you with him again last night at the café."

Oh, but did I ever have words to say . . . none of which could ever be uttered on the record. "Any comment from me or this campaign will come at three. Now if you'll excuse me, I really have to go. I expect I'll see you shortly."

I pressed "End" and closed my eyes.

I'd been so busy trying to find a solution to our debacle that I hadn't had much time to consider JP's role in all of this. Was it fair to be angry with him? Or was he just doing his job? Had Halbert's demon provoked Richard? Or had those horrible sentiments been lurking inside him, just waiting to come out? Maybe that's what evil does; it brings our worst fears and prejudices to the surface, stripping away our ability to silence those voices in favor of patience or compassion. I'd told William that I couldn't change a bad man into a good one using my skills, but maybe the devil worked differently. Perhaps he could take a good man and reduce him to his worst impulses.

In the end, I realized, it didn't matter. During the countless hours I'd spent talking with voters, it was clear that they didn't care about Richard Lyon; they cared about Levi Barnes. They wanted to see what he would do, whether he would take responsibility, if he would hold himself accountable. If so, they were prepared to move on and not wallow in the scandal.

The press, on the other hand, wanted the scandal to live on, for more details to emerge, and for side players to continue their outrageous behavior. If we could deny the media any further fuel—steal the oxygen for their fire—then the news cycle would close. Richard would disappear, Levi would apologize and announce his donation, and we would get back to talking about Lacy's conservative policies. That was what this election was supposed to be about in the first place.

EVERY PARKING SPACE AROUND THE CAMPAIGN OFFICE WAS already taken an hour before the press conference. I circled the block, finally finding a space, and walked slowly toward the office. I was in no hurry to jump into the circus. I knew it would be tense until we got through the speeches. I stepped through the mob of reporters, promising we would begin promptly at three. As I walked past the press corps, I noticed JP standing off to the side looking at me. I raised my hand to wave; I didn't see any reason to ignore him. He saw my gesture but did not wave back, and it struck me as ludicrous that I had ever contemplated a romance with someone capable of such pettiness.

I made my way to the conference room at the back of the suite of offices we'd rented. There inside, wearing worried expressions, were Levi, Gabriel, Maggie, and Patrick, but no William; I assumed he'd show up when things got started. We took the few remaining minutes we had to get organized and then walked to the front of our headquarters, where a table was set up to face the press.

"*Bonne chance*," Gabriel said to me as we walked toward the media throng. "You have done a good job of taking control."

"Do you blame me for this mess?" I asked, knowing the walk was too short for such a conversation.

"No, no, not at all," he said quickly. "The fault of this lies with the man who let his tongue slip, and no one else."

I took comfort in his words as Levi and I took a seat at the table, which was now covered with microphones.

"OK, folks," I said, greeting the assembled group. "I think we'll get started, but first, I want to give you a brief description of the format for today's conference. At this moment, campaign staff are handing out a written statement from Richard Lyon, in which he issues an apology for his outburst two nights ago. As you know, Richard made his remarks at a private party, where he was recorded, unbeknownst to him. Then, his remarks were posted online. This statement will be his only comment regarding that night. He will not be giving interviews, and he is not here today at the conference. In a few moments, Levi Barnes will make a statement, and when he is finished, we will take your questions."

I was relieved to see William slip into the back of the room just as Levi prepared to address the crowd. Levi waited until everyone appeared to have a copy of Richard's statement in their hands, and then he rose from his chair. "I'd prefer to stand, if you don't mind," he said to the assembled group.

"Let me begin by apologizing to the voters of Congressional District 15 for this unnecessary detour from discussing the issues I know they want to talk about. I also want to apologize for Richard Lyon's remarks. He is one of my oldest friends, and yet here today, in this very public way, I must say that I strongly disagree with his statements, and I wish I had said so more forcefully the other evening. Of course, I didn't know the conversation was being recorded. But I want to make it clear that I do not share Richard's sentiments. I believe they have no place in politics—certainly not as a part of the kind of campaign I am committed to running."

Levi looked up at the reporters for a moment before continuing. "The fact is that I *do* believe in the power of people to change their lives, to change careers, to reinvent themselves, because I did, and I know that many others in their lifetime will too. I think that is the fundamental promise of our country. But that promise is predicated on a few things that I think are worth mentioning: hard work, honesty and civility. Without those things, there is very little that can be accomplished, which is why I have asked Richard to step down as chairman of my campaign's fundraising operation. His presence would distract from the real issues of this campaign, but also more fundamentally, I think that his views require me to sever my ties with him for the time being. I have an obligation to lead by example, and as much as it pains me, I have asked Richard to withdraw from campaigning and to refrain from speaking publicly again until the campaign is concluded. He is now out of the country on business, and I do not expect him to return until the New Year."

Levi shifted the pages of his speech, bringing the few remaining words to the front of his pile.

"As I mentioned earlier, I believe in the power of people to change their lives. And to ensure that everyone in Silicon Valley has that opportunity, today I am announcing my family's pledge of $5 million to the Vocational Service Corps, a leading job-training non-profit in the valley. I was a member of VSC's board of directors for many years, and I admire them tremendously for the work they still perform every day. The donation is intended to establish a drop-in center where clients can walk in and immediately begin to find the information and tools they need to find new employment or transition to a new career. I hope that this will help to demonstrate my belief that all of us have the power to change our lives, even in adversity. I hope, as well, that this gesture will end discussion of the events of two nights ago and allow us to focus on the real issues of this campaign. And now, if any of you have questions, I'd be happy to answer them."

A row of hands shot up immediately.

"Can you confirm that you had no idea you were being recorded?"

I looked at Levi to signal that I would answer the question. "Yes, I can," I said addressing a reporter from a local TV station. "We only knew of the existence of the video after it had been uploaded online. We were not asked to comment prior to its publication."

"Did you know a member of the press was present at the party?"

Again, I indicated that I would reply. "Yes, we were aware that Mr. Lyon had invited a reporter to interview guests, but the conversations were supposed to be obvious on-the-record interviews, not a private discussion between two old friends at the end of the evening when they believed they were alone. It's an unfortunate reality of the world today that it's so easy to record someone without their knowledge, but we acknowledge that the comments were made and, as you can see, we were prepared to respond."

"Did you make the $5-million gift out of guilt?" asked JP, clearly determined to draw blood before this campaign was through.

Levi looked over at me to let me know he was OK to respond.

"If you check with the Service Corps," he began, "you will find that I had already been discussing some kind of gift with them for several weeks. It's unfortunate to have to do something like this under a cloud, but my donation is one that I intended to make all along. So, yes and no. I do take responsibility for Richard, and I want to make amends for his thoughtlessness, because I can."

"You said you want to get back to the campaign," JP said. "Do you have any comment on Lacy Smith's demand that you withdraw?"

"I'm sure Ms. Smith would love to spend the next six weeks talking to herself," I said, generating laughter from the reporters. "But the fact is that Levi Barnes has done nothing wrong, and there is no reason for him to end his candidacy. In fact, our research indicates that voters continue to remain focused on the real issues, such as how unemployment, education, and job creation will be managed by Congress. At this moment, the approval rating of the federal government has never been lower. The voters want to see new leaders, and they want to see the debate continue on real issues, and that is exactly what we intend to do until the election."

After that, the press calmed down. The remaining questions from reporters all related to actual government policies—not the video. When the last photog had packed up his gear and left, we all breathed a sigh of relief and returned to the back conference room. The moment we were away from prying eyes, Levi locked me in a forceful embrace that lifted me up off the floor.

"You were brilliant," he said. "We were brilliant. That could not have gone better."

"Oh, no! Please don't jinx us again," I said. "I do think we turned a corner, but let's not tempt the gods. We'll watch the news tonight and see what happens tomorrow."

No sooner than I finished my sentence, Gabriel burst through the door carrying a bottle of sparkling wine and a stack of plastic glasses. "*Très bien.* Excellent," he said. "I knew we were going to be fine, so as soon as I could, I went out to find something to celebrate with. They call this champagne . . . but we will see," he said, waggling his eyebrows to indicate his skepticism.

We had beaten the devil at his own game, for the moment at least. As the evening wound down, however, I began to have an uneasy feeling in the pit of my stomach. I knew that either Stoner or JP would be waiting for me outside. It didn't seem possible to escape without one more confrontation. William, sensing my anxiety, was quickly by my side.

"Are you expecting trouble outside?" he asked.

I nodded. "It feels inevitable."

"We'll go together," he said. "Whatever is there, we'll meet it together."

I suggested Levi and Gabriel use the back door of the offices. It didn't seem necessary for either of them to deal with anything else tonight. But before Gabriel walked out, I asked for a minute of his time.

"Now that we're finished with this mess, I want to see that recording of the robbery," I said.

"*Merde*, you are stubborn," he said, but without a trace of irrita-tion. "*Bien sûr*, I will ask Aidan to have it ready tomorrow night."

Feeling victorious, I grabbed my bags, ready to walk with William to my car. Time was a marvelous thing, I mused, in its ability to speed up and slow down depending on your adrenaline. Two days had passed with almost no sensation of their conclusion. I wondered if time felt that fast for William too.

"Sadly, no," he said, hearing my thoughts. "Not when it's centuries, instead of days."

"Does it make you weary?"

"Sometimes," he said. "But I have learned to pass the time grace-fully. Come on, let's go home."

Unfortunately, as anticipated, both JP Ellington and Stoner Hal-bert were waiting for me outside. I studied the two of them, noting their body language, and got the distinct impression that they had known each other prior to the campaign. They were standing too close to one another to be strangers. Men normally don't give their personal space away that easily, but these two were standing as close as brothers would. A lightbulb went off in my head. Was Halbert so determined to humiliate me that he would ask his reporter friend to play seducer? Perhaps that's where the video had come in. JP had needed something for Halbert, having come up short in his quest to compromise me. William's trip to Hearst Castle, it seemed, had saved me on several levels.

"Gentleman," William drawled as he held my hand tightly. "Is there something we can help you with?"

Both men regarded William warily, now unsure of themselves.

"What you do want?" I asked. "The press conference is over."

"I have it on good authority that you were not even in the house when Lyon made those comments to Levi," purred Halbert. "My sources tell me you walked out of the fundraiser—and off the job—early, for a tryst with your lover. How professional do you think that would look to the world if that bit of info hit the news?"

William started forward, but I put out my arm to stop him.

"I've got one better," I said. "How about I tell the press about your long-standing friendship with JP, a preeminent Silicon Valley reporter, and how you two conspired to have him lure me into his bed to gain confidential information, and when that failed, violated the privacy of two men by secretly recording them? What do you think the press will make of that? Shall we have a race to see who can pick up the phone faster? My instincts tell me my story will prove far more damaging to your boss. Especially when I tell the press I am engaged to be married—that it had been a surprise proposal that caused me to leave early."

Two pairs of eyes stared back at me, unmoving. This, they hadn't expected.

"Shall we get started? I'll start data mining and see if I can turn up any compromising photos of the two of you together. You know, you can never really delete things from the web."

"Bitch," Halbert said, taking a step toward us. "You think you can—"

"Shut up," JP said, pulling Halbert's arm. "For once, just shut up."

"I suggest you two leave here, *now*," William said, leaving little doubt about what would happen if they refused.

Both men glared, but they turned and walked away.

"Are you going to turn JP in?" William asked, opening my car door for me.

"No," I said, sinking into the seat with relish, my body finally realizing it was exhausted. "JP will live in fear that I'll call his editors, and that's punishment enough for him. As for Halbert, he's got one hell of a boss—how pleasant can that be? I am satisfied just to get on with my work."

"You surprise me," William said as he turned the key in the ignition. "Most people would be ready for revenge by now."

"Oh, I do want revenge," I said, yawning. "But the best revenge will be for Levi to win the race. So I would rather focus on that. Besides, I feel foolish, having almost fallen into their trap. If you hadn't come for me, I might have done something far worse to harm Levi's campaign. I hope you don't mind that I lied and told them we were engaged. It seemed like the one thing that would take the wind out of their sails."

"I don't mind one bit," he said, giving me a provocative look that spelled hours of fun later. "I say we go back to my place and make it official."

26

THE SUN, IT SEEMED, WAS TAKING ITS TIME TO SET, driving me crazy. Only when it was dark could our group assemble at the Council's offices and review the videos of the robbery. Unlike the two days before, when time had passed at the speed of light, today had dragged on.

The only bright spot in my long, restless day was reviewing the positive media coverage we continued to receive following our press conference. My ability to read people had paid off. Earlier in the day, our campaign pollster had phoned with news that Levi was widening his lead against Lacy. Even JP had surprised me. His latest story hadn't betrayed any of his venom; he had played it straight.

Finally, as the foghorns began to wail and dusk crept into the city, I called upstairs to Elsa and asked her to walk with me. She had gone up to take a nap earlier, something I'd never seen her do before. But it was understandable that she'd be tired, given the pace we'd all been working at for weeks.

On the way to the museum, we spoke very little, too wrapped up in our own thoughts, I suppose. At the side door, I placed my palm on the copper, waiting for the sensors to recognize my fingerprints and open the door. Once inside, I saw William seated at the main bay of cubicles, speaking with Aidan. Their discussion, whatever the topic, looked serious, and I sensed that I was being mentioned in some context. Gabriel was there, too, nodding solemnly. Perhaps William was simply recounting last night's finale, an episode I had yet to tell the team.

"Hello," I said, breaking into their conversation. "How is every-one tonight?"

"Olivia," Gabriel said, standing to take my hand in his for a moment. "William was telling us about Halbert's threat against you. He tells us you handled them well, but I am still concerned. This Halbert, he is about to enter a lost place—we have an expression, *au diable vert*, a place that is inadvisable."

"It was his choice," I said. "He chose the dark side. But I wonder what will happen if he loses the election. How would he and his en-tourage take the loss?"

"Indeed, that's a good question," Gabriel said, a glint in his eyes. "You have come through all of this a changed woman, Olivia. You seem more . . . composed."

"My newfound responsibilities are growing on me," I said earnestly. "Thanks to Elsa and the rest of my training, I don't feel as vulnerable. I feel more in control of my destiny."

"From what I have been told, you're more than comfortable, Olivia," Aidan said, joining the conversation. "You're becoming a leader."

I blushed at the compliment, feeling suddenly shy. I looked over at Elsa to see if she was happy, but she gave away no hint of any emotion. I found it curious but let it pass. I knew she was tired and surmised that perhaps she was not feeling well.

"Can we watch the videos?" I asked, giving Gabriel an imploring look.

"The room is set up now; we can go in," Aidan said, gesturing toward the closed door of a nearby conference room—a structure whose size and shape seemed not at all to correspond at all to the actual footprint of the building.

Once again, I marveled at how the building always seemed to

have a conference room available when we needed it. I hoped one day to be shown the spell required for making whole rooms out of nothing, but in the meantime, I enjoyed the trick—and the privacy it offered.

A large flat-screen television was mounted on the wall inside, and there was an iPad, a keyboard, and a tray with a pitcher of water and several glasses. Aidan and Elsa sat down at the head of the table. Gabriel did not join us.

"We believe we've reviewed all of the videos that popped up online in the first two days after the robbery," Aidan said. "Here is a montage of what's out there."

I involuntarily cringed as I watched the first images of the car crashing into the building. I remembered how it felt to fall on my shoulder when the car jumped the curb, the pain in my eyes as I tried to peer through the windows of the jewelry store. I watched one video, then the next. My memory of the crime was very different than the images I was looking at. My recollection was that there were very few people on the street, but I saw now that there were actually dozens more.

"Did you see me in any of these images?" I asked.

"Surprisingly, no," Elsa said. "There were smartphones filming the robbery from almost every angle, but so far, you have not shown up in a single frame. It's almost as if you became invisible."

"That's the second time I've seemed to become invisible," I said, remembering Lily's comments at dinner about how I'd vanished from her sight in the park the night I ingested peyote. "Obviously, that's impossible, so there must be another explanation,"

The images on the screen continued to whirl by when suddenly something caught my eye.

"Wait, stop, hold that frame for a moment," I said, squinting at the face of one of the robbers. "I know him."

"What do you mean, you know him?" Aidan asked.

I pointed at the screen. "OK, I don't *know* him, but I recognize him. I saw him, here, in this building."

A shot of dread ran up my spine, and it wasn't my own. The collective reaction of the group was grim.

"Where did you see him?" Aidan asked, walking briskly to close the door to the conference room. Elsa followed him, closing the metal blinds in the room completely.

I shut my eyes to get the memory straight, so much having happened in the last few days. "It was here," I said slowly. "Gabriel and I were having dinner together that night, and I was waiting for him to get his coat. This man was pacing outside Nikola's office. I remembered him because I thought at the time he looked like a soldier or an athlete of some kind. He was very tense. He was waiting, and pacing, and then the door opened and he went inside. I mentioned it to Gabriel."

"What did he say?" Aidan asked, coming to sit next to me.

I massaged my fingers against my forehead as I thought back to our conversation. "He said something like, 'Yes, Nikola knows a lot of Serbians from the Balkan Wars, and some do look quite grim.'"

William, who had been lingering in the back corner of the room, came to stand next to me, placing his hand on my shoulder. "This man?" he asked. "Did he see you watching him?"

I thought for a moment. "No, I don't think so. I was standing in the shadows, waiting for Gabriel. It was only when he arrived that I stepped into the light, and by then, the man had gone inside Nikola's office." The group's concern was growing more palpable by the second, so I said to no one in particular, "You know, I can feel your worry. Is someone going to tell me what they think this means? Do you think Nikola had something to do with the robbery?"

"We don't have enough information to make that connection," Aidan said quickly, ever the cautious diplomat. "It could be nothing but a coincidence. The Serbian community is very small in San Francisco. His visit could have been about something totally unrelated."

"Are we going to check it out?"

William and Aidan exchanged glances that told me all I needed to know. This was off-limits to me.

"*I* will look into this, Olivia, but not you," Aidan said sternly. "The Council is a fragile organization, made up of many competing interests. Certain protocols must be maintained. It would not be appropriate for you to ask Nikola about this."

Elsa peeked out through the blinds, checking, I guessed, to see who was working in the main bay. "We can't discuss this outside of our group," she said.

"What about Gabriel?" I asked.

"Yes, of course," Aidan said, "But always in private, never in open rooms, hallways, or elevators. Understood?"

His question was posed to all of us, but I got the feeling his directive was mostly aimed at me. "Understood," I said, nodding.

The meeting ended on a somewhat subdued tone, with Aidan clearly distressed about this new wrinkle. I knew from our previous conversations that he was no fan of the Eastern European delegation. Now he would have to seek them out to discuss something uncomfortable, possibly accusing them of involvement in something illegal.

William and I remained silent in the elevator. As the doors opened on the main floor, we ran straight into Nikola. I couldn't have imagined worse luck, considering Aidan's instructions to us.

"Olivia," Nikola said. "How are you? I heard that you were injured recently."

William squeezed my hand, a subtle warning not to pick a fight. I nodded, smiling warmly. "Yes, but I am feeling better. How did you hear?"

"Gabriel, of course," he said. "It's standard for the Council to issue a report when a staff member is injured under unusual circumstances. In our line of work, that kind of information can be important."

"Well, I'm fine now," I said. "I'm not sure what happened. One minute I was walking down the street; the next I was knocked down by a piercing pain in my head."

"What a shame," he said, although I knew he wasn't even remotely sorry. "Do you know anything about the robbers?"

"I heard on the news that they might be Serbian," I said.

Nikola smiled, his perfect vampire teeth gleaming back at me. "Yes, of course I have seen the news reports, but who knows what the truth is? Western media love to blame everything on Serbians. We are the perfect villains for the twenty-first century."

"You would know better than I about these sorts of things," I said innocently. "I've been so busy with my campaign work that I haven't had a chance to give the robbery much thought."

Nikola doubted me; I could feel it. But I knew I had gone as far as I could with this conversation, so I changed the subject. "Nikola, I apologize for my poor manners. Let me introduce my boyfriend, William."

They eyed one another coolly, vampire to vampire. I suspected this was not the first time they had met.

"You are full of surprises, Olivia," Nikola purred. "You become the first human to work for the Council, and then you take a vampire for a lover. You certainly like to live dangerously."

"Indeed, Nikola, I surprise myself sometimes with my choices," I said. "I hardly know what I will do next."

William dug his finger into my palm, but Nikola tossed back his head and laughed, clearly amused at my insolence.

"How exciting," he said. "I must remember to keep a closer eye on you in the future."

With that, Nikola nodded curtly at the two of us and walked into an open elevator.

When the elevator doors had closed and we were alone, William regarded me with a look that was one part amusement, two parts fury. "You can't do that, darlin'. You're not prepared physically or mentally to pick a fight with a thousand-year-old vampire," he said. "He is more cunning and far more ruthless than you."

"Maybe I'll surprise you," I said, feeling prickly, but William stopped me from saying more by touching his cool hand to my cheek.

"You should head home, Olivia. I'll join you there later."

From the look on his face, I knew it wasn't worth arguing. I sat in my Uber feeling sullen, like a small child told to mind her manners. I shouldn't ask questions, I mustn't speak in the hallways, and I couldn't pick fights with vampires who were older than me. It was petty, but I felt chided and hemmed in, and more than a bit sorry for myself.

27

AFTER SEEING OLIVIA OFF, WILLIAM RETURNED TO THE conference room, a grim look upon his face.

Elsa beat him to the question. "Why do you think she doesn't show up in any of the videos of the robbery?" she asked, simultaneously sending a text to summon Gabriel. "We watched footage of every angle of the building, at the exact time she was supposed to be there, but she doesn't register in any of the images."

William put his fingers to his lips. The door opened, and Gabriel stepped into the room, followed by Madeline Klein. Both looked unsettled. It couldn't be good news if their presence was required.

Everyone took a seat as Aidan began to speak.

"I checked the feed for traces of AI interference but didn't find anything. Olivia appears to have the ability to disappear, or at least to *appear* to be invisible when she's hurt or when she experiences acute distress," he said. "A review of several videos of the robbery filmed by bystanders didn't reveal a single image of Olivia outside the building at the time the car jumped the curb and smashed through the storefront."

Madeline grimaced. "That's absurd," she said. "She's human. It's impossible for her to have such a gift. Maybe she'd already left the area when the video was taken."

William thought he detected an almost imperceptible shudder passing through Aidan and Elsa.

"Not exactly," said Elsa.

"What do you mean 'Not exactly'?" Madeline asked. "Either she's human, or she isn't. Can she be tracked with the homing device when she's invisible?"

"Yes, we did track her," Aidan said. "That's how, in addition to hearing her pleas for help, we knew she was in trouble after the robbery. We don't know if she actually was invisible to those around her, but it would explain why the thieves locked onto her mentally and tried to blind her, instead of shooting her dead in the street."

And with that, a hush came over the room. Aidan raised his eyebrows at Gabriel, who had remained silent all this time, his lips pinched shut.

"Later," he said curtly. "I take it there's more news?"

Aidan glanced at William, urging him to speak. "Olivia recognized someone from the footage of the robbery," he said. "She said she saw him pacing outside Nikola's office a few weeks ago, while she was waiting for you."

"*Merde*," Gabriel said. "She was certain?"

William nodded. "Yes, quite. In fact she was prepared to confront Nikola herself. Aidan stopped her."

"Those damned Serbs," Gabriel said. "The whole country is crawling with the undead, and they all love to fight in wars and steal jewels."

"Calm yourself, Gabriel, it's not only the Serbs," Aidan said. "Eastern and Central Europe is full of Others with criminal records that stretch back to the Balkan Wars and beyond."

Gabriel wagged his finger. "I have asked Nikola and Zoran to remember their responsibilities to this organization," he said. "They smile at me and then go and do whatever the hell they want. They couldn't care less if the human race perished tomorrow."

"Oh, I don't know about that," Madeline said. "Croatia is a member of the European Union. As head of the Croatian National Bank,

Zoran must maintain some semblance of respectability to ensure stability in his country. Croatia's existence in the EU depends on it."

"I'm not sure Zoran even knows what's happening," Aidan said. "He's been in Brussels for weeks now on bank business. It's possible Nikola is doing this all on his own."

"Alone, together, or with one thousand of his comrades, it doesn't matter," Gabriel said. "There can be no connection between the Council and a band of jewel thieves."

"My friend," Aidan said, standing up and placing his hand on Gabriel's shoulder. "These thieves no doubt are all members of the Serbian mafia. And half, if not all, of the mafia are Others, mostly werewolves and vampires who have survived for centuries, outliving the Nazis, even Stalin. Why would they care about disturbing the Council?"

Gabriel stood up, a thin, brittle smile on his face. "I'm not a fool," he said. "I know they don't care. And I know that many of them have little regard for humans. But we must find out whether Nikola has compromised the operations of the Council. Our organization has existed for centuries, helping in subtle and not-so-subtle ways to ensure the survival of our kind. Acting as a home base to a ring of international jewelry thieves falls well outside the parameters of our mission."

"Nikola is shrewd and ruthless," William said. "He won't like us looking into his affairs."

"Then we shall have to do it with the *utmost care*," Aidan said.

28

"WAKE UP, SLEEPYHEAD," WILLIAM SAID AS HE OPENED the shutters on my bedroom windows. It took me a few moments to remember where I was, thanks to my recent vagabond status. When I finally focused my eyes, I found William standing over me, a steaming mug in his hands.

"When did you get in?" I asked, having fallen asleep soon after getting home the night before. "Wow—and you brought me an americano."

He smiled but said nothing as he handed me the cup. I sipped the coffee, savoring its warmth as I slowly awakened. Not long after, my stomach growled, reminding me that I was overdue to eat. It had been a late night, and dinner had been an early affair—mainly snacks at the Council offices as we watched the videos.

"I'm going downstairs for a bowl of cereal," I said. "Care to join me in the kitchen?"

William nodded, and as we walked downstairs, I quickly got the impression that there was something he wanted to talk about.

"What's on our agenda today?" I asked, pouring some shredded wheat into my bowl. "I can tell you have something in mind."

"As a matter of fact, I do," William said. "I'd like to take you to meet someone. He owns a school that teaches fencing and other forms of self-defense. Interested?"

The prospect of meeting a new person from William's world was intriguing. He was my lover and my confidant. But other than his band, I knew very little about where he went, what he did, or with whom when we were separated. I was eager to change that, and here was a chance to do so.

"I'm game," I said. "What should I wear?"

"Workout clothes would be a good idea," he said with a smile.

"What are we waiting for?" I said. "Let's go."

An hour after our conversation, we pulled up in front of a nonde-script brick warehouse in a part of San Francisco known as Dogpatch, an eastern neighborhood near the waterfront. There was a small sign painted on the door of the building that read SAN FRANCISCO SCHOOL OF FENCING, in large black cursive letters. William walked up to the door and knocked three times. A man opened the door, looked me over, and then embraced William. They began to converse in a lan-guage I didn't recognize. I stood there awkwardly, wondering when I would be introduced. Finally, the two of them turned to face me.

"Olivia, this is my brother, Josef," he said. "Josef, this is Olivia."

A petite, wiry man with short black hair and intriguing dark eyes peered back at me. He looked nothing like William, and then it dawned on me that he wasn't his brother by blood—at least not in the human sense.

"Your father . . ." I said, knowing I didn't have to finish my sentence.

"Josef is Czech," William explained. "My father saved him from dying alone in a field after the Nazis had wounded him."

"I was a member of the Resistance," Josef said. "I was caught outside after curfew and chased into a field, where they shot me in the back and left me for dead. William and his father had been waiting on the other side of the field to receive my message. That night, I left the human world, but I gained a brother."

"It's a pleasure to meet you," I said. "William, why didn't you tell me you had a brother?"

Josef threw an arm around William protectively. "Vampires are like onions, Olivia. It takes many peels of the layers before you know all of our secrets."

"I see," I said. "Are there any other brothers I should know about?"

William shook his head. "No, there were only the three of us, now just the two of us."

"William convinced me to move to San Francisco some years ago," Josef said. "The weather here is very agreeable. And I enjoy teaching people how to defend themselves."

Josef led us inside and shut the door. We followed him down a short hallway that led to a large workout room. A few smaller offices lined the perimeter of the space. A set of lockers occupied one corner of the room, and in another corner, a dozen or more hooks were attached to the wall. Several fencing uniforms hung from the hooks, as well as a brown leather jacket and wool cap. A portable punching bag made of red and blue leather had been placed in the center of the room; it was designed to be rolled away when not in use.

While I was examining my surroundings, I heard the front door open again and a set of footsteps came down the hallway toward us. Within seconds I sensed it was Elsa. William met Elsa in the hallway and shook her hand.

"I asked her to come," he said, turning to face me. "I meant what I told you last night, darlin'. If you want to pick fights with the likes of Nikola, then you need to be prepared to defend yourself."

"What do you have in mind?" I asked, feeling a little uneasy. I'd never raised my hand against another person in my life. I wasn't sure I could.

"I want you to train with Josef," William said. "And I thought you'd be more comfortable starting out with Elsa as your training partner."

Elsa tossed her gym bag down in the corner of the room. "This will be good," she said. "I need to brush up on my skills a bit anyway. It's been ages since I had to engage in hand-to-hand combat."

"Hand-to-hand combat?" I repeated. "When did you do that?"

"I've been alive since the sixteenth century," she said. "There were times when I had to defend myself. Often I guarded my tribe while the men were off hunting. And then, there is also the fact that time-walkers are not always welcome in villages when they appear . . . suddenly."

Josef, who had been standing slightly apart from us in the middle of the studio, was listening to our conversation. He rubbed his hands together and clapped twice. "A human and a time-walker," he said. "This should be interesting."

"Wait," I said to William. "Can you clarify what you mean by 'train'?"

"He means that you will come and work at my studio a few days a week until you are sufficiently ready," Josef said.

"Ready for what?" I asked, feeling like I was yet again entering a new phase of my life where I jumped in with both feet before looking.

"What you least expect, of course," he said. "What you least expect. Now please, let's get started. In my school, I teach a combination of fencing, Krav Maga, and savate, or French kickboxing."

"Why fencing?" Elsa asked.

"For stamina, and to build fast reflexes," Josef answered. "You have to be ready to defend yourself and to be able to quickly get away from someone who attacks you. I won't teach you to pick a fight, but I will teach you how to end one."

As I watched William in the corner of the room, I felt a mixture of both anger and admiration. I knew what he was doing was necessary. I did have the urge to pick a fight with the criminals who robbed the jewelry store, and at the moment, chances were good that I would be injured if they or their minions came after me. But I didn't like surprises or mandates, and I felt as if I had been presented with both in the span of minutes: a brother I hadn't known existed, and an obligation to work with him. What would happen, I wondered, if I refused to undergo the training?

Reservations aside, I decided to give it a try. I was in good physical shape, thanks to Elsa. Surely, I could at least hold my own for one afternoon.

Of course, I was mistaken.

Elsa and I began to spar, jogging around one another. The first time Elsa took a swing at me, I fell down immediately. I simply had no will to hit back. My body rebelled against the very act; my arm felt as if it were pinned to my side. Fortunately, we were wearing a mountain of padding, so the only thing hurt so far was my pride.

"Come on! Attack, Olivia," Josef said to me.

I gave Elsa a slight push with my hands.

"Not good enough," he said. "Come on. William tells me you taunted Nikola Pajovic. What prompted you to do that?"

"I didn't like his attitude," I said.

"Try to find that energy again. When Elsa comes forward to strike you, raise one arm to block her, and with the other palm, hit her with all your strength."

We went through the exercise again and again, and though I always managed to block her, I didn't have the constitution to hit her.

After a few more unsuccessful bouts, Josef brushed Elsa away and leaned in next to me, his lips just inches from my ear.

"Where is your energy, your passion, Olivia?" he whispered. "Perhaps you have not been properly schooled in the ways of passion? You are human after all. Maybe you need someone other than my brother to teach you. Maybe another vampire, who won't be so gentle."

At his taunting words, my body betrayed me. My cheeks turned pink, and I felt my pulse quicken. But Josef's jeering worked. With one hand, I took a swing straight at him, my palm stiff and flat, and caught him hard across the face. With my other hand, I pushed against him, using all the force I could muster. The slap made a loud noise, he took a step backward, and my stomach lurched.

Josef, however, was thrilled. "Yes! You see, you found it—your anger," he said rubbing his cheek. "Don't lose it. Nikola is ruthless. If you want to hunt him, you will need to maintain that edge."

I looked over at William to gauge his reaction. He peeled himself off the wall and came over to me, putting both hands on my face as he pulled me toward him. "Josef knows you're with me, Olivia."

"He goaded me into hitting him," I said, tears lurking at the corner of my eyes. "I don't want to do this. I don't want to fight."

William wiped a tear away with his thumb. "You can't have it both ways. You want to pursue Nikola. You want to work for Gabriel. No one wants to fight, Olivia, but when the time comes, you've got to be able to defend yourself," he said. "You asked me to accept your life, your work. The only way I will be able to relax is if I know Josef has taught you to take care of yourself."

Josef was standing in the corner, dark and brooding. I knew what he was thinking because I felt it too. There was an attraction between us. I could feel his desire. As usual, my thoughts came through to William loud and clear.

"Vampires are competitive; they covet what the others have," William said, with a gentle laugh. "It's in our nature, though some of us can ignore our impulses. But you will be safe with Josef; he is my brother."

I didn't doubt William's sincerity, but I wasn't so sure about Josef, who at the moment, seemed to hold my fate in his hands.

"OK," I said warily. "I will do the training."

From then on, training, reading, and campaigning became the three activities that consumed my time. I rose at dawn to meet Josef at his studio—sometimes with Elsa, sometimes alone—then, after ninety minutes of sparring, I would return home, shower, and drive to Palo Alto. My days were filled with political luncheons, walking neighborhood shopping districts, visiting the editorial boards of newspapers, and writing last-minute direct-mail pieces.

Flush with additional funds from generous donors, we created a very sophisticated digital advertising campaign along with radio and television commercials. In the last few days, I had been on location for hours as Levi was filmed taking walks with firefighters, police officers, and small-business owners. Our field operations were relentless. We worked every angle, pressing to locate as many hidden pockets of voters as we could before Election Day.

I reported to the Council offices weekly, meeting Gabriel in the evenings to brief him and the rest of the team. He was pleased with the progress in our race, especially since many other campaigns across the country were faltering. It was a volatile time in US politics, with the economy sluggish and so many people out of work in many parts of the nation. Incumbents of both political parties were facing tough races. For many, their only shortcoming was being the current officeholder, but when mass-group dynamics take over in a race, it can be very difficult to win.

In the midst of this frenetic schedule, Elsa moved out, taking with her the few possessions she had kept in my guest room. She gave no explanation, but I didn't need one. It was obvious she and Aidan had become inseparable. After so many years of walking the planet alone, it was lovely to see that Elsa had found a mate. I didn't pretend to understand how her penance worked—how much time she had left to fulfill her debt—but I assumed she knew, or perhaps she and Aidan were simply happy to enjoy the time they had together.

By comparison, my love life was tepid most of the time, thanks to the campaign. Periodically, William accompanied me to my appointments for the day, but he had his own businesses to attend to. He continued to perform with his band at night, though I wasn't often able to watch him play.

JP and Halbert, meanwhile, kept their distance. I saw them lurking together at a debate between Lacy and Levi sponsored by the Silicon Valley Chamber of Commerce, but neither of them approached me. JP limited his stories to current campaign events and seemed to prefer to call my staff to obtain a schedule or request a quote.

When William wasn't spending the night, I would crawl into bed and read one of the books in a stack by my bed. I could have used my Kindle but I liked being free of devices. There was something reassuring about holding a real book in my hand. Lily, who delivered some of the books in my stack personally, would stay for a quick drink or meet me for dinner. She also was very busy at work, but we texted one another every day, staying in touch as best we could.

When I was alone, I read for hours, reviewing the historical events leading up to the two world wars. It was both fascinating and frightening to see how the stage was set for World War II. Absorbed by the narratives of how world leaders had let Hitler get so far ahead of them, my curiosity kept me awake till dawn some nights. I read about the unbridled lust for power by Germany, the great ambivalence of other countries as Czechoslovakia and Poland were invaded; and then finally, the world's horror as France, too, was occupied and divided.

Through my readings, I began to understand why William, Josef, and other members of the Council seemed so deeply skeptical that society could manage its own affairs. History continues to repeat itself. The United States and Europe look more and more like their past selves in the 1930s with economic headwinds and nationalism rearing its head. The opportunity to upset the balance of power remains a constant, no matter the century. Headlines continue to announce governments suspending constitutions or eliminating their judiciary. And too often the inexplicable fringe candidate surges suddenly to the forefront, running on a platform of paranoia and hatred.

And yet, as absorbed as I was with history, my training with Josef also became a source of fascination. William didn't always accompany me, leaving me to work without his scrutiny and also perhaps so that I might ask questions to feed my inquisitiveness. I made the most of it.

Josef was also handsome, more so than William in some ways. Where William was fair, Josef was swarthy. I had to remind myself that they were brothers through a vampire bond; two very different men bound to one another through a man, not a woman.

Josef was provocative, his motives complicated. I had no doubt of his loyalty to his brother, but I remembered what William had said, that "vampires covet what the others have." When Josef took my body through its paces, knocking me to the ground, using his arms and legs to block me, lust was left hanging in the air. I would be lying if I didn't acknowledge some desire for him too. I wondered if this was a ploy by William to gauge the strength of my own fidelity.

Perhaps William had good reason to test me. After a particularly intense sparring session, as we were catching our breath on the mats, I made the mistake of telling Josef that I could read him, that I could see his aura and pick up on his emotions. William would have had a fit, reminding me to be more discreet. I don't know what caused me to push the limits like that. But when I did, Josef fixed on me the fiercest of gazes.

"Do not let other vampires know," he admonished. "We are a private sort, and do not like to be so transparent to others." He stared intently, his dark-brown eyes scrutinizing me. "It's curious that you can read vampires. Humans don't usually have the skills. It's no wonder William wants you to be able to defend yourself."

"Why didn't William tell me about you right away?"

"If you know a vampire's family, you know where they sleep," he said. "We protect our privacy."

"So the fact that William introduced us is significant," I half asked, half stated.

Josef eyed me warily. "Yes, but please don't ask me if he *really* loves you," he said in a mocking tone. "Vampires are not like a grade-school crush. My brother has survived close to two hundred years by limiting his exposure to humans. If he brought you to see me, it's because he is certain he has found his mate. He trusts you with his survival."

"Apparently, he entrusts *my* survival to *you*," was my comeback, with a twist. I shot my right foot in the air, and my timing was right. Josef was too distracted by my comment to move out of the way, and I managed to knock him partially to the floor.

"Very good, sister," he said.

"Sister," I repeated, continuing to spar. "Don't I have to be married to William to become your sister?"

"You are as good as married to William now," Josef said. "He has left you alone with me for days. If he hadn't made it clear you were his mate, I would have taken you for myself. Immediately."

Ever so briefly, an image popped into mind. I shook it away, ashamed that I had entertained it at all, but Josef caught a whiff of what my imagination had evoked. He sensed my slip and let out a loud laugh as he knocked me to the ground. He came down to the floor, hovering directly over me.

"Olivia, I believe you have a bit of vampire in you," he said. "*Now* who is coveting what she may not have?"

I lay still for a minute, feeling the outline of his body on mine. He smelled of cinnamon and cumin, like some exotic spice out of the East. I suppose I was testing his mettle as much as my own, but I could sense he was merely playing with me. He had no intention of betraying his brother. We both stayed silent, apart from my taking a few deep breaths, and then I pushed him aside and got up.

"*Au revoir, mon frère.*"

"*À bientôt,*" he said, with a mock salute. "I will see you again, yes, and soon."

Twenty minutes later, as I walked into my house, the phone was ringing. The caller ID told me it was my mother. I hesitated to pick up, cognizant of being only intermittently in touch these last few weeks. I hadn't been avoiding her exactly, but there were so many events, so many revelations, that I wasn't feeling up to telling her everything. Just learning of my injuries from the robbery could have been enough to send her over the edge.

I could feel her happiness when I answered, though I gave off the vibe that I was very much on the move yet again.

"Are you coming or going? Do you have a minute to speak?"

"I'm just walking in from working out," I said. "What's up?"

"My trip to Paris is coming up," she said. "I'm leaving in two days. I think I may have mentioned that I was invited to show my paintings at the Galerie Rive Gauche. It's down the way from the Musée d'Orsay on the Quai Malaquais."

"Two days?" I said. "Is someone already in Paris helping set up?"

"Yes, darling. You know me well enough to know I would never agree to an exhibition on such short notice. I chose the paintings weeks ago, and an assistant flew ahead to get started. The show doesn't actually begin for two more weeks, but I want to spend some time with my work to decide its final arrangement."

I was happy for her. Paris was her refuge, a place she felt welcome and safe. The customs of the French and their rituals were second nature, and I knew she would spend the next few months at peace.

"Wonderful," I said, wanting to emphasize my positive feelings.

"You sound good too," she said.

"I am," I said. "The campaign is keeping me very busy, but I'm enjoying myself. Gabriel is very pleased with how things are going. I will have to mention your show. He keeps an apartment in Paris; perhaps he'll get a chance to see it after the election is over."

Then I felt a deep pang of alarm from my mother across the phone line.

"Mom, what is it?"

"Olivia, how old is Gabriel?" she asked. "What does he look like?"

"I don't know, and I'm terrible at guessing, but I would say he's in his midfifties," I said, amused. "He has salt-and-pepper hair, dresses like a Frenchman, and has an obsession with ordering everyone's food and wine for them. Why?"

"I'm curious about this man who has so changed your life," she said, trying to mask her anxiety. "I've been meaning to ask you more about him, but it never came up."

The worry she had so clearly transmitted was gone, but I sensed she was still concerned about something. "You don't need to worry, Mom. He has given me the freedom to do great things."

"I'm your mother. It's my job to worry and to lobby for your time. Would you consider coming to Paris when your work allows? It would be nice to spend a few days with you."

I thought about for it moment and knew that it was the perfect place to escape to with William when the campaign was finished. "Sure, I'd love to come," I said. "Let me look at my schedule, and I'll call you when I figure out the dates."

"Will you be coming alone?" my mother asked, the tinge of concern back in her voice.

"No," I said. "I'll probably bring a friend."

"OK. I've taken a suite at the Ritz. Extravagant, I know, but at my age I need the pampering. There will be an extra room for you if you want it."

"*Merci, maman. Je t'aime.*"

"Love you too," she said.

After the conversation, I began to daydream about walking the streets of Paris with William. It was romantic and thrilling—except the part where I explained to my mother that I had a vampire for a companion. I wasn't sure how much she would pick up on her own or how much I should tell her. I needed to discuss the situation with William and see what he thought.

Meanwhile, my conversation had thrown me off schedule, leaving me little time to clean up. I raced upstairs, excited at the prospect of Paris in the autumn, strolling carefree through the city's magnificent arrondissements.

29

ELECTION DAY IS ALWAYS A STRANGE DAY FOR CAMPAIGN
consultants. After weeks and weeks of nonstop work, there is nothing to do but wait. When a race is in play, it can feel like the longest day of the year. The polls in California don't close until eight o'clock. Normally local results don't begin to trickle in until an hour or so later. That means that from the minute I wake up and then for another ten hours or more, I have to find a way to occupy myself, hoping that in the end, all of my hard work would pay off. Every consultant has a different way of coping. I know some who arrange long, extravagant lunches with friends. Others go into the office and busy themselves with other projects. For me, it's a rare day to get in plenty of exercise.

On this Election Day I got up early, as I had for the last several weeks. But instead of heading to Josef's studio, I had another idea in mind. I prodded William, who was lying next to me in bed, and he agreed to join me for a run in Golden Gate Park.

"Let's run to the beach and back," I said as we stretched at dawn on the sidewalk in front of my house.

We jogged through the Music Concourse, its rows of sycamores fading with autumn. A dozen senior citizens were doing their tai chi exercises, accompanied by traditional music playing from a portable speaker. We passed the de Young and then quickly turned behind the museum and headed west toward Ocean Beach. I looked up at the now-empty floors of the tower, where the Council met. The copper skin of the building was illuminated by the white glow of interior office lights, giving the building an odd artificial color in the predawn darkness.

"It's amazing to realize this building leads two lives," I said as we jogged past.

"Sort of like you," William said.

"I guess so," I said. "All of us, really."

"A necessary evil," he said. "Because in this case, the truth is more complicated than the fiction."

As we continued to run, I picked up on the distinctive caw of a raven somewhere behind us. I stopped for a moment and turned toward the noise, and there atop a streetlight was a trio of the black birds. William, who had run a few paces ahead of me, circled back when he realized I'd stopped.

"Why'd you stop?"

"I was distracted by the ravens," I said, pointing. "I've never known them to be so bold so early in the morning."

He eyed the enormous creatures with disdain. "Get out of here, you three!" he said, facing them directly. "Tell your master you've been discovered."

The ravens didn't move, nor did they make another sound. We were locked in a staring contest, making me feel like a character in an Alfred Hitchcock film.

"They can understand you?" I asked William under my breath.

"I'm guessing," he said, never taking his eyes off the trio. "You said it yourself—ravens aren't normally this active so early in the morning. I think they're spies, shape-shifters, who report to someone, perhaps Nikola."

"That's odd. I don't sense anything. How can you be sure?"

"I can't," he said. "All I have is my instincts, but their presence is odd."

"Let's ignore them," I said. "You might be right, but what could they tell him anyway?"

"OK," William said. "But don't say anything you don't want him to hear."

"You mean Nikola?"

William nodded.

"But I'd like to send him a message," I said.

"That's exactly what I was afraid of," he said. "Say nothing, darlin'. Let him know nothing of what you're thinking."

Reluctantly, I agreed. "Come on," I said, turning my back on the birds. "I feel like going over to Strawberry Hill instead of the beach. We can run up the hill and look out at the Golden Gate."

A few minutes later we turned onto the access road that climbs up to Stow Lake and followed the pavement until we reached the trail that led to the top of the hill. Morning was in full swing for the creatures of the lake. The ducks and geese were quacking and honking, waddling back and forth as they searched for their morning meals. Small pink crayfish were crawling out of the muck onto the grass, creeping slowly toward a point unknown. I marveled at the activity as we slowly zigzagged up the dirt path, the city panorama coming into view. Our climb finished, I paused with my hands on my knees to catch my breath.

"Do you remember when we first sat up here?" I asked. "I told you my story, and then you disappeared."

"That's not exactly how I remember it," he said.

"How do you remember it?"

"I kissed you," he said. "I kissed you, and then I disappeared."

"That's right," I said. "I was so disappointed. When I opened my eyes, you were gone."

"I was disappointed, too, darlin'," he said. "But I thought it better to leave."

"Did you know I would find you?"

"I hoped you would try."

"I didn't know what I was doing," I said, surprised at my admission. "I mean, I wanted you so badly, but I didn't realize . . ."

"I know," he said. "That's why I decided to leave that day."

"And now?"

"Now," he said, pulling me into his arms. "Now I know that you *know* exactly what I'm thinking."

What he was thinking is that he wanted to kiss, so I obliged, several times over. And this time, when I opened my eyes, he was still there, right by my side. That fact wasn't lost on me, and I decided to make my long-term intentions clear.

"My mother has invited me to visit her in Paris," I said. "She has an exhibition there. I told her I'd come for a few days after the election. I thought maybe you would come with me."

"You want me to meet your mother?" he asked.

"Isn't that normally what people do before they get married?" I asked. "But I need some help figuring out what to tell her. Will she be able to sense you're a vampire . . . the way I can?"

"I'm not sure," he said. "We'll have to see when we get there. I have an apartment in Paris, the one my father bought before the war. It's near the Canal Saint-Martin. We can stay there."

"You still own an apartment in Paris?" I asked. "From the war?"

William nodded. "After we're married, I'll tell you more about our holdings. We've been very fortunate over the years."

"Can we have a ceremony?" I asked.

"If you can live with a judge instead of a priest, then yes," he said. "We could even have a ceremony in Paris if you like, or wait until we're back home."

I was already imagining a small café on the Left Bank or maybe inside the Hôtel de Ville, City Hall. And then I got to the part in my daydream where we say, "Till death do us part," and I caught myself wondering what life would be like watching myself grow old when he would not.

"I can hear your thoughts. Don't worry about that now. We have many years together before that's an issue. Let's enjoy our fortune in finding each other. Even human couples have no guarantee that they will grow old together, Olivia."

"You're right," I said, taking his hand in mind. "Let's take it one day at a time."

We jogged back through the park and returned home, no ravens in sight. By the time we showered and changed, it was time for me to leave for Palo Alto. William said good-bye, promising to meet me at the campaign offices later. I would monitor things for a while from there and then move to a bistro nearby for what I hoped would be a victory party.

I passed the last few hours until the polls closed packing up boxes of confidential documents and organizing the equipment and other supplies we'd rented so they could be returned.

By seven I was ready to check in with the local news outlets and see what they had to say about other local election results. I had managed to stay calm most of the day, reminding myself that our own internal polling had shown Levi ahead in the race by a solid ten points for several weeks. The numbers for undecided voters, however, had not moved, making it possible we could still lose the race if those votes went to Lacy.

Levi had texted me earlier, letting me know he would see me at the bistro at eight. I didn't see any reason for him to arrive sooner. Gabriel was also coming around that time, and I suspected William and Lily would follow. Perhaps even Josef. At the last minute, I'd sent him a text inviting him, figuring I should include my future brother-in-law in major events.

Just as I turned on the local news, a reporter began discussing the station's process of exit polls. "It is *possible* to predict the outcome of a race using exit polling, although not always. Exit polls," she said, "show Levi Barnes as the winner."

I can only hope she's right, I mused as I tried to stay busy for the final hour of voting.

At eight we all assembled and indulged in a light dinner and plenty of wine as the first results came in. Each update revealed a slight lead, until finally at ten, with most of the precincts reporting, Levi had jumped twelve points ahead. It was astonishing, a clearer win than we had hoped for.

As we were watching the election returns, my phone vibrated in my pocket. I pulled it out to glance at the caller ID, curious, since most members of the press and campaign team were already standing within a few feet of me. The number was blocked, but I answered anyway, putting the phone to my ear to say hello.

"Are you going to claim the seat?" said a voice that was immediately recognizable from its unique salty brusqueness. Paul Levant, head of the California Democratic Party, went straight to the question, skipping any greeting, as usual.

"I'm thinking about it," I said. *Claiming the seat* meant having us declare ourselves the winner before Lacy had conceded losing. That would be a bold statement.

"Christ Almighty, you've got it in the bag, kid," Levant said. "Our own number crunchers are calling you the winner, with fifteen points to spare."

"Shit, really?" I was dumbfounded. Fifteen points was a hugely comfortable margin. It afforded a candidate the kind of maneuvering room that freed him from having to glance over his shoulder at the opposition too often. Candidates who win by two points can never say their ideas have a mandate. But win by fifteen points and the world is theirs.

"There are still a few precincts outstanding," I told Levant, unable to overcome my superstitious nature.

"Suit yourself, kid," he said. "But I'm telling you—Levi Barnes will shortly be Congressman Barnes. I'll expect a sizable donation from him to the party *tout suite!*"

The line went dead, his words ringing in my ears, my pulse in my throat.

"Who was that?" Levi asked.

"It was Levant," I said. "He says the seat is ours by a margin of fifteen points. He thinks we should call the race." Silence followed as we looked up at the television above the bar, which was now, in fact, posting election results confirming our fifteen-point lead, with two precincts left to report.

Victory chants cropped up around the restaurant. "Levi! Levi! Levi!"

"OK, let's call it," I yelled over the din. I hugged Levi. "Congratulations, Congressman Barnes! I think it's time to address your supporters."

Levi smiled and embraced me tightly. "Amazing. Amazing work, Olivia," he said. "The way you took control and stayed calm. I've never seen anyone with better instincts and courage. Thank you."

"My pleasure," I said, smiling. "It's easy to run a campaign for someone like you. Promise me you'll call when it's time for reelection."

Levi looked puzzled. "Aren't you coming back to Washington with me?"

"No, not this time. I hope you'll take Maggie and Patrick with you; they'll make great legislative aides."

Levi squeezed my hand. "You're not the same person anymore," he said. "There's something, a certainty in you that didn't exist before."

"I suppose I know more about what I want now. Perhaps it's not so much certainty, but confidence in my own decisions," I said, "which is really about growing older and knowing oneself."

"Ah, but they are *cousins*," said Gabriel, pronouncing his last word the French way. He had come up behind us while we were talking. "You cannot be certain without confidence."

Richard Lyon was with him. They both urged Levi toward the front of the room to give his victory speech. I nodded in agreement and promised to follow in a moment. As they departed, I stopped and exhaled deeply, releasing much of the pent-up stress and anxiety I had been harboring for weeks. It was over. We'd won. A weight that had been pressing on my chest lifted, and a feeling of lightness returned to my body. I was about to make my way to the front when an arm wrapped around my waist holding me in place. It was William.

"Well done, darlin'," he said, pulling me to his side. "Now that you're officially unemployed, can we kiss in public?"

"Yes, definitely," I said.

We did, quickly, and then walked forward to the main area of the bistro's dining room in time to watch Levi climbing onto a chair—a podium being too formal for such a casual space—to speak to the crowd. I glanced over at Patrick, giving him a nod as he grabbed a glass and a piece of silverware to signal to the crowd to quiet down. After a few whistles and clinks, everyone fell silent and looked toward Levi as he stood above them. Flush and happy, his blue oxford shirt rolled up at his sleeves, here was the newest member-elect from the great state of California, alone, with no entourage. *Remember this moment*, I silently urged Levi; as a consultant, I knew it was fleeting, irreplaceable.

"We did it," he said to a sea of cheers. "Can you believe it? We won by fifteen points! I'm not prepared to say much more except that I want to thank all of you, my supporters, for believing in me. I want to thank the voters who made me their choice; I promise to work hard on your behalf. Finally, I want to tip my hat to Lacy . . ."

A chorus of boos rang out from the crowd.

"Now, now," Levi admonished with a smile. "I do want to thank Lacy Smith. I may not agree with her on just about *anything*, but I respect her for raising the issues."

More applause. More cheers.

I smiled, squeezing William's hand. When you're a winner on election night, anything seems possible. Fly to the moon? Sure. Balance the budget? Immediately! It's like getting into your new car at the dealership and driving off into a brilliant orange sunset. Tonight, at this moment, these people were ready to follow Levi on a great journey, wherever he went. Would they feel the same way in sixty or one hundred days? Who knew? That is the essence of politics. I really hoped Levi would enjoy the evening, because tomorrow the real work would begin.

After speaking, Levi stepped off the chair and disappeared into a cloud of well-wishers. Champagne corks were popping, the volume on the music rose, and the group prepared to celebrate into the night. It was, after all, officially a victory party, and in politics, there is no better place to be.

My thoughts drifted to Lacy and whether she would concede. I wondered too, if Halbert would have the courage to dial my number. My answer came across a television screen as a tearful Lacy climbed the stage at her campaign party and spoke into a microphone to say she had "called Levi Barnes to congratulate him."

"This was not our moment," she said, tears streaming down her cheeks, her mascara following in streaks. "God works in mysterious ways, and I'm sure he has a purpose for us beyond tonight's defeat. This is not the end. We will continue to fight for the things we believe in."

I closed my eyes for a moment, savoring her words. I had no doubt she would live to fight another day, but for now, she was no longer my concern, nor were her advisors. Still, I wondered where Halbert was, knowing he would be furious at his loss. When I opened my eyes, I noticed reporters heading my way. My job was to lead each one of them to Levi for a one-on-one interview. I would make sure he gave them each a quote, but I wouldn't let him speculate about what he would do next. For now, it was enough to declare victory and thank his supporters.

I sent word through William to ask Richard Lyon to stay in the back of the room while the press was around. I couldn't ask the man who'd raised hundreds of thousands of dollars for the campaign to leave, but I felt no compunction at asking him to make himself scarce for a few minutes.

Levi was about finished with his interviews when I realized that one major player was missing from the room. JP had not been in the building all night. It didn't seem possible that the valley's biggest online journalist would skip the party, but I knew better than to make assumptions. His relationship with Halbert had been a revelation, one that had taught me to assume nothing.

Finally, about a half hour after most of his colleagues had departed, JP appeared in the doorway. He looked timid, as if he expected to be stoned by the crowd. If anyone had been sober enough to care, there might have been trouble. But in general, drunken winners are a magnanimous group, and JP was able to walk inside unscathed. I stood still, waiting for him to notice me. When he caught my eye, I waved him over.

I began by giving him my most professional greeting, a gracious winner's smile. "Would you like some time with the Congressman-elect?"

He nodded, a notebook and pen clasped in his hands.

"Will you be recording this on video?" I added, unable to resist.

"Yes," he said tersely. "But—"

"This is on the record?"

"Exactly," he said.

"That's certainly a much better way to go," I said, my heart not really much into scolding him further.

I caught sight of Patrick from across the room and signaled that he should join us. Since the two men knew each other, I didn't make introductions. Instead, I simply asked him to find a quiet place where Levi and JP could do an interview. I pulled Patrick aside and whispered in his ear to keep the interview short and not to allow any questions about the fundraiser that was the scene of the controversial recording.

"If he dredges up the past even for a second," I said, "stop the interview."

Patrick nodded and escorted JP out of the main dining room.

"That was very magnanimous of you," William said, coming to stand beside me again. "You could have been much harder on him."

"I don't have any energy left to be that petty. I could sense his shame the minute he walked in, and besides, he doesn't know it, but I already promised an exclusive interview to a rival publication when Levi arrives in Washington. JP will be furious, but it will make us even as far as I'm concerned." I closed my eyes again, this time feeling weary as I thought back to JP's video and the damage it had caused.

"Let me take you home, darlin'," William said, pulling me close. "You look exhausted."

I was completely spent, and serious fatigue was creeping into the corners of my body now that the adrenaline had receded. "Let me say good-bye, and then we can leave," I said, making my way through the crowd.

On my way out, I promised to meet Gabriel and our small inner circle for dinner the following evening. I scanned the room, waving to a few acquaintances and noting with pleasure that Josef and Lily were out on the dance floor, dancing cheek to cheek.

"Does he know she's a fairy?" I asked William.

"Yes," he said. "Everything is always more complicated when you mix species, but they'll be fine. They both live very openly in the human world, so it gives them something in common."

"Is he giving her a lift home?"

"Don't worry, darlin'," William said. "All of your baby chicks will get back to the nest safely."

"I'm a worrier, I know," I said, smiling. "I'll stand down for the night."

As we walked out the door, I turned back, savoring the image of celebration. Victory was finally mine again. I had overcome my demons, helped a good man win a seat in the United States Congress, and recovered my sense of identity along the way.

"Not a bad day's work, darlin'," William said. "What's next? The Senate? Maybe the presidency?"

"For now . . . Paris," I said, feeling content. "I've been thinking about places we should visit." I leaned into William, enjoying the sensation of a partner at my side. "Maybe we can take a trip to Normandy, see the coastline. I'd like to visit the memorials and maybe visit your father's grave."

I continued rattling off potential destinations, blissfully unaware that Stoner Halbert was approaching. It was only when William gave my hand a painful squeeze and I looked up to chide him that I noticed the teetering figure coming toward us. Halbert was drunk, almost to the point of incapacitation. William made a noise next to me that sounded almost like a growl.

"Halbert," I said. "What brings you here? Did you come to congratulate me?"

"You would like that, wouldn't you?" he slurred. "Shall I get down on my knees and tell you how magnificent you are? You're all the same—not happy until the man has been ruined and humiliated."

"I think you have the wrong person," William said. "Olivia has never done a thing to you."

"She's never done a thing for me," he said, his words so slurred they were almost impossible to understand.

"Halbert, what is this about? First you steal my clients, then you try to ruin my reputation as a consultant, and now you're here to what . . . hurl insults at me? You need to call a car and go home. It's one election. Sleep it off and get a life."

"You made an ass out of me," he said, coming to stand directly in front of me. "Lacy threw me out of her campaign office."

"No," I said, shaking my head. "You did that all by yourself. Now go home."

Halbert swayed back and forth, clearly trying to formulate a response, but no words escaped his lips. Finally, after a few awkward seconds, I turned my back, grabbed William's hand, and walked away.

For a moment, I felt sorry for him. The pain and disappointment of his life hung about him like a cloak. It permeated the air, giving him a rank and bitter scent. This, I mused, was an example of human betrayal left festering, and I felt some compassion for the man whose life had been so disturbed by his wife's ambitions and dishonesty.

And yet, everything that transpired since had been his choice. He chose to align himself with the darkest of paths, without a better angel to come to his aid. Now, he was left with nothing but his own reproach; he'd become a reprobate saddled with a growing paranoia that all women were out to humiliate him. Even if he won his next campaign, or the next, I doubted he'd ever find happiness again.

Halbert seemed either incapable or unwilling to move, so we left him standing alone on the sidewalk, backlit by the halogen glow of a streetlight.

"I doubt you'll ever see him again," William said as he unlocked my car door.

"You never know," I said earnestly. "Fate is a funny thing, and the world of political consultants is so small."

30

WILLIAM HEARD HIS FRONT DOOR OPEN AND LISTENED as Josef climbed the stairs to the second floor. It was early evening and they were both expected in one hour at the postelection celebration dinner. Gabriel had arranged for a celebration, a private meal for the Council and associates. He'd extended an invitation to Josef as a courtesy for his work with Olivia. But William would have recognized his brother's presence on the stairs regardless of the time or a pending social obligation. Thanks to their father, whose blood coursed through their veins, he could feel Josef's proximity deep in his bones.

"You built her a bed?" Josef asked as he strolled in to the room. "By God, you are besotted. Are you sure it's worth it? She is human, after all."

William stayed seated in his chair, a guitar in his hands, his fingers slowly picking a tune as he regarded his brother. "Don't be so provocative. You had a human lover for years, Josef," he remarked. "Why so dismissive now? Unless, of course, you would like Olivia for yourself."

Josef laughed, picking up another guitar from a stand nearby. "I prefer fairies, it turns out," he said. "They're delicious. By the way, your work is flawless. This guitar is magnificent."

"Thank you," William said. "Can we get back to Olivia?"

"You know, for a vampire, you worry too much," Josef said,

pulling the soundtrack to the movie *Cabaret* off the shelf. "Mind if I put this on?" he asked. "I'm in the mood."

William nodded as Josef set the vinyl album on the turntable.

"I'll admit she has a certain something," Josef continued, "but I have not laid a finger on her, except to train. For a woman, she has incredible endurance, far more than I would expect from a human. I will admit something about that is alluring."

William set his guitar down against the chair and stood up to face his brother. "You don't have to tell me," he said. "I remember the first moment I sensed her. She is captivating in a way that escapes her notice. But I brought her to you because I wanted someone to teach her to fight for her life, if it comes down to it. Can I trust you?"

Josef bared his teeth and hissed. "You must truly be in love if you would question my loyalty after all that we have been through."

"I intend to make her my wife, Josef. I'm counting on you to help me protect her."

Josef carefully positioned the tone arm of the record player onto the record, and "Mein Herr" began to play. "Why are you so certain she is in danger? I mean no disrespect, but she's a human female, after all. Why would an ancient vampire like Nikola care about her?"

William walked over to a small side table where a bottle of Jack Daniel's and two glasses sat. He grabbed the bottle, poured a small amount in both tumblers, and handed one to his brother.

"Several reasons," he said. "One, she is an agent of the Council aligned with Gabriel Laurent. That alone makes her vulnerable, since Nikola has little love for the Westerners and their zeal to help humans. He could harm her just to strike at Gabriel. Laurent's term is ending. Nikola is deputy to Zoran Mikic, a Croatian bank minister who is too much of a bureaucrat to really sense what's going on around him. Aidan told me the two of them are to be installed as directors next year.

"Number two, and more importantly, I don't think she is human, or at least I don't think she's one hundred percent human."

Josef raised his eyebrows as he took a sip of the whiskey.

"Come on, I know you sense it too," William said. "She's mildly telepathic, a skill few humans possess. And she can read vampires, something a normal empath woman shouldn't be able to do."

Josef downed what was left in his glass and poured another. "She told me," he said. "She told me she could read my thoughts."

"I see," William said grimly. "And what did you say in reply?"

"I told her to never let another vampire know she could do such a thing."

"You must see what I mean. She possesses skills that don't belong to a human, and that is bound to attract the wrong sort of attention," William said. "Olivia is curious, outspoken, and, above all, determined. It's inevitable that she'll run into trouble."

Josef snorted into his glass. "I can understand why you had to have her," he said. "Must be a delightful change of pace from your monkish existence these last few years. Still, I am surprised you would choose to step back into the Council's affairs. You were determined to leave humans to their own devices."

"Yes, I was. And, like all men, I was drawn back in because of a woman."

"Understood," Josef said, refilling their glasses. "But there is one thing I don't understand. Just what do you suspect she is, if she isn't altogether human? Witch? Fairy?"

"Possibly," William said thoughtfully. "I expect we'll learn the truth very soon."

I WOKE UP EARLY THE DAY AFTER THE ELECTION AND DECIDED to do nothing for the first few hours. I didn't meet Josef at the studio. I didn't read my email or make any telephone calls. Instead, I went downstairs in search of William, who had spent the night. I managed to lure him away from a copy of E. E. Cummings's poetry and into the shower, then back to my bed for several hours of lovemaking. Afterward, he left me lying in bed, returning a few minutes later with a cappuccino. The morning left me deeply satisfied. My body felt spent, worn out by my lover. My house felt like a home, the smell of warm espresso and sex filling the air.

Of course, given my habit of worrying, I immediately began to wonder what would happen after we married. I didn't want to leave my little house, but I was inclined to let my vampire husband stay in his home, which was better designed for his survival. Perhaps we would rent mine and keep it in the family until we could find a use for it. I had no idea where Josef slept; I suspected it might be inside his school. Perhaps he would enjoy living here. There would be no children to inherit my home—not unless a miracle of science occurred.

It seemed best not to dwell on those kinds of details. There was no assurance I would have had either longevity or a child with a human man, so I counted my blessings for having found someone to love, someone who returned my feelings.

I said good-bye to William around noon and went directly upstairs to throw on my workout gear and take a leisurely run to Ocean Beach. At the shoreline, I lingered briefly, despite the cold, to stretch under a clear, blue sky.

When I got home, I returned the phone calls and emails that had been piling up all day. I spoke with Levi several times, helping tie up loose ends and organize next steps. Patrick and Maggie were his staff members now, and I was eager to give them the bulk of the responsibility to arrange his move to Congress.

Fortunately, Levi had been a member of the House of Representatives once already, so his transition was not as disorganized as it might have been for a genuine freshman. When I hung up the phone for the last time early that evening, I felt confident that things would go smoothly.

My work concluded, I drew a bath and gave myself a facial, listening to a new playlist on Spotify. Without the pressures of a campaign, I was free to indulge in the little rituals that women enjoy, scrubbing and buffing until the skin on my body felt smooth and taut. Slowly, I began to feel human again. I dressed, pulling on a pair of wool capris, along with a sequined tank top and leopard-print ballet flats. I planned to wear a wool peacoat over my clothing to stay warm during the walk to Academy's private dining room, which Gabriel had rented out for the celebration.

Lily showed up at my house at six, about an hour before we had to leave. She walked through the door wearing a similar outfit, but her pants were wide-legged and silk, a fitting style for a woman of her height. She sailed into my living room all smiles, and it didn't take much for me to guess why she felt elated.

"Watch out—I think he bites," I said, adding no further explanation.

"Nothing I can't manage," Lily said confidently.

I opened a delicious bottle of white Bordeaux I'd picked up at a wine store nearby and poured us each a glass, hoping to talk to Lily about something that had been on my mind.

"What is it?" she asked, noticing I'd grown quiet.

"We spend so much time talking about the Council and William, but we never really talk about you."

"Me? You did ask about me the night I met Elsa," she said.

"I didn't really ask," I said. "I made some flip remarks."

Lily smiled. "Don't be too hard on yourself. You were given quite a shock that night."

"True," I said, nodding in agreement. "At that moment, all I could think was that everything I thought I knew was false. That maybe you'd never been my friend, not in the way I'd imagined."

"And now?"

"I guess I'm just curious about your life. Are you my age or older? Do you like being a fairy? Are you happy?"

Lily grabbed my hand and held it. "Things get confusing when you live in the world of Others," she said. "Let me put your mind at ease."

"No, don't you see? That's what *I* want to do. I want to put *your* mind at ease. Let me make you happy. Let me do you a favor or find a book that you'd like to read."

Lily's eyes grew wide. "Are you worried that I'm unhappy?"

"I'm worried that I don't really know anything about your feelings. I've been too preoccupied with my own saga to ask, and you never seem to offer up a single complaint or regret that would distract me from my own woes."

"Fairies don't complain," she said. "We don't live our lives in a state of expectation. We don't experience disappointment, at least not the way humans do. But since you asked, let me try to answer your questions.

"I am aging, but not quite as fast as you," she continued. "If I'm lucky, I will live to be about a hundred and fifty years old, which means I will start to show signs of aging a little later that most human females. In my heart, I feel like I'm living the same life as you, that of a thirty-something woman. I can even have babies, just like humans. Fairies carry them for about ten months, give or take.

"As for happiness, that's more difficult to answer. Fairies are born with one purpose: service to others. We don't wonder what to do when we grow up. We don't rebel against our parents and ask for a different occupation. It's just not in our DNA. We were born to help move the world forward. Some fairies help the salmon move upstream; others remind bears when to hibernate. Others are police officers or librarians. We are a part of the fabric of nature, a critical piece of the framework of humanity."

"Fairies remind bears to hibernate?" I said, inexplicably fixated on that detail.

"They are very absent-minded creatures," she said.

"Are there fairies on the Council?" I asked.

"There might have been a few over the years, but it's probably a rare occurrence. We help people regardless. Our work comes with no political purpose or ideology attached."

"Is our friendship out of duty or . . ." I wanted to say love, but I was too nervous to give what I felt a name.

"Maybe it's out of character for a fairy to be friends with a human, but what we have is real," Lily said. "You're not a project; you're my friend. My best friend."

I let out a breath I didn't know I was holding. Feeling confident, I decided to bring up my engagement.

"I'm hoping to leave for Paris in a few days," I said casually. "My mother is having a show, and she invited me to come and visit. I'm bringing William to meet her."

Lily smiled wistfully. "I would love to visit Paris; it's so romantic," she said. "Maybe I should take some vacation days and join you."

"I wish you would," I said. "It will make it easier for you to be the maid of honor at my wedding."

"Oh my," Lily said. "Married. Olivia, that's a big commitment."

It wasn't the kind of ringing endorsement you normally get from your best friend upon hearing such news, but I wasn't surprised. I hadn't said I was marrying a pediatrician I'd been dating for three years. This was William, a vampire, a man I'd known for only a few months. "I can sense you're worried, maybe even a little surprised."

"Both," she confirmed. "I'm happy for you. Your life was bound to be unconventional once you started work for the Council. But I'm concerned about what happens if you want out of this relationship."

"Are you saying vampires don't grant divorces?"

"That is exactly what I'm saying," Lily said.

"I doubt a piece of paper from a judge would make a difference anyway," I said. "As far as William is concerned, we're already a couple permanently. The ceremony is a formality for me."

Lily ran her finger over the rim of her wineglass, averting her eyes for a moment. She was anxious to ask me something.

"Has he asked you to drink his blood?"

"No," I said, shaking my head. "But I'd be lying if I didn't tell you I've been hoping—"

"Olivia, you *want* to drink his blood?" Lily asked, incredulous. "Once you do that, it will be impossible to separate from him; you'll be linked together forever. You'll carry his blood in your veins. You'll be able to *feel* one another's emotions, share each other's thoughts. It is an ancient kind of magic that should not be entered into lightly."

This was the second time in recent weeks that it was made clear to me that reading a vampire's thoughts was not only a skill unheard of in humans, but it was also frowned upon. I wondered what Lily would do if I told her the extent of my abilities, and then quickly I ruled out doing so. Keeping my own counsel was becoming ever more important. As much as I wanted to confide everything to her, I knew now that some things were better left unsaid.

"I didn't say I wanted to," I said sheepishly. "But I am curious. When we're together, I feel this overwhelming hunger to taste him.

We both do, and I would be lying if I said I didn't wonder what it would be like."

"If I were you, I would put off making such a decision until you've spent more time with him," Lily said. "There's no rush."

True, I thought, uninterested in dwelling on the issue any longer. I maneuvered the conversation back to more pleasant topics, such as what kind of dress I should wear for the wedding ceremony and which landmarks to visit. Our time quickly evaporated, and in short order we left to walk to the restaurant.

I hadn't been back since the night I first met Gabriel. The newspapers had posted a story announcing that the restaurant was closing for a remodel, and yet somehow our French host had been able to reserve the entire space for our private dining pleasure. It was the kind of grandiose gesture he was known for. Gabriel was unselfish in his lavishness, always ensuring that others benefitted from the extravagance.

We walked down the staircase into the main dining room, which had been festooned with dozens of candles and small vases filled with tulips and peonies. Most of Gabriel's top staff people were present, but I didn't see Nikola or Aidan in the crowd.

"*Bonsoir*," I said, greeting Gabriel with a traditional kiss on both cheeks. Lily leaned in and gave him a kiss on one cheek, grasping his hand in one of hers for a gentle squeeze.

"Good evening, ladies," he said as a server stopped by with a tray of champagne-filled flutes.

"This all can't be for one election," I remarked, hoping that there was more to celebrate than me.

"Yes, yes, of course," Gabriel said. "We won many elections across the country. Not as many as we would have hoped for, but overall our results were positive. This also is to celebrate you, the first human ever to be employed by the Council, and for you to meet a few more of the members of the organization."

It was a version of the truth, but I knew Gabriel was once again holding something back. Invariably, these inconsistencies occurred when we were standing amid a crowd of people, with no way for me to press further. I hoped that if he traveled to Paris to see my mother's show, we would have an opportunity to talk privately about whatever it was he was hiding from me.

Not long after I took a sip of champagne, I felt William's presence. I turned as he and Josef descended the staircase. They wore black suits, narrowly tailored and made, no doubt, to order. William had paired a black tie against a crisp white shirt; Josef, a silver tie against a shirt of light gray. Chic, elegant, timeless—they were easily the two most handsome men in the room, immortal and potentially lethal.

Lily's warning played in my head, her plea to delay any efforts to bind myself to him. And yet, as I watched him tonight, I could think of little else. He looked up at me and smiled, revealing in his glance that he understood the depths of my desire. There was no separation between us, no veil of mystery that new couples enjoy. Perhaps that was why we were so eager to be married.

Elsa walked in next, followed by Aidan. They stood side by side at the bottom of the staircase, clearly inseparable. I hugged Elsa, asking her how she was doing.

"I'm fine, enjoying all of my free time now that I don't have to look after you," she said with a wink. "Aidan and I are hoping to leave on a trip shortly to Scotland."

Another marriage? I wondered, but I kept my thoughts muted. "I'm hoping to be in Paris in the next week or so," I said. "To visit my mother."

"Your grandmother would be happy to know that," Elsa said. "When she was alive, she feared you two would always be estranged."

I didn't reply immediately, suddenly feeling wistful at the loss of my grandmother. She had acted as a buffer between my mother and me. Her death had resulted in an almost total withdrawal from my mother's life.

"Yes, she would have," I said. "She seemed to know a lot about my future; perhaps she saw that one day we would work through our differences."

Now it was Elsa's turn to shade her response. "She did see your future quite clearly. She loved you a great deal, and, of course, she sent me to help you."

"Yes, and I will always be grateful—to her and to you."

The unsentimental Elsa I'd grown to know returned. "I don't want your gratitude," she snapped. "I want you to use your instincts to continue to help people. What you did for Levi after that video was posted was amazing. There is no trace of the person I had to pull off the floor so many months ago."

"All thanks to you," I said. "I'll never forget what you did for me, Elsa."

"You owe me no debt."

"Maybe not," I said. "But I hope that one day, if there is anything I can do for you, you will ask."

Elsa nodded. We ended our conversation and went in search of our dinner companions. As I weaved in and out of the crowd, Gabriel picked up a knife and tapped it against his champagne flute to catch the attention of the guests.

"Everyone, please . . . if I might have your attention," he said, grinning broadly. "We are here tonight to celebrate a good season for the Council." Applause filled the room briefly before he continued. "Our election portfolio was quite good, winning a little more than half of the US races we chose to be involved in. And abroad, we helped ensure peaceful elections in several countries. All in all, it was a victory for democracy and for religious and ethnic tolerance." More applause.

"In addition to our electoral victories, we successfully managed to integrate someone special into our ranks, our first human associate. I am speaking, of course, of Olivia Shepherd, our newest campaign specialist," he said, gesturing in my direction. "As you all know, Olivia managed a win in a congressional race that was a high priority for us, despite a serious gaffe on the part of someone inside the campaign's inner circle. We're very proud of this historic alliance and look forward to assigning her even more ambitious projects."

In the spotlight, I smiled and raised my glass in salute to Gabriel. "Thank you," I said to him, and then I pivoted in a circle to smile and nod at those who were clapping.

Gabriel beamed, fixing me with a stare for a moment before informing the crowd that dinner would begin momentarily.

William was standing at my side, his arm gently draped across my back. Once my moment was over, I turned to him to see how he was faring. "OK, now I can focus on you for the rest of the evening."

"Darlin', this is your night to mingle," he said. "Besides, we'll have plenty of time alone in Paris. Do you know when you want to leave?"

"As soon as possible," I said. "I need to check the airfares. I'm sure it's outrageous unless we book ahead."

"Don't worry about the cost; it's my treat," he said. "Consider it a honeymoon gift. One among many. Just decide when you want to leave."

"Let's leave at the end of the week," I said. "That gives me a few days to pack and shop."

"I thought part of the point of visiting Paris was to shop," he said, pulling a fresh glass of champagne off a tray for me. "Pack light. We can buy all new things when you're there."

I sipped my drink and savored the bubbles as they ran down my throat. "I guess it's good to know ahead of time that my husband has an extravagant side."

"All vampires are extravagant after a certain age," he said. "It makes life bearable."

When the dinner bell rang, we moved to take our seats, searching the tables for our name cards.

"Gabriel could have done the seating at Versailles," Aidan said with some exasperation as he passed us in search of his own chair. "He excels at social management."

The first course arrived, a mixture of Vietnamese-inspired rolls, hot and cold, stuffed with combinations of shrimp, pork, cilantro, and cellophane noodles. The rolls were followed by a series of clay pots that had been simmering for hours. They were filled with sauces in every color of the rainbow: yellow curry with potatoes, green curry with shrimp and green onions, red curry with chicken. Next came bowls of noodles tossed with Dungeness crab meat. Platters bearing whole steamed sea bass followed the noodles. It was a feast, paired expertly with sweetly crisp Rieslings to keep pace with the spicy food on the table. For dessert, pot de crème was offered—chocolate pudding but made the French way, with more egg yolks and cream than one person should eat. It was a decadent but satisfying way to end a rich, spicy meal.

I glanced around the room, watching people under the sway of good food and wine. Aidan's remarks about Versailles struck me as prophetic, for we seemed perfectly suited, our small band of like-minded comrades, now sated, savoring our hard-fought victories.

After our luxurious meal, we all walked out at the same time, climbing the restaurant's steps in pairs and heading toward a steel gate located at what would normally have been the "backyard" of the Academy of Sciences. In the evening, the gate is unlocked so that guests can enter the restaurant when the museum is closed. We walked through the gate one by one, full of laughter and heady from multiple bottles of wine. We didn't hurry, lingering in the warmth of a good meal made better by good company.

As we approached the street, something shiny and black caught my eye. The entire group seemed to turn its collective head in unison. There, a few hundred feet ahead, sat a row of black Lexus SUVs. Clearly, Gabriel had arranged yet another luxury for his guests.

William and I stopped for a moment to admire the front of the Academy. It was early November, but the museum had already decorated its facade with Christmas wreaths and red bows. One of the largest natural history museums in the world, the front of the building was a mix of old and new, consisting of a set of massive glass walls affixed atop the historic stone shell of the original building, built in 1916. Steel beams run in a grid through the glass. The panels create a feeling of transparency, a fitting metaphor for the goals of an institution devoted to science and learning. Dozens of solar panels above the entryway serve as an awning in inclement weather, and provide electricity to the building.

Aidan was the first to approach the SUVs, a smile on his face as he regarded Elsa from a distance. She was trailing behind him, deep in conversation with Madeline, who'd come late to the meal. Strangely, there was no driver standing outside his vehicle—or any of them, for that matter. The absence of drivers should have made us question the arrangements, but we were too much in the afterglow of our meal to notice the details.

The moment Aidan opened his door, the car exploded.

32

THE DETONATION OF THE FIRST SUV SET OFF A CHAIN
reaction; one exploded and burst into flames, followed by the next,
and then the next. I toppled over, dazed. Thick black smoke filled the
air around us, making it impossible to breathe. Seared by the intense
heat, the steel of the museum's facade began to whine as it twisted
and bent against the inferno. The force of the explosions blew out the
building's glass entrance, and the solar-panel awnings, having nothing
further to rest on, collapsed to the ground.

It all happened so quickly. One minute we'd been standing together laughing; the next, we were trapped—on one side by a wall of
fire, on the other by a cascade of jagged glass shards falling to earth.
There seemed no way to escape. Confused and disoriented from the
deafening noise and blinding smoke, I lay on the pavement panting,
listening to the chaos around me. At one point, I thought I heard Elsa
screaming, but I couldn't be sure. I felt the heat of the fire on my skin,
but I couldn't see anything beyond where I lay.

With a pang of desperation, I noticed that William, who had
been standing next to me, was gone. I didn't know when he had vanished or how I could find him. I had no idea where to look in the
commotion all around me. I needed to move, but it was impossible to
tell what direction to go as the cars continued to explode, sending
pieces of metal everywhere. Finally, I realized that I had no choice

but to get up immediately, if there was any chance of helping anyone escape.

I pushed myself up, only to nearly collapse from a sharp pain in the back of my leg. I made an awkward pivot to my left and immediately collided with Josef, who seized me tightly and started to shout. Despite his volume, it was hard to hear what he was saying over the ringing in my ears.

"I have her!" Josef yelled. "William, I have her!"

"How do we get out of here?" I asked, worried the fire would kill even the vampires before they could escape the flames.

"We run," he said. "Now that we've found you, we run like hell."

Josef grabbed my hand and started to pull me through the smoke. I resisted—it felt as if we were heading straight for the inferno.

"What about Elsa? And Gabriel? We have to find them too," I yelled, struggling against him. I could sense the immense fear my friends were feeling, but I couldn't see them through the smoke and ash.

"Don't stop," he growled. "Not for anything, not for anyone."

I obeyed, hearing the sound of fear in his voice, something I would have thought impossible a few weeks ago. "Where is William?" I asked, wishing it were his hand dragging me through the curtain of smoke.

"He's moving the wounded to the fountain," he said quickly. "We're going to make a jump." He meant at the portal, the fountain Elsa had called the Guardian. I realized we were only a few hundred yards away. Josef's mention of the wounded brought my thoughts back to Aidan.

"Aidan?" I asked, choking back a sob as I remembered that last moment when he had turned to smile at Elsa before reaching for the door handle.

"Dead, I presume," Josef said quickly, yelling over the noise. "We couldn't get close enough to see. We were looking for you. The force of the blast threw you backward, away from the cars, but then you seemed to disappear. Until you bumped into me, William and I couldn't find you through the smoke."

Although I tried, I couldn't pay attention to his words. There was a tremendous buzzing in my ears, and I was suddenly aware that my leg was throbbing, making it was difficult to walk. Josef, unaware of my injury, pulled me toward the fountain, my shredded leg trailing behind. I leaned down, trying to locate the pain, running my hand along the back of my left thigh. My fingers returned crimson, covered in my own blood. Josef saw but wouldn't let me stop.

"Later!" he said. "We need to get out of here before the police arrive. All of us; there can be no trace."

I nodded and tried to speak, but it was a losing battle. The pain overwhelmed me. My leg began to feel chilled in the night air, thanks to all of the blood collecting in the fabric of my pant leg. I opened my mouth to tell him to leave me, that I was too injured to move, but I never had the chance. Darkness closed in, and I felt a faint sensation of falling and the sound of my name being called from far away.

I'm not sure how much time passed, but sometime later I awoke to "Drink, Olivia. Drink!" The words were echoing in my head, and I struggled to respond, unable to emerge from a deep sleep. Someone was pushing me, imploring me to wake up, but I didn't want to. I was so very tired. The relentless person on the other end of my dream, though, persisted, shaking me and rattling my bones until I regained consciousness.

I blinked, trying to make sense of the chaos and bloodshed before me. People were leaning against the walls of the room and slumped on the floor, bodies wounded, bloodied, bandaged, and disoriented. I scanned the faces, trying to piece it all together. Elsa was on her knees, hovering over a body under a sheet. Why, I wondered, were we all here? Then, as if to make the answer obvious, the searing pain returned, passing through my leg and shooting up my spine until it caught in my throat, forcing me to choke back the agony.

Now I was present, in the moment. My eyes opened wide and quickly recognized Josef's face directly in front of me.

"Drink, Olivia. You must drink from William," he implored.

William was kneeling inches away from me. He was holding his arm in front of me, revealing an open cut, his blood pooling at the edges of the incision.

Despite my injuries, I managed to recall Lily's warning about drinking a vampire's blood. "Why?" I managed to ask, my tongue rough and swollen. "Is it safe? What will happen to me?"

"It's safe enough. Besides, you won't survive unless we can stop the bleeding right away," Josef said. "You've lost a lot of blood. Drinking from William will help close the wound at the back of your leg more quickly."

William, stone-faced, nodded softly in agreement. He held my gaze, and I could hear him clearly inside my head pleading with me to hurry up before I bled to death.

I was in no position to doubt them, so I nodded.

William brought his arm to my lips, and I opened my mouth. His blood was warm and sweet, quenching a terrible thirst I wasn't aware of until the liquid ran down my throat. After a few seconds of timid sipping, my body's survival instinct kicked in, and I began to drink more robustly. Feverishly, I drank from him until finally he pulled away. I mewed like a kitten whose milk bowl had been removed, but William soothed me.

"That's enough for now, darlin," he said softly.

I heard him from a faraway place, his voice slightly muffled. I felt drowsy, maybe from his blood, and once again, I succumbed to sleep.

My rest was short-lived. I awoke a few minutes later to witness something I could hardly believe. William was stitching up the back of my leg. I came back to reality with a start, just as he pulled a stitch through my skin.

"Olivia, darlin', stay still," William urged me. "Someone come over and hold her down."

"It hurts like hell," I said, to no one in particular, tears springing from my eyes.

I was rewarded with a sharp prick in my arm, and I looked up to see Elsa holding a needle. "You're a nurse too?" I asked, my words slurring as the painkiller dulled my senses.

"Try to rest, Olivia," Josef whispered. "This will help with the pain."

When I awoke the third time, I found myself in bed at William's house. This time I knew where I was, and I sat up quickly, desperate to see William, to know that he was OK. He was sitting in a chair across from the bed, a guitar on his lap, great sadness written on his face.

"I thought you were going to die," he said quietly. "You lost so much blood. The glass from the museum. You wouldn't wake up."

I began to recall the events—the explosions at the concourse, the injury to my leg, Josef dragging me to the fountain to make the jump, drinking William's blood in a strange room I didn't recognize.

"I did wake up, though," I said. "We were in a room with lots of people, and you put your arm out. I drank from you, right?"

William looked down at his guitar. "This isn't the way I wanted it to happen," he said. "I wanted you to do it freely, to want to bind yourself to me."

"You saved my life," I said earnestly. "I would have died without your help."

"I know, but . . ."

"But what?" I asked.

"You drank a lot of my blood," he said. "Once I drink from you, our bond will be very strong."

"Go ahead," I said, holding my arm out, wrist up. "Let's finish this so we can stop worrying."

"No," William said. "You're too weak. We'll have to wait until you're better to even consider it."

I was fully aware of the depths of his anguish. His feelings were strong inside me, almost parallel sensations to my own. I wondered if it would wear off eventually, but for now, I had another question. "My leg," I said. "Will I be able to walk again?"

"That depends," said a surly voice from the opposite corner. It was Josef, walking in to the room carrying a serving tray with a glass of water, a bowl of broth, a bottle of Jack Daniel's, and two tumblers. "Do you promise to listen to your nurses and follow their instructions?" Josef asked, setting the tray on my bedside table.

"Maybe," I grumbled. "What do I have to do?"

"Your leg will be fine," William said. "I asked Nadia to come over and examine it. You needed a lot of stitches. You sustained a pretty severe cut in the back of your thigh. It will heal, but you will be stiff for several days."

"What did Nadia do?" I asked, curious to know the extent of her healing powers.

"She made a salve that she rubbed over the wound. It was already healing rapidly because of my blood, but she says her salve will help keep the swelling down and prevent too much scarring."

I ran my hands along the bandages, admiring the tightness of the wrappings. "Did you learn how to do this when you were an ambulance driver?"

"A bit," William said. "But mostly later in the Resistance. We couldn't be sure there would be a doctor around, so we had to learn to care for our own. Being the least squeamish about blood, I learned how to stitch wounds."

I paused for a moment, steeling my courage. "Did you have a lot of wounds to sew today?"

"It was yesterday, actually," Josef said, finishing his glass of bourbon in one gulp. "You've been asleep for almost a day."

His words made me feel even more separated from my friends—people I'd seen last lying against a wall, covered in blood, perhaps their own, perhaps not. I had no idea who'd survived.

"You have to tell me everything," I said. "I need to know."

William and Josef grimaced but nodded in agreement.

"Aidan is dead," William said. "He was killed instantly when he opened the door of the SUV. We left his body at the scene when we first made the jump, but Elsa went back to search for his remains. She brought back what was left."

I buried my head in my hands, trying to banish the ghastly image.

"Everyone else is alive," Josef added, pulling me out of my thoughts. "I was burned pretty badly on one arm. Gabriel suffered a series of cuts on his face from the glass."

"What about Elsa and Lily?"

"Lily broke her arm," Josef said. "It was a compound fracture, which made for a lot of blood. She's in the next room resting. She wouldn't leave until she knew you were OK."

"Elsa wasn't harmed physically," William said. "She was the farthest away from the blasts when they happened, but . . ."

"But she saw the man she loved blown to pieces in front of her eyes," I said, tears streaming down my face.

William came to sit on the bed with me, holding me gently in his arms. "Yes. She hasn't said a word since it happened. She helped hold you down so I could sew your wound, gave you the shot that knocked you out, and stayed to see that you were stable. Then she left. I warned her not to go to Aidan's house, that it might also be booby-trapped. She nodded but left anyway."

"Where's Gabriel?" I asked.

"He made a call and asked a security team to meet him at his apartment," Josef said. "He's expected back tomorrow morning."

"Were you hurt?" I asked William.

"Miraculously, no," he said. "A piece of shrapnel hit me in the leg, but it was minor. Josef and I took turns feeding after we treated your wound. Both of us are fine."

"Where were we? When I drank from you. I didn't recognize the place," I said.

"Vampire safe house," Josef said. "You know, vampires and our privacy. Occasionally, we need a place to rest or to heal after an altercation, so we have a spare house. It contains an infirmary of sorts and a doctor who's on call. She set Lily's arm. When you were stabilized, we brought you and Lily back here. She was given a very powerful painkiller to ease her pain for the next few hours. Fortunately, fairies have rapid healing capability."

The three of us sat quietly for a moment, absorbing the details. Car bombs, vampire safe houses, security teams—so much for ghost stories and fairy tales. The real version was infinitely more lethal than the fables parents send their children to bed with.

"Someone tried to kill us all last night," I said, wiping my eyes. "It wasn't some fluke accident or a case of mistaken identity, was it?"

"Car bombs are a specialty of the Serbian mafia," Josef said. "The door detonator is one of their signatures."

"Let's finish this conversation when Gabriel arrives tomorrow morning," William said abruptly. "Olivia needs to rest."

Josef bade us good night, saying he was going to look in on Lily. I wasn't sure how much I could rest, thinking about my role in Aidan's death. If I hadn't pressed him to investigate, if I hadn't taunted Nikola in the lobby, maybe Aidan would still be alive.

"This is my doing," I murmured.

"No," William said. "Aidan was a grown man with years of experience. He wasn't sloppy. He wasn't emotional. He wouldn't have done anything simply because you asked him. He was killed because he either uncovered something or confronted Nikola directly."

"That doesn't make me feel any better," I said, lying back on the pillows. My leg was beginning to throb again, and suddenly I felt exhausted. "Can I have something for my pain?" I asked.

William nodded and brought me a bottle. "Gabriel sent it over. It seems he has a pharmacist who fills prescriptions on demand. Take one—it's a Tylenol with codeine."

I swallowed a pill and laid my head back to wait for sleep. William stretched out beside me on the bed, our faces a few inches apart. Despite the pain in my leg, I leaned in to kiss him, yearning to be close to him. He returned my kiss, gently touching his lips to mine.

"That was close, Olivia," he said. "Too close. We have got to be careful until this is resolved."

I nodded, sliding my body closer to his. Before the codeine took effect, it registered with me that we still were in grave danger.

33

HARSH TONES WERE BEING UTTERED IN A ROOM NEARBY.
I struggled to regain consciousness, my head still fuzzy from the painkillers. I looked down to find my boiled-wool slippers, the pair from home. William must have brought them for me. Sliding my feet into their comforting softness, I set off toward the voices.

My body felt awkward as I tried to move without putting pressure on my wounded thigh. It was a slow process; even my uninjured leg was stiff from lack of activity. I nearly screamed in triumph after I reached the foot of the stairs without falling or knocking anything over. From the top of the staircase, I could hear the voices clearly.

"There is no evidence at the blast site, nothing to tie us to the bombing." Gabriel said. "The police will learn nothing from the crime scene."

"If you're right, then Nikola will feel empowered to strike again," William said. "He has zero risk of being linked to the bombing. And if you're wrong, and we left something behind—a trace of clothing, a drop of blood—then it would be wise for us to leave town immediately."

"We don't know that it was Nikola," Gabriel said, exasperation in his voice. "Aidan never had a chance to tell me about his investigation. We have no idea what he uncovered."

"Even worse," Josef said, inserting himself into the discussion, "our enemies have no idea what we have, but whatever it is they fear we know, they were willing to incinerate all of us to keep it from being revealed."

"It doesn't make sense," Gabriel said. "We don't conduct criminal investigations at the Council. Whatever information Aidan found would only have come to me."

"All the more reason for us to leave town," William said. "Do you have access to a private jet? We'll be more difficult to locate if we stay out of public terminals."

I'd been slowly descending the stairs even as I eavesdropped on their conversation. By the time William asked about a private plane, I was standing in the doorway of his living room.

"So I gather we're all going to Paris then," I said, catching the three men by surprise.

"Olivia," Gabriel said, jumping up to greet me. "*Ça va?* Are you OK? *Je me suis inquiété de ton santé.*"

"I'm OK," I answered, reaching out to touch Gabriel's face. His handsome lines had temporarily given way to dozens of small cuts. A small bandage crossed over one of his eyebrows, and a faint bruise clung to the side of his jaw. "How are you?"

"This?" he said, touching his face. "It is nothing. It will heal. It's you I'm worried about, and your friend Lily, her arm."

"Where is Lily?" I asked, directing my question to Josef.

"She left a few hours ago, at daybreak," he said. "She said she wanted to see her family. I expect you'll hear from her when she is feeling better."

When had Lily ever left without saying good-bye? She was no doubt horrified that she had nearly gotten killed thanks to my escapades. I hung my head, trying to absorb the magnitude of what had happened.

"I blame myself for all of this," I blurted out. "Aidan's death—if I hadn't pressed him, pressed you, about the robbery, none of this would have happened. Where's Elsa? I have to apologize."

"Elsa's gone," Gabriel said. "I assume she jumped back into another time to escape all of this. If she were here, she would have shown up by now."

"I think she and Aidan were in love," I said, my voice very low. It was difficult to find the air to speak. My chest felt tight. "She told me they were going to Scotland. I thought maybe they would be married there."

"Olivia," Gabriel said sternly. "You must not blame yourself. Aidan was *my* deputy. I asked him to investigate; he acted on my orders. I have always regarded Nikola and Zoran as buffoons. That was my mistake. I was a fool to be so cavalier, and now I have lost one of my greatest friends as punishment for my stupidity. And I put you in harm's way. Please forgive me."

"There is nothing to forgive," I said, feeling too drained to say anything more.

I hobbled over to a chair and gently lowered myself onto the seat. William came over and sat on the edge.

"I do have a question," I said, addressing the three men in the room. "Was this about Aidan, or will Nikola try again? Are we in danger?"

"At this point, we don't really know," William said, placing his hand on mine. "We need a safe place where we can investigate and decide what to do next."

"Then I was right," I said. "We need to go to Paris. It's easy to disappear there. And besides, my mother is expecting me. If Nikola does find out where I went, he'll think I left to be with her."

"We have a small office in Paris," Gabriel said. "It will not look suspicious if I move my team there for a week or so. We have plenty of issues overseas to justify the trip."

"How much time do you need to arrange transportation?" William asked.

"Not long. A few hours at the most. I will be back in touch shortly.

In the meantime, keep Olivia in your sight at all times. She must not be left alone."

William and Josef both nodded, and I got the distinct impression that the conversation had started much the same way before I had entered the room.

34

LATER THAT EVENING, FIVE OF US—JOSEF, WILLIAM, Gabriel, Madeline, and I—set out for Paris. Gabriel sent a car for us at ten, and by midnight we were in the air, traveling on Levi's private plane, with one stop in New York for refueling. Levi was only too happy to send us on what he thought was a celebratory trip after a successful election.

Scanning the news online, as we waited to take off, I read that the police were baffled by the explosions, which at this point they were labeling an act of terrorism against the museum. One journalist theorized that an animal rights group opposed to the Academy's collection of reptiles and amphibians had set off the car bombs in protest. A special team had been brought in from the FBI. But so far, no human remains had been found, leading investigators to believe the bombs were detonated as a warning, a threat of further violence.

Did Aidan know how much danger he was in? I wondered. *Did he see the threat lurking?* We would never know. I clutched my iPad against my chest and closed my eyes, contemplating the weight of what had transpired.

"Don't, Olivia," Gabriel said as he sat down beside me. "This is my responsibility, you understand? Aidan was not an amateur. He didn't put himself in harm's way because of you."

I nodded, trying hard to swallow his logic. I opened my iPad and found one of the stories I'd been reading. "I lost a lot of blood at the scene," I said. "Did you go back and bewitch the site?"

Gabriel nodded. "*Bien sûr*. Indeed, there was a lot of blood, and much of it was *not* human," he said. "I cast a spell to hide the evidence. The police will look and look, but never find a trace of DNA."

"How did you manage to get back there without being caught?"

"Magic, of course." He said. "The fog came in thick that night. But you know how this works—why are you asking?"

"I guess I needed to hear you say it," I said. "Since the moment we met, I've felt as if I've entered a world that seems to defy logic—or perhaps bend it a bit. I'm still absorbing it all. I should have died in the explosion. Instead, I'm on a plane to Paris, my leg almost healed. The force of the car bombs collapsed the front of a major American museum, but the police will never know why it happened. We, the Council, are a heavy but invisible set of hands."

Gabriel seemed poised to say something, but then he merely put his hand on my knee, gave it a gentle squeeze, and got up and walked away. I watched him make his way to the other end of the plane, take a seat, and close his eyes.

Exactly, I thought. Cheating death, misleading a police investigation, the disappearance of Elsa and Lily. It was difficult to imagine more dramatic circumstances. It was enough to leave anyone speechless.

Hours later, the plane landed at a private terminal at Charles de Gaulle. Madeline was the first to depart, promising to quickly open the bureau and settle the staff. She wasn't seriously injured in the blast, but her wounds were painful all the same. The rest of us walked off the plane a few minutes later in somber silence. As we descended the stairway, I picked up on the group's feelings that we were missing part of our team. No Elsa, no Aidan, and no Lily. Their absence was palpable, but we had no choice but move forward.

I could think of little but justice, of catching Aidan's murderer. I had intended to pressure Gabriel to develop a plan, but still shell-shocked and grieving, I couldn't find the courage to press him while we were in the air. After a day or so had passed, I would ask what he intended to do to punish Nikola. All of my instincts told me that Nikola was the one responsible for this calamity.

Revenge fantasies occupied my thoughts during the drive into Paris. After making our way through the usual maze of landmarks, we arrived at the tenth arrondissement and the Rue du Faubourg Saint-Martin, where William's apartment is located. The driver removed our bags from the car, and we bade Gabriel "À bientôt," promising to see him later that evening, perhaps for drinks.

While I marveled at the stark elegance of the nineteenth-century architecture on the street, Josef stepped under our building's awning to punch in the security code. William and Josef's apartment was just steps away from the Canal Saint-Martin and the Quai de Valmy, in an up-and-coming neighborhood where many of the city's fashionable boutiques had set up shop.

"Remind me again," I said. "What year did your father buy this apartment?"

"1930," William said. "A broker, another vampire, found it for us. This neighborhood was not always so chic. We needed a place out of the spotlight."

"Do you visit often?"

"I was here last spring," he said. "I usually come in April and leave at the end of June before it gets too hot. Despite my Southern roots, I don't care much for the heat. Explains why I like San Francisco. I've also visited in November and stayed through winter. The time I spend here hinges on where else I need to be."

"Where else do you need to be?" I asked, curious, as we loaded some of our luggage into the building's tiny elevator. Josef had decided to take the stairs.

The elevator door closed and William continued. "I own property in Paris, Zagreb, New Orleans, and San Francisco," he said. "Some are long-term rentals; others I advertise as short-term vacation places."

"And this apartment?" I asked.

"This is our family home," he said. "No one else stays here."

The family home occupied the top floor of an eight-story building. I counted four bedrooms and three bathrooms on my tour, as well as a kitchen, a living room, a formal dining room, and a roof deck that wrapped around most of the apartment, giving each of the bedrooms a small terrace. Clearly, a caretaker or concierge helped maintain the apartment. Trees and plants on the deck were healthy and lush. The apartment itself was immaculate, free of any stuffy odor that usually accompanies a home that has been abandoned or closed up for long periods of time. Freshly cut flowers had been placed in vases in every room.

The shell of the apartment maintained its nineteenth-century bones through original moldings and wood floors. Beyond that, the space had recently been remodeled to include modern appliances and conveniences. A dizzying array of art lined the walls—paintings, sketches, and propaganda posters—all of it documenting the decades marking the dawn of modern Europe. Antiques and modern pieces of furniture were paired together in great harmony, achieving the perfect Parisian salon.

"It's a magnificent home," I said, standing in the living room. "I can see why you keep it private."

William glanced over at Josef, who'd walked in with our remaining bags. "It's the last link we have to our father," William said quietly. "We've maintained and updated the property as necessary to avoid attention from my neighbors."

"It's beautiful," I repeated.

"We can live here if you like," William said, taking my hand. "At least part of the year. That is, if you don't mind Josef popping in and out."

"I would love to live here," I said. "I'll have to ask Gabriel. But since there's an office here, perhaps he won't mind."

"You don't have to work," he said. "Once we're married, I mean. I have plenty of money, which means so do you. We could disappear and enjoy the surroundings."

"Are you being romantic or trying to protect me?"

"A little of both."

I confess, it sounded splendid. Paris is a city of infinite diversions, not to mention a fabulous access point to the rest of Europe. *Wouldn't it be magical*, I thought, *to explore the world with William, lingering here and there as the mood struck us?* It was an attractive offer, and I was giving it serious thought. That is, until current circumstances brought me back to reality in the form of a sore, tired leg. I shifted my weight off the wounded limb, leaning back and forth to reduce the discomfort. It seemed our long flight was finally catching up with me.

"I need a bath," I said, fluttering my eyelashes. "Care to join me?"

"Darlin', it would be my pleasure," William said. "But you go without me. I should pay a visit to our concierge to let her know we're settled. I phoned her before we left, which is why we arrived to find things so civilized. When you're finished, meet us on the deck for a drink."

Before leaving, he walked me into the master bedroom. Spacious, its walls painted in royal blue, the room was dominated by a wooden four-poster bed with a chandelier hanging above it. If Lily were here, she'd have said the room was something straight out of a romance novel. *Too true*, I agreed as I gazed around at the antique chests along the wall, and then slowly I ran my fingers along the chocolate-brown linen duvet and matching pillows on the bed. I was no stranger to money or elegance, but living for centuries seemed to provide an advantage when it came to meaningful, timeless decor.

I entered the bathroom and studied the porcelain knobs on the bath as I ran the hot water. While the tub was filling, I decided to call my mother and let her know I was in town. Explanations would be in order for arriving early, but I decided that sticking with the partial truth—that we'd had an opportunity to come earlier by private plane—was the best idea. Any deviation, however small, and she would certainly detect it. I was spared putting my theory to the test, however, when I was informed that my mother was out at her gallery for the afternoon, so I left word with the front desk.

Near the tub was a large glass jar of bath salts. I removed the lid and inhaled, delighted by the scents of geranium and rose oil. I sent a generous scoop cascading into the steaming water and prepared to settle in. Once submerged, I let out a grateful sigh as the heat soaked through my bones and muscles, dissolving the stiffness brought on by travel and fatigue. I closed my eyes and let my mind wander, lulled by the quiet. I drifted away, pulled into a dreamlike state as I breathed in the perfumed oils. I would have gladly stayed that way were it not for Josef's voice breaking the spell.

"Be careful now. You might drown," he said, regarding me lazily from the doorway.

"Go away," I said, sending him my fiercest gaze. "I would never have pegged you as a Peeping Tom. How long have you been standing there?"

"Long enough," he said, waggling his eyebrows. "I came in to check on you because it was so quiet. I feared you were about to fall asleep."

"Unlikely, but thank you—mission accomplished," I said. "It seems your work is done here."

Josef didn't budge. Instead, he regarded me, and I mean all of me, the two of us staring at each other. Locked in his gaze, it occurred to me that this was a test; it was always a test with him. For my part, I refused to play the prude; showing any discomfort would only bring him pleasure.

"Out with you," I said, my voice made of sterner stuff this time, while flicking water at him from the tub. "You may go and let your brother know I'll join you both for drinks shortly."

Josef grinned, amused at my firm rebuke. "As you wish, my lady," he said, bending at the waist before turning out of the bathroom.

After he'd gone, I rose from the tub and wrapped a towel around myself. I dried off and returned to the bedroom. As I crossed the room to get my things from my suitcase, I noticed that my leg felt much better, most of the stiffness gone. It was amazing that I could walk at all, and I marveled again at William's lifesaving blood. My life was becoming more interesting than any science-fiction novel I'd ever read.

I pulled on a black woolen sweater dress and paired it with suede boots and a brown-and-black leopard-print pashmina shawl. I'd vacillated about whether to bring the boots. Being in a hurry usually means packing light. But this was Paris, and I was loath to arrive underdressed for the most elegant city in the world.

I gave myself one last look in a small mirror on a table and went in search of William. As I progressed down the hallway, I popped my head into each of the apartment's rooms again, admiring the decor along the way. I found the two brothers seated outside on the terrace, a bottle of red wine decanting in a glass vessel on a table next to them. Apple slices, bread, and a small selection of cheeses had been arranged on a wooden tray next to the wine. Heaters were set up around the furniture, making the outside temperature comfortable. I looked up at William, who winked at me.

"*Bon appétit, ma chère,*" he said.

"*Merci pour l'apéritif. C'est très charmant,*" I said, thanking him for a lovely meal. I was famished, having eaten little in the days prior to our trip. It felt good to sit and eat, to drink French wine, and to gaze across the rooftops. For a few moments, I pretended that none of the memories I was carrying existed—no danger pending, no death, no mourning, no loss. It was a selfish thing, burying them away. But for a few seconds, I wanted to feel happy, not be obligated to carry the lost and the dead with me in my heart.

"Did you reach your mother?" William inquired, pulling me back to earth.

I looked over and gazed at my future husband, pale and lovely in the dusk. My heart did a little flip watching him; he was mine and I was his, our blood mingled in our veins. William smiled at me, clearly hearing my thoughts. His smile was small and private, but I knew that he understood.

"I didn't reach her, but I left a voice mail and sent her a text," I said. "She's out at her gallery, so I don't expect to hear back from her until tomorrow. She'll work until very late and then go to bed. I was planning on inviting her to meet us tomorrow for drinks at a café nearby."

"Do I get to meet your mother?" Josef asked, a petulant tone attached to the question. "Are you introducing the whole family?"

Good question, I mused. *"Hello, Mom. Meet your new sons-in-law. They're vampire brothers."* But how could I not? In for a penny, in for a pound, I decided. "Yes, of course. After everything we've been through, I'm not hiding anything from my mother."

That brought a rare joyful smile from Josef. We passed the next hour amicably, making small talk while I nibbled away at the bread and cheese. Not long afterward, it was decided that we needed to experience Paris nightlife. William suggested an old jazz club in the Latin Quarter, where he knew a full bar and reliable musicians could be found. There was a taxi stand near the apartment, and within minutes we'd secured a cab. Josef slid in first, giving the driver directions in impeccable French.

"Did you speak French before the war?" I asked.

Josef looked over at William, a private memory shared between them. "No," he said. "I spoke Czech primarily. A bit of Hungarian, a little German and English. French is something I acquired in my second life."

We were heading to a club located underground that didn't open until ten, wouldn't really be in full swing until midnight, and closed only when the sun began to rise. The doorman greeted William and Josef by name, sending us inside with a hearty "*Bonne soirée*" and a pat on the back. A helpful but flirtatious woman brought us to a table in the rear of the club. Drinks were promptly served, and we sat back to enjoy the music.

A lone pianist under a spotlight began to play a sad, crisp lament that seemed to pay tribute to some far-off place. Soon, a man appeared with a bass, then another with a trumpet, and voilà, we were treated to a blues trio.

A few numbers into the set, William excused himself from the table and disappeared until he stepped onstage, a guitar in his hand. I watched, amused, as he and the pianist opened up a spirited rendition of "St. James Infirmary," the guitar and piano grinding out the notes before an upright bass joined in. I closed my eyes, listening. William remained on the stage for a few more numbers and then finally set his guitar against the wall and returned to our table.

"Play here often?" I teased.

"A bit," he said. "I know most these guys. A few of them are vampires, so it's always easy to ask if I can sit in when I'm in town."

"I'm glad, since you had to leave your band behind in San Francisco," I said, feeling guilty I'd forced William to abandon his music.

"Cat and Jack are used to me leaving periodically," he said. "They'll find a replacement. Besides, the band was something I did when I was alone to help pass the time."

"And now?"

"Now I've got other interests," he said, taking my hand in his.

Good music and an abundant list of drinks helped the night pass quickly. Eventually, I grew weary, jet lag catching up with me, and I asked if we could make our way back home. Josef scowled at first, clearly intent on staying until dawn.

"Feel free to stay," I said. "I don't want to be responsible for killing your fun."

"I'll see you both home and then go on from there," he said, picking up my wrap and handing it to me.

35

JOSEF PROVED AS SKILLFUL AT HAILING A CAB TO GET US HOME
as he had been in jump-starting our evening. I allowed myself to be
led out of the taxi and into the building. I was beyond exhausted.

I found myself squeezed into the elevator with them both. It
might have been fatigue, the tight space, the dim light of the *as-
censeur*, perhaps the vast amount of champagne I'd drunk, but whatever the cause, I leaned back on both men as we rode to the top floor.
I turned my head to rest on William's shoulder, breathing in his scent.
Josef, meanwhile, leaned in to inhale my scent at the place where my
pulse beat strong in my neck. I could feel the electricity of his lips
hovering above my skin. He pressed himself against me, so that I was
folded neatly between the men.

I felt the question in my bones, but I wasn't sure of the answer. I
briefly thought of Lily and wondered whether Josef meant something
to her. I picked my head up to face William. He kissed me deeply, his
thoughts making clear that it would be my decision, that he wouldn't
mind. I turned toward Josef, knowing what he desired, and I leaned
in for a kiss. He raised his hand to cup my face as our lips met. His
hands were as cold as William's, but they didn't feel the same upon
my skin. William, meanwhile, was holding my hand, reminding me
that he was by my side.

The elevator door opened, and, absorbed in our own world, we spilled out into the entryway, an unruly threesome. Composure regained, we approached the apartment silently, focused on what would happen next. William reached into his pocket for the key and unlocked the door. We stepped inside, and I turned to William and kissed him again as Josef stood behind me, running his hand along my spine. Together they removed my dress so that I was standing between them in little more than my suede boots. William slowly began to caress my arms, moving his hands along my shoulders, then down my back and along the curve of my backside. Josef, ever impatient and hungry, bypassed the niceties and slid his hand between my legs. His hand grew wet within seconds, my body eagerly responding. He easily tempted my body, and he knew it. Like a hungry cat playing with its prey, Josef fixed me with a ravenous stare.

It was the ferocity of his gaze that brought me out of my trance. Two vampires and one woman, not to mention a best friend back home . . . I recognized it as the recipe for a melodrama I didn't want to partake in. I smiled at Josef and placed my lips gently against his before speaking.

"I can't do this," I said. "I'm attracted to you. I won't deny it. But—"

"But you love my brother," Josef said gruffly.

"I'm not ready for that kind of life."

"Another time then, perhaps," Josef said.

I let him kiss me again, drinking in his lust. There was a part of me that regretted sending him away, but I knew I'd made the right decision.

Not long afterward, Josef left the apartment, no doubt in search of someone to relieve his tension. William and I quickly fell into bed, making furious love to each other. Later, as I was on the edge of sleep, I asked, "Did you expect me to refuse him?"

"I hoped," he whispered in my ear, spooned up against me.

"It wasn't a hard decision," I said before drifting away.

The next day, the aroma of freshly baked *pain au chocolat* lulled me out of a deep sleep. I turned over to find William's side of the bed empty, but I hadn't expected him to stay there all night.

Too much champagne, combined with jet lag, made my exit from bed a slow affair. Eventually, I tumbled out and threw on a beautiful gray wool cashmere robe that had been left nearby on a chair. It was a lovely gift, made sweeter because I hadn't asked for it. I tied the robe at my waist and walked into the hallway, on alert for the prowling brother. I was hoping he had found what he wanted the night before. I strolled into the kitchen and found the plate of *patisseries*. William had set an apartment key on the platter, along with a note letting me know he was out for the day to run some errands. There was no sign of Josef. I grabbed the key and a croissant and went back to our room to dress.

It was time, I decided, for me to find Gabriel, return to work, and locate Aidan's killer.

Museums, it seemed, were the location of choice for the Council. The satellite office, as Gabriel had called it, was located inside the Musée de l'Orangerie, a small but remarkable impressionist gallery located in the Jardin des Tuileries. It is a memorable destination for a number of reasons, but for me it is because it is home to the *Nymphéas*, the eight legendary murals featuring water lilies by Monet. As I strolled out of the Concorde Métro station, adjacent to the Tuileries, at dusk, I was looking forward to seeing the muted tones of the paintings again, set as they are in twin oval-shaped rooms with nothing to distract from their peaceful views.

Following the directions that had been emailed to me, I approached the front door of the museum and flashed a badge that had been sent by courier to the apartment. Ingenious in its design, it appeared to be a kind of temporary badge issued to visiting scholars. The guard briefly looked at it and waved me in. I used my skills to contact Gabriel, pressing hard for him to send word about where they were gathered.

"Come to the bookstore," was his crisp reply inside my head, and I walked down a set of stairs to the second level where a large gift shop occupied most of the space.

Gabriel appeared in the crowd, his ID clipped to his shirt pocket. He could have been any diligent docent, a retired teacher or accountant giving his time to the public. He smiled and beckoned silently to me to follow him. He walked toward the rear of the shop and opened a door that was almost hidden in the corner between two sets of bookshelves. Once we passed through the door, a familiar-looking landscape revealed itself, very similar to the Council offices in San Francisco. Another array of desks and touch screens occupied the space, only this time the faces of people staring into them appeared graver than they had been back home.

We continued to a small conference room. Gabriel waved me in and followed, shutting the door before he turned to face me.

"Ça va?" he asked as we stood regarding one another.

"Comme ci, comme ça," I said. "I mean, I'm as good as I can be. You?"

"The same," he said. "I have not slept well since we arrived."

I experienced a twinge of guilt as I thought of my rooftop meal, the late night at the jazz club, and my encounter with the brothers. It was all I could do to stay awake as dawn approached. But I realized for Gabriel, his mind still stuck on the loss of Aidan, peace would not return for some time.

"What have you learned?" I asked, pushing the image of my abruptly halted threesome from my mind.

"Nothing; everything," he said, distracted.

The door to the room opened, and Madeline walked in.

"Bonjour," I said, grasping her hand. I was impatient, regarding her for only a moment before pressing Gabriel with the question at hand. "When can we confront Nikola?"

"We must be careful, Olivia," Gabriel said. "Nikola is a member of the Council and next in line as deputy."

"Careful? He killed Aidan, and he almost killed us."

"Perhaps, but we have no proof," Madeline said. "At least not enough yet to ask Zoran to dismiss him as deputy."

"And what if Zoran is in on this too?"

"Olivia," Gabriel said, "Aidan's phone shows a half-dozen texts and calls exchanged with Nikola in the hours before the bombing. The day before, there were another half-dozen calls on his phone. There was no communication between Aidan and Zoran. No emails, no phone calls, and no texts. If Aidan suspected Zoran was involved, he would have contacted him."

"Well, at least we know more than we did before we left for Paris," I said. "What else?"

"Aidan's laptop had a series of files with Interpol notices containing information about Serbian mafia figures who are wanted across the globe," Gabriel said. "The man you saw visiting Nikola is listed on one of the bulletins."

"Nikola had to have known his friend was a wanted man," I said. "Perhaps that's why they tried to blind me that day during the robbery, so I couldn't see what they looked like."

Gabriel began to pace the room, his hands buried deep inside his chinos. "These are only theories," he said. "But it's not evidence that he killed Aidan. There is nothing to tie him to the bombings. *Rien!*"

"We need to find something," I said. "It's out there. We just need to look. Gabriel, you should ask William to help the Council. Ask him to investigate this for us."

Gabriel's unspoken reply was clear inside my head. *"He will have to leave you. You will not see him again for some time. Is that what you want?"*

"It doesn't matter what I want," I said aloud. "What matters is finding out who killed Aidan. You have to ask him tonight. Come meet us for drinks so we can discuss what needs to happen next."

For the next hour, Gabriel and Madeline shared a more detailed timeline of Aidan's last days, reconstructing what he had researched, and who he had contacted. His search had taken him to Interpol's most-wanted lists, Scotland Yard, and the FBI. He had contacted Nikola, too, and it was obvious they'd been having a conversation, although what they had said was not a part of our records.

I remembered my run-in with the cagey Serb; it was possible he and Nikola had spoken of nothing related to Aidan's inquiry. It was also possible they had been quite direct with one another. Only Nikola knew, and for the moment we had no intention of asking him. Our briefing completed, I excused myself from the offices and made my way down to the galleries that house the *Water Lilies* by Monet. I walked into the first oval gallery, its lights low and pale to encourage serene reflection. I lowered myself onto a bench in the middle of the room, stretched out my legs, and leaned back to regard the paintings.

"It's amazing that these were created during World War One, don't you think?" Madeline asked as she sat down next to me. "To be in the middle of war and create something of such lasting beauty."

"He brought them here to this museum to ease the suffering of the French," I said. "To give them something to help them heal after the war."

"Exactly," she said. "As a diplomat, I have always been struck by his gesture. As a witch, I have marveled that a human could create such a treasure with no help from magic. He felt a higher calling when no obligation existed."

We were not, I decided, having a discussion about the paintings. "Why are you telling me this?" I asked.

"Because you are capable of great things, but revenge should not be first on the list," she said. "I sense that you are struggling with your role in all of this. You must push yourself to see the bigger picture."

"I see a friend who has been murdered and no way to hold his killer accountable," I said quietly.

"Exactly," she said, a sad smile on her face as she walked away. "Try, if you can, to see more of the landscape."

Enveloped in the violet light of the paintings, I lingered, forcing myself to see the landscape as Madeline suggested. I stayed on the bench ruminating. Aidan's death was a blow to the Council, robbing the organization of one of its best. This was no mere chink in the armor. He had been Gabriel's top lieutenant, murdered in front of his eyes, and it had been a close call for Gabriel himself. Who would risk such a thing? What could motivate someone to be so audacious?

I began to understand what Madeline had meant: my anger had narrowed my view of the situation. My obligation should be to protect the Council, not avenge my friends.

A vibration coming from inside my purse rousted me out of my thoughts. I quickly made my way upstairs and back into the hidden offices, where I could return the call without the scrutiny of the museum's security.

"Hello, Mom," I said. "Or should I say *Bonjour, maman* . . . ?"

"Either's fine, *ma chère*," she said. "Where are you?"

"With Gabriel, at our offices," I said. "I was hoping you would join us all at a bar near the Canal Saint-Martin at seven tonight. I have so much I want to tell you. A lot has happened in the last few days. Can you come?"

I could feel her concern through the phone.

"Mom, everything is OK," I said. "I promise. Come enjoy a nice evening with me."

"Of course I'll come," she said.

"Great," I said. "I don't remember the name, except it's got the word *bar* in it and a bright-blue awning. The address is sixty-eight Quai de la Loire."

We hung up, and then I texted William to check in. He texted back that he would meet me at the apartment. I collected my things and looked around for Gabriel. One of the staff said he'd already left for the day, so I texted him the address of the bar. As I walked back to the Métro, I began readying myself for an evening I knew would be full of proverbial bombshells.

36

WILLIAM, JOSEF, GABRIEL, AND I GRABBED TWO TABLES outside facing the canal. The night air was crisp but clear, and so, with a good hat and coat, it was bearable to sit outside. William and Josef volunteered to go up to the bar and place an order. That left me sitting next to Gabriel. I leaned in closer to him to better hear our conversation over the din of traffic on the street. I hadn't mentioned that my mother was meeting us until we arrived at the bar. Gabriel's face, upon hearing the news, took on an odd expression.

"Don't worry," I said, watching the traffic pass by. "My mother is a bit of an eccentric, but she's harmless. I promise."

Gabriel smiled but said little. He seemed a bit nervous. I could feel his tension but couldn't detect the cause of his distress. It didn't concern me. It seemed natural that he would be anxious, given the last few days. As I leaned in once more to speak to Gabriel, the sound of my mother's voice caught my attention.

"Olivia, Olivia," she said, pleading for my attention as she crossed the street to join us.

I stood up as she reached our table. "Mom, hello," I said. All at once, I was overwhelmed with dread, icy cold and creeping slowly up my spine. I shrugged off the sensation, hoping to understand everyone's feelings better as the evening progressed. Since Gabriel was directly next to me, I decided to begin introductions with him.

"Mom, let me introduce—"

"I don't need an introduction," my mother said, cutting me off. "I know who your boyfriend is, and you must stop immediately."

I couldn't fathom how she knew about William, and I glanced at the bar, where he stood placing our drink order. "Mom, why would you say such a thing? I asked. "You've only just arrived and—"

"For God's sake, Olivia, the man is your father."

"My father? What on earth are you talking about?" I was baffled.

Now it was her turn to be silent. Her gaze was fixed on Gabriel, and to my surprise, he was staring back at her.

"Hello, India," he said, sorrowfully.

"You two know each other?" I asked, feeling their collective dread freezing the blood in my veins. It was obvious they had not planned on seeing one another again in their lifetimes. William and Josef arrived, drinks in hand, but paused as they read our body language. I held out my hand and drew William to my side.

"Mom, *this* is my boyfriend," I said.

India Rose narrowed her gaze, and I held my breath waiting for her to discover he was a vampire.

"I don't understand," she said.

"What do you mean?" I asked.

"All of the travel you two have been doing, the last-minute trip to Paris . . . I assumed, that he was preparing to make you his lover," she said, waving her hands frantically in the air toward Gabriel. "Never in my wildest dreams did I think you would meet Gabriel. I thought he went back to Europe and stayed. When I finally realized who he was, I had to come to warn you to stay away."

"You know Gabriel?" I asked again, realizing that neither of them had answered that question.

"Olivia," Gabriel said, remorse in his eyes.

In those few seconds, my mother's ranting became crystal clear.

"Wait," I said. "She means *you*? You are my father," I half asked, half declared.

"I was going to tell you," he said. "I came to Paris with the intention—"

"But my mother beat you to it," I said as the blood rushed into my ears. Then I spun around to confront my mother. "Mom, you knew where my father was all of these years, but you never told me?"

I was staring at my mother and Gabriel, trying to see them clearly—these two people I thought I knew suddenly transformed by their lies. I turned back to Gabriel.

"Why now? I have been working with you . . . for how many months?"

A long, cold silence unraveled before us.

"I never told Gabriel I was pregnant," my mother blurted out. "I didn't want him to take you away from me."

"Take me away?"

"Olivia," Gabriel said, "I am from a powerful family of witches. My relatives would have wanted to raise you in France."

"But I . . . I'm not a witch," I said, shocked by the facial expressions of the four people before me. I was in the minority opinion in this argument, it seemed. I looked over at William, whose face wore the grim mask of someone who had inadvertently gotten trapped in the middle of a major betrayal.

"You knew?" I asked quietly.

"I suspected," he said.

"Mom?"

"I didn't want him to take you away," she said. "His family wouldn't let him marry a human. So I never told him that I was pregnant."

"Are you telling me that you knew he was a witch?" I asked. "You must have known I would have some of his traits. Were you ever going to tell me?"

"I didn't think that far ahead," she answered. "I wanted to keep you with me, with your grandmother. I knew one day I would have to tell you, but then you refused to use your powers, and I thought maybe it wouldn't matter. Then your grandmother died and I didn't know what to do."

"Grandmother," I repeated. "She's the one who caused all of this. She's the one who summoned Elsa."

"Who is Elsa?" my mother asked, confused.

"I'm not really sure," I said under my breath.

"Elsa didn't realize who you were at first," Gabriel said. "I was the one who figured it out. She wanted to tell you. She wanted me to tell you."

"She didn't, though. And you didn't," I said. "All of you knew, but you didn't tell me. How dare you play with my life like that? How dare you lie to me!"

"Olivia," Gabriel pleaded. "You must listen. You are my daughter, my only heir."

"You can go to hell," I said. "Both of you. I never want to see either of you again."

"Olivia," Gabriel said, "there is too much to discuss. You cannot walk away."

"That is exactly what I am doing," I said, barely aware of my surroundings, my pulse in my throat. "What did you think would happen when I found out that you both had lied to me?" I continued. I grabbed my purse and began to walk away. "Did you really think this would end happily?"

I turned my back on the only mother I'd ever known and my newly discovered father. My forehead burned with anger and humiliation. All the years I had wondered and asked about my father, and my mother had known who he was. And then there was the Council. There had never been a real opportunity for me there. It was a setup from the start, from the minute Gabriel knew of my existence.

Looking back, it seemed even worse than that, for he must have known I had skills—like becoming invisible and telepathy—that I couldn't even imagine possessing. And he sat back and watched them unfold, an owner watching his pedigreed animal prance and kick to the pace of its trainer. I felt sick, wondering if anything or anyone I'd come to rely on could be trusted.

William and Josef trailed alongside me, saying nothing while they raced to open the door to the apartment. They were right to treat me gingerly. I was infuriated and horrified at being betrayed. Once we were inside, I turned to face William, my hands clenched at my sides.

"Did you know Gabriel was my father?" I asked. "Did he set this whole thing up so we would meet? Are you my compensation for him dragging me into his intrigue? Did he promise me to you in exchange for being my bodyguard?"

William glared at me and then picked up one of the nineteenth-century vases in the room and threw it against the wall. I winced at its impact, the vase exploding into a thousand pieces of ancient pottery upon the floor.

"Give me some credit, Olivia," he said. "I'm nearly two hundred years old. Do you really think I would agree to an arranged marriage to a human?"

"Ohhh, but I'm not human, not one hundred percent anyway. I'm part witch, a fact you seem to have figured out some time ago."

"I only suspected, but I wasn't certain," he said. "Gabriel told me you were his daughter the night Aidan died. He said he intended to tell you everything in Paris, but your mother got there first. He swore me to secrecy. He wanted to be the one to tell you. As usual, you fled the scene before you gave him a chance to explain."

"Explain what?" I barked. "How he tricked me into joining the Council? How he lured me into his convoluted schemes, putting my life in danger, while failing to let me know he was my father? How can he possibly provide a satisfactory explanation for any of this?"

Josef walked in to the room, a furious look on his face. As he approached, I thought he might strike me, his body was coiled so tightly. "That's enough, Olivia! Calm yourself. No vampire would bind himself, give his blood, *risk his life*, unless he was truly in love," he said. "If you want to be angry at your mother and father, fine—be angry. But don't take it out on William. Or me, for that matter. We're your allies. Maybe the only people you can trust."

Josef's words snapped me out of my hysterics, and I hung my head for a moment, feeling deflated. He was right, of course. I looked up at William, transmitting my deep regret through every fiber of my body. "I'm sorry," I said. "This is all so shocking."

William came to stand next to me, holding my hand and running his fingers across the copper bands on my finger. "I'm sorry too," he apologized. "I should have told you my suspicions."

"Listen up," Josef said. "We have bigger issues to consider. First, there is the fact that as Gabriel's heir, Olivia is technically eligible one day to assume his seat on the Council. If Nikola and his allies find out, it will give them another reason to harm her. Second, she is next in line to head one of the most powerful witchcraft families in Europe, not to mention one of perhaps a handful of children ever produced from a human-and-witch union. Rare, powerful, and in line for the throne—that is a potent trio of considerations."

I was shocked to hear myself laughing at Josef's remarks, perhaps out of distress, perhaps out of fear. "Forgive me. I think you're making too much of it," I said. "I'm not nearly that important. I was running one tiny campaign in Silicon Valley."

"Yes," Josef agreed. "Because that's what Gabriel wanted. He wanted to keep your profile low until he could assess your abilities, but then you stumbled onto the robbery and began to reveal your skills—telepathy, invisibility. He knew he was running out of time."

I stood silent, unable to think of a response.

"Olivia, darlin', stop thinking like a human," William said. "You're an Other, at least partially, and that part, however big or small, is what counts now. The rules in our world are different, and, I'm afraid, less forgiving."

I was too bewildered to speak. Lily was thousands of miles away. Elsa was missing. I was estranged from my parents and far from San Francisco, and yet I knew I could not go home again. Nothing I knew, or remembered, made sense.

"We need to get out of here," I said finally. "I want to disappear for a while, until I can figure this out."

William nodded. "I'm ready to go now," he said, clasping my hand. "But you know you can't stay hidden forever."

"I know," I said. "I just want a little time to think about all of this. Someplace where Nikola won't find us, or at least might not try to kill us."

Josef regarded us both for a moment before speaking, a knowing smile slowly appearing in his face.

"Pack your bags," he said. "I know just the place."

THE END

ACKNOWLEDGMENTS

I want to offer my profound thanks to Spark Press for taking me on as a writer. *The Others*, its fabulous cover, and its gorgeous internal layout are all possible because of the talented and creative folks at Spark. Specifically, I'd like to thank my project manager and associate publisher, Lauren Wise, for her support and good counsel. I'd also like to thank my publisher, Brooke Warner, for her leadership, vision, and creativity. It's been a wonderful collaboration, and I can't wait to start work on our next installment of The Council Trilogy.

Many thanks to my longtime editor, Cassandra Dunn, who helps me find the right words every time. I'd also like to give a shout-out to Jennifer and Marissa at BooksForward PR for their creativity and hard work. I feel very fortunate to have such a savvy team to support me.

Last but not least, I want to thank my family, including my sister Robin, for their love and encouragement.

Turn the page for a sneak preview of *The Gift*,
book two in The Council Trilogy.

THE GIFT

Chapter I

THE FORTUNE-TELLER LIT A STICK OF INCENSE AND PLACED IT IN a small holder before she spoke, her long, creased fingers steady and sure as she turned the tarot cards one by one.

"You have an enemy," she said, not a trace of surprise in her voice. "Death. The Tower. Five of Swords. Nine of Wands. Queen of Swords . . . shall I draw a sixth card for emphasis?"

"*Da,*" I said, nodding. It was the same price regardless. Ten euros, or what amounted to about ten dollars, for a basic reading. I was passing time on a sunny January afternoon in Budva, a medieval city perched on the coast of Montenegro. Everything about this tiny country near the border of Croatia pulsed with mysticism. I'd never had my tarot cards read before, but it seemed perfectly normal amid Budva's incense-filled Orthodox churches and colorful, crowded streets. I'd been exploring the ancient city when I'd come upon the woman, her small table with its bright floral cloth and two chairs set up adjacent to a church built in the ninth century.

Having recently recovered the empathic skills that were my birthright, I could tell she believed what she was telling me. Whether the cards could really predict the future was an entirely different story.

"Four of Swords, reversed," she said, turning over the sixth and final card and placing it upside down in front of me. It showed a woman lying on some kind of pedestal, three swords dangling above her head, one sword lying flat beneath her. The fortune-teller, whose long black hair, streaked with gray, was pulled tightly into a braid, eyed me suspiciously.

As I gazed back, I felt a shock of recognition pierce my chest. How had I not recognized her? We'd met before, but in San Francisco. She'd performed a spell on me to embed a map of magic locations on my arm. Nadia was her name, and she'd been introduced to me by my friend and mentor, Elsa. After everything that had happened, it felt like a lifetime ago.

Now, as then, her expression was stern. She clearly had little interest in talking about old times.

"The energy around you is strong. Too strong," she said. "You should have told me of all your powers, *chuvihani*."

I looked up, startled to hear the word. Josef, the brooding vampire brother of my lover, William, occasionally used the term to describe the types of supernatural beings that held sway in Eastern Europe, where he was born. If I'd understood him correctly, the word meant "witch" or "wise one" in Romani.

Was it possible she knew that I wasn't exactly human?

"I'm not sure what you mean," I said, drawing another skeptical look.

"Tell me, *chuvihani*, why didn't you know? You should have sensed it."

A flash of anger quickened my pulse, and pushed me to be honest, regardless of the risk. "I was lied to," I said, instinctively turning my head to scan the area before continuing. "Nobody told me until just recently that my father was a powerful witch."

"Things are changing," she said, clearly unruffled by my response. "The cards say as much. See here: Death. It usually means a break with your old life . . . leaving your past behind. But look, for your present, the Tower. It tells me you have suffered a great shock or surprise."

"Yes," I said, pushing down the anger that again surged through me. "To learn I had a father? That was a surprise indeed." And the reason I'd come to Montenegro.

I paused, feeling that I shouldn't say more. My father, Gabriel

Laurent, comes from a long line of ancient and powerful witches. He's also the head of the Council, a shadowy organization that plays a major role in the fate of humans and Others. Regardless of my grievances, I'd sworn to keep the Council's existence a secret.

"*Chuvihani,* you must assume your responsibilities," Nadia implored. "A witch is wise. She protects her village. She's the keeper of the seasons and the spirits."

Wise? Hardly. I'd been born with supernatural empathic skills, the ability to read the emotions and intentions of others. But I'd spent most of my life shunning those talents.

"A witch must embrace her strength," she continued. "She reads the minds of the living and the dead and leads her people to their destiny."

"I think you've got the wrong *chuvihani,*" I said, the sarcasm slipping out against my will. I hardly qualified as a clear-sighted leader. I'd been blindsided, kept in the dark, and manipulated by the people I loved. My mother, through omission, had lied to me my whole life, never uttering a word about my paternity. My father had recruited me for the Council but hadn't had the courage to tell me the truth about who he was—until my mother spilled the beans.

"I understand you've struggled," Nadia said, finally bestowing a bit of empathy. "But that time is over." She looked into my eyes. "The cards tell the story."

"Go on," I said, pointing at the third card in the line of six.

"Five of Swords," she said, showing me the card. It depicted a young man holding a sword in his hand and looking off into the distance. Two more swords were lashed across his back, and another two were lodged in the ground in front of him.

"You have an enemy, one who is very dangerous. A saboteur. He may be more than you can handle." She placed her hand on the card and closed her eyes. "You are taking on great evil," she murmured.

I didn't need the fortune-teller to explain. I knew exactly what "great evil" she was referring to: Nikola Pajovic, a thousand-year-old vampire. The world's financial elite knew him as a wealthy Serbian hotelier and casino owner, but I was certain he was something else: a murderer who'd recently orchestrated the bombing of my colleagues after our holiday party at the Academy of Sciences in Golden Gate Park, in San Francisco, killing my colleague Aidan Burke in the process. And it just so happened that I'd pushed Aidan to investigate possible ties between Nikola and a syndicate of former Balkan war criminals in the days before the attack. Unable to stay and grieve for Aidan, I'd had to flee to Paris to avoid the inevitable police investigation—and any further entanglements with Nikola.

"Go on," I said. "I was momentarily distracted. What do these cards mean?"

"The Queen of Swords," she said, pointing at a card with an image of a woman standing alone on a bluff, holding a sword in her hands. "You are entering a time when you will have to stand up for yourself, perhaps alone."

I nodded. I certainly *felt* alone. After the encounter with my mother in Paris, where she'd revealed that Gabriel Laurent was my father, my trust in her had been destroyed. Thankfully, William had helped me pick up the pieces and escape to Montenegro to think. His love was one of the few things that I knew I could trust. Late at night, when I tried to picture my future, it was the feel of his body next to mine that kept me from falling into despair. No matter what happened, we would be together—sometimes I imagined we might even marry—and we would find a way to get on with our lives.

Once again, the card reader's words pulled me back to the moment: "Beware, though, because the card is not certain. It could also mean that soon you will be dealing with a solitary female who has known great sadness—a widow, perhaps."

Elsa. The raven-haired time-walker and spirit guide who'd helped me access my supernatural abilities. She'd helped save my life when Stoner Halbert, a conservative political consultant and my professional nemesis, had dabbled in black magic and summoned a demon whose dark powers wreaked havoc on my once-peaceful life in San Francisco. It was Elsa who awakened my sixth sense and trained me to fight supernatural evil before the demon could destroy me. Then, after the car bombing, it had been my turn to see her life fall apart. She'd been Aidan's lover, and his death had undone her. After the explosion, she disappeared. I suspected she had jumped back in time to somewhere none of us could find her.

"And this card?" I asked.

"Yes, the Four of Swords reversed. Normally it means a time for rest," she said. "But for you, upside-down like this, it means the opposite. It means no rest. You must start work immediately. It means troubles are coming to you."

I would have laughed aloud, but I didn't want to offend her. Trouble coming? I tried to imagine what that might be. Before I'd arrived in Montenegro, I'd encountered a criminal gang of Others in San Francisco, and their supernatural powers had nearly blinded me. Then there was the car bombing. My own injuries after the blast had been serious enough that William had reluctantly shared his vampire blood to heal me. A risky gesture. All that was left to bind our lives together, at least according to my supernatural friends, would be for him to drink my blood.

"Troubles are coming," I said, repeating her phrase like an idiot. "Well, I guess I had better get ready, then." I wasn't exactly sure how to close our transaction. Saying thank you seemed like a bit of a non sequitur.

"What will you do?" she asked, scrutinizing me as she folded my dollars and stuffed them into a small cloth change purse in her lap.

"Go home," I said, not knowing what else to say. For the moment, "home" was not my cozy 1930s house in San Francisco, but a restored fifteenth-century stone cottage on an island fortress in the Adriatic.

In the summer, wealthy travelers paid a handsome sum to stay in the place we'd selected. But in late December, the place had not been difficult to book. I was traveling with William and his brother, Josef: two ancient and powerful vampires who'd lived through wars and had trained me to fight. We had Josef to thank for finding our small home in Sveti Stefan, the fortress-turned-luxury resort just slightly south of Budva.

Before becoming a vampire during World War II, Josef had lived in what was then Czechoslovakia and had traveled across Eastern and Central Europe; the cottage in Sveti Stefan had lodged in his memory as a welcome place to retreat. It turned out to be the perfect hideaway for the three of us. We were biding our time, hiding out, avoiding my family and Nikola, unsure of who to trust or how to proceed. Now though, according to Nadia, that was all about to change.

"You cannot hide from what is coming," she said, her eyes dark with foreboding.

"I need to think," I said as I gathered up my things. I didn't say it out loud, but my first impulse was to board a plane for somewhere else. Turn and run. It was becoming my habit, for better or for worse. If Elsa were here, she'd no doubt scold me for the thought. She wouldn't have wanted me to turn my back on my parents like I had in Paris. And she'd expect me to rise to the occasion now. After all, she'd picked me up off the floor where Stoner Halbert's demon had laid me out, then trained me to use my instincts and fight.

I missed her.

"You don't have much time," Nadia said. "Your fate will outrun you, if you're not careful."

"What do you suggest?"

"Assemble your allies," she said, rummaging around in a bag next to the leg of her chair. "You need to bring your people to your side and prepare."

"You make it sound like war," I replied.

"Perhaps not war, but a battle nonetheless," she said. "Now go. You'll be late if you don't leave now."

"Late for what?" I asked. I used my empathic skills to probe her feelings and sensed her certainty growing stronger as if she were being influenced by an outside force. I looked up, but there was no one else in the square.

"Just go, *chuvihani*. It's time to accept your destiny."

ABOUT THE AUTHOR

EVETTE DAVIS is a science fiction and fantasy writer. She is also the author of *48 States*, which Kirkus named one of the Best Indie Books of 2022. In 2023 and 2017, Friends of the San Francisco Public Library honored Davis as a Library Laureate. Her work has also been published in the *San Francisco Chronicle*. Davis is also a member of the Board of Directors of Litquake, San Francisco's iconic literary festival.

When she's not writing novels, Davis advises some of the country's largest corporations, nonprofits, and institutions as co-owner of BergDavis Public Affairs, an award-winning San Francisco-based consulting firm. Before establishing her firm, Davis worked in Washington as a press secretary for a member of Congress. Davis splits her time between San Francisco and Sun Valley, Idaho. For more information or to sign up for her newsletter, visit www.evettedavis.com or use this QR code:

Looking for your next great read?

We can help!

Visit www.gosparkpress.com/next-read or
scan the QR code below for a list
of our recommended titles.

SparkPress is an independent boutique publisher
delivering high-quality, entertaining, and engaging
content that enhances readers' lives, with a special
focus on commercial and genre fiction.